W9-CTI-968

THE MIRROR

Also by Marlys Millhiser

WILLING HOSTAGE
NELLA WAITS
MICHAEL'S WIFE

THE MIRROR

by

Marlys Millhiser

G.P. PUTNAM'S SONS
NEW YORK

 Published simultaneously in Canada by Longman Canada Limited, Toronto.

PRINTED IN THE UNITED STATES OF AMERICA

I would like to thank Jane Barker, Forest Crossen, Sanford Gladden, Dr. John B. Schooland, and the late Muriel Sibell Wolle for their books and articles on Boulder County history. Also the historical societies of Boulder and Nederland for the tidbits they've gathered and keep safe for us all. And more generally, A. L. Rowse for *The Cousin Jacks, The Cornish in America.*

There is no winning in life, and no losing—not really—only continuance in a state of obedience to forces that don't know a thing about us.

—Ira Wolfert, *An Epidemic of Genius*

For Jay and Joy

BACKWARD

The mirror was old. It had been old when Captain Bennet of the *Merry Dolphin* found it in the hold after his passengers disembarked in San Francisco Bay. The glass was grainy even then and reflected the light of the ship's lantern in coarse undulations.

Captain Bennet brought it to his cabin in case the owner should inquire for it, thinking that if the owner did not he'd have it pitched overboard. The stench of the oriental horde that overran his vessel on the return voyage still clung to his nostrils and he saw little possible value in any of their belongings.

That night, after a particularly violent electrical storm, certain members of the crew returned from carousing on the waterfront to find the good captain dead on the floor of his cabin.

A busy and perplexed doctor termed the cause of death apoplexy because of the profusion of blood under the skin of the face and the protrusion of the eyeballs.

The distressed widow did not share her husband's distaste for things oriental and took the mirror into her home as a memento of the captain's last voyage. She soon succumbed, however, to a strange malaise of the mind that convinced her she was not herself but someone else, and she had to be removed to a place where she could be properly looked after and restrained.

The mirror, a full-length looking glass that stood on its own base, remained for some years in her dark and shuttered parlor, until the house was sold. It was then to be found among other items of questionable origin in the dingy shop of one Edwin C. Pennypacker.

The night after Mr. Pennypacker, for unknown reasons, hanged himself from the rafters of his storeroom, hoodlums broke into the shop and the mirror along with the rest of the inventory disappeared.

It was next seen in the back of a wagon filled with a consignment of wares headed for the goldfields, and eventually stood beside the bar in a tent saloon.

Rumor has placed the mirror over the next years in deserted mine shacks, Indian tepees, a Mormon farmhouse in Utah and in a palatial bawdy house in Cripple Creek, Colorado. But the next authenticated location was the home of Charles Pemberthy, a Cornish miner, in Central City, also in Colorado, in the year 1898. It was apparently not a treasured item in the household, for when the Pemberthys left their rented residence, they left the mirror also.

John C. McCabe, the owner of this property, upon inspecting the house to discover why his renters had vacated so abruptly, espied the mirror. Having always been a man of unpredictable tastes, Mr. McCabe determined to transport it some miles over the mountains to his home in Boulder as a wedding gift for his daughter, Brandy.

Thus the mirror continued its journey. . . .

Part I

Shay

1

The Gingerbread House sat sullenly in the downpour. Water gurgled in its eaves troughs, cascaded from its peaks and false turrets, dripped from lacy trim bordering porches and railings and overhands.

The streetlight pinpointed wet speartips on the ornate fence, made dancing leaves sweep shadows across the gate swinging in the wind. A hollow clang sounded over the noise of the storm as the gate returned to strike uselessly at its latch.

In the grassy depression between the black fence and the city sidewalk, a puddle gathered, its spillover creeping under the gate.

The Gingerbread House stood aloof from the surrounding city and from the rearing wall of mountains that crouched but a few blocks to the west, insulated by the storm, by its ancient trees, by its history in a neighborhood gone neon and brash.

Storm sewers could not cope with this rare deluge and a car moved cautiously up the hill to the stop sign opposite, headlights piercing the spaces in the fence, reaching to the porches and windows of the house set far back in the protection of its lot. . . .

Shay Garrett, sitting on the window seat in the upstairs hall, leaned into the curving window as the car turned the corner. Headlights twisted through the distortion of old glass and wind-driven rain to bring fire to the solitaire on her finger.

She turned the ring so the diamond faced her palm, heard the mutter of voices downstairs, imagined a prickly tension waiting in the dark silence of the hall at her back.

As she rubbed the stiffened muscles of her neck, she felt the diamond cold against her skin and wished that it could rain inside the house, wash away the dust of decades, generations, decay, boredom.

Tomorrow a wedding band would be added to the solitaire. Tomorrow Shay would shake the dust of this house from her heels. Why then this uneasy feeling, this ennui so morbid and weighted it constricted her breathing?

"Shay?" her mother's voice came up the stairwell, sounding a bit frayed. "It's time to take Grandma Bran up. Can you help?"

Shay let her breath out slowly. "I'm coming."

"Why, the light's not even on," Rachael said below and Shay heard the switch click downstairs.

Instant light glared on new flowered carpeting and wallpaper meant to look old. The imagined, energized tension in the air seemed heavier as Shay passed the door of her room.

At the head of the stairs the wedding portrait was crooked and she paused to straighten it. The age-darkened photograph of Grandma Bran and her stiff-mustachioed husband. How could the woman in the picture be the same as the woman below, sprung from her eternal nursing home for the wedding tomorrow? Aging made no sense to Shay.

She moved down the curving stairs, half-strangled with the oppression of family relics and forebears.

"What were you doing up there with the lights off?" Rachael Garrett pushed the wheelchair to the bottom of the stairs and slid a hand under the old lady's arm to lift her.

Jerrold Garrett set his drink beside the telephone on the ancient buffet. "Probably leaning against a wall being winsomely bored."

A momentary tableau of the faces in front of Shay . . . her parents' looks of helplessness, a touch of longing . . . the rather sweet vacancy of her grandmother's stare. Shay forced a reassuring smile. "The gate's off the latch, Daddy. It's banging in the wind." She took Grandma Bran's other arm and it trembled at her touch.

"I'll get it." He grabbed a raincoat from the hall tree and the smell of soaked wood rushed in at them as he slammed the door.

Rachael smiled over the nodding white head between them, but through a mist of tears. "Well, what did you think of it?"

"Think of what?"

"Your wedding present . . . in your room. You couldn't have missed it."

"I didn't go in my room. What is it?"

"The mirror from the attic. The one you were so intrigued with, remember? We've always called it the wedding mirror because it came into the family as a wedding present. It's very old and I suspect valuable. I thought you should have something . . . of the family."

As Shay tried to remember a particular mirror from an attic stuffed with the discards of generations, Grandma Bran lurched forward.

Her mother caught herself on the banister. But her grandmother clutched at Shay, pale lips forming soundless words, sudden intentness replacing the emptiness of her stare.

"You don't think she's having another stroke?" Fear caught in Rachael's whisper as they pushed the old woman back into the chair.

A bony hand yanked at her wrist and Shay found herself on her knees in front of the wheelchair. "Mother, she's trying to talk. It's all right, Grandma." But she couldn't free her wrist. Nor believe how strong this tiny creature had become. Nor ward off the panic that seemed to pass from the frail body to her own.

"Damn gate's broken again." Her father and the rain smell entered the hall together. "Why the hell you insist upon hanging onto every piece of junk your family ever—what's the matter with her?"

"I don't know. I thought she might be having a stroke, but she seems to be trying to talk. Her color's high, though, Jerry."

The pinks of the delicate flowers on the wallpaper swam into the reds. The darkness of the buffet levitated in the blurred periphery of Shay's vision. She felt lost in her grandmother's eyes, as if she were being pulled out of herself, merging with the agony of the old woman's struggle as withered lips fought to form around something and sagging throat worked to give it voice.

"What is it, Grandma?"

"Mirror," Grandma Bran answered clearly. It was the first word she'd spoken in twenty years.

2

Shay leaned the folded canvas and metal of the wheelchair against the wall in the guestroom. Her father set Grandma Bran on the edge of the bed.

Rachael grasped her husband's arm as he straightened. "That's the first thing she's said since her stroke. Jerry, you don't think there's hope . . . after all this time?"

"I think you never give up on anything." He gestured toward the woman on the bed, whose vacant smile belied the brief lapse into reality they'd witnessed downstairs. "She's probably happier where she is, wherever she's gone. Leave her alone."

Shay still felt the impact of that emotional exchange. Her grandmother, after forcing out one word, had shuddered, looked confused and then lost all interest in further communication. "But why did she look so frightened when she said 'mirror'?"

"Oh, honey, she wasn't frightened. She just can't control her expressions that well." Rachael touched the parchment cheek and the old lady patted her hand as if to offer comfort. "I just wish it'd lasted longer. There's so much I want to say to her, ask her."

"Well, I still think it's a mistake having Bran here for the wedding." Jerry forced a creaking window open a few inches at the top. "She's not going to know the difference and she might do something to wreck it."

"She's never been any trouble. I'll watch her." When he was gone Rachael turned to Shay. "You understand, don't you? You're the only one of her grandchildren she responds to anymore. I'm not sure she recognizes her own sons. I thought she should be here."

"Mother, it's fine. I'm glad Grandma will be at my wedding. And Marek won't mind."

Rachael stared at Grandma Bran as if willing her to speak again, but the old lady was absorbed in folding her suit jacket. Sitting erect, she fumbled at the blouse's buttons. She could do so much for herself. At the table she rarely spilled her food. Her walk was halting, a barely perceptible dragging of one foot. Only in the last few years had the doctor insisted a wheelchair be kept handy so she wouldn't tire.

Shay hovered near the bed with a nightgown and hoped she'd never live to grow this old.

When Rachael returned with Grandma Bran from a trip to the bathroom, Shay helped to tuck the covers around the wasted body.

"Honey, about tomorrow. It isn't too late."

"Mother, don't—"

"Please, let me finish. I have to say this and I promise to say it only once. If you . . ." Rachael pushed back thick hair where any trace of gray had been camouflaged. "I'm not accusing you of anything, darling. Oh, I don't know how to say this. But . . . . if you—"

"Mother, I can see you're never going to get it right and we don't have all night. Let me say it for you. Shay," she tried to imitate her mother's low voice, "if you're pregnant your father and I will pay for you to have the baby at some home or even to have an abortion, but you do *not* have to marry that man tomorrow. How's that?"

Rachael sank onto the cedar chest at the foot of the bed and stared at Shay. Her face had gone as pale as Grandma Bran's. "How did you know?"

"That's getting to be pretty standard for a night-before-the-wedding talk."

"Not when I was a girl. She . . ." Rachael turned to the woman in the bed, who appeared to be sleeping, and dropped her voice, "she gave a talk on the birds and the bees."

"Wouldn't it be cool to know what her mother told her?" Shay laughed softly, switched off the light and sat beside Rachael. "Look, you're exhausted. I've tried to keep the wedding as simple as possible, but there's been a lot for you to do. There's your work and worrying about Grandma and the big dinner tonight."

"To which your husband-to-be didn't show."

"I told you about the bachelor party."

"He could've come to dinner and then gone to his party."

"What don't you like about Marek?"

"I don't dislike him. I don't even know him." Rachael stood and walked to the door. "It's just . . . just that you don't love him."

Jerry Garrett collected the remaining glasses, carried them into the kitchen, where the dishwasher rinsed its second load of the evening. On his way back he struck a hipbone on a corner of the buffet in the hall.

"Damn thing doesn't belong in a hall anyway," he muttered to the house. But the dining room had two buffets already and no room for more. They all had some family history which Rachael could rattle off at a moment's notice. Both he and his daughter had tuned that out long ago.

He sat in the one comfortable chair the house could manage and surveyed the white-and-silver wedding bows on the glass-fronted antique cabinets whose shelves were lined with knickknacks and Rachael's cobalt-blue-glass collection. This room was too little even for the small ceremony to be held here in the morning. All cut up, with its many rooms overcrowded, the Gingerbread House was suited more for tiny fluttering old ladies like Bran than for full-grown males.

"I wondered where you were." Rachael glided in with a soft swish of her hostess gown and sat in the wooden platform rocker.

"I've had the strangest feeling all day." She glanced at the corners of the high ceiling.

"That's only natural." But he'd noticed it too. So had the dinner guests. His brothers-in-law hadn't bothered to tease each other. Ever since he'd carried that crappy old mirror down from the attic and gone to collect Bran from the nursing home, he'd had uneasy sensations in his middle. "Well, did you talk to her?"

"More like she talked to me." Rachael lit a cigarette, blew smoke at the chandelier. "She didn't admit to anything."

"Is she angry with us?"

"No. She just laughed in a nice . . ." Her lips trembled and she took a deep breath. "A nice condescending way. Why, Jerry? Why?"

"She's just bored. I hear it's all the rage." He wanted to cross the room, hold her. But he didn't. "Just bored. She always has been. But Jesus, marriage. That's like jumping off a bridge to scratch an itch."

"And she's twenty years old. There's nothing we can do." Rachael stubbed out a half-smoked cigarette. "I suppose these days we should be relieved she's marrying, not just moving in with him." She stood and started for the doorway. "Mom didn't say any more, maybe it was just a . . ."

Jerry was staring over the rim of his glass at the figurine of a shepherdess on the mantel, but his mind was seeing the willowy shape of his daughter, the long pale hair, the contrast of a summer's suntan, the sudden flashes of kinky wit that would light mischief in otherwise solemn, indifferent eyes . . .

When someone screamed upstairs. When the figurine toppled, to crash against a bellows below. When the Gingerbread House shuddered to its gables with a strange explosive impact. . . .

Shay sat beside her grandmother after Rachael left. The rain had stopped but wind still lashed leaves around the streetlight and shadow silhouettes flickered across the bed.

"Mother's hopelessly old-fashioned, Grandma Bran," Shay whispered to the sleeping form. "Love! I've got to make a change sometime."

A hand moved on the coverlet and lids lifted on faded eyes that looked through Shay. "Book," Grandma Bran said, the bed shuddering as her body joined the struggle to say more.

And again Shay had the sensation of being drawn out of herself. She slipped off the bed and rubbed bare arms. Hearing even two spoken words after years of silence made her skin crawl.

If mind and speech were returning, would it be a blessing for someone almost a hundred years old?

Mercifully, her grandmother subsided into sleep and Shay tiptoed out, crossing the hall to her own room, where the flowered carpeting and wallpaper continued from the hallways both upstairs and down. If she never saw another pink-and-red printed posy in her life, Shay vowed, it'd be too soon.

Rachael'd decorated this room "little girl pretty." The frills and flounces left small space for Shay and her belongings. And with her wedding gift sitting in the middle, it was almost too cramped for air. She leaned over stacks of L.P.'s that blocked the heat from the baseboard heater in winter and opened the window. Rain and wind had brought the clean pine scent down from the mountainsides.

Shay turned to inspect her wedding gift. "Yuk! I remember you now." *Mother, I was fascinated by this monstrosity because it was so horrid, not because I liked it.* She wondered what she and Marek would do with it.

A full-length glass with a ragged crack running diagonally across the top. The crack would always cut across her face unless she stood on her head. But the worst was the frame, bronze molded in the shape of hands, long, slender but masculine-looking hands that slithered and entwined about each other like snakes, and all with talonlike fingernails. The base was a pair of hands turned downward, the mirror's weight resting on the thumb, forefinger and little finger on each hand.

Just looking at the thing gave her the shudders. After slipping into filmy baby-doll pajamas, she lifted the veil Grandma Bran was said to have worn at her wedding from its perch on a lampshade and tried it on. Another of her mother's treasures. How could Shay see well enough through the lace to descend the staircase? She giggled at a vision of herself in a heap of satin and lace at the foot of the stair, while embarrassed guests tried not to notice.

But she laughed aloud at her image in the wedding mirror. Even through the veil and the crack in the glass, her bare legs and straight hair dripping beneath the lace looked a comical mixture of time periods.

"No!"

The harsh voice startled Shay as she lifted the veil to see her grandmother swaying in the doorway, her shapeless nightgown and milky skin ghostly against the darkness of the hall.

Grandma Bran's eyes were locked on the wedding mirror.

"Grandma?"

"Corbin!" the old lady screamed.

Goose bumps prickled on Shay's arms. "No, Grandma, it's a . . ."

As their eyes met in the wedding mirror, the mirror began to hum. Waves in the glass undulated into the room on a sea of mist and swamped Shay in a sweating sickness. A cracking sound ripped the air with such force she was thrown to the floor. The carpet gave way beneath her and Shay fell in a blacked-out world filled with an old woman's screams.

3

The screams ended. Shay thought some disaster, natural or otherwise, had befallen the Gingerbread House.

She rose through layers of silent black. Sickness heaved inside her.

She whirled in sweeping circles that stopped when she reached the hardness of floor. The web of the veil's lace lay in a jumble in front of her face. Shay pushed it away and gagged.

She lay on a floor of varnished boards that smelled of oil and dust. The carpet with its gay posies had disappeared.

Pulling her knees under her, Shay raised herself on her hands. No stacks of L.P.'s, no baseboard heater. Just a foot-high baseboard stained dark brown instead of white. She swayed and fell back to the floor.

Footsteps, excited voices in the hall . . .

"What happened?"

"Sounded like dynamite. But I don't see anything's been blown up."

"Help me," Shay tried to shout, but it came as a whimper.

Blackness threatened her again and she twisted on the slippery floor to find something solid to hold to stop the swirling. Her hand met a cold talon at the base of the wedding mirror.

"Brandy?"

"What's wrong with her?" The voices were in the room now.

"She must have fainted. You men go check the rest of the house. I'll unlace her. Brandy?"

"Just some water please." Shay felt a loosening around her ribs that allowed her to breathe deeply. "What's happening?"

"I don't know. Knocked pictures off the walls and broke dishes, but we can't find what or where it exploded. Here, I'll take out your hair."

A constriction eased at the base of her skull, hair pulled as pins were removed. Who'd put pins in her hair? Hands rolled her over and she looked up into the face of a stranger.

"Lie still now. I'll get some water." The woman rose and brushed off the skirt of a gown that had a narrow waist and puffed at the bodice and sleeves. She closed the door and Shay was left staring at a queer-shaped lightbulb in the ceiling, its glass clear, its filaments visible.

The hideous mirror towered above her with all its entwined hands. It seemed to be the only familiar thing left in the room.

The chocolate-brown door that should have been white opened and the woman returned with a glass and a cool washcloth for Shay's forehead.

In profile, this stranger resembled Rachael. The same rich auburn hair, but this hair was braided and wound around the head, had a streak of gray on each side of the part.

"Mother?" Shay asked in sick confusion and tried to sharpen her focus.

"Yes, dear. You'll be all right." She placed the back of her fingers against Shay's cheek. "You're not fevered. But drink all of this."

When Shay'd finished the odd-tasting water, the woman helped her to stand.

Clutching the cold hands of the mirror, she swayed and looked down at an unfamiliar dress. It extended to the floor. The hair that fell over her shoulder reached to her waist. It was dark and curled at the ends. "Oh, my God . . ."

"Brandy!" The woman helped her back onto a narrow bed and began to remove layers of clothing, her eyes avoiding Shay's body.

"But my hair—"

"We'll brush it extra in the morning."

"Sophie?" A male voice from the hall.

"Wait." The woman pulled a scratchy nightgown over Shay's head.

"You can come in now." Sophie tucked covers around her.

Two men entered, dressed like museum pieces in baggy trousers and shiny vests. It was like watching a movie and suddenly finding oneself a participant instead of a spectator. But there were no cameras. Had she struck her head?

"Can't find much damage inside or out. Must have been an earthquake, but I never heard they made a noise like that," the older man said in a precise drawl. "And I never heard of one happening around here."

"Heavens. Do you think it's over?" Sophie asked.

"I hope so." He moved to the foot of the bed, fingered his beard and peered at Shay over tiny wire-rimmed glasses. "And you, miss, had better have recovered from your fright. Whatever happened tonight makes no difference to tomorrow. You marry in the morning, Brandy McCabe, if I have to hold you up to the preacher myself."

Sophie turned the clammy washcloth over on Shay's forehead. "John—"

"Enough's been said on the matter, woman. You two have your little talk, and to bed." He motioned to the younger man, who'd been standing just inside the doorway with a halfhearted smile. "Come along, Elton, we'll have a nightcap to celebrate the wedding."

"Brandy McCabe," Shay said when the door had closed. "I don't believe this."

"I'm afraid you had better. I can't talk him out of it. Heaven knows I've tried. Sit up now and I'll braid your hair." A brush pulled through hair that wasn't Shay's and fingers began to twist it.

Shay breathed deeply, trying to thwart the remaining dizziness and her bewilderment at being recognized easily by odd people she'd never seen. She threw away a brief thought that her parents had hired actors to play this terrible joke on her to keep her from marrying Marek. That was as ridiculous as what was happening.

Sophie flopped the loose braid over Shay's shoulder, pushed her back and drew the covers to her chin. There were tiny crumbs or grains of sand where Shay's feet met the sheets.

"Now." Sophie sat ramrod straight on the edge of the bed, folded her hands in her lap and swallowed. "There are some things you must know before tomorrow. I have no idea how much you've learned from your friends but most of that is probably in error." Sophie looked about the room, looked at her hands but not at Shay. "When a man and woman marry, the man has certain . . . privileges . . . of . . . of the marriage bed."

Sophie stood and stared at the ceiling with her back to Shay. "There is a very slight pain on the wedding night, but not after that, and . . ." She'd been speaking slowly but now she blurted out in a rush, "and all you have to do is to relax and Mr. Strock will know what to do." She turned to the bed and, with tears in her eyes, took Shay's hand. "Always remember, Brandy, to be brave, and God will be watching over you. Someday he'll reward you with children."

"Oh, whoopee-twang." But Shay's giggle ended in a gulp.

"What?" Sophie straightened. "You're just . . . overwrought, dear. Get some sleep now." She kissed Shay's forehead before Shay could pull away. "Everything will be fine. You'll see." Reaching for the lightbulb hanging from the ceiling, she half-turned toward Shay. "Whoopee-twang?"

Sophie shrugged, flicked the switch above the bulb and left.

Shay threw back the covers, placed her feet on the small braided rug, closed her eyes, gripped the side of the thin mattress and tried to ignore the throb in her head.

One, dreams are never this long or consistent. Two, I had only one glass of wine with dinner. Three, insanity can't possibly come on this quickly. Can it?

She squeezed her eyes tighter, concentrated on sanity or waking up. But the vision of herself making love on this bed with a faceless Mr. Strock, while a bearded God robed in flowing white looked on, broke her up. When God leered Shay lay down again, fighting back the laughter of hysteria.

Okay, jollies over. Let's try again. This time she made it to her feet and then to the foot of the bed. A vestige of vertigo forced her to grab the iron bedstead. *This really isn't all that funny, Shay. Get ahold of yourself.*

Shay reached above the hanging bulb as she'd seen Sophie do and switched on a light she could barely reach. The cedar chest in the guestroom on which she and Rachael'd sat this very evening was now at the foot of the bed in this room. The lace veil hung from one of the hands of the wedding mirror, and the mirror was taller. The whole room was larger.

But to see another woman's face reflecting her own distress, to see the image raise that trembling hand which didn't wear Marek's diamond to its lips and then to feel the cold touch of fingers in the same place . . . to be seeing this in a mirror that appeared so weird in itself . . .

"If you had anything to do with this, undo it!" She raised Brandy's fist to the wedding mirror . . . then moved closer. There was no crack running diagonally across the top. And the veil hanging on its frame didn't have mended lace, the satin cap beneath wasn't yellowed.

Shay stood back and shook her head. In the wavy glass Brandy shook hers.

Brandy McCabe had blue eyes instead of brown, long thick lashes and a plump little figure. Her breasts must have been two cup sizes larger than Shay's.

She was also missing a back molar on her upper left jaw. That more than anything dispelled the dreamlike quality of Shay's situation. She was in full possession of another body. What had happened to her own?

An impulse to run based on no other logic than panic sent her to the window—not to the door to the rest of the house where "they" lurked.

But what lurked outside was no better.

No motel next door to hide her view of the mountains, their shapes a dark silhouette against a lighter night sky. No city lights reaching to their bases. No sounds of traffic. No smell of recent rain. The far-off barking of a dog was her only indication that there might be anything left of Boulder, Colorado.

Shay's world was no more out there than in this house . . . or in this body. Closing the window on the chill and the scratchy hum of crickets, she sat on the cedar chest and stared at the mirror. It couldn't be responsible. Something this fantastic had to be a trick of the mind. She was ill, and delirium superimposed images of the past on those of the present. She'd felt depressed about the past weighing on this house, and her sick mind was working it out in this way.

Reason dictated that it had been Rachael and not Sophie who'd sat on the bed talking to her. And she'd been saying other things than what Shay'd thought she heard.

This was all too real and detailed for a mere dream.

The Gingerbread House was so quiet it was spooky. Shay shivered in the light nightgown. A tall metal radiator sat against the wall but it was cold to her touch.

Tomorrow she'd probably wake up in a hospital, her mother and father at her bedside, recovered enough to laugh at this whole thing.

The body was making its demands known just as her own would, shaking her conviction in a logic that hadn't been too convincing.

Well, I'll just play it out . . . find Brandy the bathroom and . . . Again that urge to run . . . *and not panic.*

Leaving the door open for light, she slipped into the hall and headed for the bathroom. It was a walk-in closet.

Shay stared at the closet for a full minute, shuddering more now from reaction than chill. Finally she moved to the head of the stairs on a narrow strip of grainy carpet. Light from below helped her find her way down bare stairs. At the bottom a table with a vase of fresh flowers sat where the old buffet had. She was stopped by males voices from the living room.

". . . crazy as a loon. Why marry her off to Strock, Pa? You could keep her home to care for you and Ma when you're old."

"If she's that crazy she won't be no good to us. But I don't think she is, Elton. Your sister had two good prospects at eighteen and she turned 'em both down because she didn't love them. Or so she said. Love! I don't know what's getting into women these days but it's got to stop, I tell you. And now she's pretending witlessness to scare men off and get out of marriage. It's not going to work. She's twenty years old and I'm waiting no longer."

Shay tiptoed around the corner, hoping the bathroom under the stairs was still there.

It was, and again she had to stretch to switch on the light hanging from the ceiling.

The toilet tank hung high on the wall with a long chain dangling from it. A metal tub, encased in wood, had only one faucet. Strange that her hallucinating mind could produce details of a time she knew nothing of. Strange she and Brandy should be the same age.

No one had flushed the stool lately and the windowless room smelled foul. Shay pulled the chain when she'd finished and the house reverberated with a frightening clamor. She stepped into the hall quickly.

"Who's working the plumbing at this time of the night?" John McCabe bore down on her. "You? And running about in your nightgown. What's this house coming to? Now get yourself back to your bed, miss, and no more of your antics or I'll take the strap to you, I will."

Shay ran up the stairs to her room and slammed the door, Brandy's heart pumping thunder.

"Old bastard," she muttered and faced the mirror.

The reflection of Brandy looked shocked and defenseless, the room behind her cloudy and warped in the ancient glass.

If you do this to me I'll shatter you with my bare hands.

Shay traced a line along the top of the mirror where there should have been a crack. She hadn't noticed before the few chips of darkened enamel adhering to bases of nails or in the ridges between fingers of the frame's hands, as if the bronze had once been painted.

The plumbing still clanged downstairs.

I don't like this world.

Throwing back the covers, she wiped the grit from the sheets and with a nasty look for the mirror switched off the light and crawled into bed.

Running around on bare floors had left more grit on her feet to replace what she'd just removed. *Tomorrow I'll wake up in my own world.*

Shay rolled over and buried her face in Brandy's pillow.

4

An odd sound awoke Shay. She lay there wondering where the roosters came from and then sat up, almost hitting her head on the ceiling that sloped past the bed to the peak in the roof.

"Oh, no!" Her tongue felt her teeth as her eyes searched the room. The molar was still missing, the room still Brandy's.

She rushed to the window. A horse grazed peacefully in a pasture where there should have been a motel.

You marry in the morning, Brandy McCabe, if I have to hold you up to the preacher myself.

Shay turned to the wedding mirror. "Take me back." She beat on it with her fists but it stood solid against her.

She caught sight of Brandy's rigid face held up so close to her that the steam of her breath evaporated on the mirror's surface. Shay dropped her arms and moved away. Why was she so sure it was the mirror?

The surge of adrenaline that had propelled her out of bed receded, leaving her limp . . . and angry.

"Brandy?" Sophie entered wearing the same dress she had the night before but covered by a long white apron. "Nora has hot water for your bath. Where's your robe?"

"How should I know," Shay said between Brandy's teeth.

"Do try to be cooperative, dear. Make the best of this situation." Sophie brought a hideous flannel robe from the closet.

The heavy woman called Nora dumped two buckets of steaming water into the metal tub and mixed it with water from the one faucet. Looking scandalized when Shay dropped the robe and nighty from Brandy's body, Nora hissed and slammed out of the bathroom—buckets and door banging.

Well, there's nothing here you won't see on yourself. Just less of it.

The water was only three inches deep. The soap was as hard as a brick and lathered about as well. But the bath felt good and Brandy needed one.

Washing someone else but feeling the touch of the cloth and the tug of water against submerged skin . . . the fingers, shorter than her own, showing no clumsiness at obeying a different mind . . .

Dark hairs covered Brandy's legs and puffed under her arms. Shay eyed the leather strap hanging from the sink. Probably the one John McCabe had threatened to beat her with.

There was undoubtedly a razor to go with that strap. Shay was tempted to give Brandy a shave, but then shrugged it off as a useless gesture. *This can't last forever.* And she wasn't about to crawl into bed with Brandy's groom tonight. The name "Strock" had a harsh sound to it.

Perhaps God was punishing her for her disdain of her mother's obsession with the past. Perhaps he was teaching her a lesson and would soon slip her back into her own body and time. Shay hadn't given God much thought since she was thirteen.

But instinct kept harping back to the mirror. Even though it'd been in the attic for years and done nothing to anyone. Even though it was not a very logical explanation.

This whole trip started with one quick glance into Grandma's eyes in that mirror.

A stab of longing for her mother and father . . . Shay wept quietly into the washcloth.

Shay sat across from John McCabe while Nora and Sophie delivered breakfast to the round kitchen table.

"You're not married yet. Get up and help your mother." His teeth were crooked, the lower ones brown-stained.

"Leave her be, John. It's all on. Where's Elton?"

"He went downtown to get the news." John McCabe slipped his spectacles higher on his nose to read a long document with a colored seal showing through when he held it up. "Well, Strock gets Brandy and the Brandy Wine this morning." He glanced at Shay with the look of longing she'd seen on Jerry Garrett's face. But it quickly vanished. "What he wants with the last, I don't know."

"There's talk of opening the mines again. Eat your breakfast, Brandy." Sophie slid an egg onto Shay's plate.

"Conger and his black iron," John said with a snort. "Bunch of nonsense."

Ham slices, fried eggs, cornbread, pancakes, and something that resembled oatmeal. Brandy felt hungry but Shay didn't know where to start.

She wore the dress Sophie'd taken off her the night before. It was so tight she wondered if there'd be room for food. The egg was the best she'd ever tasted.

When she poured herself a glass of milk, John and Sophie stopped eating to stare at her, Nora halted her fork on its way to stab a pancake.

Creamy, warm, sweet. It probably came straight from the cow. She drank it all before taking another bite.

"But you don't like milk," Sophie said in astonishment.

"Oh." In a fit of delayed rebellion, Shay refilled the glass and then wondered if it was cholera one got from unpasteurized milk, or . . . diphtheria? Brandy probably hadn't had much in the way of shots.

Sophie leaned toward her and whispered, "What's happened to your corset?"

Shay, who wasn't wearing one, was saved by a flutter of chickens on the step as Elton McCabe walked in the back door.

"Old Strock spent most of the night at Werely's." Elton winked at Shay and filled his plate. "Wagers are out he won't make it to the wedding."

"He better had," his father answered and swiped at a fly crawling across the oilcloth toward the white butter.

"Bet he spent the rest of the night on Water Street," Elton said through a mouthful.

"Elton!" Sophie rose to get the coffeepot from an iron stove that poured too much heat into the room. "Coffee, Brandy?"

"I don't know." Shay sucked a piece of food from the unfamiliar hole left by the absent molar. "Do I like it?"

Brandy's father gave her a hard look and turned to his son. "What news of the earthquake?"

"Nobody but us felt or heard anything last night, Pa."

Shay slipped out the back door after breakfast. Fat black flies. The smell of dry grass and sweet-scented flowers. A dirt path led to an outhouse and the brick garage. The latter looked much as she remembered it except for the wooden chicken shed tacked to one end. Peering inside, she found a small carriage with its tongue resting on an earthen floor instead of her father's Oldsmobile sitting on concrete.

The panic knotting Brandy's stomach belonged to Shay and it sent her running a few yards across a prairie that should have been city. The buildings of this Boulder were some distance away. She stopped. No help for her there. She couldn't survive in a world she didn't know. She needed shelter, food and, most of all, the mirror. If it had indeed performed the impossible, why couldn't it reverse the process?

The wedding mirror was her only hope and it was in the Gingerbread House.

Shay walked slowly back. The horse in the pasture whinnied and she stroked his nose. He blew warm breath to tickle down her arm. He was real; so was the sun on her face.

Drawing a hand over one of the barbs on the wire fence, Shay watched another woman's blood ooze from the cut. No nightmare could be this genuine.

"Brandy! Hurry, there's not time to dawdle." Sophie swooped down on her. "What are you doing without your bonnet, child?"

Shay sagged against the fence, helpless to stop the tears.

Brandy's mother gathered her in her arms. "It's going to be easier than you think, dear. Don't cry. You'll muss your face. You don't want to be a spinster, do you? Or a schoolmarm? Even if your father had allowed you to enter the university, you'd have had to marry sometime. You will come to love Mr. Strock with the years." But Sophie McCabe didn't sound all that convinced.

"Please?" Shay stood before the wedding mirror, tightly corseted, feet aching in tiny button shoes, Brandy's body too warm in the white gown spread over scratchy, starched slips.

Sophie'd brushed Brandy's hair till it crackled, and piled it high in a configuration Shay would never be able to duplicate. Then Sophie'd read aloud from the Bible.

Was Marek, in a future time, waiting for a bride who wouldn't show? "What's happened to my body?" she asked the mirror.

Is this what happens when you die? Did I die last night and become reincarnated or something? Backwards? This house had always been in the family. McCabe was a family name. Brandy had to be an ancestress.

What if she refused to go downstairs and wed someone else's bridegroom? *John McCabe would beat me, that's what. And then he'd probably drag me downstairs anyway*. There was no similarity between Brandy's formidable father and the gentle Jerrold Garrett.

Elton peered around the door. "Are you alone?" He slipped in, tall and handsome in his white suit. "Pa'll be here soon. You look beautiful but you shouldn't cry. Makes your face red." He wiped tears from her cheeks with his handkerchief. "It won't be so bad. But if Strock don't treat you decently, send word to me in secret. You know I'll do what I can for you, Bran." He squeezed her hand and left as quickly as he'd come.

Bran? Shay stared into the mirror. She tried to remember the face in the darkened wedding portrait that hung in the hall until . . . until the world had turned upside down. But it had been so lifeless, posed. Yes, there was a similarity.

Shay'd always heard her grandmother referred to as Bran, or Grandma Bran . . . *Short for Brandy. Oh, God.*

The veil had been her grandmother's. Rachael'd worn it too. She wished she'd listened to some of her mother's stories on the family's past. But they'd been so many, and so boring.

Footsteps on the stairs.

"Do something, please! Let me go back before it's too late." Shay pummeled the wedding mirror.

5

Shay descended the curving stairs on John McCabe's arm, in Grandma Bran's veil and Grandma Bran's body. Tears had given way to panic, panic to zero-hour logic. When the moment came to say "I do," she said, "I don't."

No buffet, no pink-and-red posies, no guests.

She hesitated at the archway to the living room and John yanked her forward. Sophie'd changed her dress. She stood talking to Elton and two strange men.

One of the men towered over even Elton, but Shay remembered Brandy's body was considerably shorter than her own. That's why the rooms seemed larger, the doorways higher.

Through the veil, Shay recognized the bay windows, the wooden platform rocker, the fireplace.

John McCabe handed her to the tall man in a black suit, a funny tie, a shiny black vest showing in pieces above the coat and below the white shirt . . . and the most unwelcoming eyes a groom ever turned on a bride.

Shay forced Brandy's throat to swallow. *I can't marry my own grandfather.*

The man beside her listened intently as the other man read from a book.

Shay concentrated on not throwing up, remembering to say she didn't when she was supposed to "do." It would be easier without guests.

"And do you, Corbin Strock . . ."

"Corbin!" Shay stared at the groom. That was what her grandmother'd said just before . . .

The minister cleared his throat and began again, "And do you . . ."

Shay swayed on Corbin Strock's arm and practically strangled the small bouquet in her other hand. A far-off buzzing in her ears.

"And do you, Brandy Harriet McCabe, take this man . . ."

It was coming. The time to refuse. Shay cleared Brandy's throat, took a deep breath.

". . . promise to obey . . ."

Her heart drowned out his voice. The bay windows behind him slipped out of focus.

". . . until death do you part?"

Now? The minister stared at her. Shay unglued Brandy's dry tongue from the roof of her mouth and . . .

"She does," John McCabe said with finality.

Sophie McCabe folded her daughter's day dress, placed it in the trunk beside the embroidered sheets and pillowcases and dragged the trunk out of the closet.

Brandy sat on the cedar chest, staring at the bronze mirror, an odd unbecoming slouch to her shoulders. Sophie'd grown up and married in more robust times, when talk was freer, manners less strict and formal. A new century, great conveniences, wonderful inventions . . . but still . . . Brandy's girlhood had been so much more sheltered than her own.

Her daughter'd been perfectly normal until a couple of years ago, bright and pretty, her father's darling. Sophie began to notice a change in Brandy about the time she'd refused to marry young Trevors. John had overlooked the occasional bouts of strange behavior since then. Until he'd decided Brandy was pretending to be touched to avoid marriage to Mr. Strock.

Boulder had noticed it early, however. There'd been no more offers for Brandy's hand until Corbin Strock.

He seemed a quiet, severe sort of man, Sophie mused. Would he treat his new wife well? He could have rented a carriage to pick up his bride, but he'd come in a buckboard, of all things. There'd been no look of softness on his face for Brandy. What kind of a future would she have with him? Still . . . it would hardly be a future at all without a husband.

Brandy startled Sophie out of her reverie by jumping up and pounding on the glass of the mirror.

"Brandy, what is wrong?" Sophie took hold of her daughter's arms from behind and tried to drag her away. "Stop this."

Finally she forced herself between the girl and the mirror. "I wish I could understand you."

Her daughter stared at her blankly.

"Come along. Mr. Strock will be waiting." Sophie hesitated in the doorway and looked back at the mirror. The wretched thing had come into the house about the time Sophie'd noticed the beginning of her daughter's unusual behavior.

Could a mirror . . . ? No. And it'd been in the attic until yesterday. John brought it home as a wedding present and then in anger at Brandy's refusal to marry two years ago banished it to the attic. A mirror, no matter how ugly, was just that—a mirror.

"Your new hat is downstairs. Nora's pressing the ribbons." Sophie put an encouraging arm around Brandy's shoulders and led her from the room. If her daughter were becoming gradually deranged, should she marry at all? What of any children? Sophie hoped they were doing right by Brandy. Not that it was much use trying to oppose John. . . .

Shay, drained of fight and even fear, walked down the stairs beside Sophie.

"Your father and Elton will bring your trunk. Here's your hat." She took a wide-brimmed bonnet with awful cloth flowers and a veil from Nora and tied it under Brandy's chin.

"Trunk? Am I going somewhere?"

"Of course. You're going to live with your husband. Don't be a silly goose and don't embarrass your father. He won't stand for much more."

Numbly Shay digested the obvious, remembering how badly she'd wanted to leave the Gingerbread House when she was herself. But now this house was the only familiar thing this world had to offer . . . and the mirror. She clung to Brandy's mother, sending the bonnet askew. "I can't leave here."

"We've forgotten your bag. I'll get it." Sophie disengaged herself and walked back up the stairs as if Shay hadn't spoken.

Shay wandered into the dining room. Tingles like the bubbles in a Coke zinged under her skin, making her shiver in the heat. The mix-up in time happened here. Could the process be reversed if she left the house?

The dining-room table was the same, the room less crowded than Rachael would decorate it.

There was probably little use in protesting. Even Sophie was losing patience with her.

She leaned down to gulp air from an open window. Dust coated the bottoms of lacy starched curtains.

Corbin Strock stood on the front porch facing John McCabe.

Brandy's father pulled a folded paper from his pocket and handed it to Strock. He worked his tongue under his lower lip and spit brown juice over the porch railing while Corbin read the paper.

"It's drawn up legal. The Brandy Wine's yours," John said as Shay wrote with her finger in the dust on the windowsill, "John McCabe chews," and thought of using another term, the humor of which had probably not yet been invented.

"And so is my daughter." He fished in his jacket for an envelope and slapped it against Corbin's chest. "I want children from this match, Strock. We'll prove to the county there's nothing wrong with McCabe's girl. And there isn't. Nothing a strong man and hard work won't cure."

"John," Sophie called from the doorway. "Can you help Elton with Brandy's things?"

"In a minute, woman." He turned back to Corbin. "My fault. I spoiled her terrible. Couldn't help myself. I'm paying you good money and the Brandy Wine to straighten her out. It's gotten beyond me."

While Corbin counted oversized bills, Shay wiped her writing from the windowsill. Brandy's father loved his daughter. Enough to pay someone to marry her. In John McCabe's world he was doing his best for Brandy. Shay knew she couldn't exist in John McCabe's world.

"Brandy? Oh, here you are." Sophie carried a beaded purse with drawstrings. "Your gloves are in your bag. You don't want your hands to freckle."

Through the dining-room archway and over Sophie's shoulder Shay saw Elton and John inching their way down the staircase with the wedding mirror on its side between them . . .

And then Shay saw her own face, not in the mirror, which was turned with its backside to her, but interposed on the room and the form of Sophie . . . her own face . . . straight blond hair flying about it, eyes wide and blank, mouth rounded in a silent scream.

The image warped . . . wavered . . . vanished, leaving Shay sticky with sweat. Her breathing struggled against the corset.

"You're shaking." Sophie led her from the room. "Is there something about the mirror that disturbs you?"

If you only knew.

On the porch, Corbin and John lifted a trunk and carried it down the steps. The mirror stood alone and Shay watched Brandy's image, hoping the vision in the dining room meant she was to return to herself. But the mirror remained passive.

"Strock says he can't take the mirror, Ma. He needs the space for supplies."

Sophie gave Shay an odd look. "Perhaps it's for the best."

Shay floated trancelike between them down steps which were wooden instead of concrete, along pink stepping-stones instead of sidewalk, through a familiar gate which now had an unbroken latch, across wooden planks that spanned a narrow ditch running full with water, and to a dirt road.

"Elton, we must open the sluices when they've gone. It's our time for water and we've missed half of it."

The trees in the parking were little more than saplings.

"And, Brandy, send letters down by coach. I've put writing paper in your trunk."

The trunk sat in a wooden wagon behind two horses.

"Put down your veil when the road becomes dusty, and give my regards to Mrs. Strock." Brandy's mother hugged Shay, stifled a sob and whispered, "Be brave, dearest."

Then Shay was crushed in the arms of Brandy's father. "Sorry about the mirror. We'll send it up. You work at being a good wife now, little one, and put to rest all these rumors about McCabe's daughter having a tile loose." He kissed her cheek, his breath strong with tobacco. Turning his back, he drew a handkerchief from a pocket under his coattail. "Take her away, Strock."

Brandy's brother lifted Shay to a hard wooden seat beside Corbin. "Good-bye, Bran. I'll be up to see you when I can."

Corbin slapped long reins down on the horses' rumps. The wagon moved forward.

In a state of shock, Shay looked back at Sophie crying on her husband's shoulder, at Elton standing forlornly by the ditch of running water . . . at the mirror without its crack sitting on the porch.

Elton raised his hand in a halfhearted wave.

6

Shay watched the Gingerbread House grow smaller. The sad grouping of Brandy's family still had not moved from the street.

Finally she turned to face Boulder, Colorado—most of which wasn't there.

Locked in Brandy's body, she felt horribly afloat now, away from the house and the mirror.

The wide brim of Corbin Strock's hat hid the upper portion of his face. But the set of his jaw below was grim.

"This doesn't make much sense you know," she heard herself say in a small voice. "My mother's maiden name wasn't Strock." Her uncles, Remy and Dan, weren't named Strock either. Shay peered under Corbin's hat brim. "And you aren't the man in the wedding picture in the hall."

"That's because Mrs. McCabe's name was Euler before she married, and we didn't take a wedding picture." He turned the horses to start down the hill. Corbin had the same lazy but careful way of speaking as the McCabes. It wasn't a Southern drawl, nor was it the speech affected by TV cowboys. It was just unhurried, the vowels drawn out, the consonants distinct.

He thinks Brandy's crazy too. Whatever Shay said would be chalked up to that. And there was no place to run. The occupants of the Gingerbread House would refuse to take her back—for her own good.

Over rooftops and low trees she could see the hill on which sat two or three buildings of the University of Colorado, out on barren prairie, alone and aloof. It bore little resemblance to the campus, crowded with buildings and trees, surrounded by city, that she'd attended until a few weeks ago.

This slip in time couldn't last. Shay would go back to Marek and to school. It had been a freak thing.

Small wooden houses, many unpainted and on large lots. Outhouses and orchards. An occasional cow, horses, chickens. A rangy dog at every lot to run into the street, bark at the horses, chase wagon wheels. The horses plodded on, paying no attention, their tails lashing flies. Corbin turned the buckboard onto Pearl Street, which was no longer blocked by an elegant downtown shopping mall.

Whenever a carriage or wagon passed too close, flies rose from piles of horse dung that dotted the dirt street.

"People are staring at us." Women with small waists and big hips, long hot skirts. Men in loose clothing with smirks to match. Everyone wearing hats. Not a bare arm to be seen in the summer's heat.

"Don't stare back," Corbin ordered and stopped the buckboard in front of a brick building where Shay'd clerked the summer before. Painted on the brick above the second story now were the words HARDWARE & STOVES.

Corbin tied the reins to a metal ring in a miniature stone obelisk and disappeared into the store.

Shay wanted to slouch in the heat but the corset wouldn't permit it. Removing the short suit jacket, she wished she could take off the long-sleeved blouse under it, wondered if she dared remove the hat and decided against it.

If I had somewhere to go, now would be the time for a getaway.

Smells of horse and dust instead of exhaust, and tar that oozed in the sun between great slabs of flagstone sidewalk. A vicious dogfight in the middle of the street. Overhead, a forest of power and telephone wires hanging on coarse tree-trunk poles stripped of bark and branches. A little boy in knee britches staring with round, frightened eyes.

Shay made a face and he ran off. She found an ironed, folded handkerchief smelling of lavender in the beaded bag and wiped moisture from Brandy's forehead.

A man with a broom swept dirt from metal rails in the streets.

Boisterous laughter across the street and three men emerged from a doorway. The sign above read, WERELY'S SALOON. They stopped when they saw her. "Looks like Strock made it to the wedding after all, gentlemen. Pay up," one of them said.

Shay turned away in embarrassment to find the little boy peering around the corner of the hardware store and the man with the broom grinning up at her.

What's the matter, never seen a crazy woman before? What if she had to remain Brandy McCabe Strock?

A trolley car approached on the metal tracks as Corbin appeared carrying a wooden box. Two men came behind him with a larger one that resembled a coffin. The wagon creaked and jerked as they loaded it and then her "husband" was beside her, urging the horses around the corner.

JACOB FAUS, GENERAL BLACKSMITHING—where there should have been a bank.

Panic, curiosity, fear, despair, excitement . . . Shay ran the gamut. Brandy's body tightened in response.

A series of railroad tracks instead of a boulevard. They turned toward the mountains. WATER ST.—a sign nailed to a telephone pole.

Where the public library had spanned Boulder Creek stood a square brick house surrounded by a picket fence.

Corbin pulled the wagon to a stop. Shay swallowed a lump.

A small sign in the window, MEN TAKEN IN AND DONE FOR.

"Is this where you live?"

Corbin's face grayed. "I don't find your jokes funny, Brandy." He reached into the smaller of the two boxes, removed a package tied with thick twine and jumped to the ground.

A woman rose from a wicker chair in the shade of the porch and moved gracefully toward the gate to meet him. Here was someone who looked comfortable, her sleeves mere ruffles at the shoulder, her dress of thin flowered material. *If she's wearing a corset, I'll eat it.*

"Well, Corbin?" Her hair frizzed around her face, her voice low.

"Marie." He handed her the package and they talked so quietly Shay couldn't hear. But Marie's eyes laughed at her over Corbin's shoulder.

The flash of another bare arm in the shadows of the porch . . . a woman's face in an open upstairs window.

A row of lopsided shanties along the creek to either side of the house. A more imposing building across the street—the sign here reading BOARDINGHOUSE FOR FANCY LADIES. Shay sat up, taking a new interest in similar houses and shanties lining the creek. *This is the red-light district and that's a whorehouse and Marie is a . . .*

Shay laughed aloud and drew a look of surprise from Marie and one of consternation from Corbin. He rejoined her, touched his hat to Marie and slapped down the reins.

Shay turned to wave good-bye to the woman standing at the gate. Marie hesitated, then waved back.

Corbin hissed and forced the horses into a trot. "I don't know if you are really silly or just acting, Mrs. Strock, but whichever, it looks as Thora K. has her work cut out for her."

"Who's Thora K.?" Something familiar about that name.

"Your mother-in-law, as I told you last Sunday. And I'm warning you now, don't try none of your foolishness on Thora K."

"You drive a bride of one hour up to a whorehouse to deliver a present to a prostitute and then have the nerve to look at me as if I were dirt."

"And you wave at her friendly-like."

"Well, *you* obviously slept with her last night. You didn't even introduce us . . . as if I didn't exist. You're blushing." She'd never seen a full-grown man do that. *He's human, Shay, be careful. He's not just a dummy in a museum.*

"Ladies don't talk of these things," he said with a finality worthy of John McCabe.

They'd angled northwest and were back on Pearl Street heading toward the mouth of Boulder Canyon. Pulling to the side of the road, Corbin took a coil of rope from under the seat and began tying the boxes and her grandmother's trunk to the wagon, his movements brisk and sure, powerful hands jerking knots so tightly the rope made snapping sounds. Shay winced. Somehow she had to get this man on her side until she could escape this body. And she'd better do something before tonight.

A whistle, the sounds of hoof and harness, and four horses came up from behind, pulling an open wagon. TALMAGE & LILLY STAGE written along its side, six men on three rows of seats within—holding onto their hats and the side bars that held up a canvas top. They disappeared into the canyon, leaving Shay and Corbin to choke on dust.

Corbin slapped his hat against his leg, removed his coat and handed it to her. They started after the stage.

"Do you live in the mountains?" With the present level of conveniences, that sounded bleak.

"I live in Nederland, as you well know."

"Nederland . . ." She'd been there with Marek just last Sunday. They'd picnicked by the reservoir, talked of the wedding, planned their honeymoon in Aspen. Marek seemed a million years away.

A railroad across the creek that hadn't been there last Sunday. Boulder Creek, twice as big and ferocious as she'd ever seen it. A narrow dusty trail that couldn't possibly accommodate two horses and a wagon.

"Put your skirts down, Brandy!" His voice was husky with shock.

"It's hot in here," she pleaded, but slid the skirt back till it reached her shoes. It was like a tent, under the sun, trapping the hot air against her legs. How had women survived these little cruelties? *If I stay here, I will be crazy.*

Occasional spray from the creek was cool at least. The horses moved so slowly. How different from Marek's sleek Porsche, which propelled them to Nederland on smooth wide pavement in less than an hour. "It must take all day to get there at this rate."

"It'll likely be dusk."

Heaps of rock piled to forever. Giant boulders that the road merely skirted. Boulder Canyon simply did not resemble itself. And rough log bridges, the road crossing and recrossing the creek to avoid the least obstacle.

Shay held onto the seat with both hands, closed her eyes in tortuous places, grew stiff and hot and hungry. The openness of the wagon and the narrow insignificance of the road made looming canyon walls appear more gigantic than she'd known them.

The railroad veered off up another canyon and the road to Nederland worsened, whole stretches of it supported by rocks piled against the bank below, a series of logs laid across mud in damp places. No springs in the buckboard. The horses sweated and strained in their harnesses, carrying Shay farther from the Gingerbread House . . . and the wedding mirror.

The man beside her seemed unconcerned with the tedium and discomfort of the trip. *I really rattled his cage by waving at old wise-eyed Marie, but he seems to have recovered.* Perhaps he was more easygoing than she'd judged him. Shay knew she'd misjudged the others, probably because of their strangeness. In their ways, all three members of Brandy's family loved her. She saw again the desolate trio in front of the Gingerbread House.

Any man the size and age of Corbin Strock who could blush had to have feelings, had to be reachable. The problem was how to go about it.

Shay took as deep a breath as the sticky corset would allow. "Corbin, I have something to tell you. I've got to tell someone, to straighten this thing out."

His body went rigid, his hands drew in on the reins and his foot jammed the primitive brake on the side of the wagon. "God, woman, you're not with child?"

"With chi . . . oh, you mean pregnant. No, it's not . . . I mean, I don't think so."

His face turned white, then red.

"Now, don't get all torqued up. For all I know, Brandy's as virginal as they come. What I want to tell you is . . . and this will sound freaky, but . . . I'm not crazy, Corbin, and I'm not Brandy." His interruption had flustered her. She had a drowning feeling but went on quickly before she lost her nerve. "I think I'm her granddaughter or rather she's my . . . let me start again. And you must listen because this is true and I need help."

"I will listen." The wagon moved forward.

"Until last night, I was Shay Garrett . . ." She tried hard to be convincing, but the further into her story, the more she realized that if anyone'd tried to tell her such things, she'd have inched away from that person until she could run. Corbin Strock merely nodded, looked into her face often and kept his own expressionless.

"I don't know how it could've been, but I think it was the mirror."

"The mirror."

"Yes, the one on the porch. That's the one that'd been in my room, it . . . oh, look. A deer. I saw a deer. And there's another, by the creek."

"You saw a deer." He didn't bother to look at the deer. His expression didn't change.

Frustrated tears all over her face. "It's no use, is it? You don't believe me and I don't know how to prove it." She fished the hanky out of the beaded bag. "Wait, I know. I can tell you of things that will happen in the future."

"You foretell the future."

"Listen, wise guy. Last Sunday when I came up with Marek, he's the fiancé I told you about, this road . . ." When she'd finished with the improvements to the canyon she went on to dredge up what little she could remember of her history studies. History had bored her all through school and she'd memorized enough to pass tests, then cleaned out her mind for more interesting details. She skimmed over the depression (oh, how Rachael'd carried on about that) and the two world wars . . .

"All over the world?"

"No, just Europe and Asia mostly and there'll be wars in Korea and Vietnam."

Corbin had never heard of either.

"They used to be called something else, I can't remember now." Shay went on to cars and television sets . . . the wildness of the canyon really did have a beauty of its own. How did they ever clear away so much of the tumbled rock and fallen trees to make the canyon that she knew?

Corbin kept his deadpan in place through airplanes but when Shay reached the point of women wearing pants and skirts above the knee he broke into sudden laughter.

Shay drooped. *Well, what'd you expect, dumb-dumb?* At least he'd heard her out. But how did one explain the impossible? How explain the future to someone who hadn't lived it or with its consequences?

Corbin's laughter died as suddenly as it'd come, replaced by thoughtfulness and then suspicion. "You aren't one of those lady authors, are you? In secret?" Disapproval in his tone.

"No." She shrugged Brandy's shoulders. "I'm just old crazy Brandy. And this is hopeless." She reached again for the handkerchief.

The road rose precipitously away from the creek on a narrow bank supported by a rock wall and tree-trunk braces. From around the curve ahead came the sound of bells.

"Damn!" Corbin glanced at her. "Sorry."

"What is it?"

"Freight wagon." He put his hand to the side of his mouth. "Whoa up, ahead!"

"But nobody can pass here."

"I'll have to back to a turnoff. You get up the hill and out of the way."

Shay ripped the hem of her grandmother's skirt as she left the wagon, fought the troublesome garment as she scampered up away from the road. She collapsed into the shade of a boulder in time to see six horses, two abreast, pull a wagonload of massive machinery around the bend. The horses stopped and the driver put his foot out on the brake to wait as Corbin backed his team down the incline.

When the wagon hit the canyon wall and a front wheel almost went over the ledge opposite, Shay was thankful he'd let her out first. She drew in a noisy breath and the driver of the freight, who was calmly dumping tobacco from a pouch onto a thin paper, looked up with a lazy smile.

He lifted his hat and nodded. "Ma'am."

Shay nodded back and let out her breath slowly, catching a glimpse of platinum blond hair before he replaced the hat.

He licked the paper, smoothed it and lit it with a wooden match he'd scraped under his boot. Taking a long puff, he looked up again.

The tanned face and sandy mustache didn't match the hair, neither did the insolent gold-brown eyes. Instant dislike mingled with the shock of recognition as Shay straightened her back at the hard stare below her.

Here, at last, was the man in Grandma Bran's wedding picture in the hall.

7

At a shout from Corbin, somewhere down the canyon, the freighter released the brake enough to let his horses move away.

Shay sat listening to the boiling creek over Brandy's heartbeat, telling herself she'd imagined the similarities between the man in the old wedding picture and the one in the wagon. The picture hadn't shown such light hair, but the picture had darkened. Corbin finally pulled up below her.

"Who was that driver on the freight wagon?" she asked when she sat beside him.

"Lon Maddon. You stay out of his sights. He's a bad one."

"Maddon." Her mother's maiden name. Her twin uncles' last names—Remy and Dan had this Lon's eyes too, as she'd had herself. Until last night.

And Shay Garrett's hair (she seemed almost a different person now) was a similar color. It'd often been referred to as "the Maddon hair" in an otherwise dark-haired family. She'd just looked into the face of her grandfather.

Brandy must unload Corbin and marry this Lon. She certainly has odd taste.

Shay couldn't get all caught up in a life not her own, knowing too much and too little at the same time. *What if Corbin Strock dies?* That would leave Brandy free to marry again. *Only, I don't want to be around when it happens.*

John McCabe said he'd send the mirror. When he did, Shay determined to have a long hard talk with it. The thought should have seemed silly, but nothing could be more incredible than the turn her life had taken since the night before.

Corbin noticed the change in Brandy after he'd picked her up. She was silent, subdued. "Did Maddon say anything unkind to you back there?"

"No." She eyed him with a sadness that made him uneasy.

She was a strange one, there was no doubting it. Unlike John McCabe, Corbin couldn't believe she was feigning madness. The best of actresses couldn't make such swift changes in personality and expression, nor so convincingly. Real tears, then startling laughter, looks of an intelligence so intense they chilled him—not the sly look of insanity he'd have expected. But Corbin'd never approved of high intelligence in women. It made them troublesome. Brandy would interrupt herself in the middle of one of her wild fantasies to exclaim over a deer drinking at the creek, or a series of small rainbows in the sunflash of spray, common enough sights in a canyon she must have traveled often.

In fact, the first time he'd seen this fey creature was at the end of this canyon, on the occasion McCabe opened the Brandy Wine. She'd been dressed in white and carried a tiny parasol, pretty and spoiled, the daughter of a wealthy man, but quite normal, playing with other children whose parents attended the ceremony. Her father had lifted her to his shoulder, announcing he was naming the silver mine for "this precious piece of baggage here."

Even before the price of it'd dropped, the silver in the Brandy Wine played out, as had, apparently, the mind of the child for whom it was named. McCabe'd abandoned the mine and was now abandoning the child. Corbin felt shame at being a party to it, but he and Thora K. would look after her. It would have been easier on them all if Brandy were not such a beauty.

Hard to believe she was the animated creature of a few hours ago. Or the girl with the brazen laughter and mischief in her eyes when they'd made that stop on Water Street, which he admitted now he'd had no business making. She'd stared about there as if she'd never seen it before. Boulder wasn't so large a place that even a well-bred girl could have missed at least a peek at the houses of that forbidden way. And it was common knowledge that the madams paid cumshaw to McCabe and others like him to stay in business at all.

No, Brandy must suffer from memory losses as part of her affliction. That would explain why she'd looked at him as if he were a stranger this morning at their wedding, when he'd talked with her in that very parlor on the two previous Sundays. And why she did not appear the same person today. He'd believed McCabe's story of her pretense then. She'd been cold, resentful, blushed often—but today . . .

To get the Brandy Wine, he'd indeed saddled himself with a demented wife. And the fault was all his own. He'd investigated the float around the mine, talked to a man who'd once worked her, and rushed off to see if he could lease her from McCabe.

After some thought and much questioning, McCabe'd stunned Corbin by offering the Brandy Wine to him as a gift, free title, and cash to boot, with only one condition. That condition now drooped next to him.

Ever since Corbin started in the silver mines of Caribou as a mucker at fourteen, he'd dreamed of owning his own mine. Work as a miner had been hard to find in the last years as the mines closed one by one. He'd swept out stores and fed horses at the livery, any sort of odd job. Now the black iron that Samuel Conger'd discovered in the area would revive mining and Corbin Strock at the age of thirty had achieved his dream at last. He owned the Brandy Wine—but the cost had been dear.

They munched on drying bread and cookies that Mrs. McCabe had sent along. Finally Corbin could stand his thoughts no longer, nor the dejection of the poor girl beside him. "What's wrong with you now, Brandy?"

She studied his face. He must not have set it right because the brief hope vanished from her eyes. "You'll just think I'm crazy." She looked away with the most heart-wrenching sigh he'd ever heard.

"I listened before. I'll listen again."

He thought she wouldn't answer but finally she said, "What if I can't go back? What if I have to live out Brandy's life? She lives an awfully long time, Corbin."

"I won't hurt you, Brandy."

"What if the mirror won't work the reverse? I'd be stuck in this body and—"

"Would you feel better if you had that mirror with you?"

"Oh, yes."

"We'll have it sent up as soon as possible then."

Her mood seemed to lighten after that. She sat straighter, seemed to take an interest in old diggings and miners' shacks along the way, but soon she drooped again. "I think this is the longest trip of my life," she said finally. "I'm used to a faster pace, I'm afraid."

"The horses are tired. I don't think they can do more."

"I didn't mean the horses, poor things. Look at the sweat on them."

"Tell me some more stories then. That will pass the time for us both."

"Stories?"

"About the future, people flying or anything." She did have a fine way with her stories, this little wife he'd acquired.

"Oh . . . well . . . let me think. I don't think you're ready for Watergate—"

"But we already have gates for water."

"Yeah. How about men going to the moon?"

"That sounds interesting."

Brandy began the most fantastic tale he'd heard yet and, as before, the words tumbled from her lips so fast he missed many, and many were either from another language or made up by her poor fevered brain. But the sound of her voice was pleasant and soothing despite her excessive energy and the tale she told outdid most anything he'd ever read. Even the novels of Mr. Wells.

"And the first astronaut gets out and says something about a big step for mankind . . . where's Tungsten? We must not be there yet."

"The ore?"

"No, the town."

"There's no town of Tungsten in this canyon. People are still laughing at those of us who are about to make our fortunes on the black iron, as they call it."

"Well, I don't know if you're going to make a fortune, but a town'll spring up along here somewhere and it'll be named Tungsten. And it'll die. There were only a few foundations left when I came up last Sunday." Brandy turned haunted eyes to him. "Isn't it scary how a whole town can be born and die in less than a lifetime? Of course, Brandy lives forever."

An eerie feeling along his spine. "What do you know of mining tungsten? I thought your father was among the scoffers."

"Nothing. I didn't know it was something you mined. It's just the name of a ghost town to me. The Brandy Wine is a mine, I take it," she added without much interest.

"Yes, and named after you. And you were not up here last Sunday. You and I were talking in your parlor. Don't you remember?" His uneasiness grew.

"No, that was Brandy. I was with Marek. We picnicked over there by the . . . where's the reservoir? And the dam?" She stared around him at Barker Meadows, the rosy flush gone from her cheeks.

"There is no such thing here, Brandy."

At times she seemed too smart by half, but she believed her silly tales and it frightened him more than a little. Corbin wondered if she would become a danger. Should Brandy be locked up somewhere?

8

The sun had gone down behind mountains and Nederland sat in dusky half-light and shadow. A different scrubby-looking Nederland, most of the houses mere rough cabins, the slopes around denuded of trees—for firewood and building materials, Shay supposed. Stumps were left standing to scar the hillsides. Desolate tendrils of smoke filed from ugly pipe chimneys, mingled with the raw smells of pine and rotting garbage. No power lines here, the only poles those propped against a few lopsided buildings to keep the structures upright in the wind.

Where was the tiny resort, tucked in its bowl of forested mountains, reflected in the aqua-blue waters of Barker Dam? *Like me, it hasn't been invented yet.* And most of the people on the rickety steps or porches and those strolling the wooden sidewalks in front of false storefronts were dead and gone to her yesterday.

Shay shivered as the horses crawled their snaillike way up the dirt Main Street.

GROCERIES & PROVISIONS—a sign hanging over the sidewalk fastened to a store with weather-worn paint. They turned a corner, crossed a primitive bridge over Middle Boulder Creek and angled across the valley to ascend the opposite side.

Brandy's body felt hungry, tired and dirty. Inside it, Shay was heavy with depression.

Only scattered shacks along the road now, and finally some trees.

"Why is everyone sitting outside?"

"It's a nice evening. What else should they be doing?"

Watching television.

Corbin turned off the road and the wagon bumped over rocks and depressions. No driveway here. A tiny cabin ahead had a covered porch running the length of its front. Corbin drove along its side and backed the horses toward the rear door. An outhouse in the trees behind.

"Is this . . . all?"

"All of what?"

"But . . . where do you keep your horses?"

"You'll have to get used to less here than at your father's grand house, Brandy. The wagon and horses belong to the livery stables."

"How do you get around without even a horse?"

"On my two feet, as the good Lord intended. When I need more I can rent a conveyance, if there's the money to be had." He jumped off the wagon and came around to lift her down.

A tiny woman, bent with the weight of a metal pail in each hand, rounded a shadowy path by the outhouse. She straightened when she saw them and approached with her stare fixed on Shay.

"Thora K.," Corbin said under his breath, and without greeting his mother or offering to help her with her burden began to unloose the ropes that tied the cargo to the wagon.

Thora K. stopped in front of her and set down the pails. A swarm of black flies settled instantly on their rims. The old woman peered up at her with such fierce concentration her eyes crossed. "I be Methodist, wot be 'ee?"

"What?" Shay backed away.

"The McCabes are Presbyterian, Thora K., and this is Brandy." Corbin manhandled the coffinlike box from the wagon bed to the board platform that provided a back step for the cabin.

"Brandy? And wot kind of man names 'is child after spirits, I ask 'ee?" Thora K. said, almost in English, and moved to open the screen door for Corbin. "And wot's this yer takin' in me 'ouse, Corbin Strock?"

"You'll see." Corbin grunted with the exertion of tipping the box onto his back, straightening his knees to lift it and careening into the cabin.

"Do 'ee carry in the water, you," Thora K. commanded, still holding the door, dirt and pine needles sticking to the hem of her dress.

Wait till I get my hands on that mirror! But Shay stooped to lift the pails and staggered after Brandy's husband.

"Be it for she?" Corbin's mother stood looking at the box, upended now, sitting just inside the door.

"No, it's for you." Corbin wrenched out nails with a hammer, tore apart the boards of the box and looked at Thora K. expectantly.

She neither moved nor spoke, her eyes riveted on the upright chest he'd uncovered.

Corbin took a blackened lamp with a glass chimney from a hook in the ceiling, lit the wick and held the lamp high. "Open it."

But the old woman backed away, sat on a rough bench by an even rougher table and put her hand to her breast. "Tez a hicebox."

"Yes." Corbin opened it to reveal shelves inside.

"'Ow did'ee get money fer that?" She sounded breathless.

"From my agreement with Mr. McCabe. I told you."

"And 'ee bought a hicebox." Thora K. sat trancelike, apparently unable to believe an icebox had happened to her.

Looking around the room, half-lit by the lamp, Shay could see why the present was such an occasion to Thora K. Strock. And if she'd felt depressed before, Shay felt totaled now. *This won't be forever.*

She stood in a corner, forgotten, while Corbin put the broken boards of the packing case into a box next to the cookstove, collected the unbent nails in a rusty can and unloaded the wagon. The cabin was one room deep with two tiny bedrooms at one end, so tiny Corbin could barely squeeze her trunk through a door that wouldn't open fully because of the bed. Unenclosed stairs ran up the wall between the two bedroom doors to what couldn't be more than a low attic in this small a cabin. And that was it.

No wonder everyone sat outside after dinner.

When Sophie had counseled her to be brave, she'd meant more than just the mechanics of going to bed with Corbin Strock.

He towered over Shay now and she backed farther into her corner as he reached behind her to take his hat from a peg on the wall. "I'll return the horses and wagon. She'll get you something to eat." And he was gone.

Thora K. finally came out of her trance. "Be careful of that, you. Tez all I 'ave left of Cornwall."

Shay turned to see the buffet that had sat in the hall of the Gingerbread House. She was staring into Brandy's stricken face in one of the twin beveled mirrors. She touched a familiar pull on a drawer. Rachael'd been so proud of those antique pulls.

Longing and homesickness engulfed Shay like a fever.

Thora K. stuck her face close to Shay's and again one eye wandered in the intensity of her concentration. "'Ee look wisht, girl."

"I don't feel very good."

"That's wot I said. Take off yer 'at and sit 'ee down here. I'll get some kiddley broth fer ya." She motioned toward the table with her thumb, an unnecessary gesture since the benches on either side of it were the only seats in the room. "Won't take they kiddley long ter boil." Thora K. poked at the coals under a lid on the cookstove, added a piece of the icebox's packing crate and set a teakettle on. "I 'ad some tay not long afore 'ee came."

Shay was still trying to translate all this when the old woman brought a slab of crusty bread to the table, broke it into pieces and placed them in a bowl. Tucking the ends of her shawl under her belt to keep them out of the way, she sprinkled salt and pepper over the bread, added a dab of white butter and some kind of herb from a glass jar.

When the kettle sang she poured boiling water over the whole mess and set it in front of Shay with a spoon. " 'Ere, stir it some. Looks funny but it do go down 'andsome when yer a mite wisht."

Shay couldn't believe how delicious it was and wondered if perhaps instant soup were not such a modern convenience after all. And it did make her feel less "wisht" if not less depressed.

Thora K. sat opposite, watching her every move. Streaks of orangy-red showed in thin graying hair pulled into a little ball on top of the old woman's head.

"Tez funny, 'ee don't look daft." She stood and turned up the wick in the lamp to study her new daughter-in-law.

"Would 'ee eat somethin' more now? The color's back in yer chacks."

Shay looked around the barren cabin. "Well, if there's enough, I–"

"Henough!" Thora K. threw back her shoulders and her shawl came out of her belt. "Don't 'ee worry, you. Us don't go 'ungry 'ere. Us weren't scat, 'ee know, even afore yer fayther's uld mine and 'is money."

"I didn't mean–"

"I know wot 'ee meant. Henough indeed. 'Ere, eat every last crumb, you, or I'll scat 'ee across the chacks, proper." She threw a semicircular thing into the bowl now cleaned of soup.

A kind of cold meat pie with potato and onion, rather strangely spiced and encased in a thick crust.

Thora K. sucked in sunken cheeks, pressed her lips together so tightly her nose came dangerously close to her chin. Her attention shifted with equal suspicion between Shay and the new "hicebox."

How could John McCabe have thought this a good place for his daughter, crazy or not? Shay wondered miserably.

Dusk slid into night over the Gingerbread House and the wedding mirror still standing on the porch. Light from the windows gave straining bronze hands a dull sheen, left the secret glass shadowed.

Elton McCabe crossed the planks over the irrigation ditch and walked through the gate. Head lowered, lost in thought, he moved slowly, not anxious to reach the house. The glum silence at dinner, the empty place at the table, his mother's sighs, his father's reaching too often for the wineglass . . . and Elton's own sense of guilt had sent him from the house as soon as the meal ended to walk quiet streets, to brood, to kick at dogs who nipped at his heels, to merely nod at others out for a stroll.

Elton sat on the steps, smelled in the residue of dampness from the irrigating, the fragrance of his mother's flowers tumbling from their beds. And felt a curious shiver along his spine. All the while thinking of his sister in the crude hands of Corbin Strock.

The door slammed behind him. "Should get that mirror in sometime. I forgot it." His father sat next to him. "She'll be all right, son. Don't take it so hard."

"And how do you know that?" Elton was ashamed of the emotion that shook his voice. "That lout Strock is—"

"Now, what else could I do? Answer me that." John McCabe spit into the grass. "As I see it, I had three choices. One was to shut her up in a lunatic house in Denver. And if she's not out of her mind she would be soon in a place like that. The second, to keep her home here."

"That would have been my choice."

"Would it?" John asked quietly.

Guilt brought a flush to Elton's cheeks. "Yes," he lied.

"And what would your chances be of finding a wife in this town, Elton McCabe, with a loony sister in the house? I don't believe she is, mind you, but she insisted on acting like it. And people have long thought it taints the blood of a family. If not yours, then maybe that of your children. Folks won't be anxious to have you courting their daughters if . . . I suspect you've noticed a few fences without gates already. Haven't you?"

"Yes." Mary Ann's mother giving him a pitying look but summoning her daughter into the house when he'd walked her home from the store. Mrs. Elliot hovering at the parlor door when he'd called on Margaret. The people of Boulder had to show respect to a McCabe but that didn't extend to endangering the future of their daughters. The cruel comments of some of his men friends. He'd tried to talk his father into keeping Brandy home and he'd felt empty when Strock drove her away. But Elton had also felt relieved. This was the reason for his heavy load of guilt tonight. "Corbin Strock is—"

"And how many beaux has the girl had in the last two years? Where was I to go for one? Strock dropped out of heaven like it was all intended. He's not uneducated, you know. Schooled in Caribou and I've heard many a miner's child who come from that school talk with a better command of the language than you, boy. He's better-read than you too."

"He's a lout," Elton insisted.

"Well, if he is, he's a strapping one. Ought to beget children by the score. And what better to prove our Brandy's a normal woman than a passel of normal children? He's a powerful man and stubborn as hell and his mother's a tough old Cornish woman. Now, if those two can't make her see sense, no one can. Your mother and I have always been too soft with her. Hope we done better by you.

"She'll have plenty of hard work, live in a healthful, bracing mountain air . . ." John McCabe took off his spectacles to polish them with his handkerchief, avoided Elton's eyes and whispered, "And already I miss her something terrible . . . just terrible."

"Pa—"

"Let's get that mirror in." He shrugged off the hand Elton had placed on his shoulder.

Sophie came to hold the door as Elton took the cold brass hands of the mirror's platform and his father the upper portion.

"Let's put it back in her room for now."

Elton imagined an odd tingling current passing through his hands as he struggled up the stairs with the heavy wedding mirror . . .

And in Nederland Shay toppled off the bench as if she'd been struck, crumpling the meat pie in a fist that tightened without her command. She felt Brandy's head and back hit the floor, struggled to bring air into Brandy's lungs and began to black out . . .

A wavering vision of herself and her parents standing by an undulating box. They spoke, but Shay could hear nothing. Rachael wiped her eyes, her other arm around Shay's body. Her father stood next to them.

Shay's body had the platinum hair pulled back into a bun, had a blank look in the eyes but responded when Jerrold spoke to it.

They all stared into the box . . . a satin-lined coffin. Inside it lay Grandma Bran, composed and peaceful . . .

"Be it a fit, do 'ee think?"

"I don't know." Corbin's voice. "Brandy?"

"Her were sittin' eatin' a pasty one minute and the next—plop on the floor, she was."

Shay felt herself being lifted, and opened her eyes to Corbin's chin. "What happened to me?"

"Hush now. We'll get you to bed."

" 'Ee get 'er to bed, I'm runnin fer they doctor."

"I saw his buggy at the Williamses'. Cara's baby must be due."

"There's a pasty fer 'ee in the cupboard," Thora K. called from the porch and was gone.

"Corbin, I'm afraid."

"It could be the journey in the sun was too much for you." He found a nightgown in Brandy's trunk and helped her to undress. It seemed to embarrass him more than it did her. "You rest now till Doc Seaton comes. I'll be getting something to eat." He patted her head, his fingers lingering on her hair, then left her to the dark, taking the lamp with him.

Shay felt weak and light-headed but scratched luxuriously wherever the corset had clutched her. The vision of herself and her parents peering into Grandma Bran's coffin repeated itself in her head. It must have been a dream but . . . the whole world seemed a dream now . . . and the hair style . . . Shay'd never worn it that way . . . the Shay in the vision seemed to be a different person . . . the freighter in the canyon, her grandfather, had a gap between his two front teeth . . . the family likeness was unmistakable . . . how could Brandy throw over Corbin for someone like that . . . Shay wouldn't have . . . so that must prove that Brandy returned to her own body sometime . . . what would happen when Corbin came in to bed tonight . . . he wasn't hers . . . the thought of sex with a stranger was tantalizing in books . . . but in reality . . .

Shay'd almost fallen asleep in Brandy's body for the second night when Dr. Seaton arrived.

"'Ere, do 'ee take the lamp. I've a candle for we," Thora K. told him, and closed the door on them.

"Well, now, I hear you fainted at the table. I'm Dr. Seaton, known as the Doc and worse things too," the little man said and sat on the bed beside her, putting his hand to her forehead.

"Hi, I'm . . . Brandy." Shay was too tired to explain to another soul who she really was.

"Known your pa for years. Set his leg once and unhinged a tooth for him while I was at it." His smile was kind and exhausted. He looked neither young nor old. Just tired.

The examination was surprisingly thorough. When he'd finished between her legs, he came back to listen to her chest again.

"The Lord works in strange ways, Mrs. Strock, and I'm not about to outguess him." He stood, wiped his fingers on a handkerchief and put his instruments in his bag. "But the McCabes are a hearty breed and you appear to be one of them. Your lungs sound clear. It's possible you've just spent too long a day in too tight a corset."

"I hate them."

"Throw yours away then. Your figure don't need one and I doubt Thora K. or Corbin'll care. You're not in Boulder now." He turned to go and stumbled, catching himself on the bedpost. He sat suddenly on the edge of the bed and covered his face with his hands.

Shay sat up. "Doctor?"

"I apologize, Mrs. Strock. I'm very tired. Give me a moment." His voice trembled and a shudder passed through his body to the bed and to Shay.

Dr. Seaton took a deep breath and stared into the air. "I just lost Cara Williams and her baby too," he whispered, as if to himself. "And I don't know how. I must get back to Samuel."

He blinked and refocused on her. "Forgive me, I shouldn't be troubling you now. Lie down." He struggled to his feet and pulled the blanket over her.

9

Shay awakened to darkness and Corbin's voice in the main room. "I told you about the rumors after my first talk with McCabe."

"But they do say her's barmy fer sure. Wot do 'ee say now ye've wed she? Be it rumor?"

A long sigh from Corbin. "The stories she told me on the way up the canyon and the way she changed from one minute to the next . . . she can't be sane."

"Wot sort of stories?"

"Oh, about a reservoir and dam to be built on Barker Meadows, a town called Tungsten in the canyon, men flying in metal monsters and going to the moon, herself being her own granddaughter because she looked in a mirror—"

"Sound like grand stories. Might be 'er read 'em in a book."

"But she believes them, Thora K. Truly believes in every one of them. We'll have to watch her."

"And 'ow is us to do that, ye bloomin' numbskull, when 'ee go off to that 'ole in the ground and me to the 'otel? Never thought of that, did 'ee?"

"We'll have to think of something."

"Well, daft er no, she'd best be able to work."

"That could be the answer. Keep her busy while we're away."

"Give she somethin' to do to keep 'er mind off not havin' one, huh? And wot if, Corbin Strock," Thora K. said slowly and in a tone that chilled Shay, ". . . she wanders off and 'urts herself or some 'un else?"

"Then we'll just . . . have to have her put away," he answered sadly.

Shay came fully awake at that. He'd seemed so sympathetic. She knew he hadn't believed her, but for some reason she'd come to trust him.

" 'Ee can't be meaning to 'ave yer way with she. The children may be daft too."

"I'll sleep on the pallet in the loft."

"Ahhh, tez a wisht uld job of it." Thora K. made an eerie wailing sound. "Am I never to 'old a grandchild on me knee, boy?" And then after a long silence, "'Edden with babe already, is 'er? Faintin' off the bench?"

"Doc Seaton says she's never been touched."

Shay lay wide-eyed and worrying long after the sounds of Corbin settling himself in the loft overhead had stopped and after Thora K.'s candle no longer sent slivers of flickering light through the cracks between the boards of the wall next to her.

The mattress was hard and lumpy, without springs beneath it. When she rolled over, sharp points poked through the ticking and her nightgown. Dull moonlight found its way into the room, shadowed by the porch overhang. The smell of pine and charred wood . . .

She'd pretend to be Brandy and go along with the Strocks until the mirror arrived. If she were "put away" in some institution before she could get to the mirror, it might be years before she returned to herself.

She slipped into dream-filled sleep where Rachael's image in the wedding mirror became Lon Maddon with a cruel smile, hands of cold bronze. Shay awoke sweating, to the shivery wail of coyotes and the stomp of some hooved creature outside.

In the morning, the cabin was icy and she pawed through the trunk for a sweater to put over what Sophie'd called the "day dress," but found only a shawl. Shay had ignored the corset and longed for a bra to support Brandy's heavy breasts. The frilled corset cover alone was little help. No one was in the main room as she dashed for the outhouse, avoiding the gruesome pot sitting at the foot of the stairs.

Rushing back from that dank cobwebby place, she belatedly buttoned up Brandy's black shoes and worked snarls out of thick hair with comb and brush. No dresser in her room, no mirror and no closet, just pegs on the wall for clothes. In an attempt to appear normal, and standing before a beveled mirror of the buffet, she braided Brandy's hair. Even Marie on Water Street hadn't worn hers loose. The shawl slipped from her shoulders and the hair from the braid as she used every hairpin Brandy owned to fasten it into a coronet on top.

The unfamiliar face beneath it responded to all her emotions as the body did to her commands. The voice didn't sound strange to her ears. But then they weren't her ears.

"Good morning. Feeling better?" Corbin shouldered through the screen door carrying a gunnysack.

She smiled and batted Brandy's eyelashes. "Is your mother up, too?"

"Yes, she's been gone a time. She helps at the Antlers four or five days a week in the summer. Remember?" A searching glance.

"The Antlers, yes." She tried to unstiffen the smile on Brandy's lips. "You told me last Sunday . . . in the parlor."

"We let you sleep late because of your illness last night." He removed a hunk of dirty ice with pieces of straw sticking to it from the bag and put it on the top shelf of the icebox. "The ice will be delivered from now on," he said proudly. "I put in a permanent order when I bought this. Come now, and I'll show you around."

Around what? But she followed him obediently along the path past the outhouse to a wooden door built into the hillside.

"We'll still keep some things here." They entered a cave lit only by the opening and he handed her a bowl filled with eggs and a metal pitcher of milk. "But many things we can keep in the icebox now. There are potatoes, onions, carrots, turnips and apples here."

Dim piles of things sat on a platform.

He filled his arms with shapes hanging from a beam and others from a table and led her to a wooden box a short distance from the cave. "This is the spring where we get our water. We share it with several of the houses along this way."

"But it's just a box."

"You lift the lid and dip the pail into it. Let it refill and you can dip another. It's a good spring in most seasons . . . but you're used to pipes and such." His dark hair tumbled across his forehead. "Nederland doesn't have piped water yet. Now, here you see a path. Follow it along the cliff and over a ridge and you're at the Brandy Wine. It's not the way you're used to getting there. But if you ever need me . . ."

"Yes?" Brandy's body answered his gaze and surprised Shay. *Easy, girl.*

"I'm never far from the house. You're not to wander, Brandy."

When they'd loaded the icebox, he showed her a vegetable garden by the front porch and implements stored in a makeshift cupboard built onto the side of the cabin, explaining that one of her duties for the day was to weed and water the garden.

"You mean carry water clear from that spring?"

"Yes. Now you're to bake the bread Thora K. left rising on the shelf." He led her inside again. "Clean the lamp and fill it. The coal oil is kept here. Sweep out the floor. Empty the chamber pot and the ash from the stove. Prepare the supper–"

"Prepare what for supper?" Shay eyed the black cookstove with panic.

"Whatever you'd like. I'll be back at midday to see how you're faring. Have some breakfast first." About ten paces from the cabin he began to whistle.

I don't know how to use that stove or clean a lamp. I'll probably burn the place down. The Strocks would think it'd happened because she was crazy and put her away.

Shay fed Brandy some cheese, a piece of dry bread and a glass of milk. She felt better and decided to take one thing at a time and not worry about the rest until she had to. She could at least haul water, sweep and hoe.

She poured lukewarm water left in the tea "kiddley" into the dishpan and washed. Having dumped the dirty water on the ground by the back step, she swore at herself for not thinking to pour it on the garden.

Shay began there immediately. But the hoe wouldn't cut through the crusty ground to get at the roots of the weeds. Perhaps she should water first and then hoe.

Wondering what mental institutions must be like in this day and age, she raced along the path to the spring. It took the pool inside the box forever to refill so she could dip the second pail, and she struggled slowly back with the load, soaking each side of Brandy's dress with sloshover. *I didn't know water could be so heavy.*

It took five such trips and most of the strength from her borrowed body to wet the soil enough to work it. She groaned as she stooped for the hoe once more.

Birdsong. The drone of insects. The rhythmic scritching of the hoe. The sound of an ax splitting wood somewhere below. Barking dogs. Children's voices and laughter from cabins down the road. How could this world appear so normal? Didn't it realize it had been dead for years?

Shay thought of poor Cara Williams and her baby. How old had Cara been?

The sun grew hotter and Shay thirstier, but she'd used all the water on the garden. Brandy's fair skin prickled, so she returned to the cabin for the bonnet. The moment she opened the door she realized she'd forgotten to empty the chamber pot. She rushed it to the outhouse and then set it in the sun to air. After gulping a glass of cold milk, she was back at her hoeing.

Shay stopped often now, to rest Brandy's back. Middle Boulder Creek foamed and sparkled. Wildflowers decorated the slopes right up to the cabins and around the tree stumps. She had to admit it was a pretty sight by daylight and she could see more substantial homes now, built across the valley and among the cabins.

But one thing was curious. Her view of Main Street was excellent, yet she couldn't identify a single building. Surely some would have survived. The Gingerbread House had, and for far longer.

As she bent back to her task, her eyes slipped by the sweep of mountain peaks that hemmed the valley to the west. Gone were the swaths of treeless ski runs. How many times had Shay passed through a different Nederland on her way to the Eldora ski slopes? Again that intense longing to be home gripped her.

Brandy's hands had begun to blister when a thought brought her up short. She scanned the western ridges, turned to the town below, to the meadow where horses and cows grazed instead of a reservoir, and then took another look at the cabin. This must be almost the spot where Shay's parents owned a cabin. Jerry Garrett came up often to get away from the Gingerbread House.

Rachael'd inherited the Gingerbread House from her grandmother—that was Sophie. And this land must have come to the Garretts through Grandma Bran, *who is me right now*. Did Brandy inherit it as the widow of Corbin Strock? Perhaps she obtained it in a divorce settlement. Her mother and twin uncles had grown up on a ranch outside of Nederland.

Shay felt apprehensive at the thought of knowing things that would happen but not knowing why. What if the mirror wouldn't work?

The garbage heap not far from the garden was thick with flies, rusting cans and broken bottles. Sun elicited strange odors from that direction and Shay was relieved to put the hoe away and drag Brandy's aching back into the cabin.

It was long past midday when Corbin realized he'd not been back to check on Brandy and he hurried over the ridge to the path past the spring. Someone had forgotten to replace the lid. He stopped to scoop out a few drowned bugs, drink from his cupped hand and cover the spring.

Timbers to repair the shoring of the adit near the breast of the mine . . . more for cribbing new shafts . . . the pump must be on its way up the canyon by now . . . the old storage shed was falling to pieces, he'd build a new one . . . most of the timbering was sound . . . cables for a tramway in the depths . . . the rails were intact and three ore cars in the adit would need repairs .. . much to do . . . he'd have to get Tim Pemberthy in to help and they could train for the double hand in the Brandy Wine . . . kill two birds with one stone . . .

The old chamber pot sat smack in the middle of the clearing for all to see.

Smoke seeped through the wire mesh of the screen.

"Brandy!" Corbin shook loose thoughts of the Brandy Wine and raced to save the girl for which it was named. "Brandy?"

More smoke met him as he entered the house but he could see her through it, trying to whisk dark clouds out the front door with a dish towel.

Feather wisps of hair fell about her face, a smudge blackened one cheek, reddening streaks crossed her forehead. Her dress was dirty and her eyes round. "The stove," she said between seizures of coughing. "I didn't know how to work it." Brandy tried one of those false smiles on him as she had that morning. "Sophie, I mean Mother and Nora always did the stove thing." A tear wandered through the black smudge and Corbin had to turn away.

The smoke cleared rapidly and hadn't been as bad as he'd thought. In the stove, the fire was out but the mystery was how she'd lit one at all. The damper was shut tight. "Are you burned, Brandy?"

"Just from the sun." Her smile was real now, if trembly. "I forgot my bonnet at first."

Corbin showed her the handle to jiggle the ashes down, how to scrape them into the bucket with the scoop, how to adjust the vent, and then he built a fire for her. He wondered at the McCabes, working so hard to find their daughter a husband but not teaching her to use a cookstove.

He found some late lunch in the icebox, knowing pride at the fact he didn't have to walk to the cave for it and neither would the ladies. Corbin watched his wife sniff a tin can of grease and ladle some into a kettle. She put small hunks of meat to sizzle. Peeled potatoes, turnips, carrots and onions were set in rows on the table.

It appeared he'd have a fine supper at least. "Brandy, do you have an apron? Your dress is getting soiled."

"Apron. Oh . . ." She rushed to her trunk and returned tying one about her waist.

Corbin marveled at a woman forgetting her apron. This woman seemed to forget many things. The uneasiness stirred within him, and something else as well. Even when mussed and dirty, Brandy was a pretty little thing.

He left her sweeping the floor to walk into town and order supplies for the Brandy Wine. But she called him back from the porch. "Corbin, you haven't forgotten about the mirror?"

"I'll telegraph the McCabes before I see to anything else." He had forgotten the mirror and the relief that lit her face now made him feel guilty. The fact that her every little expression could move him so was perplexing.

Corbin started down the slope and tried to shrug off his thoughts. There was always May Bell. . . .

10

Thora K. bristled into the cabin, a tiny hat of black straw hiding her ball of hair. "Hoed up 'alf me onions, she did. Do 'ee come out and see it." She dragged Corbin to the garden without a glance for Shay or the table laid for dinner.

Shay slumped to a bench and stared at the gay bouquet of wildflowers set in a broken bottle from the garbage heap. That small gesture brightened the room so. But Thora K. noticed only the onions.

The stove overheated the cabin to stifling, but a spicy fragrance seeped from under the kettle's lid. She'd added herbs from Thora K.'s jar.

"I'm 'ungry," Corbin's mother announced when they sat to the table. Then she added pointedly, " 'Ope there's henough."

Thora K. cut her food into minute pieces and chewed it with her front teeth. "Tez a proper stew." Surprise in sharp blue eyes surrounded by crinkles.

Corbin agreed and Shay felt better. She'd have to find out what all was in that herb jar and take the knowledge back with her. On nights when Rachael was working under a deadline or was just too involved in her writing, Shay cooked the family's dinner. And very soon she'd be cooking Marek's.

"They flowers be some pretty. Tez nice to come from working and have a good supper on me table. 'Ee worked hard but the 'oeing din't 'ave to be done all in a day." Thora K.'s thumb hooked in the direction of the garden. "Just a mite ever' morning to keep ahead of they weeds. 'Ow about some bread with this 'andsome supper?"

"Bread!" Shay's fork dropped to clang against the plate. She registered now the cloth-covered humps on the shelf in the corner.

"Do 'ee sit still. I'll get it."

Corbin stared at her. "You didn't forget the bread?"

"Ahhh! Me whole week's bread . . . edden even baked." Thora K. slapped a pan on the table. "Did 'ee even poke it down, you?" Part of the sticky dough hung in tendrils over the edge, the rest a porous drying mass at the bottom. It resembled a sponge after an attack by a maddened shark.

Shay's experience with baking bread was to thaw a loaf from the freezer, let it rise and put it in the oven. *Hurry that mirror, John McCabe.*

Thora K. was still muttering about the bread when she sat on the porch after the dishes were done and bathwater carried in and heated. Shay could hear her as she washed Brandy's battered body in a round metal tub from the loft. When she finished she joined Thora K. on the porch so Corbin could bathe in privacy and in the same water. His mother explained with a sniff that she did not approve of exposing the "whole skin" at once (it was bad for the humors) and she would sponge from the dishpan later.

Thora K. also disapproved when Corbin, washed and in clean clothes, announced he was off to town. "They kiddleywinks and King Alcohol" would be the death of him. Corbin replied that any miner worth his salt spent Saturday night in the saloon. His bored tone suggested this argument recurred weekly.

Shay wondered what women did for fun on Saturday nights. But once in bed she fell into the deep sleep of the exhausted.

"Edden' fitty to work so 'ard on the Sabbath," Thora K. grumbled when Corbin finished reading aloud from the Bible. "Acourse it can't be 'elped. 'Ave to wash tomorrow and with the whole week's bread ruined—that's henough kneadin', you. Put it in the pan." She was teaching Shay to make bread.

Corbin looked sleepy but content. Did Nederland have ladies like Marie from Boulder? *He sure isn't getting any at home.*

Do the freighters work on Sunday? Perhaps the McCabes would send the mirror up on Monday. *Wash on Monday . . . how? Take the clothes down to the creek and beat them on a rock?* Shay slammed her knuckles into a fresh glob of dough. *Why don't prostitutes ever get pregnant?*

"'Ow yer ma could a raised 'ee to such an age and not taught 'ee to make bread . . . and 'ee din't clean the lamp."

And there he sits with the Bible on his lap, all innocence.

"And last night there were water all over the floor. 'Ee 'ave to empty the pan under the hicebox."

Big callused hands, rumpled hair, curious glances at me when he thinks I don't see. He was very aware of her, whatever he'd been up to the night before. *It's Brandy he sees, Shay.* And her hair was falling down again.

"Might as well show 'ee how to make pasties if us 'ave ter heat up the 'ouse anyway."

More flour, lard and salt. More trips to the cave. Corbin left to chop wood. Thora K. rolled out pastry dough on the table and cut it around an overturned plate to make circles. Shay sliced meat and vegetables.

"And that's another thing. The stew were tasty fer supper but food that takes a long fire be better left to winter days when us need ter heat the 'ouse. Then we'll get up some coal to cook with. In 'ot weather short fires be more comfortable and us can use wood."

Corbin brought in wood and again dark eyes ran over her.

He's just watching for me to do something crazy so he can put me away. But she pushed the hair off her face and pinned it down.

Meat, vegetables and herbs were placed on one side of the pastry circles and the dough folded over to make a semicircle, slashes for steam cut in the top. Thora K. crimped the edges and rolled out more pastry.

When the first pasties had baked, they took them out to a grassy knoll overlooking the valley and ate them hot. They were wrapped in clean cloths so they could be held.

"'Ee might not know much, you, but 'ee learn fast and work 'ard." Thora K. chewed another tiny bite with her front teeth and turned to Corbin. "Her edden barmy, just needs teachin'."

Corbin looked uncomfortable and his eyes slid away.

"Next Sunday the circuit preacher's comin' and we'll 'ave a proper service. Acourse it won't be chapel. And then we'll bury Cara and 'er babe. Poor things be keepin' at the hice barn all this time."

Shay's pasty stuck in Brandy's throat. "Where you get the ice for the icebox?"

"There be only one hice barn."

* * *

Shay carried buckets of water from the spring, trying not to wet the skirt of Brandy's traveling suit. The day dress was being washed. Short hairs had separated from her coiled braid and floated about her face, tickling.

A squirrel darted across the sun-dappled path and the pines hummed to the cool breeze of morning.

Shay, determined this would be her last day in this funny old-fashioned world, decided to enjoy it. Surely the mirror would arrive today, and she tried to think of some of the many questions she knew she'd ask herself when this strange experience was over. A nagging doubt about the mirror's ability or willingness to work its magic lingered on the edge of her thoughts, but she worked to keep it at bay. She wasn't strong enough to face that kind of defeat.

"The birds sound so happy this morning." She set the pails down by Thora K. and the tub she'd bathed in Saturday night. It now sat on a plank between two sawhorses.

"Aye. Times like this do remind me of uld Cornwall."

"That's in England, isn't it?"

"Never been to Hengland. Us come straight to Faulmouth from Redruth and round the Lizzard and Land's End to the big sea." Her knife shaved paper-thin shards of soap from a yellow bar. "But I 'eard Hengland's not such a bad place." Condescension in the lilting voice and an expressive shrug of the shoulders.

"What does the K. stand for in Thora K.?"

"Tez for Killigrew, me family name. Me 'usband Harvey weren't Cornish. And I be always spending time with they Cornish women in the town. Caribou it were. Harvey decided I'd ever be a Killigrew even after takin' 'is name. So at first 'ee calls me Thora Killigrew instead of Thora. Over the time it became Thora K. and I be called that since. Even by Corbin." She soaked Brandy's nightgown and rubbed it against a washboard. "Do 'ee run along to Samuel Williams and tell him I'll do 'is wash. Mrs. Tyler be feedin' 'im. I'll take 'is wash."

"The man whose wife died?" *All laid out in the ice barn?*

"Aye. Tez the third 'ouse down along from 'ere. Edden far."

Shay walked "down along" the road counting cabins. Thora K. wasn't such a bad old broad. It was just that these people didn't seem real. Shay couldn't get away from the feeling they were all dead and didn't know it, that they were lost in time—mere playacting curiosities.

The third cabin had lace curtains at the windows and a man stepping out onto the porch. It wasn't Samuel Williams.

It was the freighter, Lon Maddon.

11

Shay stopped in the dusty track and stared at the man who would become her grandfather. If she'd had a sense of something insubstantial about this world and its people, Lon Maddon was a disturbing jolt from reality.

And if the broad brim of the hat in his hand had turned up at the edges, the black boots had higher heels and the trousers fit tighter, he would have looked like the legendary cowboy.

He returned her stare, his head cocked to one side, sun highlighting the pale Maddon hair and the flecks in amber eyes. "I ain't a ghost, Mrs. Strock."

Oh yes you are. A shiver made her grit Brandy's teeth. She took a step backward as he approached and stood over her.

Lon Maddon grinned, ran his fingers through his hair and put his hat on. "Brandy's a pretty name and you're a pretty woman."

The shadow of his hat brim lent a threat to insolent eyes.

Bug off, Shay. You're going home. He'll be Brandy's problem. Would Brandy come back to her body when Shay left it? Come back to find herself already married? *Maybe I should leave a note for her.*

"I've come to get Samuel's washing." She tried to smile. "Do you know if a large mirror came up in a freight wagon today, from Boulder?"

"No, ma'am. But I see one, I'll bring it right up."

"Thank you, Mr. Maddon," she answered primly and turned toward the cabin. *Man, you're really getting into this part, Shay.*

Someone was having a coughing fit inside and she waited for it to subside before knocking. Lon still watched her from the road.

"Come in."

This cabin was larger than the Strocks', with pretty braided rugs on the floor and dyed burlap on the walls. The man in the rocking chair spit into a bowl. "Thora K. sent me for your washing."

Samuel had dark rings around his eyes and looked at her without interest.

"That is very kind of her." Something faintly British in his cultured accent. He shuffled into a bedroom and brought her a cloth bag. "Tell her thank you." His hands shook.

"I will and I'm . . . sorry . . . about—"

"Yes." He turned and coughed into his handkerchief.

Lon Maddon was gone when she left the cabin and Shay didn't step so lightly on the way back. The racking sound of Samuel's coughing followed her up the road.

She delivered the bag of clothes to Thora K. and asked about the man's health.

"'Ee have the consumption, poor man. Came to 'ere from the East with his bride, 'oping to recover in the mountain air. And then her dies with 'er babe and all Samuel 'as left is the consumption."

Shay'd never heard of consumption. "Is the air here helping?"

"Do seem to me, him be getting worse the longer 'ee do stay." She strung rope between a hook on the cabin and a pine tree, moving leisurely but efficiently. No one seemed in a great hurry around here.

Shay hung clothes on the rope with hand-carved clothespins. "I saw Lon Maddon at Samuel's."

"Us don't 'ave nothin' to do with they." Thora K. pressed her lips tightly and wrung Brandy's twisted day dress. "They mother were a lady of the night." China-blue eyes widened. "And the fayther was hunged by the neck fer he did kilt a man."

If Rachael'd ever told this side of the family's background, Shay would've remembered it. But then her school studies on local history had never mentioned Water Street either. "They? Is there more than one?" With Thora K.'s habitual mix-up of pronouns, she couldn't be sure.

"There be just the two boys now. And one's as bad as t'other. Wild with the drink and the fallen women. Can't tell 'em apart to look at, neither."

Shay paused at the makeshift clothesline to stare at Brandy's mother-in-law. "Twins?"

"Aye. And nothin' good ever came of that. Bad luck to theyselves and others too. Queer things 'appen around twins." She nodded wisely.

Perhaps Brandy would marry the other brother. He might be more lovable than Lon. *She must come back to this body. How else could the family history go on? Unless it's really me that . . . No!*

Samuel's handkerchiefs were stained and had to be soaked in cold water before they could be washed. But rusty smudges still streaked them when she hung them up.

Is consumption contagious? Those handkerchiefs had soaked in a pail that would carry drinking water.

"Does the brother live around here too?"

"Why are 'ee so interested in they Maddons, you?"

"Just curious." *Because one of them's my grandfather.*

"'Ee be one of they ranch 'ands and do come and go."

When the clothes were partially dried, Thora K. ironed them on the table. "Don't s'pose 'ee know 'ow ter do this neither?"

"Not very well."

"Watch then. Next week 'ee can 'elp. I'll never understand that Sophie McCabe." Thora K. ironed everything, even underwear, and while she did she told Shay stories of Cornwall. About "piskies" leading people astray at night with little lights that beckoned up the wrong paths.

"'Appened to me granny onst. Way back along it were, when her were but a girl."

"Did they find her?"

"'Course they did or 'er couldn't 'ave grown to be me granny."

As my grandmother will reinhabit this body to become Grandma Bran.

And stories of the great mines in Cornwall, especially the Pednandrea, where Thora K.'s father and brothers worked until it closed and the family emigrated.

Shay had to laugh as the old woman gestured with her thumbs and shoulders and the iron. Some of the words were strange but Thora K. acted out her tales so Shay had little trouble following.

"Where's your family now?"

"I be all that's left of they. All buried in this land. But someday I'll go back to uld Cornwall an' that's where they'll bury me. Saved the money for me stone, I 'ave, and on it will be writ, 'She be buried in Cornwall, where she were born.'" She stared into the air as if she were seeing her tombstone, and nodded. "That's as it do belong to be." Sighing, she traded the cooled iron for the hot one on the cookstove. "I 'ear you tell 'andsome stories yerself."

"Corbin just thinks I'm crazy."

"'Ee don't appear to be 'ere though, do 'ee?" She poked Shay in the ribs with her elbow. "Could be ye have the sight. Corbin says yer stories are of wot will come to be. McCabe sounds like a Scottish name and them do say many of they have the sight."

Shay was having such a good time, she gave in and told Thora K. of the reservoir and dam. *I'm going home anyway.*

Corbin came from the Brandy Wine tired and hungry, but the mirror didn't come that day. He said it was probably waiting for other items to make a load and would surely arrive on Tuesday.

On Tuesday Thora K. went back to cleaning rooms at the Antlers Hotel, Corbin to his mine and Shay was left with few chores to do. After she'd watered the garden, she sat on the front steps and watched a relaxed Nederland. A faint coughing came from Samuel's cabin. Maybe she should go down and see if there was anything she could do for him. *Now don't get involved, Shay. You're leaving, remember?*

Finally she put on Brandy's bonnet and walked along a footpath that angled past the cabin and away from the road. She knew Corbin would consider this wandering, but if the mirror came today, he wouldn't have time to put her away. *And if it doesn't I'll go bananas!*

The path ended at another cabin, abandoned and sagging. She peered inside to find it insulated with newspapers glued to the walls between the joists and went in to read the insulation.

A cricket made a lonely chirping sound in the corner.

An ad for Captain Briar's Tonic that would cure warts and carbuncles and almost everything else. And below that—"Abisha Weir proudly announces a new steamship cruise of the Weir Line to the magic isles of the Caribbean on . . ." Rain and weather had wasted away the rest, but Shay was caught up by the name Weir.

Odd how little she'd thought of Marek, she who was soon to become Mrs. Marek Weir. Her homesickness was for her parents, not her fiancé. "You don't love him," Rachael'd said.

Perhaps she'd think again about that marriage when she went home.

Marek Weir had seemed so right and she'd been intrigued with him. He had money, looks, and was some years older than she. Perhaps all that had lent him an illusion of romantic mystery and sophistication.

His work at the National Center for Atmospheric Research was due to last about two years more, long enough for Shay to finish at the university, and then he'd be off to a new location, possibly even another part of the world. To Shay, suffocated by the Gingerbread House and the town she'd lived in all her life, this had appeared ideal, but now . . .

"Careful, there's rats in there and the floor's rotted."

Startled, Shay looked up into a face under an enormous bonnet at a side window. She stepped out of the cabin quickly. "Thanks, I don't like rats."

The woman's gown was covered with tiny flowers and leaves. She wore a curious half-smile.

"I'm Shay Garre . . . I mean, I'm Brandy . . . Strock."

"My name's May Bell." The direct gaze seemed to expect a reaction. "You're Corbin's new wife."

Not really. "That's right."

"He's told me all about you." Tiny pieces of sun pricked through the eyelet holes of her bonnet. She reminded Shay of the shepherdess figurine on the mantel at home.

"Are you a friend of Corbin's?"

The smile widened to a full one, but May Bell didn't answer. Instead she turned back to the path and Shay followed.

"Did Corbin send you to keep an eye on me?" Shay persisted.

"I'm the last person in the world he'd call on to do that." She straightened white gloves. A large-framed woman, very plump, a creamy dimpled face. "I'm just out for a walk. I like walking."

May Bell stopped in front of the Strock cabin. "Must be quite a come down from McCabe's house. Corbin thinks of nothing but his mine now." Her expression hardened. "But he could have prettied it up some for a young bride. Even a crazy one."

On Sunday Shay stood at the graveside of Cara and Baby Williams, Corbin and his mother on either side of her.

Samuel leaned on the arm of Lon Maddon as the circuit preacher said a final prayer over the gaping hole.

Cara had been eighteen. Her husband, tall and much too thin, stood with shoulders stooped and eyes sunken. Shay guessed it wouldn't be long before he joined his little family here on this rocky hillside.

The faraway hoot of an old-fashioned train whistle wailed across clear mountain air . . . haunting, sad.

Shay bit Brandy's lip. The pine box holding both Cara and her baby had been mercifully nailed shut. *All these people are dead and past to you anyway, Shay. Don't get so involved.*

She looked up to see Lon Maddon grinning at her from across the grave. Brandy couldn't possibly marry him. Shay was afraid of him.

And others watched her too, if less openly. Corbin Strock's crazy bride must have been big news in this tiny community. Thora K. had introduced her to some of the women outside the town hall before the funeral and to others at the church service held that morning, defiantly dragging Shay from one group to another, pretending ignorance of the discussions that went on in whispers after they'd passed. May Bell hadn't come to either service.

The musty smell of woolen clothing brought out of storage for rare occasions only, the pungency of dried pine needles crushed under shuffling boots, the dankness of raw earth torn from its rocky bed . . .

Wind and pine trees breathed a final amen with the circuit preacher.

Corbin slid a hand under her elbow and guided her between graves and over rocks to the road. Shay kept her eyes on the toes of Brandy's shoes. She didn't want to see the curious glances of the people around her, tried not to hear the shovels at work behind her. *I want to go home.*

Thora K. had stopped to talk with the preacher and now she caught up with them, a man in a seedy gray suit on her arm. "I did ask Tim up fer supper. Tim, this be Brandy."

Tim Pemberthy was the man who helped Corbin at the mine. His speech was not quite as Cornish as Thora K.'s. The four of them walked on together, Tim and Corbin's mother exchanging good-natured insults.

Thora K. stopped on the bridge over the creek in the valley and turned to look back up the hill. "Ahhh . . . 'twere a lovely funeral."

Shay stared at her in disbelief. This woman was fast becoming the strangest person she'd ever known.

Elton McCabe made a stop on Main Street to inquire the way to the Strock house.

As he urged tired horses up the hill, Elton wondered if perhaps May Bell would be free for a time this evening. He remembered a night years ago when his father'd brought him to Nederland on business. Part of that business had been to introduce him to May Bell. Ever since, he'd longed to atone for that particular fiasco.

When he reached the Strock house, he sat for a moment on the buggy seat, hoping he'd been misdirected. It was little more than a shack.

But before he could get down, the door opened and his sister rushed onto the porch, her hair braided into a funny topknot, a wild look in her eyes.

"Hello, Bran. How—"

"Elton, you've brought the mirror!" She was off the porch with skirts flying and peering into the back of the buggy.

"Ma has this notion the mirror upsets you, Bran, so she's keeping it for you at home. But she had Mrs. Keeler make you a new dress, and look." He opened the small trunk. "Your books."

"You didn't bring the mirror?" Her eyes were huge, swimming with tears.

"You know you enjoy reading. And here's some cloth for sewing." He looked from her shocked expression to the cabin, back to her little hands, red and roughened already. *God, what have we done to her*? "Maybe later I can bring up the mirror."

Elton had the strong urge to hold her against him and reassure them both but he saw Strock coming up the road. All he had time for was to slip her a small purse.

"Hide this. It's for you. Next time I'll bring more," he whispered and then said aloud as Strock approached, "Ma wondered if you had any letters for her, Bran."

"You didn't bring the mirror," his sister answered dully.

12

Shay stood her ground beside Thora K. in the squirming, raucous crowd on Main Street. The silly bonnet shaded her eyes. Wisps of hair made her neck itch.

The flag of the United States, minus a few stars, fluttered and then hung limp on its pole at one end of a raised platform of raw boards.

Beneath the flag, Corbin Strock knelt on one knee, his eyes boring down into Brandy's as if to discover Shay lurking inside. She held her breath, almost unaware of the antique people perched on rooftops and porch overhangs, of the electric excitement charging the crowd and the air. *He's not going to find it easy to stay on that pallet in the loft.*

The timer raised his arm and stared at the watch in his other hand. Sunlight flashed off the gold chain.

The milling stopped . . . and the noise.

Corbin looked away from her and picked up the shortest of the steel drills that lay on the flat-topped rock in front of him.

Both Corbin and Tim Pemberthy were stripped to the waist, powerful muscles tensed in readiness.

Standing, Tim raised to his shoulder what Corbin'd called a double jack, but what looked like a sledgehammer. She was told it weighed eight pounds.

The timer's arm started down.

The double jack was in the air, the drill flipped upright on the rock and the crowd had begun a long combined exhalation before the timer finished his "Go!"

Iron clanged on iron . . . an echo off surrounding mountains. Pemberthy's naked back rippled as the double jack rose into the air and came down again.

Through Tim's parted legs Shay watched Corbin's knuckles whiten as he grasped the drill, holding it straight for the blow. And when it came the shock passed visibly up his arm to his shoulder. He twisted the drill just a little before each strike of the huge hammer.

"Five dollars says it's over forty inches and this team wins. I hear Strock's got himself a new bride to show off for."

"Hush, man, she's standing right in front of you."

Tim Pemberthy was lighter and older than Corbin, but most of him was torso and heavily muscled. And all behind eight pounds of iron.

Against the flagpole sat a wooden keg clasped with copper bands. A rubber hose ran from it to the rock, and a man kept the hose dribbling water into the hole.

The double jack fell faster. The drill bored deeper. Pemberthy's back glistened.

Dots of sludge flew from the hole and splayed on Corbin's chest and arms.

His free hand grabbed the next drill in the line, longer than the first. Then, so swiftly that Pemberthy didn't have to slow the hammer, Corbin withdrew the old drill and inserted the new with his other hand. If either of them had misjudged that move . . .

"This is dangerous." Shay turned to Thora K.

"Aye. Many a man 'as lost 'is hand to this, and more."

"One minute!" the timer yelled and the two men changed places almost in one motion. No more than a strike could have been missed in the rhythm of the double jack.

Shay Garret was just existing, careful to appear outwardly normal, to dress Brandy's hair and body as best she knew how, to feed them both and to placate Corbin and his mother in case Sophie relented and sent the mirror to Nederland, in case the mirror would relent and send her home, in case the mirror had really done this to her to begin with.

Three judges stood around the flagpole watching intently.

Another man jumped to the platform and sponged the sweat from Tim Pemberthy's chest and shoulders and then held a tin cup to his mouth. Tim nodded thanks, grimacing at each blow of Corbin's hammer.

"Tez a true 'ole, Strock. Let 'er have it!" A voice from the crowd.

"Make old Harvey proud of his boy from the grave!"

Shay watched Corbin's back ripple now, and the clang rang louder, faster. Another drill thunked to the platform.

Since Elton's visit something inside her'd given up hope and a terrifying passivity had settled on Shay. But this strange Fourth of July celebration in a tiny mountain town, these sweating miners daring fate, the frightening clamor of the double jack, all these long-dead but incredibly alive people jostling her to watch Brandy's husband perform more nervelessly than an Olympic champion . . .

Who would have thought such a silly thing as two grown men hammering a hole in a rock could hold her breathless?

Again the men changed places, and now it was Corbin's turn to have the sweat sponged from him. His chest heaved and his lips drew back from his teeth. He knocked off his hat with his free wrist. Dark curls lay matted and soaked close to his head.

The man with the sponge dumped a bucket of water over him and the crowd roared approval. Corbin grinned; the spots of sludge, speckled across his chest, ran into dirty streaks.

Another drill thudded to the wooden platform, the crowd pressed forward. Shouts, taunts and encouragement lifted to mingle with the echoing ring of iron.

Shay peered between two of the rough logs that formed the base for the platform, to discover the bottom of the huge rock sitting on the street. The platform had been built around it, a hole cut in the floor to expose its top. No wonder the drills were getting so long.

The positions changed yet again. Both men were tiring now, and Shay realized this was a feat of endurance as well as skill.

"Why do they do this thing?" she asked Thora K.

"In the mines them do drill such 'oles fer they charges. And 'ere they be on a fine 'oliday doing it fer fun." But there was pride in her eyes as she watched her son. "Power drills be used in they big mines now and the double jack'll soon be a thing of the past.

"Me fayther died of the rot in the lungs and a brother's still buried in a cave-in in Black Hawk. So instead of marryin' a Cornishman like was expected, I married a fine big Norwegian."

"Was he a miner too?"

"By trade, not by blood. The Cornish who came to these mountains be mostly miners by blood, and I wanted to thin that out in me children. Few mines be working now and Corbin's 'ad the chance to find something else. So wot does 'ee do but marry you to get a mine of 'is own. 'Ee looks like 'is fayther but 'ee be Cornish through."

Wooden stairs ran up the side of a store building to her left and at the top was a railed landing. May Bell stood there watching the contest, her ample figure amplified by a ruffled gown.

The door behind her opened and Lon Maddon stepped out, placing his hat on his head. He was eating a large crust of bread.

Extending his arms and stretching his shoulders, he came to lean on the railing next to May Bell. She looked down at Shay without recognition but then pointed toward her, saying something to Lon. His eyes searched the crowd until they fell on Shay. Chewing on the bread, he studied her with a curious lack of expression.

Shay was pushed from behind and fell against Thora K. as people edged closer, and her attention was diverted to the contest.

The crowd applauded and whistled praise now to each sweat-stained man as he came off the double jack.

Tension grew. The hammer fell faster. The straining miners gulped for air.

"Time!" the timer called, and Corbin stopped the double jack in midair.

Tim fell back onto the platform and lay there with a half-smile, half-grimace. Corbin leaned on the long-handled hammer, one shoulder twitching.

The judges gathered around the rock, probing the hole with a long measuring rod. Nederland's Main Street was so quiet Shay could hear Lon Maddon crunch a bite out of his bread crust. She glanced up to find two Lon Maddons standing with May Bell. The twin had returned.

"Strock and Pemberthy," the timer announced in a voice worthy of the ringmaster at the Barnum and Bailey Circus. "Forty-one and three-fourth inches!"

Tim and Corbin smiled at each other and the crowd's roar was answered by an explosion that shook the dirt street.

"That sounded like dynamite."

"That's wot it were." Thora K. pointed to a cloud of smoke and dust on a ridge close to town. "Lunatics these miners be. 'Twon't be the last you'll 'ear today, neither."

While Corbin and his partner left the platform to be congratulated by a circle of miners, a new team took their place at the rock. Another section of it was marked off in chalk.

Soon the double jack rang out again.

Shay watched the Maddon twin with the bread descend the stairs. He wore an open vest and no jacket. She had the feeling this one wasn't Lon, because when he surveyed the crowd and found her staring at him, he didn't grin.

Four teams vied in the double-hand contest. Corbin and Tim lost by a fourth of an inch. Then followed the single-hand, where one miner held his own drill and swung a smaller four-pound hammer with his other hand. For any excuse a dynamite blast would go off on the ridge.

When this contest was over, the town retired to Barker Meadows for races and picnics.

Shay sat on a blanket and bit into a cooled pastry, her head aching yet from the clang of the miners' hammers and the dust holding on still air from the racing.

They'd raced everything from feet to wagons. The Maddon twins had tied for first place in the horse races.

The twins seemed to be everywhere and seldom together, so they appeared disconcertingly often, strolling among various groups of picnickers, one examining a horse's leg by an unpainted corral, the other trying to peer under a demure young lady's bonnet near a root-beer stand. This was a small tent where some women sat on wooden folding chairs under the sign of the "Independent Champions of the Red Cross."

Shay tried to hide her morbid interest in the Maddon twins. Even the term "Maddon twins" was hard to disassociate from her uncles, Remy and Dan. One of these men was their father . . . and Rachael's. The thought of her mother brought instant tears to her eyes.

"Is something wrong, Brandy?" Corbin lounged on the grass beside her.

Yes. Can you believe I'm twenty years old and I want my mommy?

"No, I just swallowed too big a bite and it stuck."

A short distance away May Bell spread a blanket on the grass and three other women joined her with a basket. Shay's mouth watered as they bit into crisp-looking pieces of fried chicken. She was getting very tired of pasties.

When the family group near them picked up their picnic and moved to another part of the meadow, May Bell and her friends didn't seem to notice. Their chatter and laughter carried defiantly to Corbin and Shay. But it was soon drowned out by a general cheering as a bald-headed man backed a team of horses and a wagon up next to the root-beer tent. He crawled over boxes to set a keg up-right at the back of the wagon.

He was soon dispensing foamy beer in glasses taken from the boxes. The ladies in front of the tent were all but trampled by the crowd that pressed around him.

One woman raised a fist and shouted something at the bald man with the keg. She was so angry she made little jumping steps sideways like a startled cat.

Corbin chuckled. "Mrs. Tyler does get riled."

"Why? Because he's cutting into her root-beer business?"

"More than that. The Independent Champions of the Red Cross is a temperance organization. Don't they have one in Boulder?"

"Uh . . . I think they call it something else."

"Well, I'm going to get some beer. Let me have your glass and I'll get you some more root beer."

"Whoopee-twang."

"What?"

"Uh . . . thank you, Corbin." The drink was half-warm and decidedly flat. "I'd love some more."

He held onto her hand instead of taking the glass from it. "Brandy,

you've not been yourself since your brother left. We'll talk your mother into letting us have the mirror, somehow, if it means that much to you. Stop fretting and enjoy yourself. Holidays are few and far between."

She watched him walk away and then saw May Bell watching him too. May Bell turned to look at her, again without recognition. But Shay was too busy considering what he'd said to mind. *Don't get so down. There's always hope, and if he's willing to help . . .*

A group of women crossing the meadow made an unnecessarily wide circle around May Bell and her friends. There *was* something different about the women on the blanket. Their way of dress was fussier, their faces less washed-out looking . . . makeup. Shay detected now the color added lightly to lips and cheeks and around the eyes.

The population had swelled with ranchers, farmers and miners from the countryside and summer visitors who'd come for vacation or health reasons. Shay studied the other women on the meadow.

A great many straight dark skirts and white blouses, summer-thin dresses with high collars like the one Shay wore, the subdued colors of tiny flowers or plaids. The summer visitors tended to congregate and their younger women wore all white and carried parasols, their hair more cleverly and smoothly coiled. They made Shay feel like a dowdy hick. She sat straighter, her hand automatically moving to Brandy's hair.

Even with the sense of displacement, the feeling she was outside of time—a mere observer of a parody of life—Shay was affected subtly by these people, drawn in by the age-old forces of vanity and fashion-consciousness. Would she become so submerged as to forget who she really was? Thora K. and Corbin were already moving from the unreal to the real.

Shay removed a piece of pasty from the hole in Brandy's mouth.

Her dress, the new one Sophie'd sent instead of a mirror, fit too tightly without a corset.

Real clouds formed above western ridges in a real sky. The actual but distant sound of thunder from that direction. A high resonant snapping of cicadas . . . a normal summer sound. The Maddon twins carried glasses of beer to May Bell's group. Their sandy mustaches were identical. Odd to observe one's own grandfather in his twenties . . . and in duplicate.

The briny scent of horse. A clatter of utensils against dishes. No paper plates or beer cans or plastic cups to be left to litter the meadow. Corbin stood in the beer line now with a glass of root beer, his back looking very broad. Thora K. tossed her head and laughed as she talked to a friend near the corral. Shay was suddenly in shadow.

The Maddon twin with the vest stood over her, a fried drumstick in one hand, his hat in the other.

Shay brought Brandy to her feet before she realized she was preparing them for flight.

"May Bell wondered if you would like this." He held out the drumstick. There was no gap between his teeth.

She reached to accept it, her eyes imprisoned by his pale hair, so like her own had been before . . . "Tell her . . . thank you."

Shay swallowed against the lump moving up Brandy's esophagus. The sound of cicadas dimmed in her ears.

He inspected her blankly, his head tilted back, as if he were experiencing her rather than looking at her.

Brandy's face grew hot and Shay said, "I . . . don't suppose I can go over there . . . and thank her myself."

"I don't suppose you can." A suggestion of laughter touched amber eyes. "I'll give her your message."

Shay was still watching her grandfather or his twin walk away when Corbin stuck a glass under her nose. He did not look happy.

"What was that about?"

"He gave me a piece of chicken." She sat down, almost spilling the root beer. People were looking at them.

"What did Hutch Maddon want with you?"

"Nothing." And that was true. His interest had not been admiration or particularly friendly. It was more a curious dissection. "Hutch is a funny name."

"It's shortened from Hutchison, his mother's maiden name."

"Thora K. said his mother was a prostitute."

"There are gentler words for that profession, Brandy. Mrs. Maddon fell upon hard times."

The chicken tasted so good, Shay forgot the root beer. Then, with a crunchy piece still between her teeth, she stopped chewing and stared at the enormous meadow with people dotting one end of it, but saw instead a memory . . .

. . . Memorial Day in Columbia Cemetery in Boulder . . . Shay watching her mother place a vase of cut flowers against a pink headstone . . . it wasn't the first time Shay'd been there, but probably the last . . . she could remember little of the inscription and no dates . . . but the name chiseled in pink granite had been Hutchison Maddon . . . her memory saw it clearly . . . Rachael'd always spoken of him as Dad . . . and the grave next to his . . . Sophie Euler McCabe . . . whom Rachael'd always referred to as Grandma . . . Shay'd been junior-high age that Memorial Day . . .

"Brandy?"

Shay Garrett came back to the salty taste of chicken and the man beside her. Where was Corbin buried? Hard to think of him as dead. He was so big and masculine and now looked so sincere.

"Brandy, you've not been listening to me."

"I'm sorry, my mind was a million miles away."

He looked worried, as he always did when reminded she was crazy.

"Oh, come on, Corbin, give me a chance. Haven't you ever had a knotty problem that wouldn't leave you alone until your mind turned out everything else and just struggled with it?"

"I've never thought of it in such words but . . . yes, yes I have. Though what problem a woman could have that's of such weight . . . She's taken care of, fed, housed. Problems of weight fall on the men."

"You, Corbin Strock, are a first-rate MCP. Do you know that? Well-meaning, but–"

"MCP?"

"Male chauvinist pi . . . uh, never mind. What were you talking about while I struggled with my unimportant problem?"

"I was pointing out that you must be careful, Brandy. Nederland's a small place and you musn't go about discussing . . . fallen women and–"

"Is May Bell a pros . . . fallen woman? And her friends over there?"

His answer was an expression of acute embarrassment.

"Corbin, if I'm to live here, I have to know something about this small place of yours. And if I can't discuss it with you, then who? Someone else's husband?"

"How do you know of May Bell?"

"This is her chicken."

"You accepted that from a–"

"I like chicken. And you haven't answered my question."

"Women discuss these things amongst themselves I suppose. My mother–"

"Would Thora K. discuss fallen women with me?"

Corbin laughed and drew curious looks from the meadow. "Sometimes you seem such a child and at other times I wonder if it isn't too bad the Young Men's Debating Society doesn't include women. From now on, I'll buy your chicken for you. And yes, May Bell is–"

"Like Marie on Water Street?"

"Yes, and you're to have nothing to do with May Bell or her friends."

I'll bet you do, though, don't you?

"Now, don't embarrass me any longer with this chatter. I've some people I'd like you to meet. Be careful what you say."

Shay happened to catch May Bell's eye as she turned to deposit the chicken bone in the picnic hamper, and gave her a surreptitious smile of thanks. May Bell, without moving another muscle in her face, lowered one eyelid slowly.

The Maddon twins were off to another part of the meadow, but there was still a good-sized male crowd hanging around that blanket. Those women were outcasts only to a degree.

Maybe it was the holiday mood, but Shay felt less of an outcast herself as she talked to Corbin's friends. The women appeared kindly if guarded, the men respectful if curious. They seemed more like people than relics of the past when she talked to them. She did her best to act normally because she wanted to please Corbin.

She overheard a Mrs. Schiller whisper to her husband as they moved away, "She don't look very uppity for a McCabe. Don't look crazy either."

"Well, Strock ain't changed his bachelor ways none, if you know what I mean," her husband answered. "Something's unnatural up at that house."

Shay's holiday mood vanished. *What do you care for anyway? He's Brandy's problem.* Would Shay have Brandy's problems to contend with the rest of her life?

Suddenly she was thinking of Hutch Maddon and his pink tombstone again.

13

Shay and Corbin sat on a raised bleacher next to the corral fence on the meadow.

The corral had been turned over to a Fourth of July rodeo. It was much like those she'd grown up with at the yearly Boulder Pow Wow, the same cruelty to animals to show off the macho of men. The difference was in apparel and the skill of the cowboys, who obviously got their practice on the job.

Dr. Seaton was everywhere, minding wounded horses as well as men. He was also a judge and by far the busiest man at the rodeo.

Across the corral from the bleachers, May Bell watched from a buggy seat. "Corbin's told me all about you," May Bell'd said.

"He ain't changed his bachelor ways none," Mr. Schiller had whispered.

But Brandy mustn't have anything to do with fallen women or the Maddons. Talk about double standards.

Hutch Maddon and a screaming black horse exploded into the oval ring. Shay knew it was Hutch because of the vest.

The horse bucked violently, his hooves seeming never to touch the ground and Hutch's seat never to hit the saddle. Clutching the saddle with his knees, he raised his hat above his head and let out a whoop.

Then he flew over the corral fence and landed with a sickening plop at her feet.

Hutch Maddon lay on his back, eyes closed, chest pumping breath, lips drawn back from his teeth as Corbin's had during the double-hand. But this grimace was one of pain rather than exertion.

Corbin knelt beside the fallen cowboy.

The black horse still reared and screamed behind the fence as Dr. Seaton sprinted toward them. Shouldering Corbin aside, he ran his hands over Hutch's body. "If you can hear me, boy, tell me where it hurts."

"Leg . . ." Hutch Maddon opened his eyes to stare back at Shay.

Doc Seaton slit a pants leg with a borrowed knife. There was no blood but there was something wrong with the angle of the leg.

"Strock, get my buggy. Somebody find a straight board and some rope."

Shay could stand it no longer. Grandfather or no . . . the way that man had landed . . .

She slid to her knees beside the doctor. Hutch hadn't taken his eyes off her since he'd opened them.

"Can you move your fingers and toes?" she asked him. "Can you feel everywhere?" *You've got to stick around to sire my whole family.*

Hutch blinked, flexed his hands and the other foot. Again that bare hint of a smile in his eyes. "Yes, ma'am," he answered meekly.

"Who's the doctor around here, Mrs. Strock?" the doctor asked.

"You are. But he landed—or it seemed he landed—on his back. I . . . thought he might have broken it."

"Now, Hutch, you wouldn't do that to me on the Fourth of July, would you?" Doc Seaton handed her a brown bottle. "Here, Dr. Strock, pour some of this down his gullet, long as you're so handy."

Shay hesitated, then moved her hand under her grandfather's head to raise it. It felt strange even touching him, and he didn't seem like a grandfather. He was younger than Corbin.

The bittersweet stench of raw whiskey rose from the bottle she tipped to his lips.

"Hutch, you gotta quit drinking so much." Lon squatted across his brother's body from Shay. "I keep telling ya."

Hutch choked and spit whiskey. He pushed the bottle away. "She's drowning me!"

Laughter from the crowd. Shay looked up to see Thora K. staring at her. Thora K. wasn't laughing.

Embarrassed, Shay slid Brandy's hand from beneath his head. It came out sticky and red. "Doctor, he's hurt his head. It's bleeding."

"Well, I'm not surprised. Probably landed on something."

"But he's lying in the dirt."

Doc Seaton poured whiskey all over his handkerchief. "Here, put this under him then. You lady doctors sure are finicky."

Shay slipped the handkerchief under the wound and held it there. She supposed alcohol was alcohol.

"Now, Hutch, you know what I got to do," the doctor said quietly.

"Yeah." Hutch's eyes watered, either from the raw whiskey she'd dumped down his throat or from the sting of it against the open wound.

"Lon, pin his arms." The Doc handed her the long knife he'd used to slit the pants leg. "Mrs. Strock, put the handle between his teeth."

"What are you going to do?" She was afraid she knew.

"I'm going to set his leg, of course."

"Here?"

"Yes, here. He's swelling already. Now, do as I say."

Shay put the leather-wrapped handle lengthwise between her grandfather's teeth. Drops of sweat pocked his face. His Adam's apple moved up and then slowly down to his shirt collar.

Lon lay across his twin's chest.

Hutch drew in his breath and closed his eyes. So did Shay.

She heard the sickening snap, heard a moan cut off sharply and felt the convulsive jerk in his body that sent Lon's head crashing into her side . . . felt her own senses snap as if a bullet had entered her head.

Her picnic lunch struggled to return. The muscles in Hutch's neck relaxed onto the whiskey hanky. He went limp against her knees. The knife came loose in her hand.

"You can open your eyes now, Dr. Strock." Doc Seaton was tying the straightened leg to a board that looked suspiciously like a piece of the corral fence. "Our patient won't give us any trouble for a while."

Hutch Maddon looked dead. His lips had parted slightly to reveal the lack of a gap between his teeth. His face had drained of life and color.

But his chest moved with slow rhythm.

The crowd made way for Corbin with the doctor's horse and buggy. If Shay could have felt anything more, she knew she wouldn't have been comfortable with the look Corbin gave her.

"I apologize, Mrs. Strock, if I was overly brusque with you. But we had to hurry," Doc Seaton said too loudly, as if he'd also noticed Corbin's expression. "For a town-bred girl, you'd make a fine nurse."

Shay watched as they loaded her limp grandfather into the buggy. The spreading stain on the back of his head looked almost black against the pale hair. Lon and the doctor held him as Corbin drove them off.

Thora K. dragged her across the meadow to the creek like an errant child and sponged dirt and a blood smear from her skirt. "S'pose it can't be 'elped, 'ee being there when it 'appened and all. There, might be this'll keep it from settin' till us gets back to the 'ouse."

"I've seen things like that in the movies but I didn't think they really happened," Shay said as they collected the picnic things. *Booze for anesthetic, knife between the teeth . . .*

"Moving wot?"

"Moving pictures."

"Might be 'ee know things I don't, you." Thora K. pushed her face close, and one eye wandered. "But I do know pictures don't move. Edden possible."

As they walked up the road to the cabin, Shay kept staring at the hand that still had a dark streak across the palm. *Someday this will be part of my blood. He couldn't be more than twenty-five. My grandfather will be dead before I'm born, and I'll never know him.*

"Brandy . . ." Thora K. stopped beside the cabin. "Yer a strange 'un, but I've come to like 'ee, child." She smiled so wide that Shay knew why the old woman chewed her food the way she did. Her front teeth were all that was left. "Tez possible 'ee 'ave the gift of healing as well as the sight."

"I didn't heal him. I just helped Dr. Seaton."

"In the uld days in Cornwall"—she dropped her voice and looked over her shoulder—"them as would a burned 'ee with the fire and hunged 'ee from a tree. But us modern Cornish know things. 'Ee edden a black witch."

On Thora K.'s next day off, she and Shay trudged up out of the valley to the north, their destination Caribou. It would be mildly famous in Shay's time as a ghost town and for its cemetery.

She, Rachael and Jerrold Garrett had jeeped the road she now walked, to gather material for one of Rachael's books.

The thought of her parents sent Shay's mind racing over schemes to get back to the Gingerbread House, since the mirror apparently wasn't coming to her. She'd considered running away to Boulder, but Brandy's shoes wouldn't permit it. There might be bears in the canyon. It'd be another instance of her behavior that could be labeled crazy. If the mirror wouldn't cooperate, she could yet be "put away."

"I didn't realize Caribou was ever this large." They stood on the main street. Empty storefronts on one side. Heaps of blackened boards on the other.

"'Twere bigger afore the fire last winter. Terrible it were. Wind ablowin' flames and men with buckets doing no more good than if them was spittin' tobacco juice. Miners be proper ones fer digging 'oles in the ground but not much fer taking time to lay pipes. So when there's a fire . . ."

About half the town stood unburned on the high mountain meadow. The elements had erased all but a trace of the paint on ugly wooden buildings. It looked like an arsonist's paradise still.

"Caribou were dying way back along. Now tez dead fer sure." Her crackly epitaph moved hollowly on a wind that stirred dust from empty streets through glassless window holes, moved building shells to groan and creak in response, sent a forlorn tin can banging down a gray and rippled plank sidewalk.

Shay followed Thora K. down a side street. A cookstove with a hole in its underside lay on a pile of rusting cans behind an abandoned house.

"What do the people do who still live here?"

"Them be mostly caretakers fer they mines now," Thora K. said sadly. "And them few as is too uld to give it all up."

She stopped before a tiny one-room cabin with a caved-in roof and sighed like the wind that blew through it. "Me Harvey did build this 'ouse fer we. A mite crowded it were, but 'appy fer a time."

The old woman straightened her shoulders and went on. That shack made the one in Nederland look like a palace.

It was a shock to come across a curtained window with glass, or yellowed long underwear strung on a clothesline among all the abandoned dwellings.

Caribou was a sad and dirty mutilation of the meadow. Nature would erase it almost totally, green over the scars, and leave only shapes of foundations, signs of earth unnaturally leveled for buildings, a few heaps of wood marking the collapse of a structure, hillocks that when dug into produced broken bottles and bedsprings. Only the rusty mining scars would remain on the ridges around.

On the outskirts Shay recognized, by its location, a large building still in fair repair. She and her mother would poke around the decaying pile it would become and wonder about it.

Shay stared at the building, remembering the future. On this spot Rachael would speak of a Thora K. . . . someone from her childhood . . . and in that book there'd be a Thora . . . an old woman with a frizzy white bun on top of her head . . . who was never without her bottle of tonic . . . what else? Shay'd helped proof the manuscript for that book, but she could bring no more to mind. Thora K. must live to be very old.

They walked up the hill toward the cemetery where Shay and her parents would be saddened at all the graves of children.

"Thora K., how old are you?"

"I be forty and five years. Gettin' to be an uld 'unman."

"Forty-five?" Rachael was in her fifties and looked decades younger than Thora K., who seemed elderly rather than middle-aged.

The cemetery was far larger than when Shay would visit it with her parents. Many of these gravesites would be erased by nature too. Trees would grow back in places. Now it had a tended look, with many weathered but upright wooden and stone markers.

Thora K. knelt to pull some weeds and rearrange rocks around one of them.

HARVEY D. STROCK, 1852–1880
GONE TO JOIN HIS MAKER

"Crushed 'is arm in a cave-in, 'ee did. In the Poorman Mine. Did turn to rot and 'ee died of it. But 'is heart were broken afore the cave-in." She nodded toward a wooden enclosure that had ornate newel posts at each corner. Inside it a solitary marble shaft pointed heavenward.

GONE BEFORE US
OH OUR CHILDREN
TO THE BETTER LAND
VAINLY WAIT WE
FOR OTHERS IN YOUR PLACE TO STAND.
OLGA MARY STROCK. B. 1873, D. JULY 5, 1879.

Shay walked around the enclosure to find another inscription on the next face of the shaft. Elsie Strock had been three years old when she died the day after her sister.

The next side was mercifully blank, but on the last face Shay found that Jane Ann Strock was only a year old when she followed her sisters two days later.

Shay felt as if she'd been punched in the stomach. "Oh, Thora K.—"

"Me babies. All did die in the summer. And the next spring me Harvey joined 'is girls 'ere on the hill." Thora K. stood and brushed off her skirt, her eyes dry, empty. "'Twere an awful time."

"But your little girls all died in less than a week."

"Fever raged the town, dipthery it were. 'Twere a new town then and most of the graves 'ere be children from that summer. Us was lucky it left Corbin. Some folks din't 'ave a wee one left."

"It's horrible. How could you bear it?" Shay sniffed back tears. "I mean three children gone in just a few days."

"Ahhh, bless yer sawl, child. Them be 'appy in heaven." Thora K. hugged Shay and kissed her cheek. "And I 'ave me a daughter again now, don't I?"

The next morning as she left the outhouse, Shay still pondered the courage of the little Cornish woman and the devastation diphtheria had left in Caribou's cemetery. She'd been depressed all the way back to Nederland. After a fitful night's sleep that depression had deepened.

"Brandy, look what I brought you." Corbin rounded the corner of the cabin with an expectant smile. "I asked Mrs. Tyler to save the next one for us."

The chicken he held by its feet still twitched. Blood dripped from a headless neck. "I told you I'd buy your chicken for you."

Corbin and the chicken blurred. Brandy's stomach rolled. "But . . . it's got . . . feathers."

"Of course it has feathers." He held it higher so she could see the blood better. "You can cook it for supper."

"That's not the kind you cook." *They come naked and cut in pieces and wrapped in cellophane and, oh God, stop twitching.* "That's the kind that lays eggs . . . or something."

"Brandy, this is a rooster."

"But I don't know how to cook a chicken with feathers." She backed away as he approached.

"You scald it and pluck it first, of course. Don't tell me you've never plucked a chicken?"

"Don't bring it any closer, Corbin Strock. It's . . . it's bleeding."

He laid the murdered bird on the ground and wrapped his arms around her waist, laughing. "Brandy, my little Brandy. You can help set a man's leg and yet grow faint over a chicken with its head cut off."

"It's not funny, and that was a rotten thing to do to me." Her voice was muffled in his shirt and soon so was her crying. She relaxed against him, thankful for a good cry, if not for the poor chicken. It felt wonderful to have some release for her emotions, to be held and comforted.

Corbin pulled Brandy's chin up so Shay had to look at him. "Don't you cry now. I'll teach you how to pluck a chicken."

"Whoopee-twang." With tears still on Brandy's cheeks, Shay began to laugh. And then Brandy was kissing Corbin, and Shay was surprised at them.

Brandy was a nubile young woman and Shay no shrinking violet. *Between the two of us, there's no telling what trouble we can get into.* She tried to draw away, but Corbin wouldn't have it. He tightened around and against her, and returned that kiss till she thought Brandy's neck would snap.

Oh, hell, who was it said, if it feels good do it?

. . . and then she felt the telltale ache of Brandy's uterus. Shay knew the signs . . . depression . . . moodiness . . . and Corbin seemed so sexy this morning and . . . *Oh, Brandy, not now* . . . had Tampax been invented yet? Even Kotex? Surely they did something.

An unwanted image of Hutchison Maddon interfered with her thoughts of Corbin Strock . . . the feel of his pain, the lurch of his body as his leg . . .

"Pardon me," a voice said behind Corbin. "But I got this telegram for Mrs. Strock."

Corbin let go of her so suddenly she fell against a tree.

Lon Maddon leered at them from the middle of the clearing.

"And why are you running messages, Maddon?" Corbin's voice was gravelly with embarrassment.

"I was in the office when it came. Deek said it was urgent, and I was coming up to Samuel's anyway, so . . ." He handed an envelope to Shay. "Ma'am."

The telegram was from Sophie. John McCabe was very ill. Brandy was being called home.

14

Home. Home to the Gingerbread House and to the wedding mirror and through it to her mother and father. *I won't marry Marek for a while and perhaps not at all. But the things I'll have to tell Mother!* Shay adjusted Brandy's bonnet. *I'll make the mirror work somehow.*

"It do sound bad, them callin' 'ee 'ome. Might be yer fayther'll be better by the time 'ee get there. All set for the trip?" Thora K. glanced at Brandy's skirt meaningfully.

"Yes and thanks for showing me what to do."

"I just canna figure wot 'ee been doin' all these years till now."

The fact that Thora K.'d had to point out the use of those folded rags and pins in Brandy's trunk seemed to shake her theory that Brandy was a witch rather than crazy. But Shay was so confident she'd be leaving this world soon, she didn't fear losing her one ally.

"I'm going to miss you so," Shay whispered and hugged Thora K.

"Heavens, child, 'tain't like 'ee edden never comin' back." Thora K. looked flustered but pleased.

No, I'm not coming back. But I hope Brandy will and that she'll like you as much as I do. Where'd Brandy been all this time?

Shay gazed around the tiny cabin almost regretfully. She'd never forget this place or this adventure.

Corbin walked her to the stage, loading for Boulder, and she embarrassed him by throwing her arms around his neck. "Take care, Corbin."

The sickroom at the Gingerbread House was the downstairs bedroom Rachael and Jerrold Garrett would use. Some of the furniture was the same.

Now it was darkened and the sound of John McCabe's tortured breathing filled it. He lay still and staring, his face a swollen gray.

Sophie rose from a chair beside the bed and held out her hands as Shay crossed the room. "Brandy, I'm so relieved you could get here before . . ."

"Elton said it was a stroke." Shay let herself be hugged.

"It was so sudden. He said your name twice in the night. Those are the only words he's spoken since he was struck down. Brandy, I think he regretted your marriage and it's weighing on him now. I know how you felt, dear, but . . . the doctor says your father hasn't much time. We didn't expect him to last the night. Don't let him die with your anger on his conscience. Tell him you forgive him."

"Will he hear me?"

"I don't know. At times he seems to respond and be aware of us."

Shay leaned over John McCabe and took his cold hand. "I forgive you, John McCabe . . . I mean, Father."

He didn't blink or show that he could hear or see her. But Sophie said, "John McCabe? Father? I've never heard you speak to him that way."

"I don't think he heard me." These little slips in speech wouldn't matter soon.

"Stay with him and keep trying, dear. I'm going to find something to eat and I'll be back." Sophie paused in the doorway, looking confused. "Brandy, are you feeling well?"

"I'm feeling fine." Shay sat in Sophie's chair and wondered what to do. She'd never seen anyone dying before. In her limited experience the old or sick went into a hospital and left the world without distressing anyone.

She hoped Sophie'd hurry. The gloomy room and the raspy breathing were eerie. She fidgeted on the chair. Brandy's skin was scraped raw from the chafing of those disgusting rags.

John McCabe stirred suddenly and Shay jumped. She stood over him in case he could see her.

"I forgive you, Father. Don't worry. Everything'll be okay. . . ."

His eyes focused from a long way off. "Brandy?" he said faintly.

"Yes, and I forgive you . . . Brandy loves you I'm sure . . . I mean I love you." Tears came to her eyes. Would Brandy have forgiven him? It'd be wrong not to reassure him at a time like this.

"Brandy . . . mirror . . . beware . . ." He sounded like a phonograph record playing at too slow a speed and his body struggled to help him speak as Grandma Bran's had done. His eyes reflected the fear Shay'd seen then too.

"Mirror? The wedding mirror?"

He choked and seemed to be trying to sit up. She slid her arm under him to lift his head. "What about the mirror? Tell me."

John McCabe stared over her shoulder. Fear and pain drained from his face. He smiled. "Joshua, oh, Joshua . . ." He fell limp against her.

"Elton. Sophie. Somebody!" Shay didn't move except to look around for Joshua. There was no one else in the room.

Elton arrived first. He laid his father back on the pillow and drew Shay away. "Did he speak at all, Bran?"

"I forgave him and told him I loved him and he answered me." Her teeth chattered with shock.

"Oh, thank God," Sophie said from the doorway.

"Ma, he died in her arms. Now he can rest in peace."

Shay and Elton sat at the kitchen table picking at their food, he mourning the loss of a father and she dying to get up to Brandy's room.

Elton seemed real, not a caricature of times past. Shay'd never had a brother, and looking at him she wondered what it would have been like. She couldn't remember her mother mentioning an Uncle Elton.

"It was so sudden, Bran. Did you know it happened in your room?"

"The stroke?" Her neck prickled. "Is the wedding mirror still there?"

"Yeah, we found him on the floor in front of it. He'd taken to brooding in there. Over you, I think. A thunderstorm was making so much noise we didn't hear him fall or call out or anything."

Upstairs, the wedding mirror sat in the corner, reflecting wavy light from the funny bulb in the ceiling. *Did you cause John McCabe's stroke?* Did strokes come on that suddenly to apparently healthy people?

One of the books Sophie'd sent to Nederland instead of the mirror was a green leather-bound diary. Shay'd been disappointed to find it blank but had brought it back to the Gingerbread House. It was a way to communicate with Brandy privately.

A narrow table stood under a slope of the ceiling, a straight chair in front of it, a pen and an old-fashioned ink pot. Shay sat down to write to Brandy:

> I hope you will return to your body when I leave it. I don't know where you've been but I feel you must know what's gone on here while you've been away.

Shay knew her handwriting was horrid and she dripped ink trying to use the unfamiliar writing apparatus but she wrote slowly and carefully.

She tried to explain Thora K. and Corbin, to soften the blow of life in Nederland and the death of John McCabe. But she avoided any mention of the Maddon twins. Brandy would make her own mistakes, obviously, or Shay wouldn't be born a platinum blond.

And she didn't go in to the future, except to admit she was Brandy's granddaughter. Shay'd come to know how awful it was to *know*.

Poor Brandy would return to find the Gingerbread House a house of mourning and herself trapped in an unconsummated marriage.

She added more of Corbin, knowing that someday Brandy would continue the family line with Hutch Maddon. Shay ached for Corbin.

It was late when she closed the diary and faced the mirror.

But the wedding mirror wouldn't work its magic that night . . . nor the next . . . nor the next. . . .

Sunlight flooded Columbia Cemetery, the trees too young to mask its glare.

Elton's arm trembled in Sophie's. She pretended to lean on him as a grieving widow should on her grown son. But in fact he leaned on her.

"Yes, it was so sudden, such a shock," she repeated for the umpteenth time, now to the president of the bank, Mr. Harker. He looked in pieces to her befogged mind, all cut up by the black threads of her veil.

Brandy stood next to the husband John had forced upon her, staring at little Joshua's grave as if she'd never seen it.

. . . the line of stilled black carriages filling the trails of the cemetery . . . spilling out onto the road to town . . . horses stomping, jingling harness . . . buzzing grasshoppers and the sweet call of a meadowlark . . . subdued voices.

The night before, Sophie'd prayed to God to forgive her for the unexpected feeling of freedom and importance the devil had sent to her when she should have been mourning. She knew it was just the attention she received as the widow of John McCabe and that Satan had used it. But the realization that John's every mood would no longer organize her day . . .

Guilt sent her through the house seeking solace. To find her son with his head in his arms at the dining-room table actually weeping, terrified at the thought of his father's business affairs being thrust at him. Strange, sensitive boy she secretly loved above all others. But who was no help to her now. She'd had to comfort *him.*

And then upstairs to find her daughter looking at her with the eyes of a stranger. Brandy, too, seemed terrified, but Sophie could sense a strength here she knew was not in Elton. She couldn't confide in the stranger her daughter had become.

People were filing toward the carriages and Sophie moved to Brandy's side. "It's time to go back to the house, dear."

Brandy's face was pale, a dark tinge marring the skin around her eyes. "Brandy had another brother . . . Joshua."

"Of course. You and Josh had such fun together when you were small," Sophie whispered, hoping no one else had heard, feeling a tightening around her heart. She prayed this behavior was due to sleeplessness, rather than serving as another indication of an unbalanced mind. Sophie'd heard her daughter moving about in her room at all hours since her return.

At the Gingerbread House, she was able to draw Mrs. Strock aside for a moment. "I'm worried for Brandy. She's behaving queerly."

"'Er do seem to be takin' it hard, poor thing. It's the age, 'ee know. Death be mystifying to they young."

"If your son won't mind, I'd like to keep her here for a while."

"That's as it do belong to be. 'Ee need she now."

That night as Sophie and Nora arranged bedding on the floor of the parlor for the out-of-town guests who couldn't be accommodated with beds or at neighbors' homes, Thora K. bustled in to help.

The Strocks weren't what Sophie would've chosen for Brandy socially but the seedy little woman wasn't the ogre she'd pictured either. "I'm putting you and my sister, Harriet, in Brandy's room. Elton's brought down a cot. I think I'll have Brandy and Mr. Strock sleep in the guestroom next to it."

Thora K., who was on her knees plumping a pillow, straightened suddenly. "'Ee mean to put Corbin and Brandy . . . oh, but . . ." she started and then seemed to change her mind. "That do sound like 'andsome arrangements, and I thank 'ee." Her smile was unexpectedly sly.

In the kitchen Brandy sat with a towel still in hand while women moved around her finishing up the dishes.

"Sophie." Harriet shook her white curls and rolls of fat simultaneously. "Your girl looks exhausted to me. She should be in bed."

"Does your throat feel sore, dear?" Sophie asked her daughter.

"No, I'm just so tired. But I should be helping you now."

"Bless you, but get a good night's rest and you can help tomorrow. The ladies will understand if you go to bed early at a time like this."

Again Sophie had that treacherous feeling of importance as her friends chimed in with sympathy and approval.

"Even with her husband struck dead, that Sophie doesn't forget how to be a good mother," someone whispered behind her as she led Brandy out.

Shay'd spent so much of her nights working on the recalcitrant mirror that when Sophie helped her slip into the strange bed she was asleep before she could identify and voice the nagging thought that the mirror might harm whoever slept in Brandy's bed.

It occurred to her again when she awoke in the night, but was erased by the shock of finding herself snuggled up to a deliciously warm body.

Shay sat up. "Corbin?"

"Go back to sleep, Brandy." His voice came strained out of the dark. "Your mother put me in here and I couldn't object . . . without causing embarrassment. I won't bother you, Brandy."

Won't bother me! Shay moved primly to the cold part of the bed and almost fell out. *They sure didn't used to make double beds very big.* And just out of a period, Brandy felt about as prim as a bitch in heat. *The only good thing about being in someone else's body is being able to blame it for any unexpected eccentricities. Down, girl!*

Shay went back to sleep wondering who she thought she was kidding.

She was dreaming shocking things about herself, Marek, and both Maddon twins when she awoke next . . . to find gray dawn seeping through window glass and Corbin wrapped around her from behind.

A warm hand moved carefully up, drawing the voluminous nightgown from her legs. It cupped around Brandy's breast.

Shay thought "cool" for about a second and then swiveled until his hand was on Brandy's back and she was facing him. Even with the tangle of bedclothes, she managed to kiss him.

Corbin stiffened and drew away. "Brandy, I'm sorry—"

"Sorry!" She drew him back. He was so big and hard and old-fashioned and those shoulders . . . "Corbin, you can have sex with Marie and May Bell and you're sorry to touch your wife? They cost money, I'm free . . . oh yeah, I forgot. I'm crazy." She leaned over to kiss him again. "Crazy people have needs too, don't they?"

Corbin shook all over. "What kind of woman are you?" He sounded as if he'd choke.

"How many kinds are there?" She ran Brandy's hand down his body. What was he wearing? Long underwear? In the summer? Shay Garrett would have giggled if Brandy'd had the time . . .

But the two of them had set something in motion, and whatever he wore, it didn't stop him long.

"Brandy—"

"You're beautiful, Corbin Strock."

Shay took a long lovely breath and Brandy spread her legs and . . .

Shay got the surprise of her life.

Brandy *was* a virgin.

Shay watched Corbin slip his long underwear into his pants, unable to believe he intended to leave her unsatisfied. She was no expert on lovemaking and although she would rather have died than admit it to her friends, Shay Garrett hadn't slept with a man until she'd met Marek. But Marek Weir was looking better by the minute.

"Thora K. and I'll be heading back, but you may stay as long as Mrs. McCabe needs you." He gathered his belongings together faster than she'd ever seen him move. "I didn't mean to hurt you, Brandy." And he was gone.

15

Hutchison Maddon slid his stiff leg under the wooden table. With his good foot he pushed the chair back on two legs and leaned against the wall. He watched people moving about on Nederland's Main Street through the mud- and fly-specked window.

Letting his mind float away the vestiges of too little sleep, he stretched the soreness from his body.

He ordered his food and then sank into the din of dishes and voices around him . . . let them combine to form a background . . . let the red-and-white checks on the tablecloth blur into pink . . .

Distant ridges, jagged with uneven pine, eased into his head . . . swaying grasses in the north park . . . the lazy movement of a steer's behind. . . .

When his food came, he smelled in the coffee steam from his cup, let tough juicy steak linger on his tongue.

The door opened and fresh air entered to mingle with the food and people smells in the room. So did Lon Maddon.

His twin shouted a breakfast order to Hank and sat in the chair opposite. "You riding back to the north park?"

"I don't know." The yellow of egg yolk . . . the warm filling taste of it on a hunk of bread.

"What's the Doc say?"

"Says it can't be done." The salty tang of a fried potato followed by the smooth heat of coffee.

"That's what he always says."

"Lon, whatever *you* got that needs saying, let it wait?" Corbin Strock's little wife leaned over him in his thoughts, as pleasing to look at as a sky over the divide with the sun going down.

Hutch'd sensed a lifetime of secrets trying to hide behind her eyes. Where would John McCabe's daughter get secrets?

"Watchin' you eat makes me sick," Lon said as his own plate arrived. "You enjoy it too much."

Hutch sat back to study the image of himself across the table. "And you just can't wait to spoil it for me. Your face says you got news."

"Wanted to know if you was riding out today, that's all. Thought I'd go with you."

"You told me you liked freighting better than ranch work."

"I do. Figured I'd ride as far as the north park with you and then I'd go on. Thought maybe I could talk you into going on with me. But if the Doc says you can't sit a horse . . ." The excitement behind Lon's grin signaled trouble. "Thought you might lend me some of that money you been saving."

"No."

"Thought I'd take off for the Little Hole and see if I couldn't double it for you. You could go along and watch me do it if your leg—"

"No."

"I suppose we could go up to Caribou, but that's a kind of trap if he hears of it. 'Course there's two of us and one of him, still—"

"Who's he?"

"Had a drink last night with a man just in from Denver. Name was Murphy. He thought I was you. Said Tom Horn was in Denver and heading this way."

"What's that got to do with me? There's no money on my head."

"Seems like Horn had a talk with Mr. James B. Collard, III." Lon paused to let that name sink in. "And Collard's daughter sent this Murphy here to warn you. Only he warned me instead. If I was her I'd let you die. No explaining women. Never was."

Hutch kept his face still, felt a little ball of fear slide down the inside of his rib cage. "Why should Collard send Horn after me?"

"Seems Collard's going to become a grandfather unexpected-like. His daughter visited a cousin at the Wind River Ranch and went riding out with this lowly ranch hand. It got so bad they had to fire him." Lon's grin widened. "Thought you quit that job, Hutch. Murphy says you was fired."

Hutch wiped his mustache slowly with the cloth napkin beside his plate and then overturned the table, the dishes and what was left of the coffee into his brother's lap.

Somewhere in the back of the place a woman screamed.

"Oh, God, the Maddons are at it again. Now, you boys stop." Hank came running. "Hutch, that leg won't take—"

Lon came out swinging from under the pile of table and dishes. Someone tried to grab him, but not before his fist buried deep into Hutch's stomach.

Hutch fell back on the wrong leg and then against the door. When he went down it was on the sidewalk outside.

A circle of faces revolved above him and square storefronts above them.

He tried to pull in some air and choked. Nothing inside him seemed to want to open up for it.

Lon pushed through the crowd and helped lift him to his feet. With one arm slung over his twin's shoulder, Hutch managed to hop along on his good leg.

"Where're we going?" he gasped.

Lon was laughing. "To get your money and then the hell out of here."

Hutch looked down at the top of Doc Seaton's head. It was the first time he'd noticed Doc's hair was getting thin at the crown.

"This is the craziest trick you boys've got up to yet." He wound the new bandage around Hutch's leg, the cigar between his teeth exhaling a sweet smell. "No damage I can see now, but riding a horse clear to Utah—if this were my leg I wouldn't even be walking on it."

"Yes you would." Lon moved restlessly about the tiny cabin. "First baby coming or case of croup and you'd hobble off to be there."

Hutch studied the picture of the late Mrs. Seaton in its scrolly frame. The lace doily under it was as yellowed as the curtains. The pretty wallpaper had dirtied in places. Dust mocked the glass-fronted bookcase.

Doc needs a wife, Hutch thought, remembering how the place sparkled before Mrs. Seaton died.

"Now you got to hold it out some and watch for trees." Doc got off his knees and shook his head. "You go tight trails and hit one, you'll come right off your horse. It's going to hurt riding with this, boy."

Hutch stood and they helped him get into his pants.

"How are you going to get on and off a horse if you can't get into your pants?"

"Lon'll help me." The leg felt good with the new tight bandage. Hutch tried some weight on it.

"You sure you got to go clear to the Little Hole?"

"Yeah. Not even Tom Horn's going to stick his neck in there."

Hutch turned his horse as the road topped the ridge. Lon reined up beside him. Nederland looked peaceful, the creek small and sun-dazzled, the buildings a pleasant contrast to the mountain valley.

"I had a reason for saving up, Lon."

"I know," his brother said quietly. "It'll wait. Besides, I'm going to double your money, remember?"

"This is crazy. You know our chances of getting out of the Hole alive. Someone gets rankled at the cards or ornery drunk—"

"And he's shooting before he's thinking." Lon finished Hutch's thought as he did so often. They headed the horses back on the road and made them walk easy. "Rather face Horn? You wouldn't face him anyway. You'd get bushwhacked. You ain't been savin' up for that. Hutch, remember the last time we was at the Hole?"

"We were just kids then."

"But we're still Maddons. We got a free ticket because of Pa."

The sun felt good on Hutch's back, brought satisfying smells from horse and leather. But the Doc was right about his leg. It wasn't going to be easy to get to Utah.

His horse was fresh with the morning and fidgeting to move out. Hutch gritted his teeth and eased the reins to see how much he could take. He groaned and pulled back so hard the horse reared.

Lon came alongside. "This ain't going to work, is it?"

"Not clear to Utah. I'll be riding so slow winter'll catch us."

"What'll we do?"

"Circle back around Nederland. Take the train from Denver."

"Train don't go nowhere near the Hole."

"Goes near enough to Robber's Roost. By the time we get there I might be able to ride that."

"Never been to the Roost," Lon said thoughtfully. "What if we meet Horn coming along from Denver?"

"You're the gambler in the family."

Lon was laughing again. He gave a whoop and turned his horse.

They managed to skirt town without being seen and without Hutch's leg catching on a tree until they came to the Brandy Wine. Corbin Strock hammered on a shed near the mouth of the mine.

"Think he saw us?"

"He heard the horses, but I don't think he looked up."

"Wasn't that a surprise–him marrying McCabe's daughter? Rumor has it she's got a tile loose."

Hutchison Maddon didn't answer, but he contemplated Brandy McCabe Strock for miles. It helped to keep his mind off the pain in his leg. He let his imagination ponder her without all those skirts on.

Thunder rumbled low over Boulder. From the window of Brandy's darkened room, Shay watched lightning streak and crackle across the sky, turned to see its reflection glow dully on the entwined hands of the wedding mirror.

If it had caused John's stroke, she could be courting disaster by spending so much time in front of it. *Shay, Brandy was alive when you left, and ninety-eight years old.* Of course, her grandmother'd had a stroke also, when Shay was too young to remember.

Rain slashed at the window as she turned to switch on the light for another session. Lightning snapped so close the room lit up as if a flashbulb had exploded. But the light hanging from the ceiling went out.

Again twisted bronze hands glowed with the lightning. The mirror's glass remained dark . . . like an empty black hole within the frame.

The glass should reflect more than the bronze, shouldn't it?

Shay had time to sense a charge on the air, as if the lightning bolt had sizzled within the room, and to hear a humming sound and the beginning of the thunderclap.

She reached out, grabbing for the mirror to break her fall, as dark mist swirled her down through the floor.

Shay thought she was on an elevator. The downward swoop stopped abruptly and the organs inside her were still falling when the elevator moved up to adjust itself to the level of the floor.

She tried to remember why she was on the elevator and then realized she was sprawled on her stomach.

A roaring approached, the floor vibrated. She opened her eyes to light sweeping by above her.

She rose swaying to her knees in time to vomit repeatedly.

Sitting back away from it, she wiped her mouth on her sleeve.

This wasn't an elevator.

Icy sweat pricked her face and back. Her hands touched cool grass.

The roar returned, attacking her senses until she cried out. She could see the blinding light coming at her now . . . and crashing by with the roar . . . the vibration beneath her . . . and far away, the beep of a car's horn.

Car! I'm back. But Shay cowered, throwing her arms over her face and ears as the next car approached and raged by.

Stars overhead. A tiny red light flashing among them. An airplane.

Shay Garrett sat in a ditch beside a road. She'd expected to come back to the Gingerbread House.

She wore Levi's, some kind of a shirt, tennis shoes. Her hair was knotted into a bun. Pulling out the pins, she let it fall, swept her fingers through it, ran them over her face. No molar missing among her teeth. It felt like the right body. *But what's it doing here?*

The familiar dark shapes of the Flatirons and other recognizable mountains against the night sky, the lights of Boulder twinkling below. Shay hugged herself and wept.

She was on the highway east and north of town. Once more the passing of a car threw her senses into turmoil, made adrenaline surge through her body as if she were preparing to resist violation.

She decided to make her way to a house and call home. Shay couldn't bring herself to flag down one of those cars even though it was the reasonable thing to do. *Must be culture shock after being gone awhile.* Brandy's world had been quiet and peaceful compared to this.

There would be homes near, if not on the highway then off on side roads.

Her body'd been moving around without her. It felt sore and tired. Her feet hurt. Had somebody pushed it out of a car? Perhaps it was sick because of some kind of wrenching when she came back to it.

All she knew at the moment was that Rachael was in for the surprise of her life. Shay intended to kiss and hug her and fall all over her. *Daddy too. And I'll stand under a hot shower for an hour . . . and the minute my stomach straightens out I'm going to McDonald's for a quarter-pounder and fries.*

Shay waited for the shock of the next car's passing to leave her. She'd forgotten how much they stank. She stumbled along the ditch.

You really should stop a car for help, dumb-dumb.

Yeah, but what if it's full of perverts?

When she came to a side road she left the shadowy ditch.

Her thoughts filled with home and her knees rubbery, Shay walked a surprising distance before she came to a driveway with a mailbox beside it. The house at the end of the drive was dark. *Maybe everyone's asleep.*

But there was no answer when she rang the bell and then banged on the door. It was locked.

She walked back down the drive and onto the road, relishing the freedom of movement the Levi's and tennies allowed her, the natural suppleness of her own body. She picked up a strand of hair that fell over her shoulder. It gleamed silver blond in the moonlight and she thought of Hutchison Maddon.

The next house was dark too and in front of it a dog the size of a pony growled on the end of a chain. Shay went on.

The houses were so far apart here she realized she was farther from town than she'd thought.

This road was graveled. Shay kicked a small rock. *I should've known there wouldn't be as many houses on a gravel road.* She could have used Brandy's tireless legs.

A mewing sound startled her. Something that might be a cloth bag squirmed in the ditch to her left. She shuddered and walked on.

Shay, you can't. You know what's in that bag.

I have enough troubles of my own.

The mewing came again, and from several throats. Hopeless. Lost.

They'll die, Shay.

Retracing her steps, she knelt to untie the knot of the bag. *Why me?*

Wriggling, ratlike bodies. Tiny eyes glowing back in the moonlight. Plaintive, heart-rending cries. *That's all I need, abandoned kittens.*

They weren't even old enough to be weaned. *They'll probably die anyway. I'm a sap.* But Shay knew what it felt like to be lost and alone. *Why didn't I stop a car?*

Farther on another sound startled her and a goat moved from the shadow behind a fence. At least it wasn't abandoned.

The goat followed her from his side of the ditch, trying to talk to her. She was, finally, coming upon a house. And another dog on the end of a chain. It was bordered on one side by tall white tree skeletons.

Shay decided she was no longer fussy. She was so very tired. The kittens in the bag cried pitifully. They needed milk.

How can I think of them at a time like this?

The house sat back from the road. She started across the yard, keeping track of the dog.

"Help! Please, I need help!"

A yard light filled her eyes. She covered them and when next she looked she saw the dog was too close and a man with white beard and hair slid back a glass door to peer out at her.

"Help," she yelled, wondering vaguely why an old farmhouse should have a modern sliding glass door, before dark mist rose from the ground and grabbed her.

16

Voices rose through the mist with Shay.

". . . but no fever. This is certainly a strange malady. And you say she's been acting queerly?"

"Yes, as though she'd just come back from a faraway place. But she's been here all the time. And look at this. It was lying open on the table. I haven't read it. It's a personal diary. But I happened to glance at the handwriting."

"It's not very good, is it?"

"Doctor, it isn't Brandy's handwriting."

"It's possible it's the shock of John's death coupled with the newness of being a bride or perhaps the early onset of a pregnancy. Frankly, I'm at a loss to—here, she's beginning to come around."

Shay struggled to open her eyes. She'd never felt this sick in her life but her head was clear enough to know it'd happened again. Her disappointment was intense.

She lay in Brandy's body and in her bed. Sophie and the strange doctor came into focus through a welling of tears.

"I have to throw up."

"Here's the bucket, dear." Sophie held it for her and pulled Brandy's hair out of the way.

"This violent retching could cause some delirium, Mrs. McCabe," the doctor whispered.

Outside the window it was still raining in Brandy's world.

May Bell ironed the last ruffle and then hung the dress in the wardrobe next to her other lovelies. When she'd worked at Miss Hattie's she hadn't had to iron. But it was better to have her own rooms, be her own boss.

She looked around with satisfaction. All the doilies and lamp shades, the comfortable chairs and bed. May Bell had found the poor Brady woman to do her wash but couldn't trust her with the ironing. And she had to get dressed to go out for her meals now, where at Miss Hattie's there'd been a dining room . . . but still, Nederland was a better place.

May Bell liked being independent and business was so good she could afford coal all year long.

When the iron had cooled she put it and the board away, pulled her most comfortable chair closer to the potbelly stove—even if she wasn't a bit cold yet—and took a chocolate from the box Hutch had given her when he and Lon came to get their money from her hiding place. She was proud of the way she played banker to a select few of her preferred customers. Although she didn't pay interest, May Bell never cheated or borrowed, either.

All in all, life was pretty good since she'd gone into business for herself. Of course she'd worry about the twins, but nothing like she'd worried and scraped in Iowa.

She knew she should be getting dressed to go down for supper but ate another chocolate instead—bless that Hutch and good luck to him—and then found her ledger book. It was fun to add up her own accounts. She reached for the packet of papers and the tobacco pouch. Tonight should be a slow one and she wasn't cold or starving. She'd have a smoke and do her ledger and then go down. The thought of the Iowa farm made her feel pampered and cozy here.

May Bell'd no more than opened the tobacco pouch when she heard the board steps outside her door creak under the weight of boots.

The pampered feeling changed to one of anger. She was good-natured but business before supper wasn't allowed and everyone knew that. Some damn summer visitor from the hotels probably. She put the paper, tobacco and ledger book in the drawer of the side table and was half out of her chair when the door was kicked open.

May Bell knew him. Because she'd been thinking about him since the twins left. Even if she'd never seen him before.

Collapsing back into her chair she grabbed another chocolate, wishing it was a stiff whiskey.

It was the crazy look in his eyes that made him so recognizable, reminded her of Jeremiah.

"My name's Horn," he said and just stood there, a rifle dangling across one arm. "Looking for a man name of Maddon. Been told you might be able to help me."

His face and body were lean, his nose long, his eyes wide open with that self-righteous look Jeremiah wore when he told her how bad she was. That her father'd had when he told her the same thing. She'd been "bad" ever since the age of twelve when her mother died and left her the female head of a family with seven children. When she was fourteen her father'd married her off to Jeremiah because God decided such things and because her father needed money and there was a sister grown old enough to take over. But after all these years it was still hard to meet the eye of a self-righteous male.

Now this man was "good" because he killed bad men. Waited behind a tree and shot them in the back.

"Hutch Maddon ain't no outlaw," she said bravely. And he surely was small potatoes for a man like Tom Horn. Was he just picking up pin money as he rode through the area?

Horn didn't move, didn't blink, didn't take his eyes from her face. One thin hank of dark hair curled across a high forehead.

"You got no right to hunt him down." She wore a negligee and her breasts hung loose beneath it. Sweat and fear made the skin slimy where they lay against her.

His nose wrinkled as if he didn't like the perfumed air of her apartment, and his mustache twitched. What if somebody'd paid him to rid the world of bad women?

No matter how hard May Bell breathed she felt dizzy for the lack of air. "He went to the Little Hole and you can't get him there."

Rumor had it Tom Horn would wait weeks to pick off his prey. Would he wait for Hutch to ride out of the Hole? May Bell felt sick with guilt, but what could a lone woman do?

He blinked finally, relaxed a little against the doorjamb. "Thought he wasn't an outlaw. Why would he go to an outlaw hideout?"

"To get away from you."

"Then somebody warned him." The rifle rose slowly to aim at her head. "Who?"

"Some man from Denver. I don't know him."

"Who?" he repeated. His voice was thin like the rest of him.

May Bell stared at the small black hole at her end of the rifle. "His name was Murphy. That's all I know."

Tom Horn turned suddenly and the doorway was empty. She heard his boots clatter down the stairs.

Her breath made humming sounds as she reeled to the door, locked it and wedged a straight chair under the knob. "Oh, Hutch, I'm sorry."

May Bell poured a whiskey and chipped a tooth when she brought the glass too hurriedly to her mouth.

Tobacco spilled on her pretty red rug as she rolled a cigarette with shaking hands. "So sorry, Hutch . . ."

Shay and Brandy were very ill. Sophie, Nora and Elton took turns at the bedside. The doctor visited daily. Everyone seemed relieved when Brandy developed a sore throat and a fever.

The second transposition of minds must have lowered Brandy's resistance to the point that she was ripe for this new illness. And then there'd been the strain of those long nights in front of the mirror. Shay remembered how sick her own body had been in that ditch east of Boulder. This switching of bodies and time was dangerous. She'd have to wait and gather strength before she tried again.

At first Shay was too weak to care where she was. But as she recovered she worked out what she thought had happened and was still happening. . . .

Her body'd been in that ditch because, for some reason, Brandy had taken it there. And while Shay'd traveled to her own time Brandy had returned to this one, acting "queerly," talking as if she'd been to a "faraway place," as Sophie had said. The mirror'd performed a switch. While Shay was trapped in this time and body, Brandy was trapped in Shay's.

If this was a strange experience for Shay, what must it be like for her grandmother? Had she married Marek Weir?

During her convalescence, Shay developed a plan. . . .

"I heard what you told the doctor about my diary," she said to Sophie one day.

"I haven't read it, dear, and I won't. I just happened to glance at the handwriting."

"Ma, I was in a hurry and just scribbled. That's why it didn't look like my handwriting."

"I know, Brandy. Don't distress yourself." Sophie sounded as if she wanted to believe it but couldn't quite. "This illness has probably been coming on for longer than we realized." She took the breakfast tray and started for the door. "Except for that night when you were first ill, I haven't heard you call me Ma for so long." Her lips quivered. "Brandy, please don't call me Sophie anymore."

"I won't, Ma." *I'm going to be a model daughter.*

"It's as though you haven't forgiven me for your marriage to Mr. Strock. And you know it was your father who forced that."

Sophie reminded Shay of Rachael again. *Strange, tracing similar features and expressions between your own mother and her grandmother before that mother's even born.* Rachael would not resemble Hutch Maddon as her twin brothers would. She'd be a throwback to Sophie.

And another day when Elton came to sit with her . . .

"Bran, now that Pa's gone, maybe we can do something about Strock. I know divorce isn't an easy thing to live with but if we let him keep the Brandy Wine he might—"

"No, Elton. I want to go back to Corbin as soon as I'm well enough." *Your mother's too alert. I can't carry on this masquerade here for long.*

"You want to live with him?" His hair was cut short as was the fashion now. It made his ears stick out like stunted wings. "Have you come to love him, Bran?"

"Yes," Shay lied and looked Elton straight in the eye. Except for his sexual insensibilities she really did care for Corbin.

"Think of a mountain winter in that shack, Bran."

I am. Ugh. But if I can take the mirror with me I might get out before winter. The only Brandy they know in Nederland is me.

"You've changed so since your marriage, I hardly know you. I'd have said you and Strock were the worst mismatch ever, but if you're happy with him . . ." He rolled his eyes and sighed. "You don't know how relieved I am."

"Well, I am. So don't worry about it."

"Here I've been imagining you miserable, maybe even being beaten, and you're happy. Wait till I tell Ma." Elton touched her cheek and left.

Shay stared hatred at the wedding mirror crouching on its hands in the corner of the room.

Thora K. had finished the beds assigned her and was carrying soiled linen down the back stairs when the proprietress asked her to help out in the dining room. This often happened on Sundays when the Antlers served the best chicken dinner in Colorado.

Enjoying the change from doing rooms, Thora K. greeted friends as she bustled about with platters of chicken and bowls of steaming mashed potatoes.

Mr. Hollingsworth McLeod, one of the special guests at the Antlers, signaled her with his water glass. She nodded and went off to get the jug. Now, there was a name for you, Thora K. thought. Mr. McLeod was always off in a corner talking business with someone.

"Power is the thing now, Harry," he was saying to the man across from him as she returned with the water. "And with the natural fall of the canyon, Nederland's the place to build a reservoir—madam, you are pouring water all over the table."

"Oh, I do be sorry, sir." Thora K. righted the jug and dabbed at the mess she'd made. "Did . . . did 'ee say reservoir, Mr. McLeod? 'Ere in Nederland?"

"Well, yes. It's still in the planning stage. I'm trying to raise the capital right—"

"Reservoir, 'ere . . . her ain't barmy then."

"I beg your pardon?"

"Her do 'ave the sight. Oh, thank 'ee, Mr. McLeod. Thank 'ee!"

Shay turned to look at the wedding mirror, lying facedown in the back of the buckboard and wrapped securely in a quilt. She'd insisted it be covered before its removal from Brandy's room in the Gingerbread House. The mirror might be capable of harming others and she was determined to be careful with it. The trunk beside it was filled with clothes for winter, all black because Brandy was in mourning for John McCabe.

Sophie hadn't been eager to let her have the mirror but finally had to admit it did indeed belong to Brandy. Like Elton, Sophie seemed relieved that her daughter wished to return to her husband.

Shay'd asked Sophie for money and there was a good deal of it in her purse. She would fix up the cabin a bit for Thora K. and for the real Brandy before trying to switch bodies again.

A stronger, more confident Shay rode up the canyon to Nederland this time. She'd survived the disappointment of returning to Brandy's world after her short tantalizing sojourn in modern times. She'd survived the ordeal of illness without modern medicine. She was even relaxed with the slow pace of the trip.

It was Corbin Strock sitting beside her who seemed ill-at-ease now. She asked him about the mine, about Thora K. and Samuel and Tim Pemberthy, anything to make conversation, but got only curt replies.

Finally, by midafternoon she could stand it no longer. "Corbin, what's wrong?"

"Nothing."

"Now stop this and tell me." She pushed his hat back and peered around into his face. "Please?"

"I admit it was my fault but . . . but good women don't act that way." His ears reddened. Confusion mixed with anguish in his eyes.

Shay knew he referred to their one night in bed together. Corbin was falling hard for Brandy and Shay'd shocked the pants off him.

"Are you sure you know all that much about good women?" *You old Victorian, you.* "I mean, have you ever discussed . . . intimate things with one?"

"Of course not!"

"Then how can you know? I was a virgin, wasn't I?"

"Strong passions must be curbed." He clamped his teeth together so tightly his ears wiggled.

"By women. But not by men. Good women just lie around and be done unto?"

"Brandy—"

"If they move a muscle or enjoy anything, they're bad women? But the man can enjoy himself with uncurbed passion?"

"He must or there'd be no children conceived."

"This has got to be the most ridiculous conversation I've ever had. Who's talking about children?"

"Brandy, you cannot separate the two. One naturally follows the other."

"Then why don't prostitutes get pregnant?"

"I refuse to discuss this any further." He slapped the reins against the horses' rumps with a fury. "Do you understand me?"

"Yes, dear." Shay sighed but said not a word until they'd reached Nederland.

On Main Street their way was blocked by a strangely quiet crowd. Sitting high on the buckboard, Shay could see a mule at its center. And with a little shock she recognized the blanket-draped thing slung over the mule's back. It was a human body. Only the boots showed beneath . . . heel up.

"What's happening?" Corbin asked a man at the edge of the crowd.

"Old Willis found a dead man in the creek, downstream from here. Shot in the back."

"Do you know him?"

"Only to speak to. Met him in the saloon one night. He was from Denver. Last name was Murphy." The man shuffled uneasily and looked away. "Someone said Horn was asking after him."

"Probably an outlaw then, and good riddance." Corbin backed the team to take a side street to the bridge.

"Who's Horn?" Shay asked.

"Tom Horn. You've heard of him. A one-man vigilante committee who's not content to leave criminals to the ways of the courts."

"That isn't legal. He'll be tried for murder, won't he?"

"He never leaves witnesses and he's long gone by now."

The smell of frying chicken met them at the door of the cabin and Thora K. greeted her with teary eyes. "So 'ee do be 'ome. I've been some lonesome for 'ee, child."

Corbin carried her new trunk to the loft because her room couldn't hold another item.

Tim Pemberthy arrived to help unload the mirror. Shay held the door as the men lifted it down and then held onto the door for support as the quilt slipped off in their hands. . . .

This vision was short-lived and Shay didn't pass out as she had on Brandy's wedding night while eating a pasty at the table.

She saw her own body dressed in a long skirt and some kind of kerchief that covered her hair. Her arm reached over a fence toward a goat. Behind the goat a tall white tree stood bleached of bark and leaves.

"Brandy, are you sick?" Corbin replaced the quilt and rushed toward her.

"No. I'm . . . fine. Just felt a little weak for a moment." Why had Brandy stayed at that farmhouse?

"Us'll 'ave to be careful she don't tire for a bit." Thora K. led her to a bench. "Her been terrible sick."

The only space for the mirror was a corner of the main room.

Corbin left to return the team and buckboard. Thora K. turned spattering chicken in the frypan. And Tim pulled the quilt off the wedding mirror . . .

"Tim, don't!"

"Wot a hugly thing it do be." Thora K. stared in amazement.

"That's . . . why I think we should leave it covered."

"Why 'ave it at all if 'ee can't see yourself in it?"

Tim Pemberthy's skin had gone white to the roots of his hair. "I do believe it's the same as stood in me brother's 'ouse in Central City."

Shay covered the wedding mirror quickly.

"It did upset the family so, they left it in the 'ouse and moved out. They was that afraid to touch it."

"Why did it upset the family?" Shay tried to sound casual, her fingers nervously smoothing the quilt.

"Their youngest did see strange things in it. Edden been right since."

"What things?"

"No one'd tell me. But I don't like you 'aving it in the house."

"'Twas a gift from Brandy's father, Tim. 'Er knows what's best to do with it, I'm sure," Thora K. said mysteriously. "Tim, 'ave 'ee heard of the new reservoir Mr. Hollingsworth McLeod plans to build 'ere in Nederland?" She forked chicken onto a platter and winked at Shay.

17

Shay'd forgotten the Antlers Hotel was open only in the summer, and she'd been in Nederland less than a week when Thora K.'s job ended for the season. It would be difficult to work on the mirror with the Cornish woman home all day.

Without asking permission to leave the cabin, Shay walked to the general store and bought red-and-white calico. She persuaded Thora K. to help her make curtains. Shay was no seamstress and her stitches looked juvenile.

They rolled the scraps and combined them with others to braid a big rug for the main room. Shay hemmed up some material Sophie'd sent for a tablecloth. The cabin took on a new look.

She helped to "put up" the garden produce and to make sausages to hang in the cave. Thora K. patiently instructed Shay at every step.

The mirror sat uncommunicative in the corner. Even covered, its presence lent a subtle change to the very air of the room. Whenever left alone, Shay removed the quilt and stood before it.

Corbin was home only for meals and to sleep. He did his best to ignore her.

Cold winds blew in from the west. The aspen high on the hillsides turned a lovely gold and Corbin brought up coal from town. But an Indian summer intervened and one day Shay and Thora K. sat on the porch sewing blocks for a quilt. The Cornish woman told stories of phantoms of the dead appearing to loved ones at the moment of their deaths.

"'Appened to me granny, it did." It seemed everything that'd ever happened had happened to Thora K.'s grandmother.

"Her were laying in bed worrying about me fayther's brother being so late home. 'Twere bright with the moonlight and 'er did get up and look out the window. And there 'ee were, walking toward the 'ouse. Her went to the door but when her opened it, no 'un be there. Soon they did bring 'im home, and dead 'ee was. Struck down by a runaway 'orse and wagon."

"Thora K., do you really believe your uncle appeared to your grandmother like that? When he was dead?"

"Aye." She put down her sewing and stared at Shay. "Tez easier to understand that than why a 'unman of twenty years don't know how ter cook, sew, preserve or anything else, Brandy," she said quietly.

Indian summer passed and so did Shay's confidence in the mirror. She put on Brandy's scratchy woolen underwear to fight the drafts that crept up her skirts.

Dr. Seaton persuaded Samuel Williams to make the trip down the canyon to the Sanitarium. His cabin was boarded up.

One Saturday night she awoke to hear Corbin and Thora K. talking. He must have just returned from the "kiddleywinks," which was Thora K.'s word for saloon. "Look around 'ee, son. Do 'ee see wot her's done to the 'ouse?"

"I think you and Brandy have fixed it up pretty." There was a slight slur to his consonants.

"Her's nesting, Corbin Strock. Her needs a babe."

"Brandy's not a bird and you know she shouldn't–"

"I did tell 'ee about the reservoir. 'Er edden daft. She 'ave the sight and can't be helping that."

"And where did Brandy tell you the reservoir would be, Thora K.?"

"On the meadow. Same as her told 'ee."

"Mr. McLeod is contracting to buy land for it up on Sulfide Flats, not on Barker Meadows. I just heard tonight." Corbin's footsteps on the stairs were none too steady.

"Well, it edden built yet," his mother called after him.

Shay'd never heard of Sulfide Flats. She rolled over in the cold bed. When she slept, she dreamed of Rachael and woke longing for her mother. Lying still in the lonely dark, her eyes dry but burning, Shay wondered why she was such a child. She and Rachael'd never gotten on all that well when they were together. Her father, Marek, her friends were becoming like fond memories. Why then this morbid fixation with her mother?

The snow came first as powder that melted with the next day's touch of sun. Golden leaves fell from the aspen. Tim Pemberthy came to supper at least once a week and spent half the meal looking over his shoulder at the wedding mirror. He told them that it'd been in the house when his brother's family moved to Central City. But he'd heard its previous owner'd found it on a garbage dump outside a "fancy" house in Cripple Creek.

Thora K. had run out of scraps for sewing and Shay was running out of patience and busywork. She read all the books Sophie'd sent up. None would have made the best-seller list.

Shay scandalized Thora K. by buying new yard goods and tearing them up for quilting blocks and rag rugs. One morning she watched from a window a real wild bear rummage through the refuse heap beside the cabin. And she wasn't even moved by the sight.

But she waited several hours before going to the spring for water, listened for his heavy body crashing around in the trees or breaking sticks.

Shay saw or heard nothing until she followed the path back to the cabin. As she approached the outhouse the trees tilted and a familiar feeling tugged at her. A thin mist rose from the ground, pulling her over.

Instead of fighting it as she had before, Shay tried to thrust herself into the fog. But it was so thin and instead of continuing to fall, she hit hard earth almost immediately, the bucket overturning on the path in front of her, spilled water staining the earth dark around it.

Shay began to swirl.

A faint image of a girl with ratted hair, bending closer, mouthing words Shay could almost hear. A modern light fixture above her head. But trees and the bucket showed through the girl as if she were translucent film.

The sickness . . . the sweating . . . Shay fought to sink deeper into the fog but the tugging weakened. The girl faded as though melting on the cold damp air.

Corbin found her lying sick and shaken on the path and carried her into bed, but she recovered in a short time. The wedding mirror was still safely under its quilt shroud.

It probably hadn't worked at this end of time—but at the other. Her grandmother must finally have left the farmhouse with the sliding glass door and returned to the Gingerbread House and the mirror. But the girl in the vision hadn't been Shay Garrett even in body. She was a stranger, had dressed like a hippie.

Whatever Brandy'd done on her side of time hadn't been enough, but it gave Shay renewed hope that a reverse in bodies was not far off.

Winter arrived on screaming winds. Snow piled in drifts against the cabin. Corbin stayed home to tunnel to the cave for supplies and read aloud Brandy's books to his mother, who could neither read nor write. With his bulk, the place seemed suffocated with people. But on Saturday nights he managed to get out to the saloon.

One such night, a blizzard wailed particularly strong and Thora K. pleaded with him not to go. By now Shay rarely spoke to him at all.

But he left and the women sat in front of the open oven. It was too cold to go to bed. Grains of snow seeped through cracks in the walls, formed little piles on the floor that looked like sugar.

They sat in silence for what must have been an hour, listening to the wind's shivery sound, and then something snapped in Shay. She stood and pulled the quilt from the mirror.

"Do 'ee come back to the stove, child."

"Thora K., I know this is going to shake your faith in me. But you're the only person I can talk to. Brandy will need your understanding when she returns."

"But 'ee be Brandy."

"No, I'm Shay Garrett." And standing in front of the mirror, with the lantern's light making shadows in the corners of the room and lending a dull sheen to bronze hands, Shay told her story. The wind screamed to get in at them and provided an eerie background for her tale. As she talked she saw the muscles of Brandy's face and throat relaxing. It was good to confide in someone at last.

When she'd finished, Shay went back to the stove. Thora K. poked up the coals and put the teakettle on.

"You believe me, do you?"

The Cornish woman broke bread into two bowls and added herbs without looking up. "Edden zackly easy."

"You believe a lot of strange things—piskies and phantoms of the dead. I thought you might be the one person who would understand."

"Well, I'm some mizzy-mazzed, I can tell 'ee." She looked at the wedding mirror thoughtfully. "'Twould explain why 'ee know things 'ee shouldn't and don't know things 'ee should, I s'pose."

They ate hot kiddley broth and listened to the wind again.

"'Ee be used to a fine big 'ouse and tez a bad winter early 'ere. Sure it edden the cabin fever 'ee got, Brandy?" she asked hopefully. "Being shut up in 'ere and all?"

Patiently Shay went through her story again, trying to fill in any gaps she might have left the first time.

Thora K. mopped up puddles where the seeping snow had melted on the floor. "And this mirror—'ow do it do this thing?"

"I don't know what makes it work. Most of the time it doesn't."

"And John McCabe did speak of it as 'ee lay dying . . . fearful-like?"

"And he had his stroke in the same room with it. I don't know how much the mirror had to do with that but I think it would pay to be careful."

"Mmmmm." Thora K. draped the quilt over the mirror. "And this'll 'elp, do 'ee think?"

"I don't know that either, but I hope so."

"This Rachael 'ee speak of would be Corbin's daughter then? Wot's wrong now, child?"

"There's no Corbin in the family stories that I remember, nor any Strock children. But my mother, Rachael, did speak of a Thora K., who was an old woman she remembered fondly."

"Do 'ee leave 'im then?"

"If I did . . . I mean Brandy did . . . why would there still be a Thora K. living with my mother's family?" Shay answered miserably.

"Him do die afore me then and 'ee don't know when?"

"No. I'm sorry I told you. It isn't fair but I'm trying to be honest about it. You're beginning to believe me, aren't you?"

"Don't want to outlive me Corbin as I 'ave the others." She reached for the teakettle. "Let's 'ave some tay."

Shay scraped a peephole in the frost on the window. Nothing outside but a strange light darkness. "Shouldn't Corbin be home by now?"

A clatter of cups at the table and Shay turned to see Thora K. blanch, her hand rise to her throat.

What have I done? Scaring this poor woman to death. "I didn't mean to worry you. I didn't listen very carefully to my mother's stories. It's really possible she did mention a Corbin and I've forgotten." Which didn't alter the fact Rachael grew up a Maddon and not a Strock.

They had tea and still Corbin didn't come home. *Please, God, don't let it be now.*

"Tell me more of this Rachael." Thora K. finally broke the uneasy silence.

"I know her only as a mother, a grown woman. She taught school before she married. She looks a lot like Sophie McCabe, but she's taller. She remembers you as completely white-haired so she must have known you when you were quite old. She grew up on a ranch somewhere near here. I've never been there, it passed out of the family before I was born and the buildings burned so there wasn't anything left to take me to see—oh, she's a writer."

"Wot do 'er write?" Thora K. kept glancing at the door, twisting her fingers.

"Books for older children."

"Storybooks?"

"Yes. Fiction about a lot of things. I haven't read most of them. I wish I had now. But the ones I have are usually located in the West and have to do with girls growing up. Most of the girls have problems understanding their mothers and getting along with them. Now that I think of it, all that

I've read do." Shay pondered that discovery and wondered why. There'd been a lacking or flaw to Rachael's novels. The other themes worked themselves out satisfactorily but always in the background the mother-daughter thing never quite resolved itself. Perhaps her mother was just being literary.

They brought their nightgowns and robes out to the stove to undress in the relative warmth. The wind stopped and the quiet was worse.

"'Ee should be off to bed, Brandy."

"I'll wait a little longer." Had Corbin had too much to drink, gotten lost in the blizzard? Did he lie frozen in a snowbank?

They had another cup of tea and again Shay asked if her companion believed in her story.

"Some of me do and most of me don't. 'Ee be a strange 'un fer sure." Thora K. sat erect. "Do 'ee hear anything?"

The crunch of snow outside. The door opened.

Corbin looked astonished to see them still up. And even more astonished when Shay ran to hug him. "I thought you might be lost in the storm."

He laughed and kissed her forehead. "It's good to know I'm missed, but I'm not that easy to lose." He held her a little longer than necessary.

By the smell of his breath, Shay figured he was stoked enough with antifreeze to sleep the night in a snowbank in comfort.

Thora K. gave a heavy sigh and trudged off to bed, her shoulders drooping. Shay felt an enormous guilt for having told her too much.

When she went to her room with a heated brick wrapped in rags for her feet, frost coated the nail heads on the inside of the outer walls. Shay lay shivering, listening to Corbin's movements overhead, and then was surprised to hear him coming down the stairs.

He stopped in her doorway. "Brandy, it's too cold for a man to sleep up there," he whispered.

Shay moved over and opened the covers to let him in. *More like May Bell didn't have time in her appointment book.* But she snuggled against him, tried to lie still and passive as he began to explore Brandy's body. *Nothing like a little alcohol to loosen the old resolve, huh, boy?*

When he slept, she considered the fact that there were no planned-parenthood clinics in this world, no pill. What did women use now? There were no Strock children in the family's history but that didn't mean none had been born. The unwanted picture of one marble shaft marking the graves of three children in the Caribou cemetery invaded her mind and would not leave. Cara Williams and her newborn. Little Joshua McCabe, Brandy's brother, had been only four . . .

She didn't want Brandy to go through the heartbreak of losing a child and at the moment she was responsible for Brandy's body. She'd have to talk to Dr. Seaton or even May Bell. Prostitutes must do something.

When Brandy came back she'd have enough problems to face without pregnancy. Though the time was drawing out impossibly, Shay held to "when" Brandy came back. It was her lifeline to sanity.

Wind scoured much of the snow away. The weather warmed and melted more of it to mud. About every other Saturday night Corbin decided it was too cold to sleep in the loft. He'd wake up sheepish and angry at himself and at her. Shay watched for May Bell out for her customary walk but didn't see her. She had no opportunity to speak with the doctor.

Christmas came and everyone gathered in the town hall around a community Christmas tree to sing hymns. It would have been boring if Shay weren't so delighted to get out of the cabin.

One day when Corbin went to the Brandy Wine Thora K. left for her meeting of Independent Champions of the Red Cross. Shay gave the mirror another chance with the usual results and then walked to Main Street to buy a chair with a back on it for Thora K. Perhaps she'd buy one for herself too. It was hard not to be able to lean back and relax except in bed. Particularly when so much time was spent sitting around the cookstove.

The air was crisp and snow drifts lay dirty on the shaded sides of buildings. Shay walked on frozen mud ruts till she came to wooden sidewalk. For once the cold winds off Arapahoe Peak did not rake the valley but she thought she could hear them in the distance.

Gray sky. Gray buildings. Brown mud. Nederland looked like something out of a war movie.

Main Street was curiously barren of people. Two women talked at the far end and a CLOSED sign perched in the window of the little butcher shop on the corner. This seemed odd since it wasn't Sunday.

She glanced up at May Bell's apartment over the saloon. For some reason the day appeared even grayer there. Would anyone notice if she slipped up the stairs? Shay wanted badly to talk contraception with May Bell. But the women walked toward her now and she recognized both as friends of Thora K. She didn't dare risk it.

A small gust of wind reached her from behind as she turned in at the door of the general store. It was even gloomier inside and empty except for Mr. Binder behind the counter.

"Where is everybody? The street's so quiet."

"All the men are off to court in Boulder today. Trying to settle that squabble over the election." It seemed that two town boards had been elected because there was a doubt in the minds of some about the honesty of the first election and another had been held. Both boards claimed to be the legal one. "Didn't your husband go down?" Even Mr. Binder, who was always polite, watched her candidly.

"No, he's at his mine."

"He's like me then, more interested in business than politics. What'll it be today, Mrs. Strock? More yard goods?"

"I'm interested in a rocking chair, but I see you don't have any."

"Don't stock 'em but I can order you one up. Only take a couple days." The sound of the door opening, the scuffle of boots, and Mr. Binder looked over her shoulder. "Well, and here's someone else who didn't go to court. Hutch, Lon, whichever one you are. When did you get back?"

"Yesterday." The rising howl of the west wind swept into the room and flurries of sawdust scooted across the floor before the door closed.

Shay turned to look up at her grandfather. Funny, she thought, that she had no trouble telling which twin this Maddon was, when others who'd known them longer did. Even without lips parted to reveal the lack of a gap in his teeth. Hutch held himself more stiffly, tended to put his head back and gaze at the world down the bridge of his nose. He wore his hat farther down on his forehead than Lon did, held his eyes fully open so all of the amber iris showed, while Lon squinted. Hutch kept his face expressionless, rarely smiled.

"Ma'am." He touched his hat.

Shay nodded and turned back to the catalog Mr. Binder'd opened for her. Recklessly she ordered two rocking chairs, very aware of Hutch behind her. He was like facing destiny.

As she left the store she avoided his eyes. Her throat felt dry. Outside she stopped suddenly to stare across the street.

May Bell stood coatless on the wooden landing by her door. She held an armload of dresses. Shay watched her dump them over the railing into the dirt and snow below and then rush back into her apartment.

Shay steadied Brandy's body against a particularly hard gust and pondered the woman's actions. Then she saw a flame curl against the inside of one of May Bell's windows. Smoke seeped through cracks between boards, to be whipped away by the wind.

18

"Mr. Binder!" Shay almost fell back into the store. "Fire in the saloon. Call the fire department."

Mr. Binder ran to the window. "What fire department?"

"Hutch, May Bell went back inside," she told him.

In no great hurry, Hutch walked to the door and opened it. His eyes narrowed like Lon's when May Bell emerged with another load of clothes and dumped them over the railing.

"May Bell!" Hutch Maddon roared into the wind. "Get your ass out of there."

Shay giggled at that and horrified Mr. Binder.

May Bell looked across at them as if she might have heard but dived back through her door.

"Damn that woman," Hutch muttered and raced across the street.

"Mr. Binder, can't you sound the alarm or something?"

"No alarm. No one *to* alarm either. All down in Boulder."

"Shouldn't we warn the people in the saloon?"

"Closed. Nobody there. All at court." He seemed mesmerized by the flames beginning to lick through the roof.

Hutch dragged a struggling May Bell down the stairs while trying to ward off her blows with the metal strongbox under his other arm.

"You know"—Shay felt somewhat mesmerized herself—"if that wasn't real fire, this would be hysterical."

"She does look hysterical," Mr. Binder answered.

"But what *do* we do?"

"Buckets."

"You can't fight that with buckets."

Shay groaned as Lon Maddon passed her the three hundred millionth bucket of water and her arm muscles screamed an answer as she handed it on to May Bell.

Brandy's skirts and coat were soaked and the wind blew fiercely but Shay wasn't cold. The town was burning and it made the air nice and warm.

"What were you doing, May Bell," Lon said across her, "smoking again?"

"Shut your mouth," May Bell snapped back, tears streaking the smut on her face. "My lovely place . . ."

May Bell's lovely place and the saloon that had been beneath it were hot rubble. So was the building beside it. The bucket brigade was working on the next one. These buildings all backed onto the creek and someone dipped the buckets into it and then passed them up the line where the person at the end dumped what water made the trip into the fire. Another line faced them, swinging the empty buckets back to the creek.

Two more brigades worked farther down trying to soak buildings in the fire's path. The Maddon twins, Mr. Binder and four or five others were the only men to be seen. But all the women and children in town had come running. Thora K. and her temperance group made up one whole brigade downstream. During an occasional lull in the roar of fire and wind, and the crashing of beams and rafters, Shay could hear them singing. Probably because the saloon was no more.

Shay kept thinking of Caribou's main street. "This is hopeless. We aren't doing any good. Isn't there any way to call for help?"

"Sure is." Lon grinned. "We got one telephone line to Boulder."

"Where?"

"In the saloon." He laughed so hard he spilled water down her front.

The smoke made it seem like dusk. Weather-dried wooden buildings fell like cards before the fire. Red flame leaped into the sky. People shouted and coughed. At the head of the line Hutch Maddon cursed as he heaved a little water on a lot of fire.

Suddenly Hutch shouted, trying to push back the line. Then he turned and ran as the building they'd been "watering" collapsed. He grabbed Shay with one arm and May Bell with the other, pulling them toward the creek.

When the wind cleared dust and smoke they saw the fire had crossed Main Street. Mr. Binder's store was in flames. Lon had to hold onto him to keep him from crossing still-burning rubble to reach it.

"Poor Mr. Binder." Shay turned to find Hutchison Maddon, his arm still encircling her waist, staring down at her in that strange consuming way.

"No," she said stupidly and pushed away from him.

It took another hour for the wind-driven fire to eat Main Street. The gusts died before the devastation reached the homes at the end. But most of the business buildings were gone.

Shay and Thora K. trudged up the hill, too exhausted to speak. When they reached the cabin they sat at the table and sighed. Shay wiped a tear from Brandy's cheek and wondered if her eyes would ever stop smarting.

They were still there when Corbin came home. "What's for supper?"

When his eyes adjusted to the dim light he took a second look at them. "What happened? Brandy, did you have trouble with the stove again?"

"No, dumb-dumb, the town burned down. And *you* can get the dinner."

"Dumb-dumb?" He glanced at his mother as if for clarification. But she just coughed and hooked a thumb in the direction of the front door.

When he returned from the porch his voice shook. "Why didn't someone come and get Tim and me?"

"Us was too busy fightin' the fire, 'ee jackass. And all they men down in court fiddling like Nero whilst the town did burn and 'ee off to yer uld 'ole in the ground." Thora K. banged a fist on the table. "Proper gate buffleheads, the lot of 'ee. Uld 'unmen and children singeing their eyebrows off—"

"But we didn't know—"

"Poke up the stove, you."

Corbin opened a can of beans, made coffee and sliced bread, turning to look at them as if he couldn't believe two women would sit there and let him get the dinner.

Shay ate hungrily even though everything tasted like smoke. Then they ordered Corbin to carry in water so they could wash.

Someone came to fetch him to help soak the still-smoldering ruins so a new blaze wouldn't start in the night. Shay and Thora K. sat by the open oven brushing their hair dry.

"Well, it do seem to me"—Thora K. cleared her throat and looked at the ceiling—"yer uld mirror didn't tell 'ee about the fire now, did it?"

"No, it didn't." Shay sighed and then began to laugh—from reaction and the pleasure of being clean, fed and safe—from the joy she found in the strange bond she was forming with this funny Cornish woman.

Thora K. chuckled and poked an elbow into Brandy's ribs. "Did 'ee see the look on Liddy Tyler's face when 'er hair caught aflame and Mr. Binder did dunk 'er head in the creek?"

They were still laughing and swapping experiences when Dr. Seaton stopped by to ask if they had any burns or injuries. "I was just going the round of the houses to be sure," he said uncomfortably.

"And where were you when Rome burned, good doctor?" Shay winked at Thora K.

"Ahhh . . . I was down in Boulder." He shifted to the other foot and scratched a grizzled chin. "An important court case. I had to be there. I was an election official, you know, and—"

"Aye and leavin' us 'unmen with the likes of they Maddon boys fer protection. Shame on 'ee." But she poured him a cup of tea.

"The Maddons are liable to be among the few men who can hold up their heads around here for a long time, I can see." He told them the twins had returned the day before. "And the first thing they did was buy the Tandy place. As wild as they were I'd have said neither would ever be worth a plugged nickel. But they say they're going to raise hay and horses. Maybe they're settling down."

"And where'd them be gettin' the money ter buy a ranch?"

"I know their mother left them some. Lon went through his like he goes through life, all a-busting. But I've heard Hutch kept his and's been adding to it. He's a strange boy, savors things," Doc Seaton said thoughtfully. "I have the feeling he gets more out of each day than the rest of us put together."

"What'll them do with a ranch if Tom 'Orn do come back?"

"Let's hope he doesn't." He shivered. "For all our sakes. I did hear that Lon gambled his brother's nest egg into a tidy sum."

"Ahhh, the wages of a sinful 'unman increased by Satan's own cards. That do be twice evil gain."

"Oh, you're too hard on them, Thora K." The doctor slipped into his coat. "They were never mean like their father, just full of the devil."

Shay stepped out onto the porch with him to speak privately. She asked about contraception and then wished she hadn't as the shock registered on his face.

"The only safe thing I can tell you is to abstain . . . but why . . . why would a healthy young woman want to avoid having a child? Motherhood is the most precious state you can obtain this side of heaven."

"Doctor, I just don't want to get pregnant right now, okay?"

"When is not for you to decide, Brandy. It's the Lord's decision." He patted her hand. "Now go in before you catch cold, and trust in the Lord."

The sound of hammering rose from the valley. The men of Nederland seemed in a fever to rebuild Main Street and probably their respect in the eyes of their women. Even Corbin shirked the Brandy Wine to help.

Shay and Thora K. stood on the porch and watched as he came up the hill for supper one evening. A building stood finished and Thora K. pointed it out to him. "Wot be the one 'ee got up already?"

"The new saloon." He ducked quickly into the cabin.

"Saloon, 'ee says! Mr. Binder be selling food out of 'is 'ouse and trying to store it in a barn and the first thing built's a saloon. And another storm coming anytime."

But the weather held through February and the building went on magically.

"Mrs. Tyler do say they two ranches on Sulfide Flats 'ave sold to Mr. McLeod fer the reservoir." Thora K. had just returned from a temperance meeting. "Wot do yer uld mirror say ter that, you?"

"I don't know," Shay snapped. She was getting so impatient with the wedding mirror she could barely control her emotions. It had made the switch twice—it could do it again. Why *wouldn't* it?

"If this Rachael 'ee say is yer mother—if 'er name edden Strock then wot be it?"

"Garrett." Shay regretted having confided in the Cornish woman, especially when Thora K. was in one of her cranky moods.

"That be 'er married name, according to yer fine stories. Wot be she named afore her was married then?"

"Thora K., will you leave it be?"

"No." She folded her arms and pursed her lips. "'Ee tell me, you, or I'll scat 'ee across the chacks."

Shay'd been about to make up a name, any name, but in her present mood and with her friend threatening her like that she spat out, "Maddon. It's Maddon. Now are you happy?"

Angry and ashamed of herself, Shay grabbed Brandy's coat and stalked out the door rather than face Thora K.'s expression. *Damn, Shay, you know it was your own fault for telling her so much. She's no dummy. That question was bound to come.*

But I had to talk to someone. I'm going crazy with worry.

The ground trembled beneath her feet and she heard the familiar muffled rumbling. It was getting late in the day and the charges had been set and exploded in the mines so it would be safe for the miners to go in the next day. Corbin would be coming home soon.

But she walked on until she came to Samuel's cabin and was surprised to see the boards off the windows and smoke coming from the chimney.

She was even more surprised when May Bell stepped out to dump a pan of water.

"Hi. I thought you'd moved to Boulder."

"Samuel said I could live here till I found a better place," she answered defiantly. "And I got it in writing." May Bell had added weight and chipped a corner off a front tooth. Her fancy gown needed pressing.

"Listen, I don't care. I'm glad you're back. In fact, I've been wanting to talk to you about something."

"Now I know you're crazy. Someone might see you."

"Not if we go inside."

"Well . . . all right." She held the door for Shay. "Corbin won't like this. How come you never told anybody about how the fire started?"

Rags stuffed around a stovepipe where it went through the saloon's outside wall had been blamed for the fire.

"I wondered why Hutch Maddon or Mr. Binder didn't."

"Hutch is a friend of mine." A ladylike blush crept up May Bell's exposed neck. "I don't think Binder figured it out."

"Maybe it'll teach the town a lesson and they'll build a water system."

"They can't. Emptied the town coffers to pay the judge in Boulder for that court case." May Bell grinned and turned to the cookstove. "Want some coffee?"

"Please." Shay sat on a chair with an elaborate needlepoint cushion and wondered if Cara Williams was turning over in her grave.

When May Bell handed her a cup and sat down with her own, Shay launched into her problem and finished up with, "You see I don't want to get pregnant and Dr. Seaton would only say to trust in the Lord."

May Bell's mouth hung open, her cup suspended halfway between it and her lap.

"Nuts, May Bell. You gals must do something with all your . . . I mean . . . uh . . . you know . . . exposure. You haven't had any babies, have you?"

"I had two once. Year apart." She lowered her cup, her coffee still untasted.

"Oh, I'm sorry. Did they . . . die?"

"Far as I know they're still in Iowa. I was just a kid and my father made me marry this old man. I didn't like the life or my husband and I ran away." She was rather plain without makeup. "I don't know why I'm telling you. I guess it's your big dumb eyes. You look so innocent and then you come in here and talk like this."

"Can you please help me?" *Careful, Shay, you can shock even a whore.* "Remember I didn't tell on you about the fire."

May Bell gulped a slug of coffee. "When I started I used a penny. I don't seem to need anything now. Some of the girls used different douches but I think a copper penny is the best. You have to get ahold of one of the old ones. They're bigger."

"A copper penny . . . how . . . you mean like a diaphragm?"

"Huh?"

Shay explained the insertion principle of a diaphragm and May Bell nodded. It was a little hard to believe, but some of the pennies were larger now than they'd be in the future. In fact Shay had one in her purse minted in the 1850's. It was slightly bigger than a quarter. "Can I ask you one more thing?"

"I just wish you'd go."

"May Bell, do prostitutes feel anything? I mean . . . is it all right if they enjoy sex? You know, have an orgasm?"

"What's an organism?"

"You see, Corbin thinks only women like you are supposed to climax."

"You sure talk funny."

"Look, what's the big secret? We're two women alone, no one to hear us. I've never had the chance to talk to a . . . to someone like you. And . . ."

Shay watched the coffee cup slide off Brandy's lap to the floor. She had a horrid weak feeling as she slithered off the chair to join it . . .

. . . the picture that flashed across the darkness of her mind swayed and warped as if distorted in an amusement-park mirror . . . a cat arched, its tail swollen with alarm . . . Shay Garrett's head flopped about on a pillow streaked with pale Maddon hair, her face almost convex-looking, the nose and gaping mouth enlarged as it would be in a camera's eye when brought up too close or at the wrong angle. The head rose from the pillow, the muscles of the neck and jaw rigid with a silent scream and a bloodied hand reared up in front of it . . .

Short chopping slaps across Brandy's cheeks.

"Brandy Strock, don't you get sick here. How would I explain it?"

"Stop hitting me." Shay saw the woman through tears stung loose by the slapping.

"You sure it ain't too late? For the penny I mean?"

"It's not that." Brandy must have looked in the mirror or something. *But just what was going on with my body?* It had looked as if someone was trying to murder it.

Shay was still shaky when May Bell helped her back up the road.

"This is as far as I'd better go. Someone might see us."

"Thanks for everything."

"Uh . . . about what you were asking. Unless it's somebody . . . in particular . . . we just pretend." May Bell poked a pointed toe into the snow and stared at it. "Otherwise it'd take too long."

"But why aren't other women supposed to have fun?"

"I think it has something to do with religion. I expect a lot of them do and keep it secret. As for the rest"—May Bell looked up with a shy grin—"if you ask me, that's why there's so many megrims and hysterics around."

Corbin still wasn't home when Shay reached the cabin. The table was set for four so Tim must have been invited to supper.

Thora K. stood at the stove, her back eloquently stiff. The warm cabin smelled of fried hogspudding, cornbread and coffee.

Two wooden rocking chairs stood in the corner where the wedding mirror had been. "Where's the mirror?"

"No room fer it now. Mr. Binder did come with yer chairs whilst 'ee be out."

"Did you put it in the loft?"

"Corbin and Tim did carry it off." Thora K. turned, a long-handled fork in her hand, wispy hair escaping the knot on top of her head. "It be gone, you. Don't 'ee bother to look for it."

"Gone? What do you mean?"

Thora K. brought the cornbread to the table and cut it while she explained that Sophie had written to Corbin. She was worried because Brandy hadn't answered her letters and warned him to get rid of the mirror if his wife's behavior appeared strange. For some reason the mirror seemed to upset Brandy and perhaps she'd improve if it were gone. "And I say 'ee be acting strange. Maddon indeed."

"It's mine. You don't have the right . . ." Shay felt betrayed and panicky.

At times she was oddly at peace here. Little news of the outside world reached her, and what did seemed remote. But how long could she survive in this tiny, restricted life? How soon would her old nemesis, boredom, make it unbearable? She remembered the vision of her own screaming body threatened by a bloodstained hand. The body of Shay Garrett could be dead.

Shay lowered Brandy's body to a bench and looked around the cabin with new eyes. *What if I really have to stay here?*

The snows of spring were enormous. The sky just kept dumping it.

Shay made cushions for the rocking chairs, read aloud to Thora K., craved fresh fruit and vegetables, and retreated to a numb, unthinking state. No one would tell her where the mirror was and she had no idea where to look.

May Bell moved back over the new saloon.

Washing hung interminably on a slatted frame behind the cookstove.

The copper penny kept falling out.

Corbin brought home news that the Maddon twins were fixing up the ranch house on the old Tandy place.

Shay thought of Hutch Maddon and pushed the thought away.

Sometime in May the snow turned to rain and the melting drifts rushed down the slopes. The creek roared from its bed in the valley and kept Shay awake at night. Main Street turned to mud and passing wagons and hooves flung it against storefronts and windows in ugly blotches.

But the dazzle of sun and sky and new grass, the scent of pine and wildflowers beckoned Shay from her lethargy.

Tim Pemberthy was bursting with hope because he'd heard the "knackers" in the Brandy Wine and knew a big strike was near. These knackers were some kind of little people who went around knocking to show favored miners where the best ore was located. Thora K. sent food with Corbin to leave for them. She warned Tim to be careful, reminding him that "tammy knackers" also knocked to warn of impending danger.

One afternoon a thunderstorm caught them with clothes on the line. They raced to gather them in as lightning snapped to the earth on the hill above. When it was over Shay hung out Corbin's overalls to dry longer.

Thora K. lifted the empty washtub off the sawhorses. "It do seem to me, tez been way back along since I seen any rags a-soaking round 'ere."

"Rags? Oh, you mean my period." Shay tried to remember when Brandy last flowed. "I can't remember just when—"

"Hush, 'ere comes Corbin," Thora K. whispered and said aloud, " 'Ee be 'ome early, you. Edden close to suppertime."

Shay turned to see him coming along the path, a strange expression on his face, sunlight dancing on raindrops still coating pine needles over his head. She slipped a clothespin on an overall strap and then jumped as the washtub hit the ground and narrowly missed her foot.

The Cornish woman bent over and held her middle.

"Thora K., are you sick? Corbin, your mother—"

But Corbin wasn't there.

"Edden me. Tez him. 'E disappeared." She straightened and clutched at Shay. " 'Twere 'is phantom."

"I saw him too, so he wasn't any phantom. Probably turned off at the cave or the outhouse."

"No, I were looking straight at 'im and 'ee did vanish." Her little eye bulged.

Shay checked the outhouse, the cave, and walked clear to the spring. No Corbin. Thora K. met her on the way back.

"What did you mean by phantom?" A tiny chill probed Brandy's neck.

"Where are you going? Thora K.?" Shay yanked her around by the arm. "Speak to me!"

"Just like it 'appened to me granny. Oh, my dear sawl—"

"You superstitious old woman, now stop this. He probably forgot something and turned back."

"'Ee be dead. Me poor beautiful lamb . . ." She finished with an eerie wail. Her eyes glazed over now, she broke away to run along the trail to the Brandy Wine.

This is ridiculous. But Shay picked up Brandy's skirts and followed. That chill was creeping down her spine.

They were stopped at the top of the first rise by Tim Pemberthy. He was reeling up the path, red streaks splashed across his clothing.

19

Shay cringed as she heard the sound, but looked out the window to see the cloud of smoke and dust rise across the valley. They were blasting out a grave in Nederland's rocky cemetery for Corbin Strock.

Shay'd wanted to bury him in Caribou with the rest of the family but Nederland officials objected. It was too far away and wasn't used any longer. His mother didn't seem to care.

Thora K. just rocked. That's all she'd done since Corbin's death.

"'Ee knew. 'Ee knew 'twould 'appen." Her voice came with a hiss and startled Shay. Thora K. hadn't spoken for so long.

"I didn't know when." She leaned against the icebox. "I . . . didn't . . . know how. That it'd be that awful . . ."

They'd had to scrape him off the walls of the Brandy Wine. He'd been setting a charge, planning to explode it later, but the dynamite had gone off in his hand.

Tim hadn't been badly hurt. The blood they'd seen on his clothes was Corbin's.

Shay sensed she would soon convince herself they'd imagined seeing Corbin walk toward them on the path. But now it was comforting to remember him whole, the sun sparkling on pine needles and raindrops over his head.

"Yer a witch, Brandy McCabe," Thora K. said hollowly. "'Ee and that mirror."

"Where did you hide it?"

"Them took it to the mine."

"The mine? I told you it was dangerous. You don't think it caused—"

"Dynamite don't need no mirror ter blow a man to bits, you."

"Was it damaged?"

"'Twere at the mouth, far from the blast, Tim said. They bury yer 'usband tomorrow and 'ee can 'ave thought fer that uld mirror?"

Shay'd never been close to anyone who had died before. John McCabe's death hadn't touched her.

It wasn't that she'd been *in* love with Corbin. But even with the strange nature of their relationship, she'd loved him and knew that in time she might well have come to be in love with him. She'd always thought of him as Brandy's husband but she realized now, that she—Shay Garrett—would miss him terribly.

A whispered sob escaped her and Elton put an arm through hers. Sophie pressed her hand. People around her looked sympathetic, all except Thora K., who stood alone at the foot of the grave, her face stony. When the service was over she ignored the people moving toward her and, without a word to Shay, walked down the hill. Thin shoulder bones made sharp patterns through her dress.

"Come home with us, Brandy," Sophie whispered. "There's no reason for you to stay now."

Shay stared after Corbin's mother. "I can't leave her."

She turned to see Sophie McCabe's stricken face that so resembled Rachael's. *I've been selfish.* "Not yet anyway. She's lost everyone. Sophie . . . I mean, Ma . . . if you don't mind my funny handwriting I'll write to you . . . and come to visit. She's all alone." Shay did something she wouldn't have dreamed possible even moments before. She embraced Brandy's mother and kissed her cheek.

Turning to follow Thora K., she bumped into Hutch Maddon's chest.

"Just wanted to say how sorry I was." He held his hat in his hand, his platinum head tilted back.

She stared up at him, an edge of panic stabbing through the numbness of sorrow.

"Oh, oh, no . . ." Shay pushed past him and stumbled down the hill to catch up with the old Cornish woman.

Brandy was pregnant.

Shay tried not to think about it but Thora K. couldn't think of anything else. It was the one thing that seemed to lift her out of her mourning. It was only "fit" that Corbin should leave behind a child to take his place.

As Thora K.'s spirits revived, Shay grew more despondent. She struggled to remember any mention of a Strock child in the family. Shay and May Bell met often for secret walks. May Bell felt "real bad" about the penny.

"Do you ever wonder what became of your babies?" Shay asked her.

"Yeah. One of 'em was a girl. Catherine. Hope she gets out of there the first chance she gets."

Tim Pemberthy still worked the Brandy Wine. They hired him to stay on for a portion of the profits. There would be a town called Tungsten in the canyon. If it was named after the ore, there must be something in all the speculation. Others were mining it and the slope-roofed mill at the west edge of town that once milled silver from Caribou was being reoutfitted to process it. A company in Pennsylvania had offered to buy all the tungsten Tim could produce.

One day in August when she knew Tim to be in Boulder, Shay walked the path to the Brandy Wine, trying not to think of Corbin, wondering why she'd never bothered to make this trip before. She was looking for the wedding mirror.

Maybe Brandy survived whatever was happening when she'd seen her last.

The path led to a road and the road soon led to another path with a shed next to a hole in the side of a mountain.

The dark hole gaped like a threatening mouth in the sunlight and a narrow railroad track lapped out of it like a tongue. A metal wagon sat on the track just inside. She waited for her eyes to adjust to the dark and then walked in as deep as she dared. A claustrophobic panic forced her to back out . . . and the grim memory of what had happened to Corbin here. There would still be stains. The mirror was no longer at the mouth of the mine. Somebody had moved it.

Tim was afraid of it. Of course he wouldn't have left it there now that he was working the mine alone. But where would he have put it?

Corbin's baby moved like a heavy sigh inside her. *What are we going to do about you and about me, little one?*

Shay didn't feel young anymore. She felt as if she'd passed from youth to old age without experiencing the life stages in between.

Even if she found the mirror, her conscience told her she shouldn't risk anything until the child was born. Even if the child was probably doomed anyway. Even if there was a live Shay Garrett to go back to. The thought of the long years ahead was more than she could bear.

A horse's high whinny startled her from her reflections.

Where the path to the cabin met the road, Hutchison Maddon stood in the shadow of pines, holding the reins of his horse.

"Hope you're not going to run away again," he said when she stopped suddenly at the sight of him.

Shay had the urge to do just that, but didn't move as he led his horse from the shadows.

"Just what is it about me that scares you so, Mrs. Strock?"

She tried to smile at her grandfather. "Oh . . . I'm just . . . crazy Brandy. Hadn't you heard?"

"Yeah, I heard." The corners of his eyes crinkled slightly. "And I'm one of the mad Maddons. You hear about that?"

"Dr. Seaton says you're wild."

"He oughta know."

Shay stepped around him to the path and he walked beside her, the horse following. She was so aware of him she could hardly breathe. "I . . . have to be getting home."

"I'll walk you there. Or are you going to run?"

"I'm not running. It's just that—"

"You know it's not right." He slapped the end of the reins idly against his leg. "Young, pretty thing like you looking so sad all the time."

"I don't feel very young and pretty right now."

He glanced down at the bulge that had been Brandy's waist and smiled. A full smile that transformed the hard cowboy into a vulnerable man.

She was hot from more than just walking in the sun and stopped to drink at the spring. When she'd replaced the wooden top and got clumsily to her feet, he was staring back at a large mountain jay on a limb above them. The man and the bird looked as if they were communicating with each other.

"What's he saying?"

Hutch blinked and looked down his nose at her. "He's like you. Won't talk to me."

"I'm talking to you."

But neither of them spoke until they reached the back door of the cabin. She hoped he didn't expect to come in and was relieved when he mounted his horse with a creaking of leather. He stilled the animal's eager prancing and leaned forward with his arm on the saddle horn. The hard cowboy was back. "I mean to have you, you know," he said under his breath.

"Yeah . . . I know."

In September President McKinley was assassinated. Nederland was in an uproar. Apparently no one had voted for him because he was against the coining of free silver, which would have brought the silver mines back into production. But he was the President of the United States and no one could talk of anything else for a month. Even May Bell seemed shocked.

Shay was unmoved. Although the people around her were becoming all too real, President McKinley was only a dimly remembered name from history.

But Thora K. had the strangest reaction of all.

Shay came home from a walk to find the wedding mirror standing flat against the wall behind the rocking chairs, the quilt tied tightly around it with enough rope to hog-tie an army. Thora K. explained that if Brandy thought something bad might happen to Mr. Roosevelt, she should untie the mirror, see what it was, and warn the new President.

Shay sank into a rocking chair and laughed until she cried.

One night in early December, her labor pains started. Thora K. ran to the Tylers' to send one of their boys across the valley for Doc Seaton and then rushed back to boil water.

Shay wasn't trained for childbirth without the help of anesthesia, had given it little thought until she knew Brandy was pregnant, and then forced her mind into a numbed state that refused to consider it at all.

That was no help to her now.

A broken arm from an accident on a swing, even the horrid illnesses from her transpositions in time hadn't prepared her for this. She passed from screaming consciousness to blessed nothingness and back again.

"This is going to be a long night," a sweating Dr. Seaton announced to Thora K. and Lydia Tyler, who stood ready to help him. "Looks like it'll be born buttocks first," he whispered, presumably so Shay wouldn't hear.

Shay was praying for death before morning when Brandy's baby was born.

They worked over her until noon and then relaxed enough to present her with a wrapped bundle.

"Brandy, I'd like you to meet your daughter." He looked haggard, as if he'd had the baby.

Shay turned Brandy's face to the wall.

"Look at her perfect head and little copper hairs," he coaxed. "Don't often see that well-shaped a head. Afraid all the damage was to the other end."

She couldn't keep herself from taking a look.

Brandy's newborn resembled Thora K. without any teeth at all.

"Have you thought of any names?"

"Yes." Shay came out of her exhaustion unwillingly. "Name her . . . Penny."

Doc Seaton returned the next day. "Sure you want to name her just Penny and not Penelope? You could call her Penny anyway."

"No. Just Penny," Shay answered dully.

"Now, see here, young woman. This mood of yours is no help to anyone, least of all yourself or the baby. You're lucky to have her. Probably the only one you'll ever have."

"What do you mean?"

"Just that this was a difficult birth and there's been damage done. I doubt you'll ever carry another child to term. Won't be wise for you to remarry, even though you're young yet. Best thing for you is to devote your life to Corbin's child. And be thankful the Lord saw fit to bless you with little Penny. Another pregnancy could be the death of you."

"Someday I will have twin boys named Remy and Dan, and a daughter named Rachael. They'll live to see gray hairs at least, and I'll live far too long. So don't try to scare me with your phony Lord business. I wonder if you men don't trump up all that religious stuff to keep women in line."

"Brandy Strock, I'll forgive you this twaddle you're talking because you've had a bad time here. I never credited those stories of John McCabe's daughter being mad, and I'll not start now. We'll talk about this when you're yourself."

After he'd left, Thora K. brought the baby from her cradle by the stove to nurse.

Shay snuggled them deeper into the covers, her heart aching with each pull at Brandy's breast.

I mustn't love her. It'll hurt too much. Besides, she's Brandy's, not mine.

Brandy wasn't even around when you married Penny's father or conceived this baby. You did this yourself, Shay.

She buried her lips in the coppery down coating Penny's head.

Penny Strock developed pneumonia and died at the age of two weeks. She would be buried next to her father when the ground thawed in the spring.

Thora K. endured quietly except for long sighs and an occasional far-off look.

Shay took to standing before the mirror again.

The first day the canyon was passable, Sophie and Elton stormed into the cabin and insisted Shay and Thora K. spend the rest of the winter at the Gingerbread House.

They were too listless to resist.

Thora K. had her first all-over hot bath in a tub and was amazed when she didn't take cold.

Some of Brandy's girl friends dropped by, and any of Shay's awkwardness or lack of memory was chalked up to her state of double mourning.

Elton drove them about town in the buggy when the snow permitted.

He took her for rides on the trolley and to a theater for corny stage plays and an opera. She'd missed having a man around and enjoyed his company.

But both she and Thora K. were ready to go back to Nederland when the long winter ended.

Sophie reminded Shay too painfully of Rachael. Any roots anchoring her to Brandy's life were in the little mining town, not at the Gingerbread House.

And here where she'd buried Brandy's dead the air was clear, free of the stuffiness of the Gingerbread House and Sophie's questioning eye.

And so Shay entered her third year in Brandy's life. She took the quilt from the mirror rarely now, and when she did, it was without hope.

On Thora K.'s first day back to work at the Antlers, Shay brought a rocking chair out onto the porch and watched Nederland, feeling too bored to sew or read. She'd never been that fond of either anyway.

She heard the creak of wagon wheels, the jingle of harness and the snorting of horses before she turned her gaze from the meadow to see a buckboard moving up the hill toward her. Even with the hat covering the pale hair, she recognized the driver as one of the Maddon twins.

Something inside her knew which one he was.

20

"Good morning," Hutch Maddon said without smiling. He was on an eye level with her, sitting on the buckboard filled with a roll of wire and cloth sacks.

Shay didn't answer, just leaned forward to see the horses' hooves pawing Thora K.'s infant garden. The growing season was too short for a very successful garden up here anyway. It didn't matter. She leaned back.

"Ma'am, Mrs. Strock." He swept off his hat. Still no smile. "I'm inviting you to go for a ride on this wagon."

"Why?"

"Something I'd like to show you on this fine day."

"Go to hell," Shay said through Brandy's teeth. His eyebrows rose slightly. He stared at the horses' rumps and shook his head. "And I used to think I was a patient man."

Laying the reins across the seat, he set the brake and slipped off the buckboard.

As Hutch walked around the wagon Shay left the rocking chair. "What are you doing?"

He moved leisurely to the steps and looked up at her under his hat until he'd had his fill. "Inviting you for a ride, like I said."

"And I told you what you could do about it."

He came up the steps and she backed to the door.

"Hell, I feel like a bear stalking a canary bird," he said with disgust.

"Hutch, listen—" Before she could swing the door open and escape inside, he had her by the waist and before she could regain the breath to protest, she was sitting on the seat of the buckboard. Until now she'd thought he was slow-moving.

"I just want to show you something."

"I can't go anywhere without my bonnet. My nose'll sunburn."

Hutch plopped his own hat on her head and backed the team until he could turn it.

Where the wagon tracks met the road, he swung south away from town, left the road not far from the Brandy Wine and turned again onto a steep wagon path through pine trees.

Shay knew they were headed for the old Tandy place. She even knew why. But she wasn't ready for it when the horses struggled to the top of a wooded rise and he stopped them at the break in the trees.

The wagon path sloped away below them and then swept across a broad valley to the house sitting on its knoll. Trees ringed the mountain valley but came only partway down the hillsides, leaving free the tall breeze-rippled grasses bright with spots of wildflowers and dotted with scattered horses. A frothy creek ran the valley's length. High wind moved a puff of dazzling cloud across a deep sky and its shadow scudded over the grass toward them.

Hutch shook himself as though awakening from a dream and prodded the team forward. A frisky brown-red colt with slender legs raced them and then tore off across the vast meadow. It reminded Shay of Penny, who would never grow to frisk and play. Life wasn't fair, even when you knew what would happen.

The house stood square and two-story, made of logs with their ends sticking out. The logs were shorn of bark and coated with something clear and shiny to give them a deep golden glow. Two corrals nearby—one old, the other new. An outhouse and a chicken coop.

They drew up beside a covered porch that stretched along two sides of the house, just as Rachael had described it. *This is where she lived,* a voice screamed in her head, but when Hutch Maddon turned to her as if expecting some comment she couldn't speak aloud. She could feel his hurt.

He lifted her down and led her up the porch steps.

Shay'd never been a nostalgia buff although it had been quite the rage when she was a teenager. She'd skied, hiked and camped in the mountains, ridden horses rented from tourist stables, but essentially Shay was no country girl.

Yet something within her recognized this fairy-tale valley as one of the lost wonders of the world.

"So you've got a ranch and a house and domesticated animals," she fought back when she could unstick Brandy's tongue. "And now you need a domesticated woman to do boring household chores—cook, wash, scrub, sew and—"

"And tell me to go to hell." His voice rasped with disappointment. He opened the door and motioned her inside.

A golden glow here as well. Planed boards, coated with the same varnishlike substance as the logs outside, fit tightly against each other and formed walls, floor and ceiling. Sunlight added to the warm feel of the main room by streaming through paned windows that looked out on a vastness of meadow, mountain and sky.

Bright oval braided rugs. Heavy, plain furniture made of the same colored boards as the room's interior. It resembled modern lawn furniture but was brightened by cushions of the identical red-flowered calico she'd bought from Mr. Binder for the cabin. Panels of that material hung at the sides of the windows as curtains.

She touched a cushion. "Looks like you've had someone sewing already."

"May Bell found a lady in town to do it for us. Lon and I put in new walls and floors these last two winters and made the furniture," he said dejectedly.

"You made the furniture?" She'd never known anyone who'd done that before.

"Probably too ordinary for McCabe's daughter."

At one end of the room a couch, chairs, rugs and tables grouped around a potbellied stove. At the other end a long narrow table with benches at the sides and captain's chairs at each end sat near a cookstove. And though the furniture was primitive in style and all of a color, it looked just right for the room, the house, the valley . . .

"It's so . . . free-and open-feeling."

She lifted her arms and turned a circle. "You could put our whole cabin in this room, and more."

So different from the dark, stingy crampedness of the cabin. So different from the ornate, dusty stuffiness of the Gingerbread House.

Three small bedrooms downstairs and two huge dormitory rooms upstairs with bunks along the walls. A shedlike enclosure attached to the house at the back door with stacks of firewood, washtubs, and other necessities.

Spacious, airy and yet snug. Plain, simple *and easy to clean.*

"Hutch, you and your brother have a beautiful home. I like what you've done with it." She returned from her tour of inspection to find him staring out a window. "And your valley is beyond words."

"Not very fancy for a McCabe."

The house was immaculate. He'd worked hard to get it ready. And all for her. She'd been nothing but rude. . . .

"You and Lon should be proud. Thank you for showing it to me."

"It'd be lonely out here for some."

"And free. Beautiful."

"I didn't want you just for the cooking and washing." He made a faint choking sound in his throat.

"Lon would have to quit leering at me," she countered.

"If he leers, I'll wipe it off his face with a fist."

"I hear you do that a couple of times a year anyway."

"We scuffle a bit." He still spoke to the window.

"From now on, you do it outside."

"Yes, ma'am."

"I'm not a very good housekeeper."

"We'd help. And I'm going to hire some hands soon."

"I'd want to bring Thora K. to live here."

"There's room."

"And I'd want a horse of my own."

"You can have your pick."

"And when no one much was around to see"—she put a hand on his arm and gazed out at the valley with him—"I'd put on men's pants to ride it."

He turned at last to look at her. "You know, I believe you would."

What am I getting Brandy into this time?

Brandy's been gone three years and probably never even heard of this man. When are you going to stop pretending?

"You sure seem taken with the top of my head."

Shay hadn't realized she'd been staring at it. "It's your hair."

She stood on tiptoe to touch it and found her waist encircled. His mustache was soft and silky on her face.

"And all this time I thought you were going to turn me down." His body shuddered.

"What is it about men that makes it feel so good to be held against one?"

"Damned if I know." His arms tightened.

Being Brandy had been lonely. Tears squeezed beneath her closed eyelids. "I've felt so lost."

"Brandy, you're beginning to come alive again, aren't you?"

She cupped her hand around the back of his neck and pulled his head down to meet her lips, the ache in Brandy's body hard and insistent.

"Are you always going to be so proper and polite, Hutch? And say, 'yes, ma'am' and—"

"No."

"Is there anyone here but us?"

"No."

"Do you think women should enjoy making love?" She kissed his throat.

"You sure are full of questions."

He's even older than Lawrence Welk. But then so am I now. And he'd unfastened all those infuriating hooks and eyes down the back of her dress already.

"You won't have to visit May Bell during business hours anymore." She sank beneath him on the soft cushions of the couch. "Will you?"

"Don't appear so."

Slow, lingering caresses told her he didn't have Corbin's hang-up about good women and bad women.

"Now," she murmured astonishingly soon.

"Now you'll *have* to marry me," he answered, and entered Brandy's body.

"You can't compromise a widow, can you?"

"I can try."

Brandy may have been missing a tooth, but everything else was in working order.

"Hutch?"

"Wish you wouldn't talk so much."

"Someday we're going to have twin sons and a daughter."

"Yes, ma'am."

INTERIM

When Brandy married Hutch Maddon, Thora K. refused to move to the ranch. And as Brandy didn't ask after the wedding mirror, the Cornish woman stored it out in the cave with the sausages and piles of potatoes.

The next year they hanged Tom Horn in Cheyenne, Wyoming, for the murder of a young boy. The Maddon twins celebrated with a three-day drunk. What they didn't know was that Tom's brother, Charley, brought the body to Boulder and had it buried quietly in Columbia Cemetery.

In 1907 a militant group led by Sophie McCabe, among others, succeeded in electing its reform candidates to office and their first act was to clean up Water Street. The prostitutes were forced to move out into the community.

Mr. McLeod's plans for a dam and reservoir on Sulfide Flats did not materialize. But when the Central Colorado Power Company bought Barker Meadows and began the construction of a dam, Thora K. gathered her belongings and joined Brandy at the Bar Double M Ranch. The mirror remained behind, still wrapped in its decaying quilt and standing in the cave.

Thora K. found she could stomach Hutch Maddon after all, perhaps because after eight years of marriage he was still so good to his wife. His brother, Lon, was another matter.

The year after Barker Dam was completed Brandy announced she was pregnant and would give birth to twin boys. Doc Seaton was most anxious about her and Thora K. knew as did everyone else that twins happen only every other generation. But true to her word and right on schedule, Brandy presented the world with another set of Maddon twins. As if one set wasn't enough. Thora K. reminded herself that Brandy was a witch and not like other women.

Brandy named her sons Remy and Dan and then asked Thora K. mystically, "Which came first, the chicken or the egg? Did I name them that because I already knew their names, or would I have anyway?"

Eastern steel companies demanded more and more tungsten as an alloy for hardening their products, and when Europe began to arm for war, Tim Pemberthy expanded his operations at the Brandy Wine, working crews in shifts. The black metal was important in the making of high-powered guns and high-speed tools.

Two new mills were built to help process the ore, one of them just below the dam. The town of Tungsten grew up around it, just as Brandy had said it would.

Brandy irritated everyone by showing no enthusiasm for the war effort and by referring to it as World War I, as if there would be more.

Nederland was in the midst of the tungsten boom. Wagons, coaches, and even Stanley Steamers streamed up the canyon. Hopeful prospectors slept in tents and on the floors of the pool halls.

The saloons had become pool halls serving soft drinks for spiking and offering billiards and card games because the reform groups had pushed prohibition through the Colorado legislature four years before the national government would act in like manner. This suited Lon Maddon, who'd never reconciled himself to ranch work. Though the Bar Double M was still his home betweentimes, he set himself up in the profitable business of supplying Nederland with booze run down from Cheyenne. This infuriated Thora K. but each time she reported him to local authorities Lon paid off in John Barleycorn and never spent so much as a night behind bars.

During the boom May Bell made a small fortune even with the influx of younger competition. And Thora K. rented out the cabin to miners for a hefty rent because of the scarcity of beds.

Samuel Williams returned, a bare hulk of himself, only to succumb to influenza when the great epidemic that swept the nation caught on out of all proportion in Nederland. The Antlers Hotel was turned into an emergency hospital with sickbeds filling even its spacious porch. In Boulder, Elton McCabe died of the disease, leaving Sophie alone in the Gingerbread House. Out at the Bar Double M Shay and Thora K. nursed the seven-year-old twins, Hutch, and three hired hands through it before falling ill themselves. One of the ranch hands died.

Nederland lost fifty-seven people to the epidemic, most of them young adults and children. The community had not yet recovered when the bottom fell out of the tungsten market with the end of the war and the finding of cheaper sources of the ore abroad. Nederland went back to sleep.

The Brandy Wine was boarded up.

The wedding mirror slumbered on in its cave in the hillside.

And one day when Dan and Remy were cleaned up for a visit to their Grandma Sophie and the Gingerbread House, Thora K. gave them each a loving pat and some cookies for the trip. Although they had the gold-flecked Maddon eyes, their hair was dark and thick like Brandy's.

She and Brandy stood on the porch to wave good-bye as they rode off on the buckboard beside their Uncle Lon.

"Ahhh, them do be proper strappin' boys now. 'Ee edden never going to want ter walk through that uld looking glass and leave 'em?"

"No, it's too late . . . Hutch, the valley, you, the boys . . . I barely knew them as uncles. When I was a child they lived in California. So I can love them as sons. . . ." Brandy leaned against the porch railing, looking a little pale. "But, Thora K., what will I do when Rachael's born?"

Part II
Rachael

1

Rachael Maddon scuffed the toes of her shoes in the dust. Sun warmed her shoulders but breeze cooled the backs of her knees, drying that sticky feeling from sitting at her desk.

She waved at old Doc Seaton, who watched her at his window.

Behind her the laughter and shouts of other children coming down the hill from the schoolhouse . . .

Rachael broke into a run to stay ahead of them, knowing without turning that there'd be groups of girls and groups of boys. But she walked alone.

"Hello there, little Rachael, and how are you today?" Mrs. Binder stood at the clothesline behind her house.

"Fine, thank you." Rachael didn't feel little. It was embarrassing to be taller than anyone else in the second grade.

"And how do you like your new teacher?" Mrs. Binder hobbled to the gate. The Binders didn't have a fence, just a gate and a birdbath.

"I like her just fine," Rachael mumbled, because she was lying. Miss Hapscot was small and dainty as ladies were supposed to be, as Rachael could tell already she'd never be.

"And how is everything out at the Bar Double M these days?" Mrs. Binder's ancient nose wiggled like a rabbit's in a lettuce patch. But this nose was after news—it really said to Rachael: "Is your mother as crazy as ever? And are you going to be crazy too?"

"Just fine, Mrs. Binder." Rachael hurried on, knowing she was being rude. But the voices behind her were catching up and she didn't want to talk about her mother to Mrs. Binder any more than to her schoolmates.

To the other children, Rachael's mother was either crazy or a witch. And her name was Brandy and Brandy was alcohol and alcohol was against the law. Even without hearing the familiar taunts except in her head, she had that bitey feeling behind her nose.

Rachael'd reached the bottom of the hill when she heard the scuffle of another shoe behind her. She turned to see the new boy Miss Hapscot had introduced to the school that morning. His elbows were big and bony below his sleeves and his pants were almost short enough to be knee pants.

Rachael ducked into the general store and soon forgot all about him. She surveyed the array of candies behind their glass panes.

"Coming in to spend your allowance on sweets again, are you now Rachael Maddon?" Mr. Binder looked even older than his wife but the smile in his eyes was young. "And what will your mother say to that, huh?"

Rachael grinned, aware of the juices squirting around in her mouth waiting for the candy, and of the assorted gaps where her new teeth had not yet come in. "We wouldn't have to tell her, would we, Mr. Binder?"

"You might not because you'll get the candy, but what's in it for me?"

"I could owe you another kiss."

"Let's see here," he said in his slurry way and took a notebook from a shelf behind the counter. "Better look in my ledger . . . why, Rachael, you already owe me twenty-seven kisses. That'd make it twenty-eight. Kind of young to be so deep in debt, don't you think?" But he reached into the case and drew out a roll of paper her impatient finger pointed to. Across the paper marched even rows of chocolate dots.

She paid for the candy and on her way to the door said what she always did at this point, "I'll pay off those kisses as soon as all your new teeth come in, Mr. Binder."

He laughed an old man's cackle. Mr. Binder didn't have a tooth in his head.

The new boy was throwing stones at grasshoppers in the vacant lot next to the store.

Rachael scraped off a row of dots with her teeth and set her lunch pail and the candy on the sidewalk. Hooking a knee over the horizontal pipe of the hitching post, she felt the sting of metal hot from the sun against her skin. Her stomach grumbled, ordering her mouth to send down the candy.

Checking to be sure the strange boy still faced the other way, she grabbed the pipe with both hands and twirled over and around and under and up—again and again—and as fast as she could so the skirt of her cotton dress wouldn't fall over her eyes, hide the view of swirling dirt street, square stores and dazzling sky. The green-and-white-checked pattern of her dress fell across her face and she stopped upright to find the new boy in front of her. Rachael felt hot all over. He must have seen her underpants.

But he was staring at the paper roll of candy on top of her lunch pail. He hadn't brought a lunch to school. Miss Hapscot had shared hers with him.

"Do you want some?" He and the sky and Mr. Binder's store were still spinning. "I might give you some if you ever said anything." She unwrapped her leg from the hitching post, aware of how long and awkward a leg it was.

"Anything," he mumbled.

He didn't rush to grab the candy as she thought he would but waited for her to tear off a piece.

It was embarrassing the way he cleaned away the chocolate dots. She ate two more rows and handed the rest of the roll to him.

"You giving it to me?"

"No. You owe me . . . a kiss someday. I'll put it in my ledger book."

He gave the candy a greedy look but tried to hand it back.

"I'm only teasing. It's just a game I play with Mr. Binder. You don't have to pay for it."

There'd been enough candy on that paper to last her a week but it was gone in minutes. "How come you didn't bring a lunch today?"

"My ma was sick this morning." The dark pupils of his eyes were as big as Thora K.'s when she wore her magnifying spectacles. His cheekbones stuck out sharply like his elbow bones. Rachael wondered if he was an Indian.

He licked the paper and then seemed surprised to find it empty. "Sorry . . . I ate all your candy."

"That's okay. My mom gets mad when I eat anything with sugar in it. Says it'll rot my teeth."

He took a deep breath, straightened his shoulders. "I'll kiss you for it," he choked out.

Rachael backed against the hitching post. "No, it was just a game. I—"

But he lunged and planted wet lips on her forehead. "Now we're even." And he ran off as if he had to get out of sight because he was going to be sick.

Rachael was still staring after him when Remy galloped Beulah around the corner and reined up in front of the store so hard Beulah snorted and danced on her hind legs. "Come on, Squirt, we gotta break Dan's record."

She threw him her lunch pail, placed a foot on the toe of his boot and reached for his hand.

"Pull up your dress so we don't split it again. Mom'll have my hide." He yanked her onto the saddle in front of him and they were off.

Beulah was all a-lather and wild-looking but Rachael could feel the powerful animal's joy in the race. When her other brother, Dan, picked her up he used the truck.

She held onto the saddle horn and leaned back against Remy's chest. As they approached the narrow bridge over the creek, Rachael let out a yell and glanced down into the startled eyes of the new boy as they passed him by. At least he wasn't throwing up.

Her crotch still smarting from the wild ride, Rachael hurried up the slope toward the house to get away from the terrible fight in the corral. She didn't know why, but she felt responsible for it. As if something she'd done or said was behind the anger the twins would unleash on each other. It'd been the same when her dad and Uncle Lon had a set-to on the porch last summer.

Rachael'd been sitting on the steps making dolls from old newspapers when her dad had pitched over the railing and Uncle Lon came flying after him. They'd rolled in the dirt and hit and kicked each other just like her brothers.

Her mother dragged her into the house and locked the door, reassuring Rachael the fight had nothing to do with her. "I think it's about money. But they should realize they're too old for this kind of thing and your father's arthritis is getting worse."

Grandma Sophie was right, Rachael thought now as she reached the porch. How could a girl ever learn any ladylike ways living here?

She opened the door on the warm honey-colored room, so large and plain. The only valuable piece of furniture was the buffet Thora K. had brought from someplace called Old Cornwall. And the picture in its heavy frame hanging next to it of her parents when they were married. Her father'd worn a mustache then and didn't look like himself and her mother's hair was piled on top of her head like Grandma Sophie still wore hers.

But the sizzle and smell of frying meat welcomed her and the thick plates and mugs arranged on the gay tablecloth. Thora K. turned golden bread out of a loaf pan and her mother's graying head bent over the treadle sewing machine by the window.

"The boys are fighting again." Rachael carried her lunch pail to the metal sink, and pumped water into the washpan for her hands.

"I expect Remy got you home faster than Dan did last night. Right?" Brandy looked up from her sewing.

"Yes and Dan said we cheated by going through the trees and not keeping to the road. But Remy didn't cheat. Beulah just went like the wind is all." Rachael dried her hands and stood beside her mother. "It scares me when they fight. Aren't you ever worried they might kill each other?"

Her mother pushed back her chair and drew Rachael onto her lap. "Those boys, as you call them, are twenty years old and I happen to know they'll live to be grandparents."

"Be 'ee that sure, Brandy?" Thora K. straightened and rubbed her back. "They do carry on so. And twins be bad luck fer—"

"I've told you. Dan'll be a used-car dealer and Remy—"

"Hush, you. Not in front of the child. Do 'ee forget the troubles the twins 'ad at school?"

Brandy laid her head on Rachael's shoulder. "You . . . don't have any trouble at school because of me, do you, Puss?"

"No," Rachael lied to reassure this woman she loved so fiercely. At times she had the uneasy feeling her mother clung to her rather than held her. "Why don't you ever call me by my name? You gave it to me, didn't you?" Last year it'd been "Squirt," this year it was "Puss."

"Ohhh . . . mothers are like that." She kissed Rachael's cheek but that odd look was in her eyes.

Were mothers really like that? No one could convince her Brandy was crazy or a witch, but she *was* different. Rachael knew.

In the small bedroom between her parents' room and Thora K.'s Rachael changed out of her school dress. It was more crowded here. Her grandma had given her some furniture from the attic of the Gingerbread House—a high dresser with a mirror that she had to stand on a chair to see into, a glass-fronted cabinet with lovely old dolls to display in it, and a desk with a top that rolled down where she could do her homework.

Rachael felt snug and comfortable with the heavy pieces of dark furniture. At night when she could see them only as shadows she imagined they stood solid guard duty to keep her safe.

"Why don't you ever bring any friends home from school?" her mother asked her when they all sat around the supper table.

"It's too far." Rachael chewed her tongue as she concentrated on cutting her meat.

"You could have her overnight or even just for dinner. One of the twins could take her home afterward."

"I can't think of anybody that—" Rachael almost felt the identical warning looks from her identical brothers.

"Must be somebody, Squirt," Dan said and his boot gently nudged her shin.

Rachael stayed quiet, hoping the subject would be dropped.

Her Uncle Lon rested his forearms on the edge of the table, his fork upside down in one hand and his knife in the other. She'd been told he and her dad used to be mistaken for each other like her brothers were now, but they didn't look like twins anymore. Uncle Lon was heavier and he still wore a mustache. It was only a thin line over his lip and he darkened it with whisker dye.

"You ought to put that steak on your eye, boy," he said to Dan and speared a slice of bread from the middle of the table. "Stead of eating it."

The twins *were* messy, even after washing up before coming to the table.

"You boys get the problem worked out?" Her dad flexed stiff hands.

"Had to stop for supper." Remy grinned through a swelling lip. "We'll work on it again tomorrow morning first thing."

"Hell you will," Hutch Maddon said. "We got cattle to move up to the west meadow." He winked at Uncle Lon. "Then you can work out your problems."

Rachael realized her mother had grown silent during this exchange. It was a different silence than Thora K.'s disapproval of the twins' fighting. Remy's eyes still pleaded across the table. . . .

"There is somebody I might ask," she blurted out and then wished she'd thought about it longer first. "But just for dinner."

Brandy straightened. "Who? Dorothy Kinshelow or—"

"Not, it's . . . it's a boy."

Dan and Uncle Lon hooted in unison. Thora K. sucked in on her store-bought teeth. Why didn't Mr. Binder buy himself some teeth?

Remy looked surprised and helpless.

Well, I'm trying, Rem, aren't I?

"What boy? Who?" Brandy asked with her mouth full. And she never did that.

"Uhhh . . . he's a new boy. I forget his name. He just came to school today for the first time."

"I ain't 'eard of no new families. Where do him live?"

"I don't know. I think he might be an Indian."

"Ooooee, Rachael's got eyes for an Indian."

"I do not either, Uncle Lon." Rachael watched everyone enjoy her embarrassment. She wished she hadn't started this.

"Is that why you want to ask him out? Because he's an Indian?" Her mother gave her dad a questioning look but he just shrugged and smiled at Rachael.

"No . . ." She was thinking fast now. "It's because . . . because he's hungry."

"Young boys are always hungry." But Remy sounded uncomfortable.

Everyone had stopped eating to stare at her. The taste of the food in her mouth went flat. She drank some milk to avoid their eyes. Tell one little lie and look what happened. Mrs. Bonnet had warned her about this in Sunday school. Mrs. Bonnet was right.

The silence lasted forever. It was the kind of fear and attention everyone gave the subject of "hard times." Rachael didn't think the times were hard. Even though the twins couldn't find jobs and strike out on their own. Why would they want to leave home anyway? And her dad couldn't hire extra hands, but to Rachael the ranch seemed crowded with men.

Thora K. cleared her throat. "Might be they's from the city. Them do say people stand in line there just fer soup. But I never did 'ear of a body going 'ungry round 'ere."

"How do you know he's hungry?" Brandy asked.

Rachael didn't know and she certainly wasn't anxious to have him out for supper. She could hardly remember what he looked like. "He didn't bring any lunch to school. Teacher had to share hers with him. And he's all bony and . . . he ate all my candy after school." It felt good to confess the truth after lying so much.

"Candy! I've warned you about—"

"Oh, leave her be, Bran. Kid's got to have some fun even in a depression," Hutch Maddon said. "Damn few have money these days to buy any."

Rachael could always count on her dad to help her out when she was cornered. When he looked at her she never felt he was trying to find something wrong. And his glance was rarely teasing like that of her brothers or Uncle Lon. Hutch Maddon's eyes told Rachael he just enjoyed looking at her and he was proud to have her for his daughter. . . .

Except during the scary times, of course, when he was too troubled to notice her because his wife was acting so strangely.

2

Jerry Garrett straddled the hitching post in front of the general store and watched Rachael hop from the sidewalk to the street on one foot.

"You keep that up and you'll break your face."

"Are you coming or aren't you?"

"Do I have to kiss you for it?"

Rachael turned suddenly and pushed him off his perch to the dirt below.

"You just try it and I'll have one of my brothers knock your teeth down your throat and out your elbow." She stood with one polished brown toe tapping the sidewalk and her hands on her waist. Her petticoat was whiter than anything he'd ever seen.

Jerry considered hitting her but that would probably mean he'd miss a real meal.

An old stock truck rumbled around the corner, its gears whining.

"That'll be Dan. Are you coming or aren't you?"

"I'm coming."

"Don't you have to tell your mom?"

"She won't care." And he'd have a chance to ask someone else about Christine, as his mother was so anxious that he do. He'd gotten up the courage to ask his teacher and Mr. Binder, but they couldn't help him.

Rachael crawled in beside her brother, and Jerry beside her. "How come he didn't bring his horse like last time?"

"That was my other brother. This is Dan. They're twins."

"And you must be the Indian." Dan grinned at him. He had a puffy black eye and was more like a full-grown man than somebody's brother.

Jerry was disappointed because he'd never been on a horse before but the ride in the truck didn't lack for excitement. This brother was as crazy behind the wheel as the other one had been on a horse.

The jolting ruts didn't smooth out till they'd swooped down into an enormous valley where horses and cattle grazed together on yellowing grass. The truck left the track and rattled across humps to stop with a sideways skid up against a corral. Dan threw open his door, raced around the edge of the corral and disappeared.

Rachael sighed and stared at the windshield.

Jerry pulled his teeth apart. "Does . . . does he always drive like that?"

"Yeah. Mr. Binder says he's wild. My mom says he's going to be a used-car dealer."

"Well, I sure wouldn't let him near a new one."

Rows of cut hay divided the valley floor into jigsaw patterns and thickened the air with a sweet, dry, country smell. As they walked up the slope to the porch of a tan-colored house the aroma of cooking mingled with the scent of hay.

Rachael stopped at the door. "Would you do me a favor and be nice to my mom? Some people aren't. I don't want you to hurt her feelings. She thinks you're my friend."

They entered a long room bright with blond walls and red curtains and delicious smells. Two women stood at the far end, one old and bent with a snow-white knot of hair on top of her head. The other woman had silver streaks lacing dark hair and she wore pants like a man. She was whipping a potato masher around in a bowl and as he approached, the masher slowed. Her big eyes got bigger.

"Mom? Here's my friend. His name's Jerry Garrett."

"Oh, my God," the woman in the pants said, as if someone had knocked the breath out of her.

The bowl slid down her front and broke on the floor. Fluffy plops of mashed potatoes splattered on Jerry's clothes.

Jerry added another bone to the pile on his plate and spread thick gravy over a biscuit, because Rachael's mother'd ruined the potatoes. Every time he looked up, Mrs. Maddon was staring at him.

"Save room for pie, Jerry," she said. But Remy handed him the chicken platter and what was left of the peas. He could tell the brothers apart only because of Dan's black eye.

Rachael's Uncle Lon wore a white suit with a vest under it, while the rest of the men wore work shirts. Jerry wondered if he lived here or was just visiting.

"Where'd you come from, boy?" Lon Maddon asked him.

"California." Jerry felt too sleepy to go into all the places he'd been.

"I've heard of people going there but never coming from. Is it a nice place?" Dan said.

"It's all right, I guess." Jerry's part of California had been dusty, dirty and hot.

Jerry hid a drumstick and a biscuit under his shirt when no one was looking. It should be enough. His mother didn't want much. He remembered to ask his question over the pie he was too full to eat. "My ma's looking for a woman that used to live here. Name's Christine Pintor. She wants me to ask people because she's too sick to go out and do it herself."

No one had heard of such a person. The same answer he always got.

"Is your father able to be home to care for your mother?" Mrs. Maddon asked.

"He left us a long time ago." Jerry had only vague memories of the man. "It's just me and Ma."

Mrs. Maddon stood so quickly she startled them all. "Remy, you and Rachael do the dishes. Thora K.'s tired. Dan, bring the car up to the door. I'll drive Jerry home."

"But, Mom, I—"

"No buts. After all he's eaten, the last thing he needs is to ride with you." She ducked out the door by the stove, returned with a basket, and began filling it with loaves of bread and other food. "Jerry, get that chicken out from under your shirt and put it in here."

Jerry soon found himself, the basket and Rachael's mother in a car that wasn't in much better shape than the truck.

She glanced sideways as they neared the top of the lane. The boy was already asleep. Easier to think of him as "the boy" than as Jerrold Garrett, who would grow up to become Shay's father.

For thirty-one years she'd been so busy living Brandy's life, she'd become Brandy, had almost forgotten the dreamlike young person named Shay Garrett. Except when Rachael would look at her a certain way and remind her of the woman she'd known as a mother rather than the girl she knew as a daughter.

And now this boy had walked into her life.

When she reached the road she woke him. "Jerry, which side of town do you live on?"

He directed her to the first turnoff and then to the Strock cabin.

"Who told you you could live here?"

"A man a couple houses back. He let us in and said he'd tell the owners to rent it to us."

Tim Pemberthy. He lived in Samuel's old cabin now and often saw to letting the Strock place to summer visitors for Thora K. He probably hadn't had a chance to inform them of the new occupants.

She hadn't been back here for years. Memories of Corbin and little Penny pierced her and memories of a long-ago girl from a future time. . . .

"Jerrold, is that you?" A woman stood in the doorway, the light behind her throwing her shadow across the porch. "Where have you been?"

"Jerry, take the basket in and tell her I want to talk to her." She braced herself to meet another of Shay's grandparents—this one would be younger than herself.

Later when she left the cabin it was on trembling legs. Driving down the hill and across the bridge, she turned onto Main Street, passing the few stores that had not closed or disappeared after the tungsten boom. Crystalline moonlight flickered across water ripples on the reservoir ahead. Several couples strolled along the shore.

She parked in front of the frame house with the stained-glass door. *I don't want to do this.* She was almost disappointed to see light behind the window shades.

Marrying Hutch and settling down on the ranch had been a safe if hardworking interlude after the upheaval the wedding mirror had caused her. But a hungry little boy and his mother shredded in a few hours the protective cloak it had taken her years to weave. She could never be Shay again. Now she didn't feel like Brandy either.

She stepped out of the car and walked up to the house, startled by the sound of her own knock at the door, half-wishing it wouldn't open. But it did.

"Brandy? Is that you? What—"

"I have to talk to you, May Bell."

"Well . . . sure. Come on in." But May Bell couldn't hide her reluctance.

"Are you alone? This is private." She walked into a dark Victorian room of worn furniture, hideous lamp shades with dusty fringe, and red-flowered wallpaper.

"I'm alone. Has something happened, Brandy? Is it Lon? Hutch?"

"No, they're fine. May Bell . . ." She sat on a lumpy chair and closed her eyes on the garish room. "I . . . think we should have a drink."

"Didn't know you drank."

"I do now."

May Bell left the room, returning with a bottle and two glasses, her many bracelets jangling. "Something awful's happened out at the ranch, huh?"

"No." She took a slug of raw whiskey and had to wait for the fire to die down, to simmer, before she could go on. "But something's happened. You better sit, May Bell. Or should I say, Christine?"

Short curls dyed an un-uniform orange plopped about on May Bell's head as she sank into a chair so hard she hit bottom. "Who told you about Christine? It's a lie!" But she emptied her glass and poured herself another. "Who told you?"

"Your daughter."

"Catherine?" May Bell's eyes seemed smaller now that she'd added so much weight around them. "I don't believe you." She had to dislodge rolls of fat from between chair arms to stand. "You get out of here, Brandy McCabe—"

"Maddon."

"Look, I know I owe you something for warning me to get my money out of the bank before it closed but—"

"You don't owe me anything. But you do owe Catherine something."

"You got no right prying into things that've been dead for years." May Bell's tentlike dress quivered and she put her hands out as if to ward off an attack. "You're a witch. Else you wouldn't know the things you do. Christine is dead."

"Well, Catherine isn't. You can be May Bell to me and all of Nederland, but to your daughter you're Christine Pintor—sometime, one-time mother."

"I was only sixteen when I left and—"

"May Bell, she's in town. Here. Now. And she's looking for you. She wants to see you."

"You're lying. After all this time . . . no, it's somebody else . . . pretending." May Bell's lipstick and rouge looked as if they'd been applied on white alabaster. "You ain't so smart, you know. And not always right either. You were a year off on the crash. I took your advice and lost a year's interest."

"Nobody's perfect. Can we get back on the subject?"

Fumbling in her pocket for her cigarettes, May Bell lit one and puffed while she paced. "I was fourteen when I had her. I'm not old enough to be her mother. She must be a grown woman now."

"Try meeting your own grandmother when she's twenty years younger than you sometime. I need another drink." Brandy/Shay reached for the brown bottle. *Who the hell am I?*

May Bell took the glass from her hand. "I'll add some water to it. You ain't used to this."

"You mean *we* aren't used to this." But her hostess had left the room.

"Why haven't we seen more of each other these last years?" she asked when May Bell returned. "You're one of the few people I feel free enough to put up my feet with."

"Because the minute your daughter was born you got all holy." She held out the watered whiskey. "And you can't put your feet up. You got to go."

"What is it about mothers and daughters?" She took a drink and let the feeling of it wash over her. "May Bell, who am I?"

"You're Brandy McCabe, Strock, Maddon. And you're crazy."

"You're right. I'm Brandy. Because there's no one else to be." *Shay hasn't been born yet. And you, fat lady, are going to be Shay's great-grandmother.* She moved a footstool under her feet and sat back. "I am Brandy and you are May Bell and we have a problem. Sit down."

"And you are a crazy witch. Every Halloween I get my outhouse turned over and I'm only a whore." May Bell lit another cigarette off the one she was smoking. "The Bar Double M ain't that far out of town. How come no one picks on you?"

"There are two sets of Maddon twins to beat the shit out of anyone who tries it. That's why. Now, back to our problem."

"Where is she?" May Bell sat across from her finally, nervous gestures stilled. "Is she really here, or just in your crazy head?"

"She's here, renting the Strock cabin. Only been here a few days." Brandy recrossed her ankles and drank deeply. The stuff burned even with water in it.

"I was pushed into marriage as a kid. She was only two when I—"

"Well, you're old enough now to be a grandmother."

"I am not!" May Bell swung orange curls wildly, looking about her as if for a place to hide. When she could meet Brandy's eyes again, she croaked, "She has a baby? My baby has a baby?"

"Yeah. A nine-year-old baby. Wake up, May Bell. I didn't have the twins till I was thirty-one. And they just turned twenty."

"But your hair's gray."

"Because I don't dye it. I'm younger than you are."

May Bell unwedged her fat rolls and went back to pacing. "What happened to little Willie? He was only a year when I last saw him."

"She's lost track of her brother. Catherine married a man who moved around a lot looking for work. He gave her a son and left them some years ago in a migrant labor camp in California."

"What happened to the farm?"

"Seems it was entailed to a younger brother instead of the children. Willie ran away a few years before Jeremiah, your husband, died. Your daughter got kicked off the farm and married a man by the name of Garrett."

"You're making this up."

"May Bell, that woman, your daughter, is destitute and she's ill. She needs help. She has a child. And you are her only hope."

"I was just a kid—"

"And you brought one into the world and so did she. You do have some responsibility for both of them, you know. I need another drink."

"How did she find me?" May Bell poured it absently. "How could she know where to look?"

"Your husband had you traced, first to Denver and then here. Catherine didn't find out about it until she went through his papers after he died."

"Jeremiah knew all along," May Bell whispered. "For years I lived in fear he'd find me and make me go back. And he knew."

"Apparently he didn't want you when he discovered your new profession. Wonder why he bothered to keep track of you."

"He was a strange man, Brandy. And I've met all kinds since." She wrapped ponderous arms across her chest as if she were cold. "But none like Jeremiah."

"Anyway, the last she knew, you were in Nederland. She either didn't know you were using another name or didn't know what it was. She didn't try to find you until she was desperate."

But what Catherine did know of her coupled with what Brandy knew of May Bell had made it fairly easy to recognize who Christine Pintor was.

"Well, what can I do? This is no place for a kid."

"May Bell, you're not still working. At your age?"

"Sometimes. And the few people that come to visit . . . the talk. I just can't take 'em in, Brandy." Her breath made little humming sounds. "The boy's not to know about me. I've liked my life just fine and I ain't ashamed of it. But he would be. That's not right for him. Maybe if I gave you some money and you gave it to them, they'd go away."

"And you'd always wonder if I made this up to get your money. She wants to see you, May Bell. She hash . . . has the right. I'll talk Thora K. into letting them stay in the cabin for nothing. You keep them in food and fuel. And tomorrow when Jerry goes to school you and I'll sneak his mother down to Boulder to a doctor." Brandy was interrupted by a hiccup. "Doc Seaton's too old, and she's too sick to take chances."

"You know if I'd stayed on the farm I'd of ended up just like my ma," May Bell said defensively. "One baby after another till the last one killed me."

"You have to help them. I would, but there's the ranch and taxes on the Ginsherbread . . . excuse me, the Gingerbread House and Sophie and Thora K., the kids. I know I couldn't talk Hutch into taking on any more." Her chair began to revolve.

"Sophie McCabe? Didn't you warn your ma about the crash and everything?"

"She wouldn't listen. Losht almosht everything but the house." Brandy set down her glass and grabbed the arms of the chair. "I don't think . . . I'm going to be able to drive . . . drive home, May Bell."

"Lon's coming soon. He'll take you back."

"He ish? What for?"

"Looks like to take home a drunk sister-in-law. Hutch's going to kill you."

"I know." She blinked as May Bell's gaudy makeup and hair blurred above her. "But I just met my father, and he's a little boy, and thash a funny feeling."

"Brandy, what am I going to say to her? Don't go crazy on me now. Help me."

"Don't want Rashael to see me like this. Must tell Lon to be sure shesh sleep."

3

Rachael found her mother grouchy the next morning and wondered if they were in for one of the scary times. Brandy would become cold and tense toward her, then change abruptly and smother her with attention. That was almost worse than her coldness.

Rachael hated these times. Everything in her world would be unsure, unsafe. She'd have that floating feeling in her stomach until she could gauge the direction of the day by the expression on Brandy's face. The scary times usually happened in winter when snow piled too high in the valley for Brandy to go out riding with the men.

Uncle Lon looked like he wanted to laugh. Things that worried others often tickled him. He pretended to choke on his coffee, his eyes dancing between her parents.

When her dad cleared his throat it sounded angry. Maybe he'd had an argument with her mother. He did have that hardness on his face.

Brandy was pale and tight-lipped.

"Can I make 'ee a wee bit of kiddley broth, Brandy? 'Ee look to be taking sick this morning."

Hutch Maddon dropped his spoon in his oatmeal, leaned back in his chair and laughed. Uncle Lon joined in until he had to wipe his eyes.

Brandy grimaced. "Please don't–"

"Wot be so funny, you? 'Er be sick."

"Sick!" And Rachael's father laughed harder. Uncle Lon left the house and Rachael could hear his rough guffawing out on the porch.

"Then you're not mad?" Brandy watched through squinted eyes as Hutch finished his coffee and stood.

"Mad? Hell yes, I'm mad. Don't you ever pull that again, woman." He grabbed his hat off the peg. "But if you do, I want to be there, understand? Sick, oh, God . . ." And he was laughing again as he closed the door behind him.

"Might be a spoon of me tonic would 'elp 'ee now, Brandy."

"Thora K., your tonic is the very last thing I need. Hurry and eat, Puss. I'm taking you into town this morning."

Brandy handed Rachael two lunch pails when they got into the car. "The other one is for your new friend, Jerry. I'm driving his mother down to Boulder today to see a doctor. She's ill and probably couldn't pack a lunch. You don't mind, do you?"

"No." Rachael was bewildered. Her father rarely laughed during the scary times.

"Give it to him on the way from his house to school so the other children won't know."

"Mommy, you don't have to do all these things for him because of me." Rachael thought her mother looked too tired to take anyone to Boulder and she was beginning to wish she'd never seen that old Jerry Garrett. "I don't like him that much. It was just—"

"Well, you'd better learn to," Brandy snapped. "You're going to marry him someday and will you *stop* banging those lunch pails together?"

"I am not either. I'm never going to get married and if I do it'll be a man like Daddy. Don't you say things like that."

"Oh, I'm sorry, Puss. I just have this headache and . . ." She reached over to squeeze Rachael's knee. "Of course you're going to marry a man like Daddy. Forget I even said that."

But Rachael couldn't forget. That was the kind of statement that caused the town to talk about her mother.

"This is Thora K.'s house," Rachael said when the car stopped.

"Tim rented it to them. He just hasn't gotten around to telling us about it yet."

Rachael carried an extra lunch the next day too. She didn't see why her mother had to make such a fuss over Jerry Garrett.

After school, while she waited by the store for one of her brothers, Mr. Binder stuck his head out the door. "Rachael, your mother stopped in to say she and Thora K. would be up to the old Strock house and you're to go on up there."

As Rachael crossed the bridge she banged both lunch pails against the wooden railing and stopped to stare angrily at Middle Boulder Creek. It was bad enough having to share her mother with all the people crowding the ranch house. Why did the Garretts have to move to Nederland anyway?

But, upon reaching the cabin, she felt a twinge of guilt when she saw the haggard look on Mrs. Garrett's face. Brandy and Thora K. were busy cleaning and cooking. They sent her out to play with Jerry and to stay out of the way.

A cool mountain breeze ruffled her hair. Grass and weeds choked the clearing behind the cabin and a pump stood on a low concrete base.

Rachael didn't see any sign of Jerry as she walked past the tilty outhouse to an old path where a thick layer of pine needles kept the weeds from growing. She searched the tree branches for squirrels.

A door stood flat against the hillside. Thora K. had warned her to stay away from it the few times she'd brought Rachael here. "All dirt 'n cobwebs and damp in there. Just a cave us used ter keep food in afore us 'ad a hicebox," the old woman explained.

Rachael looked over her shoulder and up the path. No one around. She'd been in caves before, but never one with a door. That gave it an Aladdin-like quality. Its paint worn and chipped, shaggy juniper bushes encroaching on its frame . . .

Rachael touched the door. The wood was slivery as she ran her hand down it to the handle under the rusty latch and waited with a pleasing tingle to imagine just the right frightening thing to be hiding inside. Wide cracks caused intriguing slits between the warped boards and a round hole yawned where a knot had fallen out. Her hand still on the coolness of the handle, Rachael bent down to put an eye to that hole.

All she saw was dark, a dark so thick it had a smell to it.

A dragon? A witch? An evil sorcerer? She couldn't decide, but as she straightened, her hand jarred the handle and the door in the hillside made a slight movement toward her.

Rachael stepped back. The tingle now was not so pleasurable. A chilly, musty smell of cave dirt forever buried, never cleansed by sunlight, seeped out toward her.

The padlock meant to keep the latch from lifting over its iron hook lay on the ground.

Rachael chewed on her tongue. If that door opened some more by itself she'd hightail it back to her mother so fast . . .

But it didn't. It stayed where it was, daring *her* to open it some more. A squirrel chattered above her but she didn't even look up. Why was the padlock on the ground when this cave was never used now?

Did she have the nerve or didn't she?

No, she didn't. Rachael turned back toward the path, feeling stiff as if she'd stood there for hours instead of minutes.

Yes, I do, too. Rachael swiveled around, pulling again at the handle.

The door opened a big enough space to walk through.

It was quiet, as if there wasn't anyone in the world but Rachael and that door.

The whole mountain waited for her to go in there. Warmness flooded her skin.

Rachael stuck her head in first. It was just dark. The musty smell was so deep now it reminded her of when she'd broken open a mushroom.

Something inside gave back a beckoning glow. Didn't it?

I'm not going in there. I'm not scared. I just don't like it, and that's different.

Rachael walked backward to the path and stood in a spot of sun to get warm. Her skin was still hot but she felt cold inside.

A whooping sound like Indians made in the movies at Shorty's picture house sliced through the trees and she swung around. It came from somewhere ahead and Rachael moved toward it, looking behind her only once to make sure nothing came out of the cave and followed her.

Jerry Garrett and all his bones crouched near a wooden box in the ground. The box's lid was broken and sat slantwise against a rock. Something that looked like a piece of one of Thora K.'s saffron cookies sat on the lid.

Rachael slipped behind a tree to spy on Jerry. Maybe she'd jump out when he leasted expected it.

His cupped hand swooped toward the cookie but instead of picking it up closed on air. He shook his fist next to his ear like Uncle Lon did a pair of dice. He worked with something between his fingers and put it into the box. Bringing his nose down to the box's edge, his rump aimed at the sky and his elbows sticking up like a cricket's, Jerry Garrett stared inside. A moment later he jumped up and let out another whoop.

Mystified, Rachael stepped out from behind her tree.

Sullen eyes watched her approach. They were liquid brown instead of golden-flecked like her dad's. "How long you been hiding behind that tree, kid?"

Rachael ignored the insult. "That *is* a cookie."

"So what?"

"So what are you doing?" She peered into the square box. Its bottom was wet stones sticking above rusty water. And along its upper edges feathery cobwebs threaded the corners together. "Are you an Indian? You yell like one."

"Yeah and I'm going to cut your hair off starting down at your eyebrows, brat."

She turned to run, but he had a hold of her dress. It ripped at the waist.

"Wait. I'll show you. But you got to promise not to make noise and not tell anybody. It's a secret. An Indian secret that only Indians know."

Rachael wanted to go back to the cabin, and she wanted to know what he was up to.

Jerry Garrett knelt as he had before and gave her a warning glance. His hand rested on the edge of the wooden lid.

A fly landed, and then another. Rachael counted seven flies before Jerry's cupped hand swooped across the lid.

There were now six flies either by or on the cookie and his hand was shaking dice again. He opened it to expose the stunned seventh fly lying on its back, still buzzing and kicking its legs. He pulled its wings off.

"Ich!"

"Shut up." Putting the bug on a cobweb in the box, he wiggled the web with his finger.

"I'd never marry you."

"Who the hell asked you?"

Rachael craned forward as the biggest spider she'd ever seen darted from nowhere, pounced on the amputated fly and retreated. Jerry shook the web again. The spider returned, struck, retreated, waited and then came back to wrap the fly in fine-spun web. The feeble struggle stopped. The sun went down behind a ridge. Rachael shivered and swallowed back the sour juice coming up her throat. Jerry grinned ghoulishly and whooped.

"That's nasty. You're nasty." She wanted to cry for the poor fly, but he'd never know it.

"Little girls are just scaredy-cats, that's all."

Rachael brushed off her skirt and for once was proud to straighten to her full height so she could look him eye to eye. "Little boy"—she swallowed again for the fly but pretended to pause—"I can show you something a lot scarier than that."

He laughed. Rachael squared her shoulders with a sniff and walked away.

"What?" His hand on her arm jerked her to a stop. "You can't scare—"

"Don't touch me. You're all dirty." She walked on but he followed.

Rachael pointed to the door in the hillside from the turn in the path. "There's an evil genie in there. I bet you're too coward to go in."

He stalked to the door. Hinges creaked and wood splintered as he yanked it open as far as it would go. He disappeared inside.

Rachael waited for him to come out. But he didn't.

If she went in after him he'd probably jump at her or something. He was staying so quiet in there to do just that. There wasn't anything dangerous in that cave but Jerry Garrett.

With the door standing wide open, Rachael could see some dim but interesting shapes inside. She was too far away to make them out.

She scratched a mosquito bite on the calf of her leg with the tied laces of the shoe on her other foot. Still no sight or sound of Jerry. Maybe he was feeding more spiders.

Rachael moved hesitantly toward the dark hole. She'd just look in from the outside so he couldn't play a trick on her.

It wasn't as dark as she'd thought. She could see him standing motionless toward the middle of the cave, but only his face in shadow.

A tall shape standing alone and to one side caught her attention. The light from the doorway glowed off a slender hand with long pointy fingernails. "Is it gold?" she whispered.

"Don't come in here." Jerry sounded like he had a pillow over his face.

But Rachael was already in. "Why, it's a mirror."

It had many hands all holding each other as its frame. And wavy glass like in some of her grandmother's mirrors in the Gingerbread House.

"It must be very old." The awe in her voice came hollow on still, stagnant air. Why would Thora K. keep such a valuable thing in here?

"I think you better go get your ma, Rachael."

"Why? And how come you're talking so funny?" He hadn't moved since she'd come in and he was staring at the floor. "What's the matter with you?"

A pile of clothes and a long-handled hammer like the ones miners used in their contests on the Fourth of July lay on the floor between them. "It's just some old clo . . ." But she didn't finish. A human hand lay next to the hammer and was connected to the pile of clothes by a wrist.

Rachael blinked and stepped around the huddled mass to stand next to Jerry.

There was a face on this side, a dark swollen face with eyes popping out of it.

"It's Mr. Pemberthy," her voice said, and then it started making squeaky, screaming noises that wouldn't stop.

4

Thora K. watched Doc Seaton's ancient Model T rattle off down the road and turned back to the Maddon car. Brandy sat next to Rachael, who slept in the back seat. She stroked her daughter's hair. Doc had given both children something to quiet them.

Poor Tim. No wonder he hadn't told them about the Garretts renting the place. All her family gone and most of her friends and now Tim. It was becoming harder to ignore the speed of passing years. . . .

Thora K. pushed the specter from her thoughts. "Well, there be a ranch 'ouse full of 'ungry men and us with no mite a supper started." Bless Brandy for sharing her family with an old woman.

But Brandy took the radiator blanket from the floor of the car and shook it. "She'll sleep till we get back." She handed Thora K. the flashlight. "We have things to do."

"Can't it wait?" She followed Brandy around the house and toward the path to the cave. "Tomorrow the men can bury it or—"

"What if Jerry wakes up in the night and decides to go back?"

Thora K. remembered the stupefied expression of the boy as he dragged a hysterical Rachael into the house. " 'Ee won't go near after seein' Tim."

"He might. Kids are funny."

The cave was dark enough now that Thora K. turned on the flashlight and was met with an answering flash from the mirror. It settled into rings of light one within the other, as if the glass had a depth of its own, the rings deformed by the age of the glass.

Tim had pleaded with her to destroy it when he'd helped her store it here those many years ago, but she'd been against it. Brandy might need to use its magic again and see into the future. But she hadn't consulted it in all this time, so she must be able to see her visions without it.

Although Thora K. had never quite understood how the mirror worked, she could no longer doubt Brandy's predictions. Even that Jerry and Rachael would one day marry. "Do 'ee believe 'twould 'urt the boy?"

"I'm not taking any chances. It's dangerous."

Thora K. bent to pick up the double jack that had been pushed aside when Tim's body was removed. Memories of Corbin caught in her throat. "Wot do us do with it then?"

Brandy knelt to untangle the rope from the decaying quilt that once covered the mirror. "Move it to the Brandy Wine for now."

"It be some heavy for we. I got a better idea." She raised the big hammer and almost toppled over backward. "Stand back, you. Edden going to be a danger when I'm finished with it." And she swung.

"No!" Brandy grabbed her arm and the double jack dropped to the ground, only an edge of it pinging harmlessly against an ugly claw. "What do you think Tim was trying to do when he died?"

"Wot be 'ee saying, woman?"

"I know that mirror exists unharmed except for a crack in the glass in 1978," Brandy whispered, as though the thing could hear. "The mirror survives. You don't.

"The door has rotted. Tim probably figured it wasn't safe anymore with only a sick woman and her child living here. The cabin hasn't been rented to anyone with children for years. They wander and explore, especially little boys. So Tim hunted up his double jack and came out here to make sure it wouldn't harm Jerry. You know he thought it was responsible for his niece's losing her mind."

"Be 'ee tellin' me this 'ere mirror kilt poor Tim? 'Ow could it?"

"I don't know, but I'm willing to bet Doc Seaton decides Tim died of a stroke, just like John McCabe. They found him on the floor in front of the mirror too." She threw the radiator blanket over it and wound the rope around tight. "No one succeeds in destroying it. But I think it may well take care of anyone who tries. We'll have to hide the mirror where no one'll be tempted to fool with it."

They started for the Brandy Wine, the mirror between them, Thora K. at the front end where the load was lightest trying to hold it and the flashlight where her hands met underneath, a clawlike finger poking through the blanket into her armpit. That whole side of her body throbbed with the effort and tingled perversely with her excitement at the deadly magic of the thing she carried.

Night creatures rustled just out of sight.

Except in the tree shadows, the darkness was lighter here.

Thora K. nerved herself to ask the question that had haunted her since they'd found Tim. "Do 'ee know when I'll go? Be it this year? Or the next?"

"No, I don't know." Shadows softened the deepening lines on Brandy's face and blurred the contrasting streaks in her hair. "If I did, I wouldn't tell you. I've learned that much at least. I just know you're not alive in 1978. And you haven't been for a while."

"Should 'ope not. I'm in me seventies now. Don't seem proper you'd be neither."

"I'll be too old to really know it, and Hutch . . . We'd better hurry. I don't want Rachael to wake up before we get back."

Thora K. held the flashlight while Brandy tore boards away from the opening of the Brandy Wine.

"This is too easy. I'll get the twins down here in the morning with more boards. And I'll come along to make sure they don't go inside."

"I'm feelin' so weak as a robin. Shouldn't wonder if I don't make it back to the car."

"I'll bring it around. " Brandy ripped away the last board needed to slip the mirror through. "You can wait down by the road."

Thora K. worried about Rachael alone in the car as she lifted the horrid thing one more time. Her rheumatism was acting up. Would she have the strength to help get the supper on? All she wanted now was a strong dose of tonic and a warm bed. She knew shame at the weakness with which age had burdened her. Thora K. didn't want to die this year but she was glad she wouldn't live to Brandy's 1978. The world was already getting ahead of her. Women shamelessly baring their legs, bobbing their hair, kissing and worse with men in automobiles, and drinking alcohol. It was a mystery to Thora K. how there would be a world left in 1978, the way the next generation of mothers was being raised.

Struggling with a last effort, they set the mirror up in the mouth of the mine and ducked back outside. "Tez but a thing. Not alive. 'Ow could it 'urt anyone?"

"I don't know. I wish it never existed. But then there's so much I'd never have known . . ."

"Might be us could drop it down a shaft and run, quick-like."

"Thora K., you don't understand. Everything's already happened. If that mirror is destroyed, if it can be—would time change back and none of this have happened?"

"But 'ee don't look into it no more."

"I'm afraid to mess with it now. I don't know what effect it would have. I'm so confused . . . and I'd been doing so well."

"Would 'ee become yer young granddaughter again then?"

"No, I'd probably be Shay Garrett at fifty-one in a world years removed from the one I knew, if she's even lived that long. She may be dead."

Rachael didn't remember much of that afternoon. And she didn't remember the drive home, but merely awoke there the next morning.

However, she would never again come near a cave or a dark hole without knowing panic. Her childhood nightmares would be filled with monstrous black spiders emanating from forbidden dank caverns.

Everyone seemed overly concerned with that day and Doc Seaton asked her into his little house after school to talk about it. She repeated the details of Jerry Garrett's feeding spiders until she tired of it.

Her parents took her into Denver several times to talk to another doctor who didn't even flatten her tongue with a stick and tell her to say "Ahhhhh." He asked her the same questions as Doc Seaton had. This was all confusing because she didn't feel sick. One night she awoke to overhear her parents and Thora K. talking of "trauma" and "leaving it be." Whatever a trauma was, Thora K. pronounced it a blessing.

Whenever Tim Pemberthy was mentioned everyone would glance at Rachael and look worried. She'd been told he'd died. It wasn't too surprising since he was an old man. But she didn't really want to think about it. So she didn't.

There were more serious concerns in the household.

Dan received a letter from Joe Tyler in California. His grandmother, when she was alive, had been a great friend of Thora K.'s. Joe had a job "trucking cabbages" and thought he could get Dan one too. Dan wanted to go and everybody but Brandy was against it. One night he left without telling anybody.

Her dad was quiet after he read the note Dan had left on the table. Then he picked up a chair and broke it across his knee. "Cabbages, Jesus!"

He'd always been two people to Rachael. The one who loved her and the other one who could hit back at Uncle Lon and knock the twins' heads together when they needed it.

"Hutch, take your temper outside." Her mother was sad but dry-eyed. "I told you—"

"You said used cars. And I didn't even want to believe that."

"He'll be there when the need arises. You can't keep a grown bird in the nest."

"But the ranch—"

"Is going downhill fast and you know it."

Her parents stood holding onto each other, excluding Rachael. They didn't even notice her tears.

Uncle Lon led her to the door. "Let's saddle up and take a ride." Then he said over his shoulder, "Can't bring him back, but if you want to stake me to a game or two in Denver, I might rustle up some cash."

"Get out of here," her dad snarled and lowered his face back to her mother's hair.

Things settled down some when Uncle Lon returned from Denver. But then Remy started seeing her teacher, Miss Hapscot. He even had her out to dinner, and Rachael sensed more changes coming.

Rachael didn't like changes.

She missed Dan and didn't care for Miss Hapscot sitting in his place at the table.

To her the changes seemed to correlate with the arrival of the Garretts in Nederland.

Jerry had avoided her since that afternoon at the Strock cabin. But one day when snow scudded across the road to fall into frozen ruts and Rachael was making her solitary way past Doc Seaton's, swinging her lunch pail, he came up beside her.

He slowed his pace to match hers. "How come you don't ride the bus like the other kids who live out of town, brat?"

Rachael decided the two of them had an understanding. They didn't like each other. "Because the bus only comes to the road. If I walk that far I might as well walk all the way. I do sometimes in the mornings."

He reached into the ditch for a handful of snow and tried to form it into a ball but it powdered away between his mittens like sugar. "Do you ever have dreams about Mr. Pemberthy?" he asked casually.

"No. Why should I? He just got the stroke and died." Rachael thought stroke must be something like measles or mumps.

Jerry stepped in front of her so she had to stop. "My ma says I'm not supposed to talk to you about him."

"Then don't."

"The mirror's gone," he whispered, as if telling a secret. "It was gone the next day. I looked."

"What mirror?"

"The one in the cave." He sounded frightened and Rachael was trying to figure out why when Dorothy Kinshelow walked by with Mary Powers.

"Rachael's got a boyfriend," they chimed in unison and ran down the hill laughing.

"Dorothy says your ma's a witch." Jerry turned to walk ahead.

"And you're just dumb enough to believe her." Rachael'd never been accused of having a boyfriend before. And she thought she'd caught a look of admiration on Dorothy Kinshelow's face.

She pondered this as they neared Main Street, Jerry walking ahead acting as if he wasn't with her.

Dorothy and Mary peeked at them around the side of the old meat market.

Rachael hurried to catch up with him. "I can show you where a real witch lives, though, right here in town."

"Oh yeah? What's her name?"

"Miss Smith. But the grown-ups call her May Bell."

"How do you know she's a witch?"

They were walking together again by the time they passed the boarded-up market. Rachael looked over her shoulder to see two heads pop out behind its other end. "Because when you ask big people about her they shut up and won't say anything, like they're afraid to." They walked past the general store, where Rachael should have stopped. "Her house is down this street before you get to the reservoir."

Dorothy and Mary crossed a vacant lot, running bent over. They probably thought Rachael couldn't see them.

When she and Jerry reached the livery stable, he dodged behind a gas pump. "Which house is it?"

"The one over there with the pretty glass in the door. What are you hiding for?"

"I remember the last time you tried to scare me, even if you don't."

On either side of Miss Smith's steps, a skinny lodgepole pine poked into a gray sky. The cold west wind slammed shut the trapdoor of the livery stable's unused haymow and they jumped at the sound. It blew away the heavy scent of oil.

Jerry ran to a carriage that crouched on one wheel in the dead weeds beside the stable. Weather and abandonment had ripped away the leather of its seats. Rachael followed him in case the girls were still watching.

"Just because nobody talks about her don't mean she's a witch," he whispered, his nose as red as the bright stocking cap Thora K. had knitted for him.

"Remy told me that on Halloween the bravest of the big boys in school have to tip over her outhouse. If she isn't a witch, why would they do it on Halloween? Want to peek in her window and see if we can see her?"

"Yeah . . . well . . . I guess so. But you go first."

Some boyfriend he'd make, Rachael thought with disgust.

Making a dash for the truck parked at the side of the street, she pretended to hide behind it as Jerry joined her. Rachael wasn't that afraid of May Bell Smith, nor was she convinced the woman was a witch. But if she didn't make this little adventure interesting, the boy at her side would have no reason to stay there.

Black clouds tumbled about the house with the oval of colored glass in its door. Lace curtains lay still at the edges of the windows, making the interior look dark. White foam capped the leaden waves on the reservoir and wind growled low through the lodgepoles.

"I'm getting cold. Are you going or aren't you?"

"Stay close behind me." Rachael crossed to the side of the lot where they could step over broken wires in the fence. She raced to flatten herself against the house on one side of a window while he did the same on the other.

Rachael waited long enough to convince him she was building up courage and then peeked in.

"Do you see anything?" Jerry's eyes looked enormous over his cheekbones. "Is she dead?"

"Dead? No, of course not. I can't see. It's too dark. Let's go around to the back."

This time Jerry looked in first. All I can make out is a kitchen table. I don't think no witch lives here."

"Uncle Lon says May Bell got mad once and burned down almost the whole town. How could she do that if she wasn't—"

"If she wasn't what?" a gruff voice said behind them.

Rachael whipped around with a squeal and dropped her lunch pail.

"What are you up to, Rachael Maddon?" Miss Smith seemed monstrous in a fuzzy coat that made her look like a bear. Orange bangs frizzed around a woolen scarf tied under one of her chins. She swung a metal chamber pot by its handle and breathed puffs of steam onto the air. "And who's this with you?"

The children stood frozen. Behind the outhouse at the back of the yard Middle Boulder Creek roared into the silence, trying to crash the ice forming at its edges.

"Well?"

"Jerry Garrett," Rachael heard herself say in a tiny voice.

"Jerry . . . Garrett," May Bell repeated softly, her little pig eyes moving to him. "But you're so . . . so big." She raised a hand as if to touch his cheek.

Jerry pushed past Rachael and darted across the yard to the hole in the fence.

Rachael turned to follow but May Bell grabbed her shoulder. "You forgot your lunch pail." She still stared after Jerry. "You keep him away from here. You understand?"

"Yes, ma'am." Rachael watched a tear roll down the fat woman's cheek.

5

One Saturday Rachael was playing in the horse barn when Uncle Lon returned from one of his trips. She'd snuggled into the hay with a couple of cats to keep warm and was pretending one of them was Dorothy Kinshelow and the other Mary Powers. He didn't see her when he entered carrying a crate of bottles and hunkered in front of a window. His breath steamed in the dusty light as he took a jar of paste from his coat pocket and stuck a piece of paper onto an empty bottle.

One cat took a sudden notion to spit at the other and her uncle looked up into her eyes.

For a moment he reminded Rachael of an outlaw like the ones in the old-time wanted posters Mrs. Sweeny kept tacked on the wall at the post office as a joke. "What are you doing, Uncle Lon?"

He grinned and the outlaw went away. "Can you keep a secret, Rachael?"

"Gross my heart." Still clutching a rangy tom, she left the hay and sat on the floor beside him as he drew a bottle from his overcoat pocket. "Why, that's molasses. What's it for?"

Lon Maddon glanced over his shoulder as if he worried that the mare pawing her stall behind them might overhear. Then he squinted and leaned close to Rachael. "I'm making up some tonic for Thora K."

"I didn't know *you* made it."

"Neither does she," he whispered. "That's the secret. 'Chief Geronimo's Tonic, Magic Elixir of the Fabled Apache Medicine Men. Offers wonderful relief from the grippe, neuritis, neuralgia, rheumatism and pains in the extremities,'" he read from the colorful label he'd pasted on the empty bottle. "'Guaranteed to restore hair when applied regularly to the scalp.'"

"That's like the one on her tonic in the kitchen. Where'd you get it?"

"Took an old label into a printer and had him make me up some more of the same." With his tongue over to one side and between his teeth, Uncle Lon carefully poured Thora K.'s bottle well over half full of whiskey. "You see, Rachael, as she gets older the tonic Thora K. buys at the medicine show on the Fourth of July don't last as long as it used to. I told her I saw a store in Cheyenne that keeps it in stock."

He drank from the whiskey bottle and coughed. "Now this stuff ought to grow hair on something," he gasped, and wiped his eyes.

"But Thora K. hates whiskey."

"That's what the molasses is for."

Rachael watched gooey black strap slither down the sides of the tonic bottle and thin when it met the whiskey. He corked the bottle and shook it till the amber and black had combined to cloudy dark.

"I don't understand. All that molasses without sugar or anything'd taste ick."

"Whiskey without molasses tastes good and that makes it bad." He touched the cork to the end of his tongue and wrinkled his nose. "But whiskey mixed with molasses tastes bad and that makes it tonic." He laughed suddenly and a startled cat jumped from her lap. "And that's good."

Rachael laughed too . . . but she still didn't understand.

Lon passed the tonic under her nose and the mixture's fumes made her think of rotting things soaked in motor oil. "Must need something. You're still sittin' upright."

He brought yet another bottle from his pocket, this one small and amber with no label. "Now this here's the kicker."

"What is it?"

"Chloroform."

Brandy Maddon caught a cold that winter and the cough lingered even after the other symptoms had disappeared. Thora K.'s tonic proved to be a fairly effective if bad-tasting cough medicine.

Several blizzards snowed them in and Rachael braced herself for a scary time. It started as usual with her mother snapping at everyone.

Despite Thora K.'s efforts the meals grew tiresome. "I don't feel like cooking tonight. Let's just warm that roast over and cut it up for sandwiches," Brandy would say wearily.

Or . . .

"Rachael, will you stop that racket! Pencils are for writing, not clicking against the paper." And the skin around her lips would turn white.

"This house is driving me bananas," Brandy yelled at the ceiling and Rachael curled up in her chair and tried to make herself small and quiet.

Mrs. Sweeny called on the telephone from the post office and read the mail to them.

"God, if they can get phone lines out here, why not electricity? This damned antique world. Hutch, can't you at least pipe water in from the spring? I'm going crazy without plumbing."

"Got water into the sink. Hell, woman, what do you want? Man can go broke trying to buy the latest doodad."

"An indoor bathroom for one thing. We live like animals here."

"Calm down, Bran. You're scaring Rachael."

"Well, what about me? The same routine day in and day out. It's deadly."

There was no clue to Brandy's behavior in the stories Rachael read or heard in school or Sunday school. Did other mothers, even such respected ladies of the community as Mrs. Kinshelow, get in these moods in the privacy of their homes, and did their families keep it a secret like the Maddons did? Everything she'd been taught about true ladies and proper mothers indicated they would never badger a good man like her dad, but suffer in silence far worse indignities than her mother ever dreamed of.

One day Mrs. Sweeny called to read a letter from Dan. His job didn't pay much but he'd saved enough for Remy's train ticket to California if he wanted to come.

Remy promised to wait till the meadow had been dug and they'd got the water on to irrigate the hay in the spring.

As soon as the roads cleared enough, Brandy drove down to the Gingerbread House for a visit and to "get away." There she could use the plumbing and listen to the radio.

The visit was to have lasted a week but three days later Brandy Maddon returned, tearful and apologetic. "I don't know why I get that way. I love you all so much."

Remy left at the end of June. The house seemed empty without the twins. Brandy's cough finally began to lessen but Catherine Garrett went into the hospital in Boulder. Jerry came to stay with the Maddons. Rachael enjoyed trying to teach him to ride but didn't enjoy the fuss her mother made over him.

On the Fourth of July, Brandy dropped the children and Thora K. off in Nederland and drove on down the canyon the see how Mrs. Garrett was feeling after her operation.

They stopped to watch some of the double-hand contests and then wandered on to the vacant lot by the old meat market where Chief Geronimo once again held forth on the wonders of his elixir.

He paced along the side of his truck, the tails of his bright headdress sweeping down his back, long iron-gray hair parted in the middle and gathered to the sides under each ear.

Rachael could never quite follow his long sentences to their conclusions. But there was no mistaking his ability to convince. He could frighten people or make them laugh, and more by the way he spoke than by what he said.

"Little girl!" Chief Geronimo turned on Rachael with an accusatory finger. She and Jerry had slipped between adults to join the children sitting on the ground in front. "Tell these people here the truth. Have you ever, I mean *ever* seen a bald Indian? The truth now."

"No sir, I haven't but—"

"No sir, she hasn't. Did you hear that? Do you know why? Because there aren't any and do you know why there aren't?" he shouted. The chief always shouted and stared directly into eyes. "Because, my good friends, the Indian has always known the secret formula of the elixir. When I was a young boy, my father . . ." And he went into a long story about his childhood with many funny little stories in it that pleased the small crowd and its laughter attracted more people. The story had nothing to do with why there were no bald Indians but Rachael soon forgot this in her delight over the magic of his words.

Pictures of Indians and lettering all in yellow and red decorated his black truck. The weeds lay crumpled over where he paced beside it. He gestured flamboyantly and often, shaking the fringe on his sleeves. Wetness darkened a circle on his buckskin shirt under each arm and formed a triangular patch between his shoulderblades.

The air was still and hot for a mountain day and thunder growled behind Arapahoe Peak.

Mr. Binder stood on the sidewalk between two men. One of them wore the uniform of a county sheriff and the other was dressed like a banker, with his hair slicked down and his brown shoes polished to gleaming. He was the handsomest man Rachael'd ever seen.

Then she realized they were all three looking at her. Mr. Binder motioned her to join them. "Rachael, these gentlemen wondered if your uncle came into town with you for the celebrations this morning," he asked uncomfortably.

"No, but he and Dad are coming in for the rodeo pretty soon."

The warning in Mr. Binder's eyes was unmistakable but Rachael'd noticed it too late.

"That's all right, honey. We just want to talk to him," the handsome man said, and stepped backward, narrowly missing Miss Smith as she walked behind him. May Bell Smith crossed Main Street faster than Rachael would have believed possible for so heavy a woman.

"Now you're probably wondering what all this has to do with a bald head and this famous elixir," Chief Geronimo bellowed. "Well, I'll tell you."

Rachael turned back, anxious about Mr. Binder's warning look and why the deputy and his friend wanted to talk to her uncle. But she had to know how the chief was going to tie together all those details in his talk and relate them to elixir.

"Neuritis, neuralgia and rheumatism, my dear friends, sneak up on you like a snake in the grass on a warm afternoon." His s's hissed and his arm wriggled like a snake but his eyes moved nervously toward the sheriff's deputy on the sidewalk. ". . . like a robber in the darkness of night. They spare no one, neither the wealthy nor the poor. But you are too young to worry about them, you say? Well . . ."

Chief Geronimo launched an attack on something called dyspepsia and though Rachael listened closely she never discovered how the ancient Apache medicine men discovered the cure for all the ailments mentioned. Nor did this Indian ever say outright that the elixir would help someone who had them. But when the deputy wandered off, Chief Geronimo shuffled through a hurried dance accompanied by bells tied around his ankles and started selling tonic.

Lon Maddon leaned against the truck and brushed a speck from the jacket of his summer suit. "We're gonna be late for the rodeo, dammit. Get a move on," he yelled at the screen door.

Hutch came out of the house on the run, his good shirt unbuttoned and hanging out of his pants. Lon heard the snap as the spring on the door broke again. "Well, you don't have to hurry that—"

"Lon, you got any hooch stored on the place?"

"Some in the horse barn, why?"

"Jesus H. God! Get in the truck." His brother had the motor running and was backing to the barn before Lon could get off the running board into the seat. "May Bell just called from town. A sheriff's deputy was asking Rachael about you. And she told him we were coming in for the rodeo."

"Hutch, you know old Skinner and me got a deal."

"Wasn't Skinner. Some deputy she's never seen before and he had a man with him that looked like government to her."

"A fed?" Lon helped his brother load the nine or ten cases that were left of the last run and to fork hay over them. "Probably just some dude visitor up from Boulder, all dressed up."

"Well, this dude wanted to talk to you and if anybody knows which way the stripes run on a man it's May Bell Smith."

Thunderclouds rolled in fast overhead and Lon began to catch his twin's fear as the truck bounced up out of the valley. This wasn't the first time he'd wished there was another road out of here. "Hell, we're just going to meet them head-on. The way you're driving, those bottles will bust. They'll smell the evidence coming right to 'em."

"Can't let them find it on the ranch. May Bell said they were still hanging around town."

"Waiting to catch me?" A plop of rain the size of a half-dollar splashed the windshield. "Why not come out to the house?"

"Maybe waiting for us to get settled at the rodeo so they could sneak out and search the place when nobody's around. Maybe they don't have a warrant." Hutch stopped the truck. "You hightail it up to the road and see if they're waiting for us."

Thunder threatened the treetops around him, sparse heavy raindrops spattered the dust at his feet as Lon Maddon approached the road that led to Nederland one way and Central City and Denver the other. As he was turning around he happened to raise his eyes up the mountainside across the way. Just the top boards covering the mouth of the Brandy Wine showed above the tailings.

Lightning accompanied his dash back to the truck, and a bit more rain. "Nobody in sight. Let's go."

"We can dump the stuff between here and Central City."

"Hell no, I got a customer for it. We'll stash it and me in the Brandy Wine for now. You go on to the rodeo."

"They're going to connect that mine with us eventually, Lon, and go looking there when—"

"It won't be there then. I'll deliver it to my customer tonight, by hand if I have to. He's local. Then I'll take a little trip. If they ask where I went, say you don't know. 'Cause you won't. I'll be back in a month or two."

They parked the truck in the trees across the road from the mine and carried the wooden cases up the mountainside in several trips, rain striking their faces like cold pellets. Entering the Brandy Wine was no problem. The boards across the entrance were new and firm but the wood of the framing where they were attached had rotted. Pulling some of the boards loose on one end, they let them dangle with the nails still in them and stacked the crates inside.

"How am I going to get the haying done with you as well as the boys gone?" Hutch flexed his arms and shoulders, rubbed his neck. He looked fit for fifty-seven, lean and hard from ranch work. But Lon knew the day was coming when his twin would have all he could do to get his arthritis out of bed in the mornings. He stuffed a wad of bills in Hutch's hand.

"Here, hire a haying crew this year. Maybe this is all May Bell's imagination and I won't have to go nowhere. I'll scout around after dark and find out." Lon noticed a tall shape hovering behind Hutch on the other side of the entrance. "What the hell's that?"

Whatever it was, it was wrapped in a dirty blanket tied on with rope and stood almost as tall as they did.

"Probably something of Thora K.'s. You better keep this money for your trip."

"Naw. I'll get paid for the hooch tonight. You get yourself and the truck into town. Don't worry if you don't hear from me for a while. Somebody might be watching the mail."

They shook hands and Hutch ducked out into the rain that fell hard now. It might delay the rodeo but it would also wash out any tracks they'd left in the dust. Lon settled down beside the whiskey. He selected a bottle from one of the crates to keep him company.

He took a nip and blinked as lightning flashed through the opening. Something resembling a metal claw gleamed at the base of the blanket-wrapped shape across from him. The covering rippled as if wind had gotten under it and couldn't get out.

Lon put down the bottle and rose to untie the rope, letting the blanket fall to the floor of the mine.

"OOeee, now if you ain't the ugliest thing I ever did see." It was a full-length mirror surrounded with hands and claws made of what looked to be brass. But that was impossible unless someone came in regularly to polish it. There was no sign of tarnish.

Lon had gone back to his whiskey before he realized there was more wrong with this mirror than its appearance. He sat facing it but it was not reflecting his image. And it was making a humming sound.

"Queer," he muttered to no one, and raised his bottle high. The surface of the mirror ignored the movement completely. "Goddamn queer's what it is."

Perhaps this batch of hooch was bad and affecting his mind. But he'd drunk so little of it.

Again lightning flashed, briefly flinging the mirror's contorted shadow across the rusting tracks along which ore cars had once traveled. But it made no impression on the cloudy darkness within the bronzelike frame.

Wind stirred the blanket at its feet and the heavy scent of wet pine needles drifted in as rain splashed against the glass. Instead of beading and sliding down the slippery surface, the raindrops seemed to disappear on contact. Thunder rattled bottles in the crates behind him.

Bewildered and forgetting his distrust of the whiskey, Lon brought the bottle to his lips and drank. When he lowered his head the haze had vanished. Prickles crawled among the roots of his hair.

There was a picture in the looking glass now, but it was not Lon Maddon's reflection, nor the reflection of anything inside the mouth of the Brandy Wine.

6

Lon stood, backed against the crates of illegal whiskey, the opened bottle overturned at his feet, its amber contents spreading out across the rocky floor of the mine.

He watched a silent movie playing for him alone and with dizzying speed on the mirror's surface. Random scenes flashed across the glass.

A willowy girl with pale straight hair and a filmy costume that allowed the darkness of her nipples to show through and bared her legs to the crotch. A crowd of scantily clad people standing still on moving sidewalks. A giant machine that flew, hovered, and crawled across a concrete landscape.

"Naw," he said aloud, and shook his head, but couldn't look away.

Another girl in an old-fashioned dress. She looked like Brandy as a young woman. A city of tall buildings encased in glass under water. People appearing and disappearing when a man pressed a series of square, lighted buttons. Stooped people hovering naked around a fire, their jaws heavy and slack, their hair matted.

Lon wanted to go behind the mirror to discover the secret of these projections, but fear and the tantalizing images kept him rooted. He was aware of the rain having stopped as he watched the mirror pictures. Thunder grew distant. The sound of water dripping from the trees outside . . . sunshine filtering through the opening . . . the grind of an engine down on the road . . .

In a more rational moment he would have picked up a case of whiskey and flung it, shattering the mirror. But being confronted so unexpectedly by the impossible destroyed his self-control.

With a huge effort, fed by terror, he pulled his eyes away and noticed a mist writhing along the floor from the direction of the mirror and toward his feet.

He lost any control that might have remained and for the first time in his adult life Lon Maddon screamed.

Then he was running . . . in the wrong direction . . . toward the inky bowels of the Brandy Wine.

On the road below, Chief Geronimo, known to his mother as Edward Slack, heard the scream over the sick rumblings of his truck. He was so startled his foot jerked from the gas pedal and killed the engine. He leaned out the window and looked up the slope of old tailings, rubbing shivers from the back of his neck.

Was there murder going on up there? It had sounded like a man's scream. The intelligent thing to do would be to leave the scene quickly. Chief Geronimo Slack grabbed the hand crank from the seat beside him and slipped out of the truck quietly so as not to irritate anyone feeling murderous up on the mountainside.

Steam seeped from under the truck's hood. He'd meant to fill the radiator before he left Nederland but his uneasiness over the presence of the sheriff's deputy and the ominous-looking man with him had caused the chief to leave town in haste and after just one show. The labeling on his medicine bottle didn't bear looking into any more than did the contents.

The chief loosened the radiator cap, using a chamois skin to protect his fingers. He kept water in the truck for just this occurrence, but if he poured cold water into the radiator without waiting for it to cool, he'd have a cracked block and no truck at all.

He cursed himself and looked nervously up the tailing pile. These hills were full of old mines.

The sound of another vehicle coming along from town was just as distressing. His truck blocked the road and it might be the sheriff.

"Lord, you get me out of this and I'll quit tonic and go back to working kidney pills," he promised silently, and crept up the side of the tailings to where he could see the road and the partially boarded entrance to the mine at the same time. What if there was some old coot up here with a gun? The chief flattened himself on the ground and instant sweat covered his face as he recognized the sheriff's deputy driving the approaching car. The gent with him was probably the one he'd seen in town.

When the deputy turned off on an old ranch road and disappeared into the trees with no more than a glance at the truck, Chief Geronimo slipped his fingers under the iron-gray wig and scratched his barren scalp.

The sound of the engine faded gradually, as if the car had kept going rather than stopping for the men to circle back and inspect the truck. No sound from the mine either. A robin bathed in a puddle in front of the opening where some boards hung loose, then cocked his head and hopped inside. He returned a moment later, showing no concern, and began to peck the ground between the metal tracks.

Chief Geronimo gave a slight sigh and the startled bird flew off. "You're gettin' too old for this business, Ed." But he stayed where he was and watched the ranch road for a while.

At first he thought he imagined the smell of whiskey. But then he made out the shape of an overturned bottle just inside the mine entrance. That scream he'd heard could have been some drunk having a nightmare. Nothing in there to even scare a robin.

He hesitated and chided himself for being so skittery. To prove himself to himself he peeked into the opening. Nothing fearsome came hurtling out of the dark. He stepped inside. His eyes adjusted to the dimness and focused on stacked crates of bottles like the one on the ground, only these were full.

"Sure would make a lot of tonic," he thought aloud. "Hello? Anybody here?"

He looked around outside. No sound. No sheriff. Should he risk it? "Maybe just one crate."

When he had it safely in the truck and no one had challenged him, Chief Geronimo Slack decided the radiator was still too hot to fill. So he dashed back up the mountainside for another case. This time as he was about to duck back through the opening he caught a movement out of the corner of his eye and almost dropped the precious load. It took him a moment to realize the man he stared at was himself reflected in a mirror. "Ed, you better have a swig of this stuff to settle your nerves," he said as he returned to the truck.

As long as no one was about, he thought he might be able to carry two cases at once and double his wonderful windfall. But the odd-looking mirror made him uneasy so he covered it with the blanket that lay on the ground in front of it. Wondering why anyone would keep a spooky old mirror and a stack of hooch in a mine tunnel, he filled the radiator and then sat with the truck running. "Oh hell, I can't go off and leave all that."

When he returned to the mine the blanket had fallen off the mirror. Watching himself steal made him feel superstitious so he covered it once more and tied it with a rope that had been on the ground under the blanket. More secure now with the sound of the truck engine running and ready to go, Chief Geronimo cleaned out every last case and as an afterthought pulled the dangling boards into place, pushing the nails back into their original holes. True, he hadn't found them like that, but if the deputy returned this way and decided to wonder about the truck that had parked below, the mine would look as if it hadn't been entered in years. Perhaps then no one would investigate and find any tracks he might have left.

One day when Brandy and Hutch were shoveling manure out of a corral, Thora K. sent the children to fetch Brandy to the telephone. They stayed to sit on the fence and watch Hutch work.

"Did Uncle Lon leave because those men were looking for him?"

"You just forget all about those men, Rachael."

"But you told them you didn't know where he was."

"And that's true, I don't. You know your uncle, he's always going off. He'll come back when he's ready."

When Brandy returned she asked Jerry to walk with her and they strolled off across the meadow without even a glance for Rachael.

They sat on a boulder by the stream. He had his knees drawn up to his chin and his arms wrapped around them. Brandy tried to put her arm across his shoulders but he pushed it away.

Jerry stayed alone on his boulder all afternoon. Rachael wanted to take him some food but Brandy wouldn't allow it. "His mother has died, Puss, and he's asked to be left alone for a while. We must be very kind and careful with him now."

Toward the end of August Jerry left for Pennsylvania to go to a school where, because he was an orphan, his living expenses and tuition were to be paid by something Rachael's mother called the "Smith Foundation." Rachael had Brandy to herself again.

One night in February, Thora K. died peacefully in her sleep. The ranch house grew emptier. In the spring, Hutch Maddon made several trips trying to locate his brother but there was no word of him anywhere.

"How is it you know things ahead of time but not where Lon is?" Hutch said at supper one night. "It doesn't make sense."

"I don't remember Rachael even mentioning him," Brandy answered vaguely.

She'd had a running cold since December and it had left her so weak that Rachael helped more and more around the house. They all missed Thora K.'s willing hands.

By summer her mother could do little more than sit around and cough.

"I've heard dying people sound better than you do, woman. You get in to see a doctor about that cough."

Grandma Sophie came for a visit and she agreed with him.

"I'm sure it's nothing. I don't think Brandy was ever ill until her stroke," Brandy said. "Rachael, why did you always talk so much about things and so little about people?"

"You see, Sophie? She's not even talking sense anymore. You stay with Rachael. I'm taking her in to the doctor."

"Hutch, I live to be at least ninety-eight. . . ."

The changes in Rachael's life that started two years before were not over. One by one family members had left the ranch house. And now her father would live there alone. Rachael moved into the Gingerbread House with Grandma Sophie, and her mother entered the Sanitarium in Boulder.

7

One day as Rachael fingered the beautiful shepherdess on the mantel, her grandmother came into the room. "Be careful with that, Rachael. It came all the way from Germany with your Great-Grandmother Euler."

Sophie explained the history behind each knickknack and stick of furniture until Rachael began to feel they were old friends that her grandparents and greats and great-greats had left behind to comfort her. "You seem to appreciate my treasures like your mother never did."

In the attic they explored trunks full of old clothes and Rachael dressed in long dresses. "What's in this one, Grandma? It's locked."

"I think it's just stuck. Your mother's wedding dress and veil are in here." Sophie lifted out cascades of delicate lace all gathered to a little hat. "Perhaps someday you'll want to wear this at your wedding, dear." But her voice broke and she lifted the veil to her face and wept.

"Grandma?"

"I lost her. The day Brandy wore this I lost her, forever." Sophie replaced the veil and closed the lid. "I didn't mean to, Rachael," she whispered, "I don't know what I did."

On Sunday afternoons her father came down from the ranch to visit her mother. Then he and Rachel would ride the bus or go to the drugstore for ice cream. He seemed a sad and lonely man.

"When is Uncle Lon coming back? He could keep you company at the ranch."

"I don't believe he is, Rachael. I've had the feeling for a long time that something's happened to him."

One Sunday he told her Miss Hapscot was going to leave school in Nederland at the end of the term and go to California to marry Remy.

"Does that mean he's not going to come back? Or Dan either?"

"According to your mother they won't be back for a long while."

Rachael looked up at the Gingerbread House as they approached it, and it seemed to say to her: "You can't count on people. But I have been here since your Great-Grandfather McCabe built me."

The leaves had fallen from the trees and made whispery, scratchy sounds as they scuttled across the street. Rachael wore new white gloves and held Sophie's hand as they stepped across the trolley tracks that were no longer used. She could barely breathe as they stood waiting for the bus and hoped she wasn't coming down with "TB" like her mother.

"Now, you may not run up and kiss her. You must sit quietly and, whatever you do, don't upset her. Talk about happy things."

When they reached the Sanitarium Rachael was reluctant to get out. "What if Mommy won't like me now?"

"Don't be silly." Sophie led her along the sidewalk. "Long illnesses do change people though." She stopped to straighten Rachael's hat. "She will look different but you mustn't say anything and, dear . . . if she seems . . . Oh, never mind."

The building was of dark brick and the steps at the entrance were overhung with a heavy shroud of ivy that encroached upon the sides and from which the leaves had not yet fallen. They'd begun to turn a dull orange that blended with the closed door to form the illusion of a shadowed hole. Rachael saw another hole that yawned in her mind as it had in many a dreadful dream. Her fear was automatic and shoved against her lungs.

Sophie reached into the dark hole, pulled open a door and pushed Rachael inside. "It'll be all right, dear."

When she could breathe again they were walking down a gray hall that smelled of boiled cabbage and ammonia. Rachael covered her nose and breathed through the filter of her glove. A muffled coughing from behind a door. The squeak of a nurse's shoes as she hustled past. They turned into a room.

The woman in the bed had her mother's eyes but her hair was limp. The woman in the bed was fat. Her face was puffy. "Hello, Rachael." Something in her tone told Rachael she'd never be "Puss" again.

The lady in the other bed smiled at her encouragingly and went back to her knitting.

"I have a new friend at school." Rachael tried to sit still. She wanted to leave. "Her name's Arlene."

Only the knitting needles clacked in the silence.

Her mother scratched at the pink sleeves of her bed jacket. "You never told me about this," she accused Rachael. "You never told me I was in this place for months, maybe years. Or did I not listen?"

"Don't be ridiculous, dear. How could Rachael know this would happen, any more than the rest of us did?"

"She knew. Years from now, she knew and didn't tell me." Brandy Maddon turned her head to the wall. "And all this time wasted."

"If you're going to live to be as old as you say you are, you'll hardly miss it." Sophie laughed uncomfortably and looked at the other patient, who'd stopped knitting to stare at Brandy.

"But Hutch won't. I'm missing what time I have left with him."

Although Rachael would visit the Sanitarium often over the next five years, she'd never think of her mother as being there between visits. She would close her mind to the dark hole of the ivy-shrouded entrance and think of Brandy Maddon sitting easy and slim in the saddle, her hair fluffed by the wind as she rode the valley of the Bar Double M.

Her father razed the old Strock cabin and, mortgaging the ranch, he built a small comfortable cottage on the site. It had electricity and indoor plumbing and it was built for two. His arthritis prevented him from working the ranch alone now and he leased the valley to a neighbor. Hutch moved into the cottage and waited for Brandy.

Rachael was thirteen and a good head taller than her mother when Brandy left the Sanitarium. Brandy spent a few weeks at the Gingerbread House and the constraint between mother and daughter was more marked than ever. They were strangers.

Rachael ached to bridge the gap but Brandy's only interest was in her husband. "All the years of his life I've wasted in that Sanitarium . . ."

So Brandy moved to Nederland. But Rachael stayed in Boulder because, she was told, the cottage was small and besides she had friends in Boulder.

Rachael didn't consider friends a substitute for parents, but she was allowed to spend most of the summer months at the cottage. And many weekends Hutch would drive down for her.

Remy had a job training horses for a movie studio. (Rachael told her friends in school that her brother was a movie star.) Dan had married a girl whose father owned a used-car dealership in Los Angeles.

By the summer of 1939, when Rachael was fifteen, Remy and Elinore had two little boys and Dan had a daughter. The Bar Double M sold to a big outfit for a good price and several companies asked permission to inspect the Brandy Wine with an eye to leasing it. Tungsten from cheaper foreign sources was being diverted to Germany and Japan.

"So we're sitting better than we have for years right now, Bran," Hutch said one evening as the three of them sat in the living room at the cottage.

"I want you to get on the train and go out and see those grandkids of ours before they get any older. Bring back pictures."

"But I can't leave you—"

"Holy Jesus, Bran! I promise I won't die for a month. You watch me like I got one foot in the grave. Nobody ever died of arthritis. You make me so nervous I'm afraid to go to bed at night."

"Well, it would be nice to see the twins again." Brandy'd lost her sanitarium fat, and it seemed to Rachael that she looked years younger than Hutch.

It took a good deal more persuasion but her mother finally boarded the train in Denver. Rachael and her dad drove home in silence.

They turned off on the ranch road to the Bar Double M. One of the things they'd planned to do while Brandy was away was to clear out the remaining Maddon possessions stored in the ranch house. The buildings would stand empty, as the new owners intended to combine the valley with a neighboring ranch to form one giant spread.

Hutch stopped at the top of the lane and they sat looking down at their old home and the valley. Even at this distance the empty house looked sad and betrayed.

"We had a good life here." Her dad cleared the huskiness from his voice and spit it out the window but it was back when he spoke again. "I remember that first day I brought your mother here." He leaned over the steering wheel and chewed on his thumb.

Rachael blinked back tears. "Why does everything have to change?"

"She was sitting beside me as you are now. Only on the seat of a buckboard." The lines on his face deepened under silver-gray hair. "You know, she told me that day we'd have twin boys and a girl?"

"How does she know things ahead of time?"

"She says if she told me how, I'd think she was crazy. I just quit asking her."

"She's not crazy like people say."

"It's like living with a witch." The car started down the lane into the valley. "But I wouldn't have missed her for anything."

Most of the personal items had been removed from the house but some of the furniture remained.

"Dad, can I have this? There's room for it at the Gingerbread House." Rachael pulled out a drawer of Thora K.'s old buffet. The beveled mirrors were clouded with dust.

"Take anything you want. The rest we'll sell if anybody'll buy it." His voice carried hollow across the emptiness of the house. "About the only thing your mother's interested in is me."

"It's funny she didn't want your wedding picture." It still hung on the wall by the front door.

"Take that too if you want."

Rachael decided she would. That way she'd have her parents with her at the Gingerbread House.

Early the next morning they walked along the path behind the cottage to the Brandy Wine and pulled the boards off the entrance. Investigators from a mining company were coming to determine whether or not it would be worth starting up again.

Hutch stood back from the opening, the last board still in his hands, as if he didn't want to go into the dark hole any more than she did.

"Last time I ever saw your uncle was right here. Left him and ten cases of hooch in there." He was really talking to himself. "Eight years ago."

Rachael bent down to wipe a streak of dust from one of her anklets. Why did her father have to dwell so on all the sad happenings of the past?

"When I came back, the place was boarded up and Lon and the hooch were gone. Never saw him again."

"We don't have to go in there, do we?"

But Hutch was smiling to himself. "Jesus, we used to fight dirty."

"Dad, what's that?"

"Hm?" He tilted his head back so he could see under the rolled brim of his cowboy hat. "Oh, that's been there for years. Figured it was some old thing Thora K. stored here and forgot. Better get it out. Just be in the way."

Rachael couldn't bring herself to go inside and help, though she didn't like him lifting things. She knew whenever he overdid he'd be in such pain he couldn't sleep nights. As it was, he moved differently than other people. She'd overheard one of his friends remark that Hutch Maddon walked like he'd got a wagon tongue stuck up his rear. Which wasn't very nice but was a fairly good description of his unnatural stiffness.

Hutch stood a tall object in front of her and removed the blanket and rope that covered it.

"I remember this . . . from somewhere." She was looking at her tall awkward self in a full-length mirror. As usual, Rachael wasn't happy with what she saw. Her shape was like a pear's, all hips and no bosom. Little wonder boys never looked at her twice.

"If you'd seen it once you wouldn't forget it, that's for sure." He touched the molded metal hands of the frame. "Funny. Feels warm. You'd think it'd be cold after sittin' in there."

Rachael caressed a smooth bronze hand. The warmth seemed to be cooling even as she touched it. "Do you suppose it came from Cornwall like the buffet? Maybe I've seen it in Thora K.'s old cabin when I was little."

"Question is, what do we do with it? Might just haul it to the dump."

"But, Dad, it must be ancient. You can't throw it away. Let me have it."

"Rachael, what are you? A young lady or a pack rat?"

"Please?" She looked at the back of the mirror, which was covered with some kind of black wood. "We can take it down to Boulder in the truck with the buffet."

"Your grandma's got a houseful of junk now. Where's she going to put any more?" But the gold-flecked eyes told Rachael she'd have her way.

He tied the blanket back on to keep it from getting scratched. "Although a few scratches couldn't hurt its looks none."

As they rounded the curve by the cave in the hillside, Rachael had the sudden thought that that's where she'd seen the mirror before. But she didn't like to think of caves. So she didn't.

The next day they loaded Thora K.'s buffet onto the truck at the ranch and when they returned with it to the cottage a county sheriff's car was parked in front. Mr. Skinner, a deputy, several local men and one of the mining-company inspectors were gathered around it, smoking.

Her dad leaned out of the truck. "What's going on, Skinner?"

"Hutch, I think we found your brother," the deputy answered solemnly.

8

They buried Lon Maddon and held the inquest before Brandy returned from California. The probable cause of death was determined accidental.

"Nothing she can do about it now," Hutch said. "She'll find out soon enough when she gets home. No sense in spoiling your mother's vacation. Can't help but wonder if somebody didn't push him down that shaft and steal the whiskey."

Brandy bubbled with news of the twins and their families when Rachael and Hutch picked her up at the depot in Denver. They waited until they reached the cottage to tell her of Lon.

"Oh, God, I knew I should have moved it." The blood drained from Brandy's lips. "But I kept putting it off."

"What are you talking about, Mom?" Rachael poured her a cup of coffee.

"You're not the only one who doesn't think about things she doesn't want to, Rachael." She took a deep breath and closed her eyes. "Thora K. and I once stored a large free-standing mirror in the mine to—"

"We found it. And as Thora K. would have said, it was 'some hugly.'" Hutch spooned sugar into his cup. "But your daughter had to have it so we took it down to Sophie's along with a few other things Rachael wanted. That girl's going to grow up to be a junk collector."

Brandy stared at Rachael through the steam of her coffee. "So that's how it gets back there. You."

Her mother's gaze was haunted and so direct that Rachael squirmed. "We'll bring it up here again if you want it. I—"

"No. What will be will be, I guess. I just wish I knew how to get rid of it. Or what would happen to me if I did. Exactly where is it in the Gingerbread House?"

"I wanted it in my room but Grandma made us put it in the attic. She doesn't like it either. She said it was a gift to you from Grandfather McCabe a long time ago. Why did you keep it in the mine?"

"Oh . . . to get it out of the way. It's a big thing. Was it covered at all when you found it?"

"There was a blanket tied over it."

"Are you sure? That's odd. Maybe it didn't have anything to do with it. Maybe . . ."

"Anything to do with what?" Hutch asked.

But Brandy would say no more. Her delight over her trip to California seemed to have evaporated.

On December 7, 1941, the Japanese bombed Pearl Harbor and May Bell Smith dropped dead of a heart attack at the age of sixty-six. There was no known connection.

"You said December 11," Hutch said of the air strike.

"The only dates I can keep absolutely straight are 1492 and Rachael's birthday," his wife answered.

The Brandy Wine and several of the larger mines in the area were in full production. Nederland and the smaller town of Tungsten just below the dam showed renewed signs of life. No boom this time, but steady employment for the miners still in the area and others that would come. The Wolf Tongue Mill just above town belched forth steam for the war effort and dumped its wastes into Middle Boulder Creek.

Rachael was in her first year at the university in Boulder on the proceeds of the leasing of the Brandy Wine. She'd enrolled in liberal arts with an eye toward a teacher's certificate because her mother said she would become a writer and Rachael was out to prove her wrong for once. Her figure had reapportioned itself more to her satisfaction and she'd begun to date.

In January the abandoned house on what had been the Bar Double M burned to the snowy ground. Rumors of Nazi spies and "Jap" infiltrators sending signal fires made the rounds in Nederland. But Deputy Skinner told Hutch winter winds had whipped up the poorly doused remains of a fire left there by some cowboys who'd camped in the house the night before.

On Decoration Day Rachael helped her aging grandmother decorate the family plot in Columbia Cemetery in Boulder and then drove to Nederland in the secondhand Chevy her folks had given her on her eighteenth birthday.

When she reached the cottage her father was out, but her mother, as usual, refused to accompany her to Nederland's cemetery.

"Graveyards remind me of pink granite tombstones," was all she'd say.

Rachael walked across the valley. Decoration Day was often late in

Nederland because the cemetery sat on a shaded hillside and would normally be piled high with snow. But this year the thaw had begun early and though she picked up some mud on her penny loafers, she didn't have to walk in snow.

Flowers would still get pinched by night frost here, but she carried a trowel and clippers. Snow melt trickled down the gullies beside the road. Drifts hovered yet in the shadows where pines stood thickest.

Thora K.'s grave was bare of snow and Rachael cleared away winter-dried weeds. She rearranged the ring of white rocks that outlined the plot.

> Here lies the body
> Of Thora Killigrew Strock.
> But her spirit is in Cornwall,
> As it do belong to be.

Thora K. had talked so often of returning to Cornwall. But death hadn't waited.

Rachael straightened the weathered wooden marker where little Penny Strock slept beside her father, Corbin. Rachael wondered what he had looked like and why Penny's name had not been Penelope.

A sad job, but comforting in a way . . . as if these mounds of earth retained an essence of lost loved ones. She left Lon Maddon's grave till last. She didn't like to think of him lying all those years in the dark hole of the Brandy Wine.

Rachael brushed the dirt from her hands. Someone had laid a wreath on old Doc Seaton's grave. Nearby, Mr. and Mrs. Binder slept side by side, hemmed in together by a low concrete wall.

The faint scent of spring's beginnings pushing green through rocky soil . . . the cool dampness that retreating snow left on the air . . . the musty dirt smell clinging to her still . . .

A cloud covered the sun, taking away the warmth, muting the contrast of spring and winter colors.

Rachael shivered, slipped her arms into her sweater sleeves and picked up her trowel and clippers. Shaking off her thoughts of the past, she noticed a solitary figure standing between her and the road.

He had his back to her and wore the dark blue of an officer of the United States Navy.

She felt an unreasonable resentment that he should bring the present and a reminder of that awful war to this quiet place of the past.

As she walked behind him he turned. His liquid brown gaze skimmed over her without recognition. But Rachael stopped short.

Jerry Garrett had grown into his bones. She could no longer look him eye to eye.

He stood before two graves secluded in a darkened hollow formed by three pines and a bare thorny bush. Snow obliterated all but the small close-set headstones.

Catherine Garrett's stone leaned toward the newer marker of May Bell Smith.

A broken branch of the bush swayed on a silent breeze, trailing an ancient cobweb across Catherine's last resting place.

He seemed to realize Rachael hadn't left and he turned to her again, his look questioning and as cold as the snow on his mother's grave.

"Jerry?" she said a little nervously, still trying to adjust to the transformation of that boy into this broad-shouldered young man. "I'm Rachael Maddon. Remember?"

Rachael blushed with the memory of Brandy's prediction that she'd someday marry him.

"Rachael Maddon," he repeated as if his thoughts were returning from a distant place.

He glanced her over in a fashion more in keeping with the U. S. Navy. "You've changed some, Rachael Maddon." A brief smile.

Rachael felt like an awkward girl again. "Have you been back long?"

Jerry turned to the graves in the hollow. "I'm on my way to San Diego and the war," he said, as if reporting in to his mother.

"Won't you stop by the house when you're through here? Mom and Dad would love to see you too. They live in town now. Dad built a cottage right where you and . . . Catherine used to live."

"There's nothing here," he said with a last look at the hollow. "I might as well go with you now. I didn't really expect there would be anything," he added defensively and followed her to the road.

They walked slowly, pausing often so she'd have time to fill him in on the people he'd known during his year in Nederland, the sale of the ranch, her life in two houses and two towns. "I feel like a yo-yo. But here I've been yacking on like an idiot. You probably don't even remember half these people or the things I've—"

"I remember some of it. I remember finding that dead man in that cave, I can tell you. Had dreams about it for years."

"You found a dead man in a cave near Nederland? That would have been news I'd have heard about. You must have it mixed up with some other place."

He stopped. His hands had been jingling loose change in his pockets.

That stopped too. With his head tilted, Jerry Garrett looked at her in the oddest way.

"What's the matter?" Rachael wondered if anyone noticed her standing in the middle of the road with this tall, good-looking serviceman.

"You really blocked it out, didn't you?" He removed his hat by its bill and smoothed his hair, replacing the hat in the precise manner she'd seen young officers do so often of late.

"I see a lot of uniforms like yours on campus. The navy has a language-training course at C.U. Are you going to take it?"

"Just finished it. I leave for San Diego tomorrow."

"You mean you've been here—what—six weeks? Why didn't you get in touch with us?"

"I don't know, Rachael Maddon. I thought about it. But . . . I don't know." He shrugged and started jingling change again. "Who is May Bell Smith?" Jerry looked back up the road toward the cemetery.

"You know, I didn't know until last year? It was supposed to be a secret and Mom didn't tell us till May Bell died. Come home with me and ask Mom, she—"

"I'm asking you." He held her arm gently so she wouldn't continue down the hill. "Why is she buried next to my mother?"

"Because she's your grandmother."

"The bogus Smith Foundation that supported me through boarding school and a year of college?"

"Yes. Would you like to see the school? It's changed but—"

"My grandmother was Christine Pintor, not May Bell . . . May Bell. Was that the fat lady with the orange hair? You said she was a witch and she caught us peeking in her window."

"And you ran away, leaving me to face the music. I've never forgiven you that."

They were standing on the road between Doc Seaton's old cabin and the house that had been the Binders'. The birdbath and the gate were gone. Rachael wanted to be gone too. But he tightened his hold.

"Christine and May Bell were the same person? Why didn't she tell me then? Why all this Smith Foundation business?" The loneliness she remembered in the little boy had stayed to mature in the man. It echoed in his voice, hollowed out his eyes. "Why?"

"Because she was the town prostitute. And she didn't want you to know."

He let go of her arm as if it was hot. "You always did like to drop bombs on people, didn't you?"

They walked in silence down the hill and through town, Jerry studying the toes of his shoes. He paused on the bridge to stare into Middle Boulder Creek.

Rachael dared to slip her arm through his. "Jerry, my Grandfather Maddon was hanged for murder and no one even discusses my grandmother. It's not such a terrible thing."

"It takes a little getting used to, though." But she could feel his body relaxing.

"Stay for dinner and talk with the folks. They've spoken of you often. Wondered how you were doing."

He considered her solemnly over the edge of his shoulder. "Do I have to kiss you for it?"

Rachael laughed. "Oh, so you remember that too, do you?"

Before she could remove the arm she'd slipped through his, Jerry Garrett's arm swung at the elbow and came up behind her. It pressed along her back, tucking her against him, till his hand was on her neck under her hair.

His brief smile returned, with a hint of mischief this time and a rather startling maturity.

Rachael tried to regain her balance and think of some suitably flip remark. But he wrapped himself around her, kissing her not just with his lips but with his whole body. A series of dangerous squirming sensations prickled where she was caught up against his leg.

9

Jerry Garrett disappeared without trace after dinner that night, without even asking Rachael to write. She knew that one of her mother's predictions would prove wrong at least. He had no roots in Colorado. She'd never see him again. Or have any way of knowing if he were killed in the Pacific.

She must forget him. Yet she thought of him every time she saw a navy uniform or crossed the bridge over Middle Boulder Creek.

By the end of that summer Rachael didn't have to cross that particular bridge any longer.

Hutch Maddon had a heart attack in late August and moved into Community Hospital in Boulder. Brandy rented the cottage to a miner's family and moved into the Gingerbread House to be near him.

There were several offers to buy the cabin but Brandy refused them. "Jerry will need it to get away from this mausoleum sometimes."

"Jerry? Jerry Garrett? What's he got to do with it?" Rachael asked.

"Oh . . . he'll show up. One of these years."

When Hutch recovered enough to join them at the Gingerbread House, a weak heart plus his arthritis made him a semi-invalid and he chafed against the added restrictions on his life.

Brandy worried about him constantly.

He worried about the twins, truly separated now, Dan in Africa and Remy in the Pacific.

Rachael worried about the war spreading to the United States and the enemy dropping bombs on the Gingerbread House.

And Sophie worried about the men who came to call on Rachael. They were generally older servicemen with medical discharges or home on leave. Sophie thought they drank too much and wanted only one thing of her granddaughter.

When Rachael took up smoking and came home with alcohol on her breath, Sophie worried they were getting what they wanted.

One night when Rachael was a junior, she returned from the campus library to find the Gingerbread House ablaze with lights and her father on the living-room floor. Brandy knelt beside him holding his hand.

"We've called the doctor," Sophie said. Her head had the permanent nodding quiver that very old people often have and she used a cane to steady her balance. "I'm afraid it's his heart again."

Rachael sank down on the other side of him but when he opened his eyes they saw only her mother. "Bran?"

"I'm here. Don't try to talk."

". . . twins, Bran? This war—"

"They'll be all right, Hutch. They come back alive. I'm sure. I know . . . Hutch?"

But he stared past Brandy with a look of confusion. "That you, Lon?" Then he was just staring without seeing.

Rachael and her grandmother watched with horror as Brandy put the heel of her hand against his chest and gave it a swift hard blow with the other hand. "Oh, dear God, it's been so long since I've seen this done." She socked Hutch's chest again.

"Mom?" Rachael said in a half-stupor. "Mom, he's . . . Dad's dead."

"I know."

"Rachael, what's she doing? For heaven's sake stop her." Sophie waved her cane over them.

But Rachael could only sit on her heels and blink away tears as her mother tilted back her father's head and, with one hand pinching his nose, began blowing into his open mouth in slow, evenly measured breaths.

"Rachael, she's gone mad. Do something."

"Mom, please." She reached over Hutch Maddon's body but Brandy's outstretched arm shoved her back. This was a nightmare beyond any Rachael'd known as a child. Through a buzzing noise in her ears she heard the chime of the doorbell, was aware that her grandmother had left the room.

"Leave him be, Mrs. Maddon. Leave him be, I say." The doctor pulled Brandy to her feet and Rachael's dad stared sightlessly at the chandelier. "Rachael," the doctor said gently, "your mother needs you now."

She had to push on the floor to stand. *My mother needs me now.* Her legs wobbled under her but she managed to walk around her father and catch up Brandy in her arms. *My mother needs me . . . finally.*

Rachael steeled herself to make all the funeral arrangements. Brandy came out of her daze only long enough to cling, childlike, to her daughter. "It's all right, Mom. I'll take care of you."

She hoped now they'd finally establish that closer relationship for which she'd yearned so long, but when not clinging, Brandy was as elusive as ever.

The family plots in Nederland were full and they buried Hutch in Columbia Cemetery, leaving a space by John McCabe for Sophie. Rachael ordered the stone and it was later placed on his grave. When Brandy seemed a little more lifelike Rachael asked if she'd like to see it.

"No. It's pink granite and I don't want to see it."

"But how did you know?" And then Rachael remembered that day her mother refused to decorate graves because cemeteries reminded her of pink granite tombstones. Had she seen into the future?

Brandy sighed and shook her head. "Life will be so different now. Hutch was many things. But he was never boring."

Sophie Euler McCabe passed away two days before President Roosevelt did the same. She left the Gingerbread House to Rachael.

A month after the surrender of Germany, Rachael graduated from the University of Colorado with only Brandy left to attend the ceremonies. Her mother's graduation gift was enough money to pay for repairs on the roof and porches of the house.

By the time Japan surrendered, Rachael had a contract to teach fifth-graders in a Boulder school.

She'd been teaching only a few weeks when her mother announced she was leaving. "I can't stand this house all day. I've always wanted to see Mexico. I think I will before—"

"But why? You have a home here and I have a job."

"And you have your own life to get on with, Rachael. Your dad left me pretty well off and if I'm careful I ought to be able to see some of the world."

"But I thought we'd use that money to fix up the house. It needs so much."

"The house is your problem and you're welcome to it."

Rachael was alone for the first time in her life. And lost.

10

Rachael saved enough money to have the house painted that winter. On weekends she painted woodwork and stripped furniture.

The first year on her own, she discovered two things about herself. The tedious process of painting, sanding and varnishing drove her nuts.

So did fifth-graders.

"Why don't you try writing?" her mother wrote the next summer when Rachael had admitted this in a letter. Brandy was now in Canada.

"I'll be damned if I will," Rachael thought, and went back to weeding a flowerbed. "The old know-it-all, anyway."

But as she daydreamed among weeds and blossoms and sunshine, she thought of a young girl and boy exploring a cave and discovering a body there. Then she thought up a set of circumstances that would bring them to that cave.

Before she knew it she'd looked into their backgrounds and personalities, considered names for them . . .

Rachael set her trowel down and stared at a scarlet petunia. When had she begun to fashion stories out of idle daydreams?

As she ate her solitary dinner in the gloomy kitchen she thought of all she'd do to this room if only she had the money.

The imaginary children scampered, just out of sight around the corner of the pantry.

Vowing she'd never mention this to her mother, Rachael hauled the typewriter she'd used for college papers down to the kitchen table and set to work. She sent the completed story to *The Saturday Evening Post.* It returned with a printed rejection and an unkind remark about her spelling.

The school year had begun and she put aside her lesson plans long enough to correct the spelling, retype it and send it to another magazine. The story came back with a suggestion that it be slanted toward the children's market. This she did and it returned again. Had she considered expanding it into a book-length manuscript for children?

It would soon be Christmas and Brandy planned to stop in to spend the holidays before going on to Florida. Rachael hid all signs of her writing life and seethed over the money her mother frittered away on travel, while she worked so hard just to make the house livable.

"How's *The Secret of the Lost Cave* coming?" Brandy asked the first evening after her arrival. "Or is it *The Mystery of the Lost Cave?*"

"I don't know what you're talking about." Rachael felt as if the bottom had fallen out of her stomach. She decided to rename the book she'd fashion out of her rejected story, *The Hidden Cave.*

"Well, you must be getting to it one of these years."

Two days before Christmas Rachael had a blind date with a sailor whose sister was the other fifth-grade teacher. After a movie he led her around a corner and down a flight of stairs to a basement door under a store. "Buddy of mine's giving a party."

"I didn't know there were apartments here," she said.

"Wasn't meant to be, but all the G.I.'s coming back for school—you gotta be Truman to get a room in this town."

At first Rachael could see nothing through the cloud of cigarette smoke. The air was even staler and more packed with the human smell than a fifth-grade classroom.

The first voice she recognized was Frank Sinatra's. He moaned over the buzz of conversation from somewhere.

"Larry? You got here, you son of a bitch. I want you to meet . . ."

Larry disappeared into the smoke. A glass was shoved into Rachael's hand and the press of bodies pushed her back onto a hard bench.

Steam pipes crossed the ceiling. A concrete floor, two daybeds along the wall, a table, a stove and a refrigerator.

Men outnumbered women. Wild gestures denoted planes diving and bombs exploding. Wives and girl friends sat around the edges looking as bored as Rachael felt.

Her interest picked up instantly when the crowd parted and she saw a man sitting on a mattress on the floor across the room.

He looked older, thinner, harder. His hair had grown out from its military haircut. But he was still the man who'd kissed her on the bridge over Middle Boulder Creek.

All my mother's predictions, Rachael thought, staring into her drink. *It's as if I don't have any control over my own life.* Melting ice left a tiny eddy of foam in the center of the bourbon and Seven, reminding her of a whirlpool. She imagined herself being dragged down into one, imagined what it would be like to know you'd drown in a few seconds. She decided it'd be similar to having a fortune-teller for a mother.

If she weren't so polite, she'd walk out the door and home right now. But Larry would think she'd ditched him. *Rachael, just because he's in town doesn't mean you'll marry him.*

Larry carried two glasses across the room and tried to hand her one. "Sorry, I got sidetracked. Didn't mean to leave you over here like a wall flower."

Rachael refused the drink. "Listen, I have a headache. Would you mind if I just walked on home? It's not that far from here."

"I'll walk you home."

"No, you stay and chat with your friends." She slipped into her coat. Jerry had gotten to his feet across the room.

"Well, if you don't mind . . ."

"I don't. Really. And thanks for the movie." She was soon in the fresh cold air and up the concrete steps.

"Rachael? Rachael Maddon?" Jerry said behind her.

She stopped under the streetlight and shrugged. "Hello, Jerry. How are you?"

Jerry had registered at the university on the G.I. Bill and was due to start the second semester. He'd been out of the service for over a year, wandering. "I was so sure I wouldn't live through the war I hadn't made any plans," he said as they walked toward the Gingerbread House. "Sounds melodramatic, but—"

"Why did you choose Colorado? You've lived so many other places." It must be strange to have no particular place or people.

"I don't really know. I remember liking the mountains. Even though my mother died here, I had some good memories of the place."

Rachael thought it would be horrible to have nothing personal, of one's own. To be dependent on the kind of thing like the party they'd just left.

She was suspicious of the welling of sympathy she felt for his aloneness, of her awareness of him beside her, of her mother's inane predictions . . . "I'm damned if I will!"

"What?" He stopped jingling the change in his pocket. Snowflakes began to fall. They stuck in his hair.

"Nothing. Looks like we may have snow for Christmas after all." Christmas . . . an awful time to be alone. "This is where I live." She stopped at the gate of the Gingerbread House.

"You've changed, Rachael. You're different."

I'm an old tired woman at twenty-three. "So have you."

The streetlight on the corner accentuated the hollows around his eyes. "Well . . . it was good seeing you again . . ."

"Jerry? I'm starving and I think I'm going in there and scramble up some eggs. Would you like to come in? My coffee's not the best but my eggs are out of this world."

"I had the feeling you were trying to avoid me tonight."

"I thought you probably had a date with you," she lied. "And wouldn't want to renew old acquaintances." She opened the gate and paused to look at the Gingerbread House. The repairs and paint made it look happier, even at night with snow falling.

"Do you rent a room here?"

"My grandmother left it to me. Mom is visiting for the holidays and by the looks of all the lights on she's probably still up." *And she won't be a bit surprised to see you. Damn her eyes.*

INTERIM

After Brandy left for Florida, Rachael wrote *The Hidden Cave.* It was published, but not before an editor changed the title to *Secret of the Lost Cave.* She sank the small advance into improvements on the Gingerbread House.

She continued to see Jerry Garrett because she couldn't help herself. They were married the next Christmas. Rachael wore her mother's wedding veil.

Brandy returned for the wedding and the night-before-it talk. "Now, the first thing is, there's more to a successful marriage than sex."

"Well, I should hope so. Mom, this really isn't necessary. I know about male and female anatomy. I'm twenty-four years old, for heaven's sake."

But Brandy went beyond ovum and sperm, penis and vagina. "I know you've discovered you have one. What I'm saying is, there's nothing wicked in using it."

"Mother!"

"You're still a prude, aren't you?" Cobalt-blue eyes twinkled. "Rachael, that's a healthy young man you're getting there. If you're going to have to wash his socks the rest of your life, you might as well enjoy him."

* * *

The renovation of the Gingerbread House slowed as Rachael invested her earnings as a writer and teacher into living expenses and helping her husband through law school.

Up in the attic the wedding mirror slumbered on under its dusty blanket, forgotten.

Brandy had invested in Dan's used-car business and so on the proceeds expanded her travels worldwide. Every year or so she'd stop for a few weeks at the Gingerbread House, and Rachael and Jerry often caught her writing in a leather-bound diary.

"Do you suppose she's writing her memoirs?"

"Probably her version of *Gulliver's Travels.*" Jerry thought his mother-in-law a dear but slightly batty old lady.

When Jerry settled in an established law firm in Boulder (he was offered an excellent position in Poughkeepsie but Rachael wouldn't move), she quit teaching and devoted herself to her writing. The Gingerbread House gradually acquired an all-new heating system, electrical wiring and plumbing. Whole rooms were replastered.

But other large houses in the neighborhood were being chopped into apartments for student housing or torn down. Rachael attended town-council meetings to fight proposed zoning changes as downtown Boulder crept nearer.

The Garretts wanted children but as the years passed they began to give up hope. The doctors couldn't tell them why they remained childless. Rachael blamed her mother's advice on that night before her wedding.

"Nonsense," Brandy said on one of her visits. "You'll have one child. A daughter. And with your writing and obsession with this house, one will be all you can handle."

"When?" Rachael asked defensively. "Since you know everything."

"Nineteen-fifty-eight," her mother replied. "Which reminds me. I haven't seen the Orient yet."

"Mom, don't you think you should settle down?" Brandy would be seventy-five on her next birthday.

"Far too much time for that. The nursing home looms."

Brandy was in Hong Kong when the triumphant letter reached her. "The baby's due in early May," Rachael wrote.

Huh-uh. May 23. That's one date I remember for sure. Brandy sat on a high-backed rattan chair in her hotel lobby and stared at the letter. *This baby I've got to see. It ought to be interesting. There'll be two of us.*

She planned to arrive on May 22, but due to a missed plane connection in Hawaii, Brandy's taxi drove up to the gate of the Gingerbread House about ten-thirty on the night of the twenty-third. It was dark and locked but she found the hidden key on the porch and had the driver carry in her bags.

"Must be at the hospital having me," she said to the quiet house. Carrying her cosmetic case and leaving the other suitcases in the hall for Jerry to bring up when he returned, she mounted the stairs. She was too old and tired to carry suitcases anymore or to travel either, she decided. This last trip had about done her in. *But still pretty spry for seventy-eight,* she thought with satisfaction. There'd even been an article in *Time* magazine last spring with her picture, entitled "The Amazing Traveling Grandmother."

Brandy flipped the switch inside the door of the guestroom. She sat on the bed with a grateful sigh to remove her shoes.

Rachael had redecorated the room again. A rocker that had been broken and in the attic for years sat beside the bed, repaired and refinished. New paint and carpet. "That girl, honestly."

As she turned her head, something burnished glowed at the corner of her eye. "Oh, no . . ."

She rose slowly to face the wedding mirror, polished and dusted, proudly displayed beside the wardrobe. "Rachael . . . it's always Rachael . . ."

Brandy's body shook but she straightened Brandy's shoulders. "We may be old and travel-worn, you ancient hunk of ugly garbage, but we're still fit and a long way from any stroke, so . . ."

The mirror didn't reflect her image. Instead it showed her a moving picture of Rachael writhing on a table, her sheeted knees drawn up and parted.

A ripping sound exploded in her head as the glass of the wedding mirror cracked in a jagged diagonal line across the top.

At that moment, some ten blocks away, Rachael gave birth to Shay Garrett in Community Hospital.

Jerry returned later that night to find the Gingerbread House lighted and unlocked, suitcases in the hall and his mother-in-law unconscious on the floor of the guestroom. When he couldn't revive her, he carried her out to his car and raced back to the hospital.

Rachael's delight over her new baby was diminished by her mother's stroke.

Completely paralyzed at first, Brandy Maddon was removed to a nursing home, where in time she regained the use of her muscles. But her speech did not return and her eyes looked on the world with a blank disinterest. She would walk when led, eat when food was set before her, dress in clothes that were handed to her. Sometimes she'd smile as if a happy memory had floated past. On Sundays Rachael would bring her to the house for dinner so she could have some contact with her mother even if it was only physical.

When Rachael had unpacked Brandy's bags she'd found a parcel wrapped in brown paper, and written across the wrapping, "For Shay Garrett on her wedding day."

"She even knew the baby's name." Rachael shivered and put the parcel in the bottom drawer of the buffet that Thora K.'s family brought from Cornwall.

Rachael redecorated the guestroom again, as if to erase what had happened to Brandy there. The wedding mirror returned to the attic.

Shay Garrett entered kindergarten the year someone assassinated President John F. Kennedy. She was attending Boulder High School when the war ended in Vietnam and when Nixon was pardoned for the Watergate scandal. And in the year of the nation's bicentennial, Shay enrolled as a freshman at the University of Colorado.

Several times as she was growing up and happened to be in the attic with her mother, Shay uncovered the mirror and asked about it.

"A wedding present from your great-grandfather to my mother. It's very old," Rachael would say in a reverent voice, and cover it up again so it wouldn't get dusty.

With the end of World War II the mines had closed in Nederland. The town subsisted on summer visitors and eventually developed into a bedroom community for people working in Boulder and Denver who desired to live in the mountains. A ski area opened to the west of it and provided additional income in winter.

The cottage Hutch Maddon built on the site of the Strock cabin deteriorated with years of careless renters and in 1973 Jerry Garrett had it torn down. In its place he erected an A-frame cabin as modern and as different from the Gingerbread House as he could devise.

By this time tourists and fire had eradicated almost all signs of the short-lived town of Tungsten below the dam.

Shay's twin uncles and her aunts, their families grown and gone, returned to Colorado to retire because California had grown too crowded. They moved into condominium apartments near a country club and its golf course. And so they were on hand when Shay met and eventually announced she would marry a man named Marek Weir. . . .

Part III
Brandy

1

The Gingerbread House stood aloof on its hill at the edge of town. Moonlight sat in puddles among its gables and along the miniature widow's walk. It traced the intricacies of the wrought-iron fence in shadow patterns across the irrigation ditch.

A carriage drawn by a skittish horse approached on the road beside the ditch and turned to descend the hill. It brought a drowsy whinny from the pasture next to the house.

And then all was still once more . . . a silence made up of the mere brushing together of leaves and the peace of sound that is so familiar it isn't heard, doesn't disturb. A brief rustling from the hen house. The far-off chirp of a prairie-dog sentinel. The background clatter of crickets. A breathy hiss from a prowling housecat.

All color drenched in the softness of moonlight and shadow. All scent muted by the spice of drying grass and sage.

Brandy McCabe poured steaming water into the dishpan.

Nora clanked plates against the metal sink. "Don't know what you young folks expect nowadays." She made a clucking sound to show her disgust.

"The time has long since passed, Nora, when fathers choose marriage partners for their children." Brandy kept her voice controlled so the shaking inside her wouldn't show. *But most people don't have John McCabe for a father.*

"Well, at least Mr. Strock is young."

"Nora—"

"You could've married Tom Trevors or the Arnett boy before that. What do you expect your father to do, now you've waited so long?" Nora slipped a plate into the dishpan of rinse water.

"I don't wish to discuss this any further." Brandy picked out the plate and dried it by feel, her eyes on the night silhouette of mountain range outside the kitchen window. Her own rigid reflection and the dim globe of the light from behind her looked pasted onto the landscape.

Brandy tried to ignore the murmur of the argument still waging in the dining room, the occasional outburst . . .

"But, John, you've not even given us time to see to a trousseau."

What possible need would I have of a trousseau living in a miner's shack in Nederland? Brandy knew her mother was trying and she was grateful. But she had little hope that Sophie McCabe could dissuade her husband from a course he'd set his mind to.

Brandy, unlike her mother, had always been able to reason, cajole, tease or flatter him into at least considering her wishes. She'd held out these last two weeks and through Mrs. Strock's interminable visits in the parlor, assured that she could delay and eventually cancel the wedding planned for her in the morning. But Brandy'd realized at the table tonight this time her father was determined she should not have her way.

She clearly had no choice but to carry out her half-formed plan. After wiping the last kettle, Brandy hung the dish towel to dry and removed her apron. *I just pray I'm brave enough to carry it through.*

As she stepped into the hall, John McCabe exploded from the dining room. "That's my last word," he said over his shoulder. "I'll hear no more of it, woman."

Then he saw his daughter and added, "Or from you, miss. Tomorrow at this time you'll be Mrs. Corbin Strock."

Brandy, holding her head as proudly and defiantly as she dared, lifted her skirts and ascended the staircase without answering him.

She had no real power to oppose him and would probably have none with a husband. As if she'd been nothing but a pampered slave all her life and just discovered the fact.

"Bran?" Her brother stepped out of the shadows of the upstairs hall.

"Oh, Elton." She clutched his arm and for a moment wanted only to be weak and cling to him.

"Listen, I have a plan. I'll talk to Pa. Convince him you're not sane. He couldn't let you marry then. I'll remind him of every crazy thing you've said lately and make up a few to boot. It's worth a try."

"Thank you, Elton." *For all the good it will do, beloved brother.*

"I'd have said something before now but I thought sure you'd be able to talk him out of it. He always used to listen to you."

"Be careful, Elton." She raised on tiptoe to kiss his cheek and turned into her room.

Brandy stood on her toes again to reach the switch above the lightbulb and caught her reflection in the mirror that stood next to her writing desk. A wedding veil of fine lace hung from a bronze hand on one side of the mirror's frame.

"You. This is all your fault," she whispered.

If she'd never seen the intriguing pictures in its glass, she might never have had the lofty idea of attending the university without any conception of what she wished to study.

"I feel unformed," she'd told her father when she'd backed out of her betrothal to Mr. Trevors. "I want to learn . . . anything, everything. There's so much we don't know, cannot imagine."

"Nothing unformed about you, girl. You've got the figure of an hourglass. Only women up there are them that're too ugly to get themselves a man," John McCabe answered. "Or too dumb to want one. A man, that's what you need. And babies. They'll settle you down and make you forget all this nonsense."

Brandy touched a cold hand on the mirror's frame. "If you're so magic, help me escape this abominable marriage."

If she'd never spoken of the pictures she'd seen in the mirror, there wouldn't be such malicious rumors about her floating around the town. And other beaux would have called at the Gingerbread House. Her father wouldn't have been forced to pounce on the rough miner from Nederland to wed his only daughter.

"There'll be sleek and powerful machines racing across the nation on ribbons of paved roadways," she told Mr. Heimer at the baker's shop when he'd joked about the concept of the horseless carriage. "Horses, even the trolley and locomotive will be replaced by machines that'll fly and glide and hover and carry people wherever they wish to go. I've seen it. I know."

Or at the dinner table, in a fit of euphoria, she'd broken out with, "I've seen men walk on the surface of the moon and under the seas—"

"So have I," her father said. "At Werely's Saloon. Sophie, the girl's got into the liquor."

But Brandy didn't tell where she'd seen these fantastic things, of sneaking up to the attic to see if the wedding mirror was in a mood to perform its magic, of waiting hours before it—sometimes with a candle in the middle of the night. Until Brandy figured out that it worked only during electrical storms or if its frame felt warm to the touch.

When there was no storm but the hands felt warm, the pictures in the glass were of a different nature. Always of one figure. A young woman with pale hair and darkened skin, in a strange form of dress that was often more a state of undress. Embarrassed, Brandy'd wanted to look away but couldn't.

She'd cautioned herself not to speak of these things—of giant animals browsing on trees, a primitive people tearing meat from bones with their teeth.

But every now and then she'd forget herself. And that was enough to seal her fate.

She knelt with her elbows on the hard lid of the cedar chest at the foot of the bed. *Dear Lord, give me the courage to do what I must do tonight. And please forgive me for . . .*

Brandy's eyes flew open. Could she really expect help from that quarter? The Lord, after all, was another man and the Bible spoke clearly of obeying one's elders and "cleaving unto" a husband and then obeying him. . . .

Our Father, who art in heaven—just this once Brandy wished God was a woman. There might be more understanding of her plight in heaven if that were the case. But she finished the Lord's Prayer for good measure and went to sit by the window.

She'd have to wait until the house was quiet and everyone slept. She leaned out to breathe in dry cool air, hoping to regulate the alarming spasms of her heart beat.

The carriage horse stood, a motionless shadow, near the open-ended shed that sheltered him in unpleasant weather. He was no saddle horse but both she and Elton had ridden him bareback around the pasture when their father was away.

Tonight Brandy would attempt to ride him to Denver. Not by the road, but along the tracks of the interurban where she'd be less easily seen. With only the moon to light her way. Astride a carriage horse with her skirts drawn up, shamelessly exposing her limbs. Why hadn't she provided herself with a riding costume that had a split skirt?

Because she was no horsewoman. Hadn't needed a costume. She'd probably fall off and break her neck. Or lead the horse to step into a prairie-dog hole.

Her plan was mad. But she had no other.

When she arrived, if she did, Brandy would throw herself on the mercy of Aunt Harriet Euler, plead to be hidden until she could make further plans. Brandy was a favorite of her aunt's and Harriet Euler disliked John McCabe to the point of hatred. Since she was a spinster there'd be no added male interference.

The thought of marriage and the intimacies implied by "cleaving unto" held nothing but terror for Brandy. Largely because she didn't understand the nature of those intimacies.

They must be nasty because they were never discussed.

Her observations of animals at certain periods of the year did not reassure her.

Curiosity had led her to examine her body in the bath, using her fingers to feel what she couldn't see. The result had led more to confusion and guilt than to illumination.

Scarcely aware of the high-pitched but quiet hum at her back, Brandy went on with her tortured reasoning.

Were the strange sensations that sometimes attacked her body connected to this cleaving? Did they happen to others or just to her?

How could these experiences she feared be so terrible when many timid women went through them calmly, happily?

There were times when certain gentlemen seemed most attractive to Brandy. . . .

But not Mr. Strock. And not in a forced marriage. This was the twentieth century, if only the beginning, and . . .

The hum grew in intensity, broke into her thoughts.

Brandy turned to see the wedding veil float to the floor in a billow of lace. She bent to pick it up, realizing the mirror was preparing to do its magic.

Standing back to look at the glass, she saw not her reflection but dark gray twisting clouds that made the entwined hands surrounding it glow faintly green.

Brandy didn't understand. It wasn't storming.

She dropped the veil and put her hands over her ears as the humming tried to pierce her head. It had never seemed so loud before, or so threatening.

Brandy started to back away, but the clouds seeped from the base of the mirror to swirl across the floor and imprison her.

A sickness worse than the typhoid clamped upon her body.

A cracking sound ripped the air and she was thrown down, submerged in the horrid cloud. There was no floor beneath it.

Brandy fell into a blackness filled with the sound of harsh guttural screams.

2

The awful screaming ended. Brandy knew she had died.

She rose through silent layers of black. Sickness heaved inside her. Was she rising toward heaven after all? She'd imagined it to be a more pleasant experience.

She whirled in slow sweeping circles that stopped suddenly. Had she arrived?

No. The web of the wedding veil's lace lay in a jumble around her face. Brandy pushed it away and gagged.

Why would a veil go to heaven? Perhaps it was an angel's gown.

Perhaps she'd merely swooned and imagined the rest.

But she lay on a cushion of some kind with red and pink figures that her blurred vision couldn't identify.

Brandy raised herself on her hands. Nearby on the cushion lay a long crumpled shape. She blinked and focused on the wizened face of an ancient woman . . . with the sightless stare of death in her eyes.

Brandy swayed and fell back to the floor. The dizzy swirling began again. *This isn't heaven, but a dream. I must waken to be rid of it.*

She fought the sickness and the suffocating texture of the cushion to push herself over onto her back.

The wedding mirror loomed above her, looking immense from her position. How did it get here?

Because this is a dream. Wake up, Brandy McCabe. Wake up.

"Do you think lightning struck the house?" someone said far away.

"Shay? . . ." A man's voice, closer.

Brandy raised her head to see a white-framed doorway. A rush of movement and a lady and gentleman entered together, bumping against each other in their haste.

"Shay?" The man knelt next to Brandy. "What happened?"

"Mom? My God!" The lady fell to the floor beside the ancient woman.

"Not Shay. Brandy," Brandy explained to the man through the sick dryness of her mouth. His hair was fluffy and so long it covered the top half of his ears.

"Do you think . . . well, okay. Lie still, honey. I'll get it." He rushed from the room.

Brandy clamped her eyes tightly until colored lights played across the inside of her eyelids. But when she opened them the dream hadn't ended.

"What was it? An earthquake?" the lady asked Brandy. "It must have frightened her to death." Her face crumpled as she drew the dead woman to her breast and wept into snow-white hair, rocking back and forth.

These people spoke so rapidly Brandy had trouble separating the words to make sense of them. At least they spoke English.

The man returned to hold a glass to Brandy's lips. She realized that her hair was loose and down. But before she could wonder how or when it had happened, she'd swallowed some of the liquid in the glass. It wasn't water. It exploded on her tongue to burn down her throat. She sat up gasping. Tears blurred the room away.

"That was brandy!"

"Well, that is what you asked for. Here, let's see if you can stand," the man said gently. "Rachael, stop that. Help me with Shay."

Dizziness forced Brandy to cling to him as he drew her to her feet. "Can you tell us what happened, Shay?"

Brandy could only stare at her bare legs and feet. Both pairs seemed too long and thin. She wore a gossamer garment that stopped at her . . . *Dear God, I'm all but naked.*

She looked up at the man in astonishment but he seemed to notice neither her embarrassment nor her exposed state.

And then, in the wedding mirror, she saw it wasn't her he held but the young woman with the pale hair and darkened skin Brandy'd seen in the same looking glass at the Gingerbread House. But where he clasped the woman in the mirror, Brandy felt the heat of his hands on the same place —on bare skin, for the garment had no sleeves either.

A jagged crack ran slantwise across the top of the mirror, where none had been before. It slashed the strange face in two.

Brandy swayed and so did the woman with the light hair.

"Shay? God . . . Rachael, will you help me here?"

But Rachael moaned and continued rocking her lifeless burden.

He guided Brandy to a ruffled bed, set her on the edge and picked up a shiny white object.

Turning it over, he poked square buttons and put one end to his ear. He sat beside her taking her hand in a familiar way. "It's all right, honey, I'm calling the twins."

Brandy, too stunned to pull away, sat half-naked on a bed with a strange man holding her hand.

"Hello, Remy? Jerry. I've got bad news. Your mother died . . . just now. Sorry to break it like this . . . on the floor in Shay's room . . . I don't know. Did you feel an earthquake out where you are? No? Must have been a sonic boom or something. I don't think lightning would do that and there's no fire. Anyway, it shook us up here and broke a few things. Might have frightened your mother into a final stroke . . . yeah, we'll never know. Listen, Remy, could you and Dan get back here quick? And bring Ruth and Elinore. I've got two hysterical women on my hands and need help."

"That is a telephone," Brandy announced when he replaced the ear- and mouthpiece all in one.

"Yeah . . . uh . . . listen, we better get you and your mom out of here, huh?" He lifted a strand of her hair, as she imagined a lover might, and drew it out away from her shoulder.

The hair he held gleamed pale blond but she could feel the pull on her scalp as it moved through his fingers.

I'm in the body of another. That was why these people could know her when she didn't know them. She studied the ring on the body's finger, a lone diamond set in a plain setting. It caught the light and cast dazzle spots across the ceiling. "This is madness."

"Hey, it's going to be all right. Your old dad can handle this." He didn't look old enough to be the father of a grown daughter.

"You're shivering. You look like you're in some kind of shock. What a night for the old lady to kick off." He actually patted her bare leg as he rose from the bed.

This room was very much like hers in shape, but smaller, more crowded. The closet from which he brought a robe was in the same position as her own. The robe, a quilted thing of powder blue, had matching fuzzy slippers.

"Here, these'll warm you up."

Brandy was grateful not so much for the warmth as for the more modest covering.

This body was named Shay. These people were Shay's parents. The dead woman was Shay's grandmother. These facts whirled about her in the confusion.

Where is Brandy?

"Rachael?" He lifted Shay's mother to her feet.

She turned in his arms and hid her face against him. "Oh, Jerry."

"You knew this had to happen soon." Jerry stroked Rachael's hair. "She was ninety-eight. Now I want you two to go down and make some coffee. Shay, come help your mother."

Shay's head throbbed and Brandy felt none too steady on the new legs. But she didn't want to stay in this room.

When Brandy took her arm, Rachael leaned against her. As they left, Brandy turned to see Shay's father pick up the strange telephone again. What she'd thought was a cushion was really a rug that fit to the baseboards. It continued into the hall.

Rachael stopped at the head of a staircase and lifted a framed picture from the floor. "At least it isn't broken," she said dully. "Must have been an earthquake. What else would knock things off the wall that way?" She held it up. Tears streamed down her face. "Oh, Shay, she's gone forever."

Brandy stared. It was a picture of herself, Brandy McCabe, and a man she'd never seen. A photograph she'd never sat for.

This dream fascinated her more and more. Would she remember when she woke? As if . . . as if instead of watching the entertainments in the wedding mirror she was now a part of them . . . living them. Did its magic extend this far?

Jerry came up behind them. "Girls, I thought I told you to go to the kitchen."

Her thoughts in a turmoil but her senses painfully acute to her surroundings, Brandy descended a staircase with the same curve as the one at home. But here the steps were cushioned with that figured rug and the walls papered with the same design, tiny red and pink flowers gathered into nosegays. The air was close in this house.

Brandy stopped at the foot of the staircase. The buffet was unfamiliar, but the entry hall, the coat tree . . .

She ran a hand over the balustrade. Black walnut inlaid with rosewood, just as Grandfather McCabe had ordered it made when the house was built.

"Is . . . is this the Gingerbread House?"

The people turned to stare at her. They looked so lifelike.

"I'm in a dream. You are not real."

"Oh, baby," Rachael said. "I've been upset. I didn't realize . . . I mean, you were there. Jerry, I'm worried. Look at her eyes."

"That's what I've been trying to tell you. The brandy didn't work. Let's try some coffee, quick."

"Is that what you do for shock?" Rachael drew Brandy around the base of the stairs and into the kitchen.

"Hell, I don't know."

The kitchen was where it should be, its windows and doors in their proper places, the cupboards had increased in number, but the strange and gleaming objects . . . the floor covered with small bricks that were really one piece of linoleum made to look like bricks . . . white walls . . . red and copper tones . . . a strong shielded light set close to the ceiling.

This is the Gingerbread House in a future time. Brandy's excitement grew. The wedding mirror had outdone itself.

She and Rachael sat at a table with a booth arrangement for seating. The man, Jerry, made coffee. His pants and shirt fit shockingly close to his body.

Rachael's gown clung to her slender frame with no sign of stays beneath, her face was painted, her lashes darkened. Traces of red lip rouge lined her mouth.

The planes of Rachael's face were similar to Sophie McCabe's, her hair thick and with the same red tints but without the streaks of gray. Was this woman a descendant of Elton's perhaps? The Gingerbread House would go to her brother on the death of her parents.

The coffee was made quickly and tasted like it—all the bitterness without the rich flavor and smell.

"I forgot, you'll want milk in that," Shay's father said when Brandy made a face.

"I don't like milk."

"You don't like milk?" He slid into the booth next to his wife. "Then tell me why the milk bill's gone out of sight."

"Perhaps you lost it."

"This is the strangest night I've ever lived." Rachael rubbed her forehead. "Next you'll be telling us you don't like chicken."

"I'm not terribly fond of it."

Rachael took a paper package from a pocket in her gown and shook out a prerolled cigarette. It was the longest cigarette Brandy'd ever seen.

The man makes the coffee and his wife smokes the cigarette!

"Jerry, we have a problem here," Rachael said through a cloud of tobacco smoke. "Do you think we should call a doctor?"

"Nobody'd come to the house. We'd have to take her into the emergency room. This isn't physical anyway. I'll talk to Gale in the morning if she isn't more like herself. Shay, drink all that coffee."

"Morning . . . Jerry, the wedding."

Brandy choked on Shay's coffee and looked again at the gleaming diamond on the long slender finger. So Shay was to have a wedding in the morning also.

"Oh, Jesus, I'll have to call Marek. Where's that party of his?"

"At the Dark Horse. It's a singles bar. They won't page him there. I'll be all right now. You better drive out."

Two older couples arrived to take charge. The men were twins and apparently the dead woman's sons and Rachael's brothers. One stouter than the other. They were both bald except for gray fringes.

But their wives . . . gray-haired ladies wearing men's pants!

Others arrived to carry the dead grandmother out the front door.

Someone pressed a sandwich into her hand. It was made of nearly raw beef and pasty-textured bread that glued itself to Shay's teeth.

Rachael sighed and gave way to tears again.

"Now, Rachael, it was a blessing and you know it," one of the aunts said. "Be happy your mother's released from that zombie state."

"You're right, Ruth, I know. It's just the shock. We'll have to postpone the wedding now." And Rachael added as an audible whisper, "That's one good thing that came of tonight."

This dream is lasting too long. It's all very interesting but I must wake in time to ride to Denver tonight. What if she wakened too late to avoid the marriage to Mr. Strock?

Jerry returned with Shay's bridegroom, Marek. His clothing fit even tighter than that of the older men. He slid into the booth and kissed the end of Shay's nose in front of a room full of people before Brandy could jerk it out of the way.

Black hair fluffed at an angle toward a sun-brown face and completely covered his ears. He smelled of spice and alcohol. Violet eyes probed hers.

"You all right, Shay?" he whispered.

Brandy couldn't keep Shay's mouth from falling open when, under cover of the table, he slipped a warm hand through a space between the robe's buttons and then between Shay's legs, pressing her thigh snugly against his own.

3

Brandy McCabe stood before the wedding mirror in Shay's room and in Shay's body.

She'd closed the door, pulled the shades and undressed. Curiosity had overcome embarrassment.

When the mirror's hands felt warm to the touch and it had shown her the image of this body before, Brandy assumed the shape to be distorted by the age of the glass and the mysterious nature of the mirror.

But it was the same now. Tall, with straight, slender angles. Willowy, shapeless, underfed. The tiny breasts high and pointing. The teeth straight too, perfect, every one in place and evenly spaced. The armpits as hairless as a child's.

In a thin band across the nipples and another across Shay's lower private parts the skin was white, more in keeping with the fair hair.

Brandy stared back at the widening gold-flecked eyes in the mirror. Sun? *Dear heaven, she didn't go out into the broad daylight wearing no more than what would cover those light bands?*

She pinched the body's forearm and felt the pain, watched gooseflesh rise on naked skin and felt the chill.

Blushing and feeling rather wicked, Brandy redressed in the two-piece garment of yellow fluff and slipped into the robe.

Marek had jolted her conviction that this was a fantastic dream devised by the wedding mirror. There could be nothing more real than the feel of his hand between her legs. Even if they weren't her legs.

She was torn between wanting to investigate some of the objects in this room and her haste to be back in her own world and off to Aunt Harriet Euler's.

I mustn't succumb to panic but must find a logical solution. How did one apply logic to the impossible?

If she fell asleep in this body, would she wake in her own and just in time for the wedding she'd planned to avoid? Or would she wake still in this time and therefore avoid it anyway?

I don't have the knowledge to exist in this world long. Or the immodesty, I'm afraid. She'd be found out soon enough. And then what?

A crackling noise startled her, like fire eating away at small sticks. She traced it to the metal baseboard stretching along the wall under the window. Heat emanated from a crack in the . . . *not a baseboard but some version of a radiator*. Why would anyone stoke a furnace in the summer?

Or was it summer in this time? Brandy raised the shade and the window. The screening had been pushed out at the bottom on metal poles.

The smell of recent rain. Had there been a thunderstorm in this world that caused the wedding mirror to work and bring her here? Another odor, acrid and disagreeable, reminding her faintly of pitch. Giant trees dressed in summer leaves.

Where she'd known a pasture, a large building loomed, blocking all trace of the mountains. Atop the building an enormous orange word in lights. The letters spelled LETOM but the L and the E were backward.

No carriage horse to take her to Aunt Harriet. There'd be no Aunt Harriet in this world.

She placed a hand on each side of the mirror's cold frame. All traces of the enamel chips had been polished from the bronze. "You've enticed and toyed with me enough. Whatever you've done, you must undo."

But the wedding mirror stood hard against her, the glass clear of all but the body of a woman called Shay and the frightening distortion caused by the crack that separated her eyes from her nose.

Was this a punishment from heaven because she d planned to run away rather than marry Mr. Strock?

Brandy knelt at the side of Shay's bed and prayed for forgiveness and aid.

Knowing that a watched pot never boils and having used up her meager store of ideas, she sat on the bed to wait for God or the mirror to do something useful and tried to think of other things.

A white box sat next to the telephone. Everything in the room was either white, pink or red. There were numbers on a disk on the box's side and below that a button. Brandy pushed the button but it didn't move, nor would it pull out. It did turn however, and she moved it around until it would go no farther . . .

"Rattle, rattle, rattle!" the box screamed and Brandy jumped up to hit Shay's head on the sloping ceiling above the bed.

"Rattle, rattle, rattle, Rattle your boodeez." It sounded like several young men whining in unison above a cacophony of musical instruments tuning up to play.

Brandy was still staring at the screaming box when Rachael burst into the room and turned the button until it clicked and the box stilled. She held her hand over her heart.

"Listen, honey, baby, sweetheart," she pleaded breathlessly. "I know you're upset, but dammit, so is everybody else."

"What . . . is a boodeez?"

"Boodeez? I thought they were saying booty, but then I haven't understood the words to a song for so long I'm used to it. I thought you got all that stuff." Rachael had washed the paint from her face and was even lovelier with the tiny lines showing at the outer corners of her eyes. "I know what the problem is, all that coffee your dad poured down our throats tonight. And I have the answer right here." She opened a hand to reveal a small bottle. "Come on."

Honey? Baby? Sweetheart? These parents were certainly fond of their daughter. Brandy wondered what they'd do if they discovered someone else lurking inside that daughter as she followed Shay's mother down the hall and into the linen closet.

But now it was not a linen closet. A shiny water closet sat on a commode and a porcelain sink was enclosed in a cabinet. The sink had one spigot but two handles.

Rachael pulled a small cup from a rack on the wall and filled it with water. She pressed on the bottle cap with the heel of her hand and turned it until the cap came off. Taking out a pill, she shoved it onto Shay's tongue and pushed the edge of the cup after it so quickly that Brandy was forced to swallow.

She coughed. "What . . . was that?"

"A sleeping pill." Rachael swallowed one without water.

"Sleeping . . . oh, no . . ."

"Listen, darling, I know you don't approve of them. But we all need help tonight."

Rachael pulled Brandy back down the hall, removed the robe and tucked her into Shay's bed. "Sit tight. These are powerhouses." She turned out the light with the button beside the door. "You won't even dream, believe me." Shay's mother was gone.

"I mustn't sleep." A sleeping compound was the last thing she needed this night. If it was anything like laudanum . . .

I have to get to Denver. The body'd already been tired and Brandy already sleepy.

The bed was eiderdown-soft, the sheets like silk. *I must get to Aunt Harriet's . . .*

Brandy woke to sunshine and birdsong, a heavy head and a swollen tongue. Shay's tongue.

I'll miss the wedding.

The mirror stood innocently in the center of the room, sunlight streaking mellow sheen along bronze finger ridges and clawlike nails. How long did it plan to keep her here? How long could she pretend to be Shay? No matter what happened, she was caught between the horse and the barn door.

She took Shay down the hall to the linen closet and on her return met Jerry with a breakfast tray. "Morning, princess. How do you feel?"

"Strange."

"It's that sleeping pill." He propped her up against the pillows and laid the tray across her lap. "Don't remember ever serving you breakfast in bed before. Must be getting old."

His smile was so pleasant Brandy found Shay returning it.

"That's better. I was beginning to think your face'd gotten stuck." He wore a snug-fitting suit and broad, patterned tie. "We've contacted the guests we didn't get ahold of last night and managed to have the funeral services planned for tomorrow. So you and Marek can work from there about rescheduling the wedding. Well, I'm off to the mortuary and then a few hours at the office."

Brandy held Shay still as he kissed her forehead. He turned in the doorway. "There's no rush, you know . . . about the wedding."

When he'd left she drank the fruit juice and the awful coffee to alleviate the dryness in her mouth, reflecting that her own father and this one certainly had opposing views when it came to marrying off their daughters.

The toast was evenly browned but flavorless. The dry flakes sprinkled with sugar tasted like nothing at all. She added milk from the pitcher on the tray and then had a soggy mess that tasted like nothing at all. No wonder the people in this house were so thin.

The telephone object rang. She stared at it as it rang again and then again. It would look suspicious if she didn't answer.

"Hello?" Nothing. Brandy turned the object end for end and tried again. "Hello?"

"Shay? This is Marek." He sounded sensual even over the telephone. "Did I catch you in the shower?"

"Shower?" It wasn't raining.

"It took you so long to answer. Are you feeling better? You were so cool last night, I—"

"Cool?" Actually she'd been overwarm in the stuffy house.

"What are you, a parrot this morning?"

"I'm not . . . fully awake."

"Well, will you tell your mother that I've notified my best man the wedding's off for now? And, Shay, things went to hell with the computer about two o'clock this morning. If you don't need me I think I'll go out to work today. See you tonight?"

"Yes, that will be fine." *Surely I won't still be here tonight.*

Rachael appeared in the doorway wearing pants. Brandy delivered Marek's message.

"Your dad says you're still feeling strange this morning." She sat on the bed and took the tray onto her lap. "Honey, Grandma had a full and a good life even before that stroke twenty years ago." But tears came to her eyes. "I realize I must have scared you as much as she did last night and that explosion or earthquake or whatever—there wasn't a thing about it on the news this morning, by the way—but you're twenty years old, about to be married. We just can't protect you from everything anymore. Now, you go take your shower and get your head straight. I need help. People are finding out about Grandma and calling. We'll work through today together and take on tomorrow when it gets here. Okay?"

"That sounds like a wise idea."

"Now, do you want to wear blue jeans or shorts or what? Some of your things are still down in the laundry room."

"Will you choose for me, please?"

"You stopped listening to my advice on what to wear at about the age of two. Oh, all right, I'll bring something into the bathroom. But you can scrub yourself. Are you really feeling strange or just helpless this morning?"

Brandy McCabe looked around the linen closet, at the sink, the commode and a door made of clouded glass in the back wall. Inside, a tiny room with slippery porcelainlike floor and walls. If she closed the door, would it be similar to a hip bath? She gave the knob on the wall an experimental turn and screeched as cold water cascaded onto her from a nozzle she hadn't noticed above her head. *Shower . . . of course.*

The glass door opened and Rachael reached in to turn off the water, her face white.

"Don't you think you should take off your robe and pajamas before you shower?" The suspicion in Rachael's eyes frightened Brandy.

Brandy rubbed Shay's hands along the bronze hands of the mirror. *Help me!*

She'd never felt she was delicate in matters of taste or sensibility, had considered herself open to change and thus to self-improvement. Her curiosity alone would have prevented her from ignoring new ideas. But to go abroad dressed as she now was in tiny useless drawers beneath "blue jean" pants—the inner seams of which pressed so tightly up against the female parts they created odd and surely forbidden sensations.

And no corset or corset cover. Merely a narrow strapped garment to cup the busts that Rachael'd called a bra and which was clearly outlined under the clinging shirt.

The costume could not but be a siren call to the baser instincts of gentlemen.

Please take me back. I promise to be vigilant against curiosity. Brandy shook the wedding mirror. It wobbled on its claw base. *I don't understand this world.*

The bronze hands grew hot and Brandy opened Shay's mouth in a startled scream as she was flung backward.

Transparent and dim, as an apparition, between her and the mirror—not in the glass itself—an image of her own body, dressed decently in her traveling suit and hat, standing beside the dining-room table, Sophie McCabe walking toward it with Brandy's beaded handbag.

She leaned forward. "Ma!"

The image contorted . . . rippled . . . vanished, leaving Shay's body sticky and struggling for breath.

In the parlor, where she recognized some of the furniture, Brandy found the small figurine of the shepherdess Grandmother Euler had brought with her from Germany. It lay broken on the hearth.

She fingered the demure face with the downcast eyes and sweet lips, lifted a piece of blue skirt with a ragged edge of milky pantaloon peeping from beneath it. She felt as shattered as the shepherdess.

Holding back tears, she stood and squared Shay's shoulders. Self-pity was never of use.

She'd pretend to be at ease in the unfamiliar clothes and in this unfamiliar time to avert suspicion until she could return to her own. Brandy'd been taught that with proper strength of character and purpose one could achieve almost anything.

In the kitchen, Shay's mother set Brandy to peeling hard-boiled eggs for lunch while she emptied an odd cupboard with slatted rubber shelves that pulled out into the room.

Rachael'd carried a tray of goblets into the dining room when the telephone rang. It hung on a different wall now but looked to be the same boxlike affair Brandy's father'd had installed.

"Get that for me, will you, Shay?"

Brandy took the wooden receiver off the hook and a touch of homesickness gripped her at the familiar feel of it. "Hello?" she said into the iron mouthpiece.

No one answered and the ringing continued.

"Hello . . ." She jiggled the hook and looked up to see Shay's mother in the doorway. "It doesn't seem to be working."

Again that hard suspicion in Rachael's eyes as she took the receiver from Brandy, replaced it on the hook and opened the front of the telephone box. Inside was an oblong ear- and mouthpiece all in one like that on the bedside table in Shay's room.

Brandy slipped out the back door to discover the source of the roaring noise she'd heard all day and to get away from Rachael.

She took two steps in Shay's ugly canvas shoes and stopped.

The outhouse and the hen house were gone. So was the prairie. Tall trees and buildings surrounded the Gingerbread House. Metal automobiles, as sleek as those the wedding mirror had shown her, roared by on the hard-surfaced road. The air was foul.

Keeping close to the familiar house, Brandy walked around to the front. Across the street an unusual building with a paved yard and a sign, CONOCO.

The irrigation ditch was no more than a grassy depression outside the wrought-iron fence.

A young girl, dressed much like Shay's body, approached on a thin, clicking bicycle. Without pausing or glancing at Brandy, the girl pulled something from a bag and threw it. It struck Shay's chest and fell to the grass inside the fence.

When Brandy bent to pick it up, it unfolded into a newspaper. *Boulder Daily Camera.* It was dated June 16, 1978.

As changed as things were in this world, she would have thought she'd been transported to the year 2000 at least.

Rachael Garrett watched her daughter from the dining-room window.

Shay'd walked around the house as if she were in a trance, had looked about the neighborhood as if she'd never seen it. Now she stood staring at the evening newspaper, her lovely hair rolled into that ridiculous bun at the back of her head.

Rachael could stand it no longer and went out onto the porch to call Shay inside. Again that slow stiff walk, the other-world expression in her eyes as Shay came toward her.

A sick feeling moved from Rachael's stomach to her chest.

Inside, they poured coffee and sat down with the *Camera*. "Let's see if they got Grandma's obit right. Here it is. I'll read it to you. 'Brandy Maddon' . . . that's the headline. What's the matter?"

"Brandy?"

"You knew Grandma Bran's name was Brandy, didn't you? Oh, you must have. You just never listened when I talked family. 'Brandy Maddon,'" Rachael began again . . .

Brandy Harriet (McCabe) Maddon died yesterday at the historic Gingerbread House on Spruce Street, which is now the home of her daughter, Mrs. Jerrold Garrett. Mrs. Maddon had been living for many years at the Eternal Care Nursing Home here in Boulder and was visiting her daughter at the time of her death. She was 98.

She was born on August 7, 1880, at the Gingerbread House to John and Sophie McCabe. Her grandfather was James Elton McCabe, prominent Boulder pioneer who built the Gingerbread House in 1867. She graduated from Boulder Preparatory School in 1898 and married Hutchinson Maddon of Nederland in 1902.

The Maddons lived near or in Nederland for the next forty years and most of that time on the Bar Double M Ranch, where Mr. Maddon raised cattle and horses. After his death in 1944, Mrs. Maddon traveled extensively and was the subject of an article in *Time* magazine entitled "The Fantastic Traveling Grandmother."

Mrs. Maddon is survived by two sons, Remy and Dan, who have recently retired in Boulder; a daughter, Rachael Garrett, also of Boulder; four grandchildren and six great-grandchildren.

Private services will be held at Rowe Mortuary. Interment will be in Columbia Cemetery.

"Seems so short for such a long life, doesn't it?" Rachael looked up into the shocked eyes of a stranger.

"But . . . *I* am Brandy Harriet McCabe," her daughter said.

4

"That," Rachael whispered slowly and carefully, "is Brandy . . . Harriet . . . McCabe . . . Maddon."

Brandy stood between Shay's parents beside the casket holding the ancient body. Jerry supported her with an arm around her waist.

"You are Shay Catherine Garrett. Repeat that."

"I am Shay Catherine Garrett," Brandy lied obediently. Why had the obituary not mentioned Mr. Strock?

The woman next to her was her daughter. The aging twins behind her, her sons. She'd never heard of the man named Hutchison Maddon, whom she would marry, and she was inhabiting the body of her granddaughter.

When I go home I will know my own obituary.

Brandy searched her memory for Bible references to explain this phenomenon she was living. She could think of none. But then her mind had always wandered during Bible readings in church and at home. "One pays for such transgressions," Sophie McCabe had warned.

The coffin looked too large for the tiny Brandy. The eyes were closed to staring death now. *What is this nursing home where I will spend the last twenty years of my life?* Twenty years . . . that was all the life she'd known.

She couldn't relate the dead Brandy Maddon to herself. The thin white hair. The still, empty face. The spotted hands folded across—it was inconceivable that she should be looking at herself in her own satin-lined coffin seventy-eight years after yesterday. . . .

Brandy had no warning of the vision that appeared suddenly, superimposed over the dead body. A vision of herself, still dressed in her traveling suit, lying on a rough plank floor. And kneeling beside her, a woman with a topknot made of her hair and . . . Corbin Strock.

"Let's get her out of here, I think she's fainting," Shay's father said.

She stumbled beside him through the door to the lobby and then outside.

Jerry Garrett watched Marek Weir drive off with Shay and let the curtain fall back. *God, I hope I did the right thing.*

"I don't think we should have let her go out with him tonight," Rachael said.

"Let her? We had to make her. Maybe an evening at a disco will snap her out of it."

"I had to choose her clothes for her again. You know that pink top she loves and you hate? She was going to wear a bra under it." Rachael straightened a picture with trembling hands. "Can you imagine Shay Garrett being caught dead at a discotheque wearing a bra? Did you talk to Gale?"

"He's out of town for a week."

"There are other doctors."

"Not one I'd trust with my only daughter." He hated to think of Shay going to see any shrink at all.

"And yet you let her go off with Marek while she's in a half-crazed condition."

"Rachael, that's the man she'd be married to right now if—"

"He's a walking sperm count and you know it."

"She's twenty years old and for all we'd like to think otherwise, no innocent." *And just who are we kidding besides ourselves?* Marek Weir had a good job and a future. He was a lot better than most of the punks she'd brought home. Nobody would ever be good enough for their Shay.

"He's years older than she is and she hardly knows him."

And when he takes her away, he'll take our last excuse to stay together. You'll be left with your house and your books and I'll have nothing. "She can take care of herself."

"Can she? Did you see her try to cut up her artichoke with a knife and fork at dinner tonight? Our slouchy daughter is suddenly sitting ramrod straight, doesn't like milk, wears her hair in an old-lady bun, calls me Ma instead of Mother and tries to answer the kitchen phone through the antique mouthpiece." Rachael stubbed out her cigarette and flopped down into the platform rocker. "She decides she's Brandy McCabe and you say she can take care of herself."

"Rachael, she isn't suddenly crazy. Just upset and vague right now. People don't act normally all their lives and then go off the deep end in one night. She was probably preoccupied this morning when she turned the shower on herself with her clothes on and—"

"This afternoon I asked her to do up the lunch dishes. She did them in the sink. Not two feet away from the dishwasher."

"Maybe she was trying to conserve water."

"Now who's hiding his head in the sand? Jerry, she took the bar of hand soap and shaved slivers off it with a butcher knife. Tried to dissolve them in water. And when she'd washed them and dried them, mind you, then she put them in the dishwasher."

Jerry knew his wife was strung tight. Bran's death, Shay's worrisome behavior—who could blame her? It was just that Jerry couldn't help her anymore. Things had gone too far. "Well, take her in to Haffenbach then."

"He's an M.D."

"Maybe the shock was physical in some way too. At least ask him what he thinks. He's been her doctor for years." Jerry pushed up the knot on his tie and slipped into his jacket. "I have a few things to do at the office if I'm going to the funeral tomorrow."

"Yeah, sure." Rachael emptied the ashtray into the fireplace.

"I'll be home before the kids get back from the disco."

The intensity of the silence throbbed in the room. He made it to the doorway before she spoke.

"Jerry, I know you plan to leave me." Her voice strained under her attempt to control it.

"Hell, I'm just going to the office."

"I mean . . . when Shay's gone." Rachael came up behind him. "And I know what's been going on up at the cabin in Nederland."

He leaned into the side of the archway and rested his hand on Thora K.'s old buffet in the hall.

"Jerry, it's not that I've blocked out what you've been doing because I couldn't face it, like you think I do with everything. It's just that . . . just that I haven't known how to talk about it."

The familiar ache clamped the air from his chest. "Rachael—"

"Let me finish. I won't be unpleasant or try . . . try to hold you. All I ask is that you stick with me until we're sure Shay's all right."

He could hear the repressed tears, see the crow's feet at the corners of her eyes even though she stood behind him. See the brave, drawn expression, the still-slim body. "I need you now."

No one had needed Jerry since his mother died except his daughter for a while . . . and God those years had gone fast.

But Rachael had her anchors, buoys to grow old with. Her damned house filled with family relics to which she'd always belong, inanimate things she seemed to love and trust more than she did people. The safety valve of escape into the imaginary world of her writing. Neither of which he could share. Oh, yes, Rachael'd be fine without him. Not even menopause slowed her down.

All Jerry had was the looming prospect of retirement. Was it really any wonder that he turned to others who needed too? Escaped to the cabin that he had designed and built, instead of some ancestor of Rachael's? Of course he'd stay until Shay left, but after that . . .

All these things Jerry wanted to say but they wouldn't form into coherent words and sentences when spoken aloud, as most of his personal thoughts would not, so he mumbled, "She's my daughter too."

And he hurried out of the Gingerbread House as if he were being chased.

Brandy McCabe sat alone in a secluded booth, tingling with the excitement of her first outing in an automobile. She and "the family" had walked the short distance to and from the mortuary to view her dead body.

This was also the first time she'd gone abroad with her limbs bared. Shay's skirt came only to the knees. Beneath it—nothing but the tiny silken drawers. If Sophie McCabe ever learned of this, she'd succumb to the vapors.

And yet Shay's loving father had insisted she come to this place. It was no more than a saloon. Brandy'd never seen the inside of one before. The rampant curiosity that had allowed the wedding mirror to place her in this fix to begin with almost overwhelmed her now.

She sat surrounded by foliage. As if the proprietor hoped to give the impression this saloon was a jungle. Rough earthenware pots hung from open rafters by twisted ropes that flared to form nets around the bowls. The rope ends dangled beneath in frayed strands that resembled horses' tails.

Leafy vines showered from the pots, forming curtains around three sides of the booths. Hooded lightbulbs above each plant provided the only lighting in the room and it was dimmed to suffocation by the forests of greenery.

At intervals between plants, rectangular panels of leaded and beveled glass hung from chains like useless windows.

Through the protective foliage she could see Mr. Weir leaning against the bar.

Brandy fought the temptation to forget she wasn't Shay, to learn and experience as much of her granddaughter's wicked but interesting world as she could before she returned to her own.

In the booth across from her a youthful couple embraced and kissed and felt each other, heedless of their presence in a public place. His hair grew so long he tied it back with a leather string, while hers was short and frizzled, forming a close-fitting dome around her head.

Brandy felt as suffocated as the lights by the rapidity of new sensations and sights. She gasped stale air into Shay's lungs to ward off faintness.

Marek Weir stood in front of her holding a goblet of green foam and a smaller glass. He was tall and slender like her brother, Elton.

"Your favorite." He set the goblet in front of her and slid in the other end of the booth and around beside her with that relaxed ease of movement so unlike Elton.

"Do you realize that at this moment we would be in Aspen on our honeymoon if your grandmother hadn't died last night?" He sat so close their arms and thighs touched. "You'd be Mrs. Marek Weir."

If Brandy moved away from him she'd fall off her end of the booth's seat. So she leaned forward to sip Shay's favorite drink and at least get Shay's bare arm away from his.

It was more than foam. Almost liquid ice cream, with the taste of limes and sugar. Salt coated the rim of the goblet, its taste mixing with the others. The combination was delicious. "Is . . . this a lady's drink?"

"Well, it's no martini." He laughed as if she'd joked.

A rasping sound descended from the ceiling, followed by the odd music Brandy'd heard from the box in Shay's room.

Rattle, rattle, rattle,
Rattle, rattle, rattle,
Rattle your boodeez.

She turned to Marek. "What is a boodeez?"

"Boodeez?" He cocked his head to listen. "I thought it was boobies." Violet eyes laughed into hers seductively. "Shows you on what level low minds gather, doesn't it?"

Brandy gulped at the sweet-sour concoction in the goblet. She seemed to be having some difficulty with the language.

His arm encircled her and drew her back against the cushions.

Brandy sucked in Shay's breath.

His shirt had short sleeves and opened partway down the front. Black hairs along his arms, more peeking from the shirt opening. Firm muscle rolled from beneath the sleeves.

Gooseflesh rose on Shay's skin.

"I don't understand this sudden change in you, Shay." His breath tickled her neck. "It's not like you were that close to your grandmother. She was practically a vegetable."

The music changed to a throbbing clamor that kept time with the pulse rhythm Brandy's reactions caused in Shay's veins. "It was disturbing to see her die that way."

"It must have been. You're like a different person since it happened."

Brandy was fighting the devil on his own ground. She'd had no idea all she'd been protected from. She'd heard much about sin in her life, but . . .

She tried to ignore the amorous couple and their disgusting antics across the way.

She tried to ignore the warm body so snug against Shay's, the arm with its muscle and hair that held her so casually. Shay's body did not cooperate.

Brandy leaned away to drink from the goblet and Marek's arm loosened to allow the movement, slid down so that his hand rested on her . . . lap.

Brandy drained the goblet. Even the hanging vines seemed provocative now. Marek was handsome. Even when she wasn't looking at him. She'd have to tell him she wasn't Shay.

"You're cold. When you get chilled your nipples swell under that thing you're wearing."

"Nip . . ." The audacity of the man to refer to . . . She glanced down to see that his observation was correct. Rachael'd pointed out that if she wore a "bra" under it the straps would show.

"Let's dance. Warm you up." His thigh bumped Shay's and Brandy had either to stand or to fall on the floor.

She protested but he drew her to a sunken parquet area. Blue light played upon it. Hypnotic music made her senses swim.

Marek Weir began to writhe. Sensual, heathenlike writhing.

Brandy wanted to look away. But she couldn't.

Shay's body swayed in answer to the primitive music and the look in Marek's eyes.

The body felt light and the head lighter.

The kissing couple joined them, contorting themselves.

And then another couple. These two wore beards.

Brandy McCabe passed beyond shock.

The twangy music increased in tempo and drumbeat, like wicked native dances she'd heard a missionary from Africa tell of at a church meeting. He'd described much the same thing—sensuous music and movements, half-clad bodies.

Brandy wanted to run. Shay wanted to sway.

"Relax, Shay. Loosen up," Marek said, looking like the devil incarnate with dark hair and tanned skin. "It'll do you good."

There was a warm moistness in the area of Shay's private parts. *Dear Lord, please forgive me.* Brandy felt locked into the dance.

Surely God would come to her aid at a time like this. Where was he? Testing her? If he really had the legions of heaven at his disposal, he could spare one angel to help Brandy now. But that missionary from Africa had seen his wife butchered by natives, and the Lord hadn't done a thing except to make that a lesson to him.

Marek Weir could be Satan. But the dance floor was by now crowded with Satans and loose-jointed women who didn't seem to mind. Satan Weir didn't touch Shay's body once. He merely moved and so did Shay.

"You even dance differently," Marek said when the noise stopped. "Hardly move at all." He led her back to the booth and went to the bar.

He returned with two more drinks. "That's all you get," he said as he put another foamy goblet in front of her. "I've ordered snacks. You're not only freaked and different, you've never handled booze that well."

"This has alcohol in it?"

"I'll admit that's a bastardized version, but, Shay, you've been drinking margaritas since before I knew you." He sat away from her now, studied her. "The night before a family funeral's no time to take your fiancée dancing. This was your dad's idea, not mine. Your folks are worried about you. So am I. You sure it isn't more than just your grandmother's death that's got you so fluffy?"

A girl delivered a tray of crunchy tidbits, all of them salted. Brandy longed for more of the drink to quench the thirst they inspired. Of course, she *had* seen Sophie McCabe take an occasional sherry before she'd joined her temperance committee.

Brandy took but a small sip.

"Let me put it another way," Marek said. "I'm thirty. I've found what I want to do in life. I've avoided permanent relationships." He stretched out, rested his head on the back of the booth and stared at the rafters. "Then I meet this beautiful blond, slightly spacey but interesting, and I think . . . what would it be like to share my life with her?"

He lowered his head to watch lemon rind swirl in his glass. "Before I know it I've asked her to marry me. Immediately I begin to doubt her and myself. I mean, marriages don't have long life spans anymore."

Marek lifted Shay's chin and stared into her eyes as if probing for Brandy. "And then my bride-to-be suddenly gets spacier, looks at me with round innocent eyes and I doubt my doubts, go all macho, corny and protective. Do you know what I'm trying to say, Shay?"

"No," Brandy answered, hypnotized by the man, unable to move as he leaned over and kissed Shay's lips.

Marek Weir sat back, his eyes narrowed. "Who are you?" he whispered.

But Brandy didn't tell him.

5

Brandy McCabe watched her casket lower into the yawning hole.

Beside her, Rachael sniffed behind a paper handkerchief. Jerry's worried glance rested on Brandy over Rachael's head.

She could feel the presence of Marek Weir behind her. And across the hole, the solemn elderly twins and their wives.

No hats. No gloves. No church service. No one wore black. Very few people. *And I shall come to this. . . .*

The rasp of locusts buzzed in her ears. The din of automobiles not far away. Sun gleamed on the black motor hearse that'd brought her body here and on those for the mourners waiting in a line behind.

The last time she'd come to the family plot in Columbia Cemetery these giant trees had been saplings and a line of horse-drawn carriages waited in the drive. They'd buried her little brother Joshua, so long dead, so sorely missed. And now the plot was full.

Elton rested beside Joshua. His life sadly short.

And next to him her father, who'd died the very summer the mirror had taken her away. She realized she'd rather have married Mr. Strock than to see John McCabe's grave.

Her mother, the newest addition to the plot, would outlive all but Brandy herself.

Next, the pink headstone of Hutchison Maddon. What would he be like?

The mirror had given her a look into the future. It'd been a cruel trick. *I really didn't want to know.*

Over all hovered the Rocky Mountains. Brandy saw them through tears.

"What happened to Mr. Strock?" she asked Rachael as they turned away.

"Mr. Strock," Rachael said blankly. "Oh, you mean Thora K.'s son? I didn't realize you even knew of him. He's buried in Nederland with

Thora K. My mother was married before she met my dad," she explained to Marek, "and widowed in a year or two."

Rachael talked quietly with her brothers, and Marek took Brandy aside. "Did you see this? I read about it in that local history column in the *Camera*." He pointed to another pink tombstone directly across the grassy path from Hutchison Maddon's grave.

In Loving Memory of
Tom Horn
1861–1903

"Tom Horn." Another name Brandy knew. "The one who kills outlaws?"

"Not anymore, he doesn't."

Brandy stood before the wedding mirror, Shay's eyes swollen from Brandy's grief over the graves of her loved ones. Elton hadn't survived to carry on the name. She'd seen the last of the proud McCabes in Columbia Cemetery.

"Haven't you done enough?" she said to the mirror. "I've learned my lesson." She'd go back and marry Mr. Strock even though she knew he hadn't long to live. "Please don't show me any more."

But how could she return, knowing all she knew? The knowledge would be a curse to haunt her nights and days. *How can I stay here? I'm too weak to withstand the temptations of this world.*

Brandy had lain awake for hours the night before, her thoughts full of Marek Weir.

In the Garretts' living room, Marek shifted uncomfortably on the antique settee made for long ago and shorter bodies. "I tried to draw her out last night. She wouldn't talk. Look, I'm not hiding anything from you."

Rachael prowled the room. "Marek, Jerry and I have talked this out and come up with absolutely nothing. We thought you might at least have a fresh viewpoint."

"I have a crazy idea I can't get out of my head and it's as fresh as hell, but I don't think you'll believe it any more than I do."

"Try us." Jerry stared into the scotch he wasn't drinking.

"This'll sound strange coming from a so-called scientist, but . . . Shay seems like another person. I'd almost swear you switched twins on me."

"Where is she now?" Jerry looked over his shoulder toward the archway to the hall.

"Last I knew she was upstairs talking to a mirror."

"That's not so crazy, Rachael. I've talked to mirrors before," Jerry snapped. "So have you."

"Only when practicing to give a talk. And, Marek, that thought wasn't so fresh."

"I haven't finished. You've heard of dual or multiple personalities? More than one inhabiting the same body but who surface alternately? I sense a stranger looking at me from Shay's eyes."

Jerry stared at Marek over his glass. Rachael stopped pacing. They'd felt it too.

"The thing about this theory that doesn't work is, at least from what little I know about it, this occurs in people with a history of instability. For it to happen literally overnight to a normal—"

"She's had chickenpox, strep, colds, flu, a broken arm and her teeth straightened," Rachael said. "Never anything mental except the bitchy fours and the rebellious teens. I read all the books. I'd have noticed."

"There's always possession." Jerry rolled his eyes. "I mean, as long as we're getting fresh. Maybe she's possessed."

"And Gale doesn't get back for a week." Rachael opened a glass-fronted cabinet, took out a blue glass bottle and put it back.

"Let's just keep her calm and call Gale the minute he gets back," Jerry said. "She's always liked him."

"Well, the three of us had better keep an eye on her." Rachael gave Marek a hard look.

He thought it ironic they should include him in a three-way deal. He'd sensed their opposition to his marrying their daughter. They clung to Shay but wouldn't admit it. No man on earth deserved the treasure they'd created.

His ailing mother'd been pleased at having her last son finally settle down. Louise Weir was of the opinion that no man could survive without a wife. His oldest brother now lived with his third wife. The middle brother was on the verge of divorcing his first. But Louise didn't know that. She wanted only to see her youngest safely settled before she died.

Had his mother's wishes anything to do with Marek's sudden proposal to Shay after a brief three-month courtship?

He considered this again that evening when Shay sat beside him in the Porsche. "I want to run out to NCAR for a minute. Then I thought maybe a movie. There're several in town you wanted to see."

"Yes, that will be fine."

Her hand clutching the armrest whitened as he turned a corner, came up as if to ward off a blow as he stopped behind another car. A sharp intake of breath when he stepped on the gas . . .

Marek almost ran a red light watching the odd play of expressions.

Delight. Wonder. Dismay. Her head swiveled as if she were sightseeing in an exotic vacation spot. Here in the town where she'd lived her entire life.

When she looked at him, he read fascination mixed with distrust and fear. They didn't jibe. To be able to read Shay's face at all was a new experience. Before, she'd cloaked her emotions with sophisticated boredom or the protective deadpan Marek saw everywhere and knew he wore himself.

The display on her face now was almost childlike. But at the same time he sensed a mature woman behind those wide amber eyes. It was just that the woman wasn't Shay Garrett.

Marek was shaken and intrigued by the other woman who was Shay. She regarded him with shocked innocence one moment and something resembling infatuation the next.

None of it made sense but the dual-personality theory was becoming more plausible. He couldn't believe in possession.

"National Center for Atmospheric Research," she read from the sign she'd seen dozens of times, and sounded mystified.

As they left the rows of houses to climb the graceful curves to NCAR he pointed out a deer and her fawn grazing on the green-belt area which the city had closed off to the destruction of developers.

Shay merely glanced at them. He could remember her making him stop for half an hour at such a sight when he'd first known her. But now she looked at the mountains and then back at Boulder as if to get her bearings.

This isn't in your field, Weir, not something you can punch into the number cruncher. Leave it for the shrink.

He pulled into the parking lot on top of the mesa. Shay gaped at the concrete towers.

"You've never seen that building before, have you?" A growing dryness in his throat.

"No." She couldn't seem to drag her eyes from it.

Shay Garrett had driven up here just four days before to collect him for a luncheon date.

Marek walked around to open her door. "You'd better come in with me."

She hung back as he led her to the sidewalk. Her arm trembled when he took it and he glanced up at the futuristic building . . . an impression of a series of towers connected by cubes, colored a muted pink to blend with the green of pine and reddish-pink rock of the mountain backdrop. Blue-green tinted windows like square eyes, the tiny balconies between like noses. Impressive yes, but not frightening.

Shay hesitated at the glass doors but he drew her into the lobby. Because of the change in his fiancée, Marek was suddenly aware of the sterile straight lines of the place. The silence broken only by the echoing click of their heels on terrazzo.

"Dr. Weir," the guard greeted him from behind his waist-high enclosure.

Shay stared at the television monitors.

"Evening, Harry." Marek signed the off-hours register and led her to a back elevator.

"Shay, it's not only this place. You don't know me either, do you?" he asked when the door had closed on them.

She grabbed his arm as they descended to the basement, looking at the floor and then the walls. "I think you must be the devil himself."

She flung her arms around his neck when the elevator door opened.

"Then why did you come out with me this evening?"

"Because I'm weak and can't resist the chance to ride in your wonderful automobile." The strange woman inside the familiar body seemed suddenly to realize her position. She blushed and moved away. "And because I have a foolish curiosity to know more than I need to. It's sure to be the death of me."

The exaggerated slowness of her speech, the rather archaic arrangement of her words . . . *and she's even forgotten what it's like to ride in cars and elevators.* Marek considered amnesia and rejected it for insanity. Yet there was a consistency about her that appeared sane.

"This place has no scent," she whispered as they walked down the hall. "All places smell of something."

"What did you expect, the smell of sulfur?" He looked into frightened eyes. "Shay, I don't know what's happened to you but I'm not meaning to scare you. This is just the place where I work. It isn't hell and I'm not the devil."

He checked the monitor outside the computer room to see what stage his program had reached and found it listed in the output status. "Relax, please. There's nothing to be afraid of."

But inside the computer room the normal clicking, clacking, sloshing, rattling of various peripheral machines all at different rates and tones over the constant roar of the cooling system seemed to belie his words. He grabbed his stack of cards and the printout from a shelf in the output bin and got Shay away from the place.

Back in the elevator, he glanced over the printout sheet of the numerical storm model he was building and decided his theories were all awash here too. "I want to drop this off in my office," he said to Shay and then thought aloud, "Either the programmer goofed or . . ."

Marek was so irritated with the errors in his model that he walked into Martin as they stepped into the hall.

"Shay, you remember Martin Black." Marek stopped to pick up the book he'd knocked from Martin's hand. *No, you probably don't.*

"How do you do," Shay answered formally.

"Sorry to hear about your grandmother, Shay, and the postponement of your wedding. Don't wait too long, will you? The world'll be a safer place once you get this young swinger out of circulation." Martin laughed, patted her shoulder and disappeared into the elevator.

When Marek unlocked the door at the end of the hall, Shay seemed reluctant to go outside.

"I promise I won't throw you over the parapet."

"This is like a strange castle," she said as they walked the open catwalk to his tower room.

"Well, you've already seen the dungeons so it can't get any worse, can it?"

Marek laid the computer cards and printout on his desk. Shay moved to the window.

It was barely dusk but the automatically timed lights blazed the map of the city streets below.

"So many lights . . ."

"So much for the energy crunch, huh?"

"I hadn't realized the town had grown this vast."

"Yeah . . . uh . . . Shay, let me take another quick look at this."

Sitting at the desk he scanned the printout sheets. He could hear her moving about the room, writing on the blackboard.

Marek looked up once to see her examining titles in one of the bookcases. He went back to his coded numbers, only to be interrupted again.

"You must be the devil." Shay pointed to the photographs of thunderclouds and lightning on one wall. "You made the storm that caused the mirror to . . . no, that's foolish." She covered her face with her hands. A lock of platinum hair escaped the puritanical bun she'd affected.

"If I'm the devil, I could make a storm or a mirror or whatever. But I'm not and I don't make them, I study them . . . storms that is." In his heart, Marek knew hers was a disturbed mind, a case of sudden insanity. But his mind wouldn't buy it.

"Shay, to my older colleagues I'm a cloud dynamicist by day and a swinging single at night. To your parents I'm the monster who's offered to take their daughter away from them." He stood to hold her but she moved away. "To you, I thought I was the man you were going to marry, but suddenly I'm a devil. Right now I don't know who I am." *I'm not a bit sure who you are either.*

Then he noticed the ornate chalk scrawl on a lower corner of the blackboard. *I am Brandy.* It wasn't in Shay's handwriting.

"Brandy, who—"

"We buried her this morning," his fiancée said.

Something in her voice sent a superstitious thrill along the higher reaches of his spine.

Marek watched Shay sit silently through the movie, her body stiff, her eyes never leaving the screen. *As if this is her first film.*

"What did you think of it?" he asked as they walked back to the car.

"It was a very . . . interesting play. But cold. Such horrid things happening to those poor people." A streetlight glistened on wet cheeks as she looked up at him. "And no sympathy for them . . . no hope."

Marek had come to expect nothing but cold technique and brittle feeling in films. He had come to accept and enjoy it. But if this'd been the first he'd seen, would he have said much the same thing?

"This abortion that was done to the young girl," Shay said thoughtfully. "Was it really to kill an unborn child?"

"Yes. But it didn't happen, Shay, in that movie any more than it would in a play. It's just a story to . . . ?" Marek stopped, wondering at the need to make so inane an explanation to an adult.

"But this abortion is practiced in life here . . . now?"

"Yes."

Marek took Shay to her old favorite, McDonald's. They had a running joke about her taste for the fast-food fare and usually went there after a movie.

But tonight the quarter-pound burger was undercooked, the bun soggy, the fries too salty and she asked if there was alcohol in her Coke.

Merek wondered if the wedding would take place at all. The change in Shay seemed so complete. Was it wise for her parents to wait for their friend Gale to return before seeking professional help?

He had a powerful urge to take her to his apartment as he probably would have the old Shay. But he couldn't take advantage of her confusion now.

She pushed the half-finished meal away and looked directly into his eyes, quickening something in him he hadn't known was there.

6

Brandy sat at the breakfast table with Shay's parents. The marvelous clothes-washing machine hummed in the pantry. The electric coffee maker gurgled on the counter and her head pounded from late-night pleading with the wedding mirror.

And then, over it all, Brandy McCabe heard the sound of church bells. "Is it Sunday . . . here?"

"It's Sunday everywhere, Shay." Jerry looked up from his newspaper.

"I would like to go to church," Brandy whispered.

"Church." Rachael carefully lowered the spoonful of grapefruit she'd just brought to her lips. "What church?"

"The Presbyterian church, of course."

"Of course." Rachael exchanged a glance with her husband.

"Didn't I . . . my grandmother go there?"

"Bran? She didn't belong to any church, did she, Rachael?"

"No. But *my* grandmother, Sophie McCabe, took me to the Presbyterian church when I lived with her. Thora K. hauled me into Nederland to Sunday school. I don't remember Mom ever going along."

"I would like to go to Sophie McCabe's church then." Just saying her mother's name brought tears to the borrowed eyes. "Please?"

"Okay, honey. Don't cry. Jerry, can you find yesterday's paper? It'll have the time of the services."

"You'll have to take her. I've got a golf date with your brothers." He left the room and returned with another paper. "Why not the Lutheran church? That's where you dragged us during your famous six-month conversion when you were thirteen."

As they hurried to finish breakfast, Brandy marveled at their eagerness to please their daughter. Even when they suspected her mind. Rachael helped her choose proper clothing without comment and they rushed to the carriage house, which had a cemented floor now and barely enough room to contain the large automobile.

It wasn't until she identified Boulder Creek that she realized the broad boulevard along which they sped was the Water Street of her time. Gone were the railroad tracks, the shacks of the poor, the houses of prostitution and gambling. Seeing the latter abominations missing on such a beautiful Sunday morning, Brandy thought it possible that God had not abandoned Boulder after all. She felt a welling of relief and determined to put the wicked Mr. Weir from her mind.

The Gingerbread House seemed to be almost all that was left of the Boulder she'd known. Except the mortuary, which she'd recognized as the Trevors' mansion, where she might have become mistress had she married Mr. Trevors. Odd how the sturdy buildings, meant to last the ages, had disappeared in less than a century.

The First Presbyterian Church was now but a corner of a far larger building tacked on around it. To the right of the entryway, doors opened to the sanctuary and Brandy was comforted to see it much the same as she remembered. Except that it was empty on a Sunday morning. She turned to Rachael in surprise.

"You must be visitors." An elderly lady with legs as bare as theirs came up to them. "That's the chapel now. Lovely isn't it? Used to be the sanctuary. It's been restored you know. The new one is over here. You'd better hurry, I think the service is about to begin." She led them to a vast auditorium that was so crowded they had to sit in a front pew.

No subdued chatter of friends. No crying of babes. Scarcely any coughing or clearing of throats. Just a man playing a piano softly. Brandy glanced over Shay's shoulder, amazed to find so many people congregated in such silence, apparently as much strangers to each other as they were to her. She saw only two youngsters.

An enormous wooden cross, straight and unadorned, seemed built into the wall in front of her. Below it, she made out the chancel by its raised platform but was at a loss to identify the altar. There was only a long narrow table, a few chairs and a lectern.

Members of the choir sat robed and expressionless.

Cold white walls and sharp graceless angles reminded her of Marek's NCAR, which to herself she'd dubbed the devil's castle.

A man appeared at the lectern to discuss collecting money from the congregation for a new organ and Brandy felt more at home. But the sum required was staggering.

The choir sang. The minister led them through a program of singing, speaking and answering unfamiliar to her. She understood his lengthy sermon even less but gathered he'd made a minute study of the least-known portions of the Bible and surmised that mankind could survive only by finding the key to unlock the mysterious solutions hidden in the Scriptures. He did assure them that God still existed.

If God was in this place, he didn't speak to Brandy. But the congregation followed the minister's words with rapt attention. The young man sitting next to her actually took notes and Brandy could feel his intensity. Was there nothing relaxed about Shay's world?

She longed for the stirring words of the Reverend Dr. Wilson and the warm presence of Sophie and Elton. John McCabe gave generously of his wealth to the church but rarely attended.

Beside her, Rachael Garrett squirmed and tried to hide her yawns.

When it was over, they were admonished to shake hands with those next to them. The intense young man stuck his pencil between his teeth, gave her a clammy handclasp and stared right through her.

On Monday morning Rachael announced she must work because of something called a "deadline" and would Shay please stay nearby in the "den."

She led Brandy to the cellar, where instead of the coal bins, fruit-and-vegetable storage, and giant furnace, there was now a series of smaller rooms. The one in which she left Brandy had a cushioned carpet, deep sofa and chairs, and walls lined with bookcases. At one end stood a polished box with a glass front resembling those she'd seen at the devil's castle with Marek. "Zenith Solid-State Chroma-color II" was printed on a panel beside the gray glass and beneath these meaningless words two rectangular buttons. One labeled "Chromatic" and the other, "Off/On."

The Off/On wouldn't turn so she punched it. The box began to talk and she backed away until she was sure what else it would do. A flash of colored dots on the glass formed into a moving picture of a slender woman running along a sidewalk.

"Aren't you glad *you* use Dial?" the box asked.

Brandy backed to the sofa and sank into it.

The runner vanished and, while music played, the picture of a large room appeared where many women sat in elevated rows of chairs. A lone woman sat on a platform in front of them.

A man who looked young but had silver hair walked among the chairs and held out a stick on the end of a black rope. A woman would stand, lean toward the stick and ask a question of the lady on the platform.

The discussion had much to do with love, sex, self-stimulation, intimacy, foreplay, climax, masturbation, sexual intercourse, orgasm, and the stupidity of men while making love. All this constantly interspersed with the words "you know."

She slid deeper into the cushions of the sofa with the guilty suspicion she was witnessing a public discussion of cleaving unto. Shay's face grew hot. Brandy's curiosity had already gotten her into enough trouble.

But every time one of those women said "you know," Brandy wanted to shout, "No, I don't know."

She scanned the spines of the shelved books until she came across a dictionary. Brandy didn't know the correct spelling and it took her some time to locate "masturbation," which led her to "genitals" and "genitalia." She decided it meant the self-abuse she'd read of in a book on health that had warned such activities led to insanity and the mysterious female diseases.

There followed a series of game shows. People jumped about, screaming and acting embarrassingly silly.

And constantly interrupting all of this were short plays to advertise an array of wares. Here women, all as slender as Shay, set great store by the scrubbing of floors, ovens and windows. By the polishing of commodes and the spots from glassware.

Yet the entire time Brandy'd been in Shay's world she'd yet to see Rachael so much as pick up a dust rag.

But after dinner that evening Brandy demonstrated she could load the dishwasher and fill it with soap powder.

Then she went back to the picture box in the cellar.

When she climbed the stairs, Shay's eyes burned, her body felt sluggish. Too exhausted to plead with the wedding mirror, Brandy fell into bed, only to wake often from bad dreams.

But the picture box held her captive for the rest of the week while Rachael worked next door, often clicking a typewriting machine much different from those Brandy'd seen used in the bank.

"At least it keeps her from wandering," she overheard Jerry tell his wife.

One morning a young couple arrived to solve the problem of how Rachael kept the Gingerbread House so tidy by ignoring it. Laughing, quarreling, cursing, they swept through the upstairs and down. Dust flew. A noisy metal machine sucked grit from the rugs.

The girl, Sarah, wore three earrings dangling from holes in the lobe of one ear. Chris stared moodily through thick spectacles but moved swiftly. Just before they left he handed Rachael a sheaf of papers.

"Christ, I've told you I don't know anything about poetry and other than the little magazines I don't know where you'd find a market for it. Everybody's writing it, but nobody's buying it."

"Little Mags don't pay anything. Think I want to clean houses all my life?"

"Then write something someone wants to read."

"Don't see why anybody'd want to read the garbage you write."

"Have you ever read any of it?"

"I know it's for kids and it isn't poetry so who needs it?" He grabbed the papers and the money she offered and slammed the door on his way out.

"Don't mind him." Sarah rolled her eyes under a heap of hair with frayed ends. "He doesn't buy poetry either."

Rachael settled herself in a chair across the desk from Gale Sampson in his office. "Well?"

"Well, nothing. She wouldn't talk to me." Gale relit his pipe and tossed the match into an ashtray filled with matches instead of ash. He was one of those men who smoked matches. "Oh, she was coolly polite but whenever I broached any topic to get her started, she looked at me as if I were being impertinent and clammed up."

"She's known you for years—"

"And acts as if she's never seen me before."

"Amnesia?"

"Amnesiacs don't forget how to take showers or shave their legs. Rachael, I want you to go over everything again, from the beginning."

She started with the night her mother died and tried to remember any odd action, reaction or word. There were many.

". . . and when her friends call, she refuses to see them. She loves to ride in the car but won't drive it. She never cared much for TV and now she has it on till it's driving me bananas. She never plays her stereo anymore. Her attitude toward her fiancé has changed. I can't explain it . . . almost like a schoolgirl crush. At least she's stopped telling us she's her grandmother. But, Gale, it's a total personality change. As if she's experiencing things for the first time like . . . well, as I've said, she told us she learned to shave her legs and shampoo her hair properly from a TV commercial."

Gale sucked on a dead pipe and doodled on his notepad. Finally he looked up with a frown. "I don't know why the term 'culture shock' keeps popping into my head."

"But this is the culture she was born to."

"I know. There are pieces of all kinds of things here. But no recognizable pattern. I'd like a full medical report. Who's she seeing?"

"Jeff Haffenbach. He's checked her quickly since this . . . thing started and found nothing, but he didn't have time to schedule a complete physical till the end of July."

"I'd like to see her again next week. Keep me posted and keep a watch on her. I can't tell you what this is, Rachael." He reached across the desk and took her hand. "But I can tell you one thing. It isn't remotely normal."

7

The box everyone called TV came to control Brandy's life. It was a way to numb her terrible homesickness.

Jerry tried to coax her on walks or for rides in his automobile. She finally asked him to leave her be and then felt remorse at the look of pain that crossed his face.

Marek left for Wyoming, where his mother lay near death. Brandy decided if he were Satan this world was filled with them.

Rachael and her husband began to quarrel and Brandy withdrew further.

The wedding mirror remained vacant but for the image of Shay Garrett. Several weeks passed, interrupted only by her visits to Dr. Sampson. She couldn't convince Shay's parents that she didn't need a doctor and that the man only irritated her. Rather than cause unpleasantness Brandy sat through sessions that grew increasingly uncommunicative. TV taught her he was a doctor of the mind and not the body. She resented his attempts to invade the privacy of her thoughts.

Marek returned, saddened at the death of his mother, but soon left again for something called a field station at a place named Grover.

One day, Brandy realized she'd slept through a whole afternoon of TV's entertainment. That night she lay awake and wept for her family, for the quiet, gentle world she'd left.

The stories on the TV became repetitive, different people doing the same things with the same result.

Brandy took to long naps during the day on Shay's bed. Once she awoke to crashing thunder and dashed to the mirror to see if it would perform its magic and send her home. But the storm passed almost before it had begun and the glass remained passive.

The days blended into a hopeless lethargy. Rachael's eyes seemed constantly reddened. Jerry grew silent, wistful. Brandy didn't know how to comfort them. Marek telephoned her often from Grover and she had little to say to him, but looked forward to hearing his voice.

Rachael drove her to see Dr. Haffenbach again. He was interested in bodies. Too interested. A large-boned nurse threatened force if Brandy wouldn't cooperate with the horrid things planned for Shay.

Still smarting from the hateful examination, Brandy refused to speak to Rachael on the way home. How could she put someone she loved through such indignities if that person weren't even ill? Brandy could no longer feel any sympathy for this woman who would become her daughter.

The next evening after dinner, Brandy lay on her granddaughter's bed thinking of Marek Weir. She wondered if the wedding mirror had maliciously punished her by leaving her in this world long enough to fall in love with Shay's intended. What more could it do?

As if in answer there was a stealthy footstep in the hall and she opened Shay's eyes enough to peer through fair lashes.

Rachael stood in the doorway a few seconds, then quietly pulled the door closed. Brandy sensed that if the door'd had a lock Rachael would have used it.

Uneasy, Brandy slid off the bed and into the hall. She stood by the wedding portrait of herself and the long-dead Hutchison Maddon until Rachael reached the bottom of the staircase. Then she descended far enough to see that the entry hall was empty.

"It's all right. She's asleep. That's about all she does anymore, sleep," Rachael said from the parlor. "I'm worried, Gale. I think she's getting worse. But Jerry won't listen to me."

"Hell, what do you want me to do? Put my only daughter in a nuthouse or something?"

"Hey, I know things are getting tense around here and I can understand why." Dr. Sampson's voice. "But if you're going to help Shay, you have to get ahold of yourselves."

Brandy flattened Shay against the wall beside the buffet. Eavesdropping was a nasty occupation, but whatever they schemed for the body she inhabited was her business too.

"There's a further complication," Dr. Sampson said. "I've discussed this case with Dr. Haffenbach as you agreed we should and—"

"There's not something wrong with her physically as well?"

"Rachael, your daughter is in excellent health. It's just that she's pregnant. About two months along."

Brandy stifled a whimper. *Dear God in heaven!*

"Weir! I'll kill him. He took advantage of her in the state—"

"Jerry, the child was conceived before the change occurred in Shay's behavior. If the wedding had taken place as scheduled—"

"Are you sure?" Rachael's voice sounded muffled by shock and breathlessness. "Absolutely?"

"There's no doubt. I'm sorry."

"But she was on the pill. I found them several days ago on a shelf in her closet when I took down a blanket."

"Women have been known to get pregnant on the pill. Many have ended up that way by forgetting to take them regularly. The fact remains your daughter's going to have a baby."

"Do you think this . . . change in her is temporary?" Rachael asked.

"No, I don't. It's too complete."

"But she can't have a baby when she's . . . unstable like this. Or even marry."

"I wouldn't let her marry that bastard now if . . ." Jerry's voice broke. "Oh, God, what do we do?"

"Her mental condition isn't improving," Dr. Sampson said. "She's withdrawing further every day. Frankly I recommend around-the-clock professional care, and soon."

"You mean an institution? A mental asylum? Do you know what they do at those places? Do you want my daughter treated like a prisoner and raped by sadistic orderlies and—"

"Jerry, you're being hysterical. There are fine clinics for the mentally disturbed and you know it. You and Rachael can afford the best for Shay. I'm surprised you believe that kind of glop. Have you ever been in a hospital for the—"

"Yes. I got a client out of one once. It was horrible."

"But what about the baby?" Rachael insisted.

"There are two alternatives, as I see it. Let her have the baby and put it up for adoption or . . . well, it is early stages. A medical abortion would certainly be appropriate under the circumstances."

Brandy let Shay's back slide down the wallpaper. Asylum, abortion, rape . . . was there no end to the wickedness of this world? She looked down at Shay's middle.

"I've never liked the idea of abortion," Rachael said. "But to put her through a pregnancy and childbirth in her condition . . . Jerry we can't let her have this baby." Rachael's strangled whisper was just loud enough for Brandy to hear.

The door chimes sounded, the same tune they'd played to notify the Gingerbread House of callers in Brandy's time but gone a little thin. Now they seemed to sound a warning.

Brandy drew in Shay's long legs and huddled tight to the side of the buffet, one eye peering around it to see Rachael open the door.

Marek Weir stepped inside and even now Brandy felt Shay's body react to his easy smile. A smile that was unaware of the conversation in the parlor.

John McCabe might well have shot him on this evil night.

"Oh, no . . . Marek, this isn't a good time for . . ." Rachael put her hands to her mouth.

"Marek!" Jerry exploded into the hall. "You son of a bitch, Weir, you got her pregnant."

"Jerry, please." Rachael moved between them. "Gale, help me."

Marek raised his eyebrows in surprise.

The mind doctor stepped out of the parlor.

Jerry pushed Rachael aside in a brutal motion that knocked her to the floor. He cracked a fist into Marek's face. It sent an answering snap to Shay's head, brought a strange chill to the skin and left Brandy dragging air into the borrowed mouth.

Marek fell against the hall tree and it toppled over on him. Dr. Sampson held onto Shay's father from behind. Shay's mother raised up on an elbow and made a gurgling sound in her throat. Shay's fiancé lay unmoving under a jumble of coats.

No one had noticed her or was facing her now. Bringing Shay's body to a standing position, Brandy eased it around the staircase, into the kitchen and out the back door.

Where can I go? No Aunt Harriet here. But the body took her through the gate by the carriage house as if by its own volition. It sought shadows as it raced from one alleyway to the next.

I am Brandy, God help me! I've never even lain with a man.

A low growl. Then a hellish series of barks. A heavy body lunged at the other side of the solid board fence next to her. Hundreds of tiny explosions ignited in her granddaughter's blood. The legs leaped into a frantic pounding of paved earth.

Dogs, more frightening because they were unseen, sent up the alarm in every imaginable tone. From inside houses. From behind fences. Alerting others ahead of her as she flew across streets and beneath streetlights to the next alleyway. She turned Shay's ankles in the shadow puddles of potholes.

The smell of fear rose from the body. The wetness of it oozed into the clothes. Trees and buildings reared up around her. Alleys became darkened tunnels with streetlights at the end of each to guide her through. But tunnel and beckoning light began to sway, tipping to one side and then the other as if she raced on a gigantic ship at sea.

The ugly canvas shoes and the blue jeans lent her a freedom of movement she hadn't known in her own button shoes and long skirts. The body was lean and lithe but not strong. Exhaustion shot pain up the legs, set the lungs ablaze, filled the ears with hammer blows until dogs near at hand sounded distant.

A massive beast with pointed ears hurtled over a fence. Snarling, it tried to block her way but when she didn't pause it turned to avoid a collision and ran beside her, veering to crowd against her. Brandy grazed the side of a building and bounced into the animal's flank. It snapped air and slobbered but didn't harm her.

Brandy was afraid of him but had lost control of Shay's body. She continued the mad flight to nowhere with the dog running easily beside her.

Brandy heard the noise of automobiles somewhere but met none. She glimpsed a man strolling toward her on a sidewalk but didn't see if he looked up. Where had all the people gone in this crowded city?

Did the dog wait for her to collapse? He was big enough to halt a horse if he so decided.

The body was in pain and slowing but couldn't seem to stop.

A heavily lighted area ahead. The sound of automobiles over Shay's hoarse breathing. Brandy saw the street only dimly. The dog fell back at the honking and screeching.

She'd reached the raised portion dividing the street when she heard the thud, the animal's high-pitched yelps. But her granddaughter's body drew her on. Wheels screamed near, drowning out the dog's cries. *Why won't she stop? She'll kill us both.*

But they reached the safety of the far side before the grinding crunch of colliding metal sounded behind.

On they went, without the threatening dog. Their pace slowed to a sagging jog. Darkened streets and business buildings. A fence they were too weak to climb barred their way. They turned and headed north.

I must be truly mad now.

They reached a graveled road at the edge of the city. The jog became a walk.

What are we doing to your baby, Shay?

But the fate awaiting that unborn child, and the body as well, kept them going.

Shay and Brandy crouched in the borrow pit beside the road when the lanterns of automobiles bore down on them. And then, too tired to stir, they slept. Only to awaken damp, aching and stiff. The night had deepened.

Another broad ribbon of highway, divided by a grassy area, and the red rear lanterns of an automobile that'd passed.

But once across they met a fence so they followed the borrow pit away from the sprawling city, dropping to the grass when a vehicle approached.

Shay grew light-headed, her stomach churned. But Brandy realized how far they'd come and still avoided capture. *There must be a way, Shay. If only we can think of it. Perhaps God is with us after all.*

A cloud appeared in front of her where there had been none a moment before. At first Brandy thought it a swarm of gnats rising from the tall grass. But it enveloped them. Pulled them down as if there were no earth beneath it.

The falling stopped. Brandy rose through a mist of dizziness and nausea. When that motion ended the sickness remained.

Thunder clamored and the borrow pit shuddered beneath her.

She opened her eyes to a lightning flash against a rain-smeared windowpane and then the blackness returned. Her groping hand found not the grass of the borrow pit, but a hard wooden floor with cracks between the boards, and farther on, the cold metal of ridges like . . . *Fingers! The wedding mirror . . . thunder . . .*

This was the Gingerbread House. And there was no cushioned rug on the floor.

She was home. She moved her tongue along her teeth and felt the space left by the tooth that was pulled the summer before. *I'm Brandy. Oh, thank you, Lord. I'll marry Mr. Strock. I'll do anything. And I'll forget all about Marek Weir and . . .*

Had he been badly injured or even killed when his head struck the hall tree?

Flickering light replaced the darkness. "Brandy, I've brought you a candle. The lights . . . dear, did you faint again?" Candle shadow softened the beloved face.

"Ma, it's so good to see you, to hear you . . . it's been so long."

Sophie knelt to feel her forehead. "Only since dinner, dear. Here, I'll unlace you. Why, you've left off your corset again." Her voice was so much gentler than Rachael's.

Brandy put her fingers to her lips. "Ma, I think you'd better fetch the bucket."

"There's one in the linen closet. I'll hurry." Her mother and the candle left, barely returning in time.

Sophie had to support her so she could keep her head over the rim of the bucket. Then her mother helped her into her nightdress, took down her hair and tucked her into bed. "I'll braid your hair later. Rest now. I'm going to empty the bucket and freshen it. Try not to be sick until I get back."

Sophie McCabe didn't seem very happy to see her. *Only since dinner.* Had time stood still while she was away?

The bed felt hard and gritty after Shay's luxurious one. Brandy longed to rid herself of the stench of sickness, to take a hot shower and wash her hair with the scented liquid soap of Shay's world, brush away the evil taste with the minty tooth polish.

But she looked at first one familiar object in the room and then the next. Even by the candle her mother'd left on her writing desk, Brandy could see that no crack jagged across the top of the wedding mirror.

Sophie returned with the bucket and placed it beside the bed.

"Oh, Ma, it's so good to be home."

"Yes, dear." The cruel suspicion in Sophie's eyes heightened her resemblance to Rachael Garrett. "Brandy, I'm going to call Dr. Jackson. You've been too tired since your father's funeral and now tonight—"

"Funeral!"

But her mother'd left. Brandy saw again the stone of John McCabe in Columbia Cemetery. And Elton's next to it. No, time had not stood still. *Pa's already dead and in a few years, my brother.* It would be so awful to know.

Rain lashed at her window. The candle flame danced in the wedding mirror. Had the storm caused it to yank her back to her own world? Was its dangerous magic haphazard? Did it control her destiny by a mere whim of fate and nature? Did no reasoning power rule it? Not even God?

Beside the candle lay a green book with gold lettering on its front. It hadn't been there when she'd left.

Dizziness assailed her as she slipped from her bed and she sat quickly in the desk chair.

The gold lettering read "Diary." Unlike most of her friends, Brandy'd never kept a diary. Had someone used her room while she was away?

Knowing she shouldn't, she opened it. The handwriting was messy and unfamiliar.

> Dear Brandy, I hope you will return to your body when I leave it. I don't know where you've been but I feel you must know what's gone on here while you've been gone.

Brandy looked up. *Shay. While I've been her, my granddaughter has been me.* No wonder Sophie showed no surprise at her return.

She read on to find that she was already Mrs. Corbin Strock. That she'd "had sex" with Corbin only once so probably wasn't pregnant. That his mother, Thora K., was really a "neat old broad," and would Brandy please be kind to her. It appeared that her body was now at the Gingerbread House, because Shay returned with it for John McCabe's funeral.

> He died in my arms, Brandy, thinking I was you. And I forgave him for you. Hope I did right. He seemed very sorry for making us marry Corbin. His last word was "Joshua."

The writing stopped. Tears filled Brandy's eyes. *Pa . . . I forgive you too.*

Brandy returned to her bed and was soon forced to use the bucket for her efforts. Poor Shay. She would come back to her body to find it in a borrow pit. Probably unaware that she carried Marek's child. That her parents planned to murder it and lock her up in an asylum for the mad.

Brandy dozed and dreamed of the wedding mirror. She awoke determined it should be destroyed. It caused too much evil in people's lives. Brandy stared at it with hatred.

Lightning flashed into the room, paling the candlelight to insignificance. Thunder rolled in behind it and the mirror hummed. Misty clouds twisted across the glass.

Brandy pulled the blanket over her head but the mist seeped through the weaving and drew her down through the bed. . . .

8

Voices rose through the mist with Brandy. "Rattle, rattle, rattle. Rattle your boodeez."

"Oh, no. No, please—"

"Stop that now. Everything's going to be all right. Here's the bowl," a man said close to her ear.

Something cold slid under her chin and she opened her eyes in time to see the round container before she gagged into it. But Shay's stomach was empty.

Brandy lay on a bed in one corner of a kitchen. An elderly gentleman with flowing white beard and hair rinsed the bowl in the sink.

A radio box sang on the table.

A cat nursed her kittens on the foot of the bed.

Brandy turned Shay's face to the wall and clamped her eyelids on tears. *I didn't even have the chance to talk to Elton.*

She didn't care how this body'd come from the borrow pit to wherever this was, only that she'd been torn from home again.

"Twenty-year-old Shay Garrett," the radio box said, "was missing from her home at Fourth and Spruce this evening. The young woman is in urgent need of medical and psychiatric care. She is five feet, seven inches, approximately one hundred and twenty pounds, with brown eyes and blond hair, and probably wearing a yellow shirt, blue jeans and tennis shoes. She was last seen crossing Twenty-eighth Street at Mapleton on foot, where she caused a series of rear-end collisions. No major injuries were reported in that mishap. Anyone with information concerning Miss Garrett is requested to call the Boulder Police Department or Jerrold Garrett, 444-1008. The young woman is not considered dangerous and foul play is not suspected in her disappearance."

The old man turned off the radio and came to stand by the bed. "Sounds like somebody we know, don't it?" His eyeballs protruded.

"I don't care. I don't care if they kill the baby . . . or about anything." Tears spilled over, ran down her cheeks. "I hate this world."

"You mean these babies?" He scooped up two of the tiny kittens, and the mother cat moaned a warning.

"No, this one." Brandy placed a hand on her granddaughter's abdomen. "And then they're going to put me in a madhouse."

"It's all right, Stina." He patted the cat and replaced the kittens. "The baby they're going to kill ain't born yet?"

"Not for about seven months."

"Someone's going to murder it when it's born?"

"No. They're going to do it now and call it abortion because they think I'm crazy."

"Crazy. Ahhh, we heard that word a time or two, ain't we, Stina?" He sat on the edge of the bed. Seemingly lidless eyes roamed the ceiling and walls, lips pursed and then constricted. "Sometime last night, Stina here (she's Swedish, you know) slipped out of the barn to do a little mousing and left her kittens alone. And do you know what happened?"

He had a wild look about him. Brandy pressed back against the pillow.

He leaned toward her. "A big"—he spread his arms—"scraggy old tom" —he clapped his hands and Brandy jumped but she could see the tomcat in her mind—"snuk up quiet-like and"—he raised bushy white brows— "and he ate up all Stina's newborn babes." The old man stood suddenly and the bed bounced Brandy and the felines. "Found a half a little body left this morning."

She stirred from her despair despite herself. "But her babes are there . . . with her now."

"And then . . ." He raised his arms again and swirled. His cuffs had no fastening and the sleeves fell back to withered muscle. His hands were brown but his arms white. ". . . all the day long Stina cried. In the barn. In the house. In the yard. And I felt her misery." His hands flew to his chest. "Till, Shay Garrett, I felt her great sadness here and I cried with her."

Brandy sat up, seeing the old man and the cat weeping together. "But her kittens are here."

"AND THEN!" Even Stina jumped to her feet at that, and the kittens mewed in protest. "A beautiful lady with silver hair fell into the front yard with this." He produced a dirty cloth bag and waved it before her face. "You know what was in this?"

Brandy cringed, fearing he meant to put it over her head and smother her.

"Kittens. FIVE KITTENS!" He threw the bag against the wall, pushed Stina down with the babies and flopped back onto the bed. "Now what do you think of that?"

"Uhh . . . well . . ." Brandy blinked.

"And Stina and I ain't cried since the beautiful lady and her sack of joy arrived. But the lady has tears on her face."

"I'm the lady?"

"And then I hear on the radio that she's got the police and her folks after her. And what should I do?"

"You'll probably take me back to them and I'll be—"

"I THINK that you was sent to Stina." He seemed ever to ask questions of her but have no interest in her answers. "So I can't let them find you, can I? After all, Stina's Swedish."

Brandy nodded Shay's head, though she couldn't really make out his reasoning.

"First thing's to get somethin' down you that'll stay. What's the one thing do you think'll stay put when everything else comes up?"

"Tea?"

"SEVEN-UP!" He took a green bottle from an icebox with rounded corners instead of square like Rachael's and poured a glass of clear bubbly liquid. "Drink this here and I'll see if my granddaughter left anything around the place for you to sleep in."

The mouth was dry and the bubbles cleaned the scum of sickness from the tongue. Brandy wondered if the odd gentleman truly meant to help her, if Shay'd come back to this body when Brandy left it to find them a refuge after all.

"Bit of a rag but looks clean enough," the old man said when he returned with a baggy cotton garment.

"Thank you, Mr. . . ."

"St. John."

"Saint John?" Brandy looked at the clutter of piled newspapers, dirty dishes, and the sagging sofa across the room. This might be a refuge but it certainly wasn't heaven.

"Ansel St. John." He stroked the cat. "And this here's Stina Mark. Them Swedes make awful good mothers, you know."

Stina Mark curled her body around the sleeping kittens and purred.

Marek Weir poured water out of the plastic bag and added more ice cubes. He lay on the couch with the bag against his bruised face. But the area on the back of his head where the doctor'd taken two stitches wouldn't permit that for long. "Oh, hell."

Marek mixed himself a martini at the bar beside the fireplace and filled his pipe, which he smoked only when greatly agitated, since the surgeon general had finally scared him off cigarettes. Even striking the match against the moss rock hurt his head.

He sat in his favorite chair and propped the ice pack across the swollen eye. With the one that would still open he stared out onto the patio but he saw instead gold-flecked eyes, bewildered, frightened.

Why hadn't she been found? When he'd walked into the Gingerbread House he'd had a vague impression of someone behind the buffet at the foot of the stairs. He couldn't remember if he'd seen a knee, a head or what. But before he'd had time to pull it into his consciousness an outraged father'd busted him in the face. When he came to, Shay was gone.

Running alone. Carrying his child. He had no reason to doubt it was his. The helpless look of the new Shay tore at him.

The police had reported a sighting of Shay running across Twenty-eighth Street. Marek's apartment was on Thirtieth. He'd searched the grounds and given up.

She'd had plenty of time to get here. The patio drapes and door were open to entice her, welcome her.

Shay'd assured him she was on the pill. How had she become pregnant? What would the child look like if it were allowed life?

Come home, Shay. Here's where you'd be living and safe now if we'd been married on time. I'll find a way to keep you out of Sampson's clutches, if I have to fight your parents and the police.

Ansel St. John sat at the table eating oatmeal. He'd removed his teeth to eat. They lay, complete with store-bought gums, between the radio and the teapot. Brandy decided she was the only sane person left in Shay's lunatic world.

She'd managed some of the acrid tea and a piece of toast after she bathed Shay's body in the bathroom that opened into the kitchen.

Shay's body felt feverish with aches that moved to every part and back again. Brandy didn't know if it was because of the baby, or the exhausting escape of the night before or the terrible wrenching of bodies caused by the mirror switching her and her granddaughter in time. She could only hope that the wedding mirror would switch them again, and soon.

She longed to see her mother once more, and Elton before he died. She'd do her duty by Mr. Strock if only she could return to the peace of a world she could understand.

By lunchtime Mr. St. John had to spoon her a poached egg while the radio announced failure in the search for Shay Garrett. Stina Mark and her adopted kittens were in a paper box with rags for a floor.

And then Brandy lost track of mealtimes and of nights and days.

John McCabe drove the buggy down Pearl Street and she ran behind, calling to him. When he looked over his shoulder he didn't seem to recognize her.

"Pa?"

"I ain't your pa." Ansel St. John propped her up and held a spoon to her lips. "Got some nice soup here. Want you to take it all."

Her mother and Elton stepped off the trolley at Chautauqua Park with a picnic basket.

Brandy ran up to them. "Ma, Elton, I'm home."

Sophie McCabe slid her arm through Elton's and they both drew back. "Who in heaven's name is that? Where's Joshua?"

"I don't know her, Ma. But Joshua's dead of the typhoid and I think she has it too."

"Typhoid? But don't you see I'm—"

"No, ain't typhoid." Ansel St. John's eyes bulged above her. "Just a bug from running around all hours of the night probably. You're young. You'll pull through. Here, drink this."

Clouds of mist rolled across the glass of the wedding mirror, thunder shuddered the floor beneath it, lightning flashed the bronze frame to green. The entwined hands writhed until they disentangled themselves, reached out to her with fingers parted, the face of Marek Weir formed from the smoky mist, dark curls fluffing toward his face, sharp features half-shadowed.

9

Brandy heard the cock crow before she opened her eyes, and wondered why that ordinary sound should make her so happy. It meant it was time to rise and help Nora with the breakfast, bring up coal for the stove, let the hens out and . . .

Something furry with prickly nails moved along her neck, nudged her cheek. Brandy sat up with a gasp even as her eyes flew open.

The bed was alive with wobbly kittens. One lay on her lap, where it had fallen when she'd sat erect. Another wrapped its front paws around her foot and tried to bite through the covers. Yet another squatted to wet on the bedclothes. Five in all.

Oh yes, Stina Mark. Tears pricked behind her eyes and nose. Why couldn't dreams be reality?

Mr. St. John snorted and rolled over on the sofa.

The odor of cat and sickness permeated the room.

Shay's body felt weak, hungry and filthy.

Brandy caught a kitten about to topple over the edge of the bed, stuffed him and his siblings into the box and put it on the floor.

In the bathroom she ran a tub of hot water and scrubbed Shay's body.

"Shay Garrett, you up and feeling better then?" Ansel St. John called from the other side of the door.

"Yes. Could you find my clothes, please?"

At the breakfast table Brandy consumed three eggs, toast and tea. "You've been so kind, Mr. St. John, I don't know how to thank you."

"I'll tell you how. Drink all that milk."

"I don't drink milk. I—"

"It's not for you. For the little one." His eyes grew wild and threatening. His beard dipped into his tea. "Do as I say now. Ain't ordinary milk. It's goat's milk." He finished eating and replaced his teeth.

Brandy choked down half the milk and then lay on the sofa while he stripped the bed.

"I'm going into town to the Laundromat and to get some food. You rest now. Got Happy chained out front. He'll keep anybody from the door."

Brandy's little display of health had exhausted Shay. They lay quietly drowsy, but clean and fed.

Stina Mark entered through a flap door cut into the side of the house and crawled into her box, calling to the kittens. They tumbled from all corners of the kitchen for their morning bath and breakfast. Stina purred while they nursed, her eyes black slits in pools of yellow.

A dog growled outside the wide glass door. It must be Happy. With a name like that he apparently wasn't Swedish.

Where had Shay found the kittens? And how had she come to be at this place? What was she doing with Brandy's body now?

The rattle of the electric icebox kept time with Stina's contented noise. A clock above the sink ticked soothingly. Brandy slept.

"Wake up, I say. High time you was eatin' something. It's four o'clock in the afternoon."

Brandy hadn't heard Ansel return. The table was set for a meal. Ears of corn, sliced tomatoes, peas, green beans and carrots.

"Just picked from the garden out back and steamed. Now, what do you think of that?"

"Mr. St. John, it looks like a feast." *Except for the goat's milk.*

Ansel cut his corn from the cob and mashed it and everything else on his plate with a fork.

Brandy politely looked away from the dentures sitting next to his glass and ate until Shay could hold no more.

"Got you a toothbrush in Boulder. Took some old things my granddaughter left around into the Laundromat and went to the Salvation Army store for more like 'em. You'll want to be getting out of the house one of these days and you can't be seen in that outfit. And that hair gets hit by sunlight, it'll shine like a beacon. Bring every cop for miles. You tie it up in a kerchief and people'll think Lottie's back and won't take no notice."

"Mr. St. John, why are you doing all this for me?"

"Told you. For Stina Mark there. And"—he stood to orate, waving his fork and shirt cuff—"because I don't think you're rowing with just one oar, any more than me." He seemed to have a great deal of energy for so old a man. "You see, Shay Garrett, the WORLD is crazy. You and me know where it's at."

He flopped into his chair and gummed the last of his food. "Now, if you feel up to it, you can do the dishes while I do the chores. I'll bring your bedding in off the line."

No dishwashing machine here, but there was the luxury of hot water piped into the sink. Every dish in the place seemed dirty, stacked wherever there was room. Nora would have been aghast. The cupboards were almost empty. Brandy washed them out first and then began filling them with clean dishes. When she finished she was tired but had gone a long way toward cleaning up the clutter.

She crawled gratefully into the washed and aired sheets, awakening rested and stronger the next morning.

She talked Ansel into removing the piles of newspapers and then swept and scrubbed the kitchen and bathroom floors. She slept all afternoon.

The next day he brought her a long patterned skirt, a baggy blouse and a kerchief to cover her hair.

"Time you met the others and got some fresh air," he said when she'd dressed.

"There are others living here?"

"Come on, I'll show you." He led her past stale-smelling rooms, out a back door, along a path by a vegetable garden and rusting metal machinery to a board fence and a series of sagging sheds.

"This here's Olina," Ansel announced as a nanny goat bounded up to him. She was joined by her billy, "Oscar," and two frolicking kids, "Arvid" and "Luvisa."

Brandy laughed and was surprised at how it felt. "I suppose they're all Swedish."

Ansel's big eyes watered. "You're a picture when you smile. Even in that get-up. It's a JOY to see you mending." On the word "joy" he raised his arms to heaven. There was something almost religious about him.

"Mr. St. John, you said I was sent to Stina Mark with the kittens. Do you think God sent me?"

"God's for the young and the rich. Us old folks and animals got to look out for ourselves."

Tall whitened tree trunks lined one side of the goat yard, barren branches pointing like dead fingers toward the blue depth of morning sky. "What happened to them?"

"Used to be an irrigation ditch run through here. Dried up because of the town and the drought. Trees couldn't take it. God don't care about them neither."

"The town is very close." Boulder sprawled out along the base of the mountains to envelop the prairie until it reached dwellings and roads to the bottom of the long rolling hill on which they stood. "Do you truly believe you can hide me from the police?"

"They don't bother me none. It's the Chamber of Commerce that's got me worried. We're still county here, but this used to be peaceful farmland as far as you could see."

"Before that, prairie with scattered cattle grazing on it." Brandy heard the wistful note in Shay's voice.

"And before that, the land of the Arapahoe and the buffalo." He drew out the o's until she saw buffalo instead of goats. Ansel St. John was almost as magical as the wedding mirror and didn't even use pictures.

"Come along. Haven't met everybody yet." He drew her on to a barn, unpainted and leaning away from the west wind. Where there should have been cows and horses, chickens ran wild, and more cats. At the far end, more goats.

"That's Hooligan and his wife Stina Mark. Watch out for Hooligan. He's a mean one. Stina can handle him though. Swedes make awful good wives, you know."

"But Stina Mark is the black cat with the—"

"THIS is Stina Mark." His tone broached no argument and Brandy felt uneasy about him for the first time since she'd begun to recover.

The goat had soft brown fur with eyes to match and streaks of white along her flanks. She butted Ansel's hand gently, her stubby tail in constant brisk motion.

Ansel led Brandy around the front of the house, where derelict automobiles sat on tireless hubs among the weeds. A dog was chained in front of the wide glass door that slid half back on itself to provide entrance to the kitchen.

"Happy, I want you to meet our visitor."

Brandy had seen the dog through the door already and was confused as to his naming also. When she asked her host he merely replied, "Because he's happy."

"He doesn't look it." The animal's lips curled in a snarl. He was medium-sized and fairly stout.

"That's cause you're lookin' at the wrong end. See his tail?"

Happy's tail did indeed wag but the look in his eyes was cold and unloving. He sniffed her hand, then her skirt. Brandy shivered, remembering the silent dog at her side when she'd fled through the alleyways and streets of Boulder.

As she turned to go into the house, Happy growled low in his throat.

Rachael Garrett lay on the bed in which her Grandmother Sophie had given birth to her mother, where her Grandfather McCabe had died. Where she and Jerry conceived and later snuggled with the baby, Shay, sharing their delight at the good fortune that had finally befallen them.

Now she watched her husband dress. He sat on the edge of the bed with his back to her, one shoe on, holding the other, probably lost in the same remembering as she, unable to share it with her as once he would have.

He cleared his throat, put on his shoe and stared at the wall.

Another day. More false leads or nothing at all. Rachael no longer cared about the book she was writing. She spent more time listening for the phone than getting on with her work. Hoping it would be Shay come to her senses. Or at least word that she was alive and well. Afraid that it might be news of finding her body. She could be in another state by now, dead or alive, anywhere.

Jerry'd hired a detective, broadcast a reward for news of their daughter. People called, some trying to help, others just being cruel.

And again, as in every major aspect of Rachael's life, her mother had been instrumental. Even in her last act of dying. The trouble with Shay began the night Brandy Maddon died. Brandy's control of Rachael's life was complete to the end.

"Remember"—Jerry said his first word of the day "when we took a picnic up to Fourth of July Campground that time and Shay fell into the stream? She kept yelling, 'Daddy, Daddy.' "

"Even after you'd pulled her out and were holding her. And that fisherman came along and decided you were running off with somebody else's kid."

Jerry turned, looked into Rachael's eyes with feeling. "She couldn't have been more than five." He blinked away the feeling. "Maybe somebody really has run off with her now."

"Let's at least have breakfast together. I'll fix it quick."

"No. I'll get something downtown." The familiar sound of withdrawal. He stood and walked to the door.

"Wait, I'll get dressed and we'll both go out for breakfast."

"Rachael, I don't need—"

"Well, maybe I do. Dammit, Shay isn't the only one who needs you, you know. She was mine too. Whether you like it or not, we do share a common grief."

"Don't say 'was'!" Weight had mellowed the lonely eyes. The longer hair style, salted with gray, softened the bone lines of his face. "You've got your historic house and your career. You never needed me except as another piece of furniture to fill out—"

"Jerry, you still love me. I know that."

But her husband was gone. Rachael waited to hear the front door slam before she rolled over to cry. She decided to try again that evening after he'd had his scotch.

But Jerry Garrett didn't come home that night. Rachael knew he was up at the cabin in Nederland and probably not alone. When he hadn't returned by the next morning, she called the police and asked them to relay any messages about Shay to Marek Weir.

Then Rachael packed a bag and walked out of the Gingerbread House.

Marek Weir doubled his jogging distance that morning, looking for a platinum-blond head he knew he wouldn't see. The sting of sweat seeped into his eyes by the time he reached the door of the apartment. He fought the pain of ragged breathing and overpumping heart as he stripped out of his sweatsuit and stepped into the shower.

Marek listened without hope to the morning news during his bachelor breakfast. Shay's mother would have called him about any development, even if Jerry Garrett did hate his guts.

The extra mug of coffee and the double exercise couldn't dispel the listlessness left by a night of nightmare and yearning on the controlled warmth of the king-size water bed that'd once lulled away disturbing thoughts.

He grabbed the notes he should have worked on the night before and left the apartment. As he locked the door, the girls living next to him did the same. One was interesting, the other not. Both invited him with their eyes.

"Fucking world," he snarled, to their apparent delight, and stalked off down the hall, leaving them giggling behind him.

The rumble of the Porsche didn't satisfy him this morning. The rush-hour traffic the length of Boulder set his teeth on edge. Gone was the last yellowness of the bruise Shay's father'd left on his face. The stitches were cut from the back of his head and much of the hair grown out where it had been shaved away from the wound.

But the wound inside Marek had grown. His mother'd visited his dreams, asking, "Where is your wife, son? Where is your child, Marek?"

The weird part of the whole damn dilemma was he liked Shay better crazy. He couldn't account for this unreasonable instability in his emotions.

"Emotions, Jesus," he said to the Porsche as he whirled it up the mesa road to NCAR. He thought he'd learned to control them better at his age.

Marek breathed deeply of the fresh air as he headed for the building Shay had called a castle. Martin Black had invited him on a hard-rock jaunt for Saturday. Marek decided to accept. That was the way to exhaust and exhilarate himself out of this agony, this mood that kept him driving streets and back-country roads till all hours in a hopeless search.

"Hell, she's probably dead or in Alaska by now," he said to the elevator button, and jabbed it.

Shay was right. The place was odorless.

No more whispered talk about the strange disappearance of his fiancée that would end suddenly when colleagues and secretaries discovered he was near. Fads in gossip were over quickly in this busy world.

No one teased him any longer about getting rid of the Porsche and joining the station-wagon set.

He nodded to a few people, hated the sympathy still in their eyes, was glad to get to the open air of the catwalk.

Old girl friends called him again. He received invitations to parties. But he didn't go. The good times had paled.

Throwing his notes on the desk, he stared at the city from his tower office.

Then Marek turned to the scrawled writing on the blackboard, the haunting message circled so the janitor wouldn't wash it away. *I am Brandy.*

10

Brandy McCabe stood before a line of graves bordering one edge of Ansel St. John's junk-filled yard.

Weeds had been cleared away here and the mounds ringed with milky quartz pebbles. Five tiny graves and four large ones. At the head of each a white cross with lettering carved in the wood and painted gold.

The same words on all nine crosses. STINA MARK.

Wind billowed her long skirt. Metal clanged on metal where her host worked on some rusting machine on the other side of the house.

Were these the graves of other goats and cats with the name so common in this place? This odd burial ground increased her anxiety about Mr. St. John.

An automobile traveled too slowly along the road. Brandy crouched behind a windowless hulk, raising her head just enough to peer through a portal that'd once held glass. The torn seats gave off a smell like that of moldy blankets.

A familiar silver-green vehicle dazzled in the sunlight and turned into the drive.

Happy barked and lunged at the end of his chain.

Marek Weir stepped out and stood looking about him from behind darkened spectacles.

Brandy experienced a glut of emotions at the sight of him. Relief that he'd not been killed by Shay's father. Horror that he'd tracked her down. Longing to feel just once more before she returned to her own world the heat of his breath as when he'd kissed her in that saloon with the hanging plants. Shame at the betrayal of these thoughts. The urge to flee before he could take her back to the Gingerbread House.

But she slumped to the weeds and covered Shay's face instead. The diamond had slipped around and lay cold against her skin. She began to pray fervently but was interrupted by Mr. St. John's curt command to Happy. The incessant barking stopped.

Brandy crawled up to peek again. Ansel walked toward Marek, wiping his hands on a rag. Ansel nodded, gestured, shrugged. Marek stood with hands on slim hips, head lowered to watch the old man's face.

Finally they shook hands. Marek slid into his automobile and drove away.

Brandy watched Ansel stroll toward the machine he'd been working on, as if nothing of importance had occurred.

She skirted around the back of the house. "Mr. St. John, what happened? What did he say?"

"Said his name was Marek Something-to-ruther." Ansel leaned his weight on a long metal handle and grunted. "Said he was looking for you."

"You mean he doesn't know I'm here?"

"Hand me that there hammer." He beat the handle with the hammer and yelled over the noise, "Told him I hadn't seen you. Ain't nobody can lie as good as me. Here, you lean on this and we'll both try."

Brandy moved to help him and she could hear his joints crack as they tried to force the handle.

"Eh . . . dang thing. Take a blowtorch to get it off. Never mind. Don't hurt the little one." He stood back and wiped his forehead on his sleeve. "That young buck give you this?" He touched Shay's engagement ring. "And the baby you're growing?"

Brandy felt a hot blush on Shay's cheeks. "Yes." *I assume so.*

"Ought to be some baby then. Why'd he want it killed, I wonder."

"It's not him. It's her . . . my parents. They mustn't find me."

"They won't. Thought you was pickin' corn for supper. Hunt up some eggs to go with it while you're at it."

She'd seen no sign of a chicken house. "Where do the hens lay their eggs?"

"All over. That's why you have to hunt 'em."

Ansel St. John didn't approve of eating meat and although Brandy missed it she found the fresh eggs and vegetables, lightly salted and buttered, more satisfying than the highly seasoned food Rachael cooked.

They sat now over such a meal and Brandy obediently fed Shay and her baby some goat's milk.

"That Marek fella sure sounded torn up about losing you." Her host stroked mashed food from his beard. "Could hear the TEARS in his voice."

"What kind of man gets his fiancée with child before he weds her?"

"Any kind that can get away with it. I ain't for judgin' neither of you. But that boy's hurtin' deep."

"I don't wish to discuss Mr. Weir."

"Sure did when you was sick. Kept callin' his name over and over."

"I did no such thing."

"Did so." He buttered a slice of dark bread and dunked it in his tea to soften it. "Told me a lot of things. You was awful sick for a while. Said you was Brandy McCabe and looked in a mirror and then you was Shay Garrett."

Brandy set down her ear of corn and stared. "What else did I say?"

His lips pursed out and then retreated around toothless gums. "Spoke of some people I used to know of when I was a kid. Sophie and Elton McCabe. Nora Labsap. Them McCabes was big news way back then. My pappy used to haul coal to the Gingerbread House, you know. 'Course I never knew John. He died before I was born but the stories about him outlasted his dying for many a year. Raised more hell than ten men put together in his day. Owned half of Water Street too."

"He did not!"

"Did so. Biggest joke in town when old Sophie led the crusade to shut it down after he was dead. Then she couldn't figure why her income shrunk so. Real religious, that Sophie. Livin' off whores and gambling and booze and not knowing it."

Brandy jumped from her chair much like he did when preparing for an oration. "You're lying."

"SIT DOWN!"

Stina Mark started up from her box of kittens, but Brandy sat. "You think I'm mad too."

Ansel pointed his fork at her. "I can outfib a politician if I want to. But I ain't now. You eat some food for that baby and I'll talk. Else I won't say another word. Ain't you a bit curious as to what happened after you left?"

Brandy took a bite of egg. "What happens to Nora? I know about the others."

"Nora Labsap? Married some bartender at Werely's Saloon. Your ma and her friends put him out of business. Moved to Cheyenne, as I remember. Don't know what came of them. Your brother Elton died of the great influenza. Like the plague it was."

"He never marries." *Don't listen to him, Brandy. He may be your savior now but he's got a tile loose somewhere.*

"Never did. Today you'd call him gay. Back then the words was harder. Got affianced once but discovered his field of interest laid in other directions. Old Sophie did her best to cover it up."

"Gay? Elton is a very solemn young man. He—"

"Real joke was after Sophie lost her money she kept the Gingerbread House goin' off her daughter's husband. He was a Maddon. Big a hellraiser as old John McCabe till he met Brandy. Had a ranch out of Nederland. His brother run booze during prohibition. They was twins. Stories about them two'd burn a lady's ears. That Brandy tamed 'em though. She was a woman and a half. Little thing. Surprised everybody. Rumor had it she was crazy too, but if she was, she sure knew how to use it."

"But I am Brandy."

"No, you're Shay Garrett. Better get used to it. Won't be easy, but you're a scrapper. Never saw nothin' fight for life and breath as you did when you was sick." His eyebrows moved up into grizzled hair. "Now, if it was me, I'd do some worrying about that mirror. Don't seem right to let it loose in the world." He scratched his chin under his beard. "That Maddon twin Brandy married, his old man was hung for murder and his mother was a whore."

Brandy covered Shay's ears, but it didn't help.

"That boy was a legend, and so was his brother. Them Maddon twins could outcurse, outride and outbastardize—"

"Mr. St. John!"

"Sorry. Keep forgetting you're from a different time than Lottie, even if you're much of an age."

"You . . . believe me then? What I said when I was ill? That I'm—"

"Never heard of a mirror could do what that one did to you. But there's a lot of crazy talk in this world. Old Ansel's learned to filter out the RING OF TRUTH when he hears it. Anybody your age who'd treat somebody mine with respect, callin' me Mr. St. John . . . I mean you ain't from *this* world. Ain't seen anybody scrub a floor like you do since . . ."

He patted her shoulder. "Think we need some ice cream or dessert. Lottie don't believe in sugar but when the cat's away . . ." He opened the icebox, produced a colored paper box and spooned ice cream onto her plate. "Get much more addled and I'll start buying coffee again."

"I do miss coffee."

"You too? Lottie talked me off coffee and sugar. She's into stuff you wouldn't believe, my granddaughter. Had a TV once. Good company for an old man. Lottie stuck a shovel through the screen. She was right about the stupid stuff it said but I was old enough to know better. But then she raised the money against the taxes to keep my place from the bulldozer. Passed the hat amongst her friends and they don't have scratch."

"Where's Lottie now?"

"She's like the hens. All over. Last I knew she was raisin' money to save a prairie-dog colony and living in a shack with three men. She has appetites, does Lottie."

"Living with . . . alone? You mean—"

"Sleepin' with 'em. Hurts your lady ears, I know. But that Lottie'd made a fortune on Water Street in your day, even paying cumshaw to your dad. Now they only get board and room and call it liberated instead of business. But Lottie makes out. She ain't no fool."

"How can you permit her? Are her parents dead?"

"Mother's out East somewheres, a social worker. Never met the father. Beth's married and divorced so often I lost track. So did Lottie."

"What does a social worker do?"

"Nothin' for their own, I can tell you. But that Marek now—"

"I don't wish to discuss him."

"He don't appear to be the kind to let go of his own. If that's his baby you're carryin' you better set your mind to being Shay Garrett and Mrs. Marek whatever. That boy's one problem's going to keep comin' back."

Late the next day when Ansel drove his rattling truck off to town Brandy explored the unused portion of the house. A dining room, a parlor, three bedrooms upstairs. All furnished and covered with dust and cobwebs, rotting dust sheets and curtains. One bedroom had been more recently used. Lottie's most likely. Books, shoes, a radio box and pictures on the walls. Large unframed photographs of naked men . . .

Brandy knew she shouldn't look. But she did.

Her curiosity about this sinful world was outdistanced only by her desire to return to her own.

She fled outside to the sky and earth, to the mountain range she could trace from memory.

At the back fence, Olina, Oscar, Luvisa and Arvid—the smelly Swedish goat family—rushed up to greet her.

Brandy scratched Olina's hard neck with Shay's fingernails, and felt a dizziness she supposed to be caused by this body's condition. A vision . . . a picture . . . the body of Brandy McCabe leaning on the door of a small cabin. Mr. Strock and a man Brandy'd never seen lifted the wedding mirror from a buckboard.

Heavy with weakness, Brandy collapsed to the weeds, Arvid and Luvisa peering at her between the boards of the fence.

Shay has the mirror with her in Nederland. She can make it work from her end of time now that I can't be near it.

Of course, she'd be returning not to the Gingerbread House but to Nederland and Mr. Strock. Still, if she could believe Ansel St. John and she was destined to tame the ferocious Maddon twins, she must be capable of convincing Corbin Strock that she needed long visits to her family in

Boulder. That would be better than being completely cut off as she was now.

Brandy wished she could meet the real Shay Garrett, but supposed they would pass through the sickness of time as before and never know each other.

Hurry, Granddaughter. Marek Weir is a devil and I haven't the strength to resist him.

11

Jerry Garrett was surprised to find the door of the Gingerbread House locked. He fished out his key, let himself in, and headed for the liquor cabinet. Pouring a scotch, he took it to the kitchen.

The house had a tense, empty feeling.

Usually by this time Rachael had preparations for dinner under way and the room smelled of cooking. He checked the bulletin board beside the refrigerator for any messages and found only a grocery list.

What the hell, she's got a right to come and go. It was just she was such a creature of habit. Her schedule rarely varied.

He sipped the drink on his way back to the entry hall and the buffet where she left the mail for him.

A faint humming broke into his thoughts. Jerry stared at the staircase over the rim of his glass.

He hadn't been able to bring himself to mount those stairs since the night his daughter ran away.

There was something that alarmed him about that sound in an otherwise too-silent house. And it seemed to be coming from the second floor. Was Shay home? Was that the sound of her stereo warming up, or her electric razor or . . .

Jerry bounded up the stairs and down the hall, scotch dribbling over the edge of his glass and wetting his fingers. "Shay?"

The room was empty. But the noise hummed louder here. Perhaps a wire had shorted on her radio and somehow turned it on.

He crossed to the radio, placed a hand on it and found it cold. The humming came from behind him now and he could almost count the tiny hairs as they stood up on the back of his neck.

Jerry turned. The old mirror Rachael'd planned to give Shay as a wedding present glowed. In the glass was a picture of two men unloading from a horse-drawn wagon the same mirror with a blanket half-draped over it. A young woman in old-fashioned dress clutched the door of a rough cabin as if she were about to faint. And then another girl appeared, dressed like a gypsy. She reached over a fence to pet a goat and slumped suddenly to the ground. When she drew her hands away from her face he saw she was Shay.

Jerry sloshed scotch down his jacket as he drained his glass. He blinked and the picture was gone. The humming stopped.

He sat on the bed, sweating.

Mirrors don't do tricks. But the mind does.

He watched it out of the corner of his eye. It reflected a portion of the room and his knees like it was supposed to. As always the mirror reminded him of the cave where he and Rachael found it and the body of that miner. Then he realized the cabin he'd seen was familiar, much like the one he and his mother'd lived in that year in Nederland.

Jerry stood in front of the mirror and saw himself. He walked around behind it. Just an ugly old mirror.

He walked down the hall to the head of the stairs and looked at the wedding portrait. The girl clutching the cabin door had been Rachael's mother as a young woman. *A trick of the mind.*

He decided the torture he was undergoing had arranged familiar images into a dream pattern that he thought he'd seen in the mirror's glass. Gale Sampson probably had a fancy word for it.

Downstairs he started to pour another scotch and thought better of it. He found a wedge of leftover roast and made a sandwich, trying to forget the vision of Shay he thought he'd seen upstairs.

Rachael should have stayed home to take any messages if the police or the detective called.

Perhaps they had and Rachael'd rushed off to find Shay.

Jerry called the police department and learned that his wife had asked them to relay any news to Marek Weir. And no, there hadn't been any.

He checked her closet. The suitcase she kept on the shelf above her clothes was gone. He called his brother-in-law but Remy Maddon hadn't heard from Rachael in three days.

Jerry was swearing as he headed the Oldsmobile across town. When he reached Thirtieth Street he turned off at a row of apartment complexes and pulled in beside the Porsche.

In the hallway a bottle blond stepped out of the door next to Weir's as Jerry knocked. He searched for a buzzer or doorbell.

"If you're looking for Marek, I think he's in the pool," she said and giggled unnecessarily.

Probably with a bevy of admiring women, Jerry thought as he retraced his steps and circled the building to a courtyard.

But Marek Weir swam alone, the deck and chairs empty except for a towel and the splashover from the man's swimming.

Marek beat the water like he was trying to kill it, kicking off from the ends, lapping the pool again and again. The piercing smell of chlorine surged into the air. Lowering sun flashed the flying spray to glitter.

Copper skin stretched over lean muscle. A tight red swimsuit. No wonder Shay had . . .

The black head emerged dripping. Marek hoisted himself out of the pool, his chest pumping.

"Your . . . daughter's . . . not here, Garrett," Marek said between heavy intakes of breath.

"I'm looking for my wife."

"She's not here either." The odd light eyes were cold under brows frizzed by vigorous toweling.

"Rachael's gone. I wondered if she'd told you where." Jerry followed Marek across a patch of grass to the enclosed patio.

"Your wife doesn't check in with me." Marek stood aside for him to enter the sliding glass door.

"She left word with the police to call you if there was any news about Shay. Why?"

"They've got my home and office number. Maybe she thought they could reach me. You tend to be gone a lot. Fix yourself a drink. Scotch in the bar." Marek trailed his towel into the bedroom and closed the door.

Lush carpet, moss-rock fireplace, expensive car, the best scotch . . . didn't kids ever start out at the bottom anymore? He poured himself a double and found ice in the tiny kitchen. A good smell came from the oven. Jerry remembered the half-eaten sandwich he'd left at home, heard the shower running. *Stud probably eats little girls for breakfast.*

Two paintings that had hung above the couch now leaned against the wall. In their place a hand-drawn map of Boulder and its environs was thumbtacked to the paneling, red lines, arrows and X's all over it.

Marek emerged dressed, without the chlorine smell, and with wet hair plastered to his head. He mixed a drink while Jerry studied the map.

"The lines are where I've been. The big X's where I've talked to people. The small ones where there was no one home."

"You think you can find her when the police can't? That she's still in the area?" Jerry flopped down on the couch and faced the bastard. "Or even alive?"

"She'd better be."

"Listen, I hired a detective. I drove around looking too. She's my kid—"

"And she's carrying mine." Marek raised his infernal martini. "I'm going to find her. And you better stand back when I do. No abortions, no Dr. Sampsons, no mental hospitals."

"If she were still on your map the police or someone would've found her. I even offered a reward—"

"And stalked off to your cabin, let your wife wait around for the phone to ring."

Jerry jumped to his feet. "You stay out of—"

"Don't push your luck." Marek set down his drink, rose slowly. "I stood still for you once. You had the advantage of surprise."

Jerry felt foolish, staring across the room at his daughter's fiancé like an old dog preparing to defend his territory. He kneaded the skin around his eyes. "Rachael might leave me, but not the house. Not when Shay . . . I'm afraid something's happened to her. She's never done anything like this before."

"People change." Marek left to answer the ring of his telephone in the bedroom.

"The police?" Jerry asked when he returned. "About Shay?"

"Rachael. Checking in to see if I'd heard anything."

"Did you tell her I was here? Where is she?"

"Could be anywhere. She dialed direct. Would you like some dinner? I made enough for two nights. We bachelors—"

"Dammit, Weir, what did she say?"

"Said for you to remember the bills are due the first of the month, the house cleaners come on Thursday mornings and if her agent calls—"

"What does she think I am, her secretary?" Jerry drained his glass and headed for the door.

"What do you think she is?"

Pausing in the doorway, Jerry stared down the hall. "She didn't even want to talk to me?"

"She especially didn't want to talk to you."

Brandy McCabe stood once again by the Stina Mark graveyard and thought of Ansel St. John. She'd asked him about these graves more than once but he ignored her questions.

As fall had deepened, the mountain foothills browned, the weeds around the collection of junk vehicles began to dry. And Shay's pregnancy became more evident.

At times Brandy felt almost at home with her host. After dinner when he read his paper she'd mend his clothes. Brandy'd often sat in the parlor of an evening sewing with her mother while her father and Elton played checkers or read.

In Ansel's parlor she'd found a sewing basket with all she needed to repair the poor man's shirts and trousers. In the basket was a thimble engraved with the name "Stina Mark."

Anyone who accepted her fantastic story as easily as did Ansel had to be wrong in the head. Was she really safe here?

When Brandy told him she knew she'd be going back to her own time soon because of her granddaughter with the mirror in Nederland, he'd dropped his paper to stare at her. "Them times are interesting to talk about but nobody that lived 'em should ever want to go back."

Brandy bent to pull some burrs from the hem of her skirt. At least two of those graves were large enough to contain human bodies.

No. She wouldn't think of that.

She'd asked the old man if he knew of a midwife or doctor they could trust. Just in case she was still here when Shay's baby was born.

"Don't need none. Delivered Arvid and Luvisa when Olina got in trouble. Calves and a few lambs in my day. Even a stuck kitten now and then. Figure I can whelp a human kid."

Brandy was the oldest of the McCabe children. Elton was born a year after and Joshua the year after that. Sophie had three miscarriages that Brandy knew of. The last one left her ill for several years.

Brandy's best friend in preparatory school, Violet, had married at seventeen, died in childbirth at eighteen.

At Violet's funeral the minister had honored the dead girl. "She gave her life in God's noblest cause."

The same minister had once preached that man was born in pain because Eve sinned against the Lord by eating forbidden fruit in the garden of Eden. And all women were cursed with this painful obligation from then on. *Poor thing. She was probably inflicted with curiosity like me.*

Brandy had seen a mare foal once . . .

12

Moonlight caught a spark of gray-white in the depths of the lilac bush by the back step of the Gingerbread House. Branches snapped, and dried seed pods from last spring's blossoms showered to the earth.

On the two-story building next door the motel sign blinked its orange letters backward. Drapes were pulled on all the lighted windows.

A dog yapped somewhere down the alley and a shadow moved from the protection of the garage, vaulted the wrought-iron fence and landed with a rustle of fallen leaves.

"Davenport?" A voice from the lilac bush.

Chris Davenport sprinted the length of the yard as a gray-haired man stepped from the bush and knelt by the back door.

"Is he still in Nederland?"

"All settled for the night. Where's the truck?" Chris asked.

"It'll be along as soon as the next patrol has checked those business buildings across the street." Keys jingled as the man tried first one and then the other on an enormous key ring. "Ahhh, this is it."

He pulled Chris into the stale darkness.

"You're sure you don't know when the lady of the house plans to return?"

"I told you, we didn't even know she was planning to leave. Sarah and I kept showing up on Thursdays to clean and the door was always locked. Then some friends of ours kept seeing Garrett up in Nederland so—"

"Yes, well, fill me in on the layout."

"This is the kitchen. Nothing much here." Chris turned a flashlight on the floor and led the way to the dining room, where the man decided on the chandelier and most of the furniture.

In the hallway he exclaimed over the buffet and had Chris shine light into each drawer as he opened it. From the bottom he lifted out folded tablecloths. A package wrapped in brown paper lay beneath. The man slit the wrapping with a pocketknife and held a green leather-bound book to Chris's light. "Diary" was lettered in gold on its front.

"No." The diary dropped onto the pile of tablecloths. "We'll empty all the drawers and take the buffet."

Chris led him into the living room, shielding the light with a cupped hand, hoping it wouldn't show to anyone in the street. "How do you think you're going to get all this stuff into the truck without being seen?"

"Remarkably easy once you get the hang of it. Ummm . . . a signed Tiffany. This is a transient neighborhood with a goodly portion of businesses closed for the night. Ideal, really. Worst problems we have anymore are dogs and joggers. And the health nuts ought to be in bed by now. This cabinet is French. We'll dump the blue-glass collection and take the cabinet."

They went through the rest of the house, the man making his choices quickly. He deemed everything in Shay Garrett's room worthless but paused at the ugly mirror with hands.

"Definitely oriental. Oriental is out now but . . . give me more light here. Garish thing isn't it? The bronzework suggests India, the design is more China? Or someplace in between perhaps or . . . Tibet? No . . ."

"Who'd want it?" Chris was sweating. His heavy glasses kept sliding down his greasy nose. He felt the tingle of imminent danger and it was not altogether unpleasant.

"No one maybe. Mrs. Garrett ever mention where she got it?"

"I never asked."

"Give me the flashlight." The man inspected the back of the mirror. "I wonder . . . there's a tiny etching in the bronze here. Could well be a temple sign of some sort." He laughed. "That or the western equivalent of a curse . . . or both. A flake resembling enamel here. The fingers at the top of the frame might possibly have held a jewel at one time."

"I wouldn't cross the street to look at it, let alone buy it."

The man laughed again. "Chris, where is your sense of mystery and romance? And you a poet. Some collector of weird *objets d'art* might take a shine to this. We'll have it."

They hurried down to the back door, where a low whistle brought two more men hurtling over the fence.

With little noise and a minimum of light the four of them set to work stacking chosen articles in the kitchen.

Chris and the gray-haired man had just deposited a rocking chair next to the growing collection when the other two carried in the odd mirror with only its claw-hand base showing beneath Shay Garrett's frothy bedspread.

"The spread is worthless and we have cover pads in the truck."

"The mirror felt funny when we lifted it so we covered it. Seemed like it was tingly or electrified somehow."

"Gentlemen, that object was made long before the age of electricity."

"How do we get all this stuff across the yard and over the fence?" Chris asked.

"We don't. We bring the truck to the door."

"But the fence—"

"Was conveniently altered this afternoon. Now hurry. We can move a few things closer to the door. We no longer need an aisle through all this."

Chris heard an engine outside and when they'd filled the aisle the door opened to the dim interior of a truck. He was sure now they'd be discovered.

They moved furniture and other items up a board ramp, the open doors of the truck serving as wings to shield the operation from passersby.

When all had been loaded and the ramp drawn back, the other two men drove through a gap in the fence, turned into the alley, switched on the truck lights as they entered the street and were gone. The entire process had taken little more than a half-hour.

Shoving Chris outside, the gray-haired man locked the door behind them. "Quickly now, help me with the fence."

For a long section between the corner and the gate to the alley the iron posts were pulled loose from the crumbling concrete base. That section of the fence now lay flat on the ground.

"A repairman worked on this, this afternoon. Poor-quality work, wouldn't you say, Chris? In some respects he resembled me."

Chris helped him lift the fence and set the posts back into their holes. Even in moonlight he could see chips of concrete that'd been pried loose from the base to pull the posts. Several that apparently wouldn't cooperate had been sawed off at the bottom. So had the upper and lower cross rails at each end of the section.

"Didn't anybody notice in broad daylight?"

"I dressed properly, acted as if I belonged and no one even paused to question me." He patted the fence affectionately. "It should stand. Until someone leans on it or tries to open the gate. Let's go."

The man walked Chris to his car and handed over the payment.

"Sure nobody'll connect me with this?" Chris asked.

"They'll question you. But we wore gloves. You should be all right. Just remember to spend your new wealth slowly. Nothing big and flashy. Don't worry. You won't see me again. I never work the same area more than once. The world's full of suckers." He laughed and walked down the sidewalk with his hands in his pockets.

Chris drove away still wondering how his nameless benefactor had come to strike up a conversation with him in a bar. Someone had fingered Chris. Who?

What would old successful Rachael look like when she walked into the Gingerbread House and saw what'd happened? Some people had it all their way. They needed a little knocking down. He didn't blame Shay Garrett for running off without a trace.

If he ever had anything of value, he'd install burglar alarms or buy a guard dog.

The only thing that bothered Chris at the moment was that he'd enjoyed the evening so much.

Rachael sipped her coffee, watched couples lean cozily across tables, gesture in whispered conversations.

She missed the Gingerbread House. *Why do I cling?*

She'd eaten a late but splendid dinner she hadn't had to cook. Soon she'd go upstairs and sleep in a bed she wouldn't have to make in the morning. Rachael could do anything she wanted. *I can't be too old to change.*

The waiter refilled her cup and slipped a tray with the bill under her nose.

Rachael'd given up on the book with the deadline and begun a new one about a pregnant teenager who'd run away from a home in which her parents were on the verge of divorce. Was Shay confused and frightened, needing Rachael and unable to contact her?

Was Shay dead?

Rachael left the elegant but subdued atmosphere of one of the dining rooms of Denver's Brown Palace Hotel, passed through the ornate lobby so rich in history and color, mounted the staircase to her lonely room.

By midmorning the wedding mirror was halfway across New Mexico, still heading south in the dark interior of a truck.

It stood next to the buffet that Thora K. Strock's mother had brought to this country from old Cornwall over a hundred years before.

Brandy McCabe rested on Lottie's bed that afternoon with a book propped on her granddaughter's stomach.

She'd taken the obscene pictures from the walls and moved into this room some time ago.

Brandy'd helped Ansel put up his garden vegetables and cleaned the house from top to bottom while waiting for her granddaughter to make the wedding mirror work its switch in time.

Marek Weir's child moved with an odd rolling motion like a boat floating loose on a gentle wave and the book rose and fell with it. A tweaking sensation in Shay's abdomen. The prickle of taut skin stretching more.

Brandy fought an emotional attachment to the helpless being growing inside Shay Garrett. It had no more connection with her than its father. But she knew that even after her return to 1900 (and she *would* return) she'd always wonder what had become of this child.

Turning a page of the novel, she tried to force her attention back to it. Lottie's books were as lewd as the pictures of naked men that had hung on the walls. Brandy knew she shouldn't be reading them. Another temptation of this evil world she couldn't resist.

But from them she'd discovered what she'd long suspected but hoped wasn't true, people coupled just like animals. And in the books she'd read so far, they spent a great deal of time and energy doing just that. Moreover, they were rarely married to each other.

Although the authors made the process increasingly clear, one aspect confused Brandy completely. In these stories women seemed actually to enjoy the sordid business.

The stairs creaked and Brandy hid the novel under her pillow as Mr. St. John opened the door without knocking. His unpredictability was more and more a worry to her.

He stood now, panting as if he'd run too long a distance, a quivering finger pointing rudely in her direction. "Out the back way and TO THE BARN with you."

"But Mr. St. John, what—"

"Hurry! Lottie's walking up the road. Must of hitchhiked."

Outside, Happy raised the alarm.

Chris Davenport's gray-haired friend overtook the truck containing the wedding mirror as it began to angle east. Except that now the man's hair was a deep chestnut brown.

His car and the truck traveled in convoy as they crossed the border into Texas.

13

Hooligan lowered his head and rammed the partition next to Brandy. She stepped back and her shoe crushed an egg nestled in a hollow of straw.

The goat reared as if to jump the partition to get at her. Hens squawked, fluttering to the far corners of the barn. A cat hissed from the ladder to the loft.

"Hush, all of you," she whispered. Lottie would surely hear all this commotion even up in the house.

Fear tightened above the baby and below Shay's throat. If she were discovered now, Brandy'd flee again before she'd allow them to murder the child.

As much as she'd tried not to, Brandy was growing involved with this tiny being. *After all, this is to be my great-grandchild.*

She crossed to the pitchfork leaning against a far wall as voices sounded outside.

Hooligan kicked an upright post supporting the floor of the loft. Dust seeped from cracks above her. Even the gentle goat, Stina Mark, eyed her with suspicion as Brandy took a stance behind the door.

A chill fall draft blew through the cracks in the barn wall by her ear. The pitchfork trembled in her hands.

"You crazy old coot." A woman's voice. "You're lying again." She giggled.

"Am not."

"You expect me to believe you cleaned that house? You've got yourself a girl friend somewhere and I'm going to find her. At your age too."

"Lottie, I told you—"

"Come on, Gramps. I don't care. I just want to meet her. After the way you treated Grandma I can't believe you'd take in another woman but me. Where is she? I'm staying until you introduce us and I promise I won't laugh." Lottie laughed anyway. "Or does she only work days?"

"Don't know where you get such ideas."

"Is she in the barn?"

"No."

The door opened and Brandy was pinned behind it.

"Well . . . if it isn't a girl friend, who cleaned the house? No man your generation would suddenly get so busy at woman's work."

"The social worker sent somebody out to do it."

"You'd sic Happy onto anybody from welfare. I know you. Gramps, you got yourself a girl. And I'm hurt you won't tell me about . . ."

The door pulled away and Brandy found herself facing a young woman whose merry smile faded.

Massive man's boots peeked beneath a long skirt. A shawllike garment —knitted, with only a hole for the neck and much like one Brandy'd once seen on a shepherd—covered most of the rest of her. Lottie's dark hair bushed in frizzed snarls resembling Sarah's, the girl who cleaned for Rachael.

Shock on Lottie's face left her mouth agape. "But . . . you're too young. You're . . ." She shrugged. "Sorry, I thought—"

"Leave me be, you." Brandy lowered the pitchfork to Lottie's breast.

Lottie backed into Ansel. "Oh hey, I mean . . . I didn't—"

"Shay Garrett, put that thing *down!*"

"Shay Garr . . . oh, Gramps. She's not . . ." Lottie turned a whitened face to Ansel. "Tell me she isn't the one from the Gingerbread House everyone's been searching for. Gramps, she's pregnant."

"Now Lottie, you listen to—"

"And you." She whirled her skirt and hair around to Brandy. "All this time you took advantage of a crazy old man? It's incredible. I just don't believe this." Lottie pushed the pitchfork aside and walked out, leaving Brandy and Ansel staring at each other.

They were about to follow when Lottie reappeared, looking almost sick. "Gramps, you . . . you didn't get her pregnant . . ."

"'Course not. You don't stop talking long enough for a man to get a word in. She came sick. Run away because they was going to kill her baby with an abortion and lock her up in an asylum."

"So she's crazy too. That explains it."

"What would you of done, turn her away?"

"I'd have turned her in." Lottie's pretty face hardened to ugly. "And claimed the reward."

The truck carrying the wedding mirror and the car traveling with it pulled into a field near a low-roofed building. Other trucks parked on brittle grass outside the paved area surrounding it and people moved through chill shadows.

November wind scattered dust and paper food containers across the field, up over the concrete lip of the parking lot and against the side of the building, whipping the loose edge of the painted sign that faced the road —ANTIQUE AUCTION.

The man who had changed his hair from gray to brown stepped out of the car and signaled the men in the truck where he wanted them to park. He moved his shoulders in a circular motion and stretched his neck to either side. It'd been a long drive. They'd stopped only to eat and to take on a load, legally acquired and paid for, stored along the way.

As his companions approached, their breathing clouded on the air. Dead grass crunched as it broke beneath their boots.

"Where's that motel? If I'm going to unload this in the morning I need sleep."

"Not yet, my good man. There's much business to be transacted tonight."

"But the auction doesn't start till noon tomorrow."

"The choice items sell by flashlight tonight." And many of the stolen articles from the house in Boulder, Colorado, would be scattered to the four winds in twenty-four hours, possibly even before the theft was discovered.

The door opened on the back of a nearby pickup camper. Light, smoke and the smell of coffee poured out to them. "Frederick, is that your voice I hear?"

"It is." The man who'd stolen the wedding mirror stepped inside the crowded camper. "And wait until you see what I've brought this time. I hope your flashlights and checkbooks are in good order, gentlemen."

Brandy Harriet McCabe stared at the ceiling. She pondered the strange turn her life had taken. If anyone had told her six months before she'd be sharing a bed with a harlot, Brandy would have been outraged.

Lottie turned a page of her book, her head propped on a folded pillow. Her small slim figure made Shay's tall body, now swollen with child, seem awkward and ugly in comparison.

The book hit the floor and so did Lottie. "I can't concentrate. This is all so . . ." She lifted her hands toward the ceiling in a gesture suggestive of her grandfather. "So . . . I mean . . . I'd turn you over to your folks tomorrow if I didn't think Gramps would get in trouble for hiding you."

She rummaged in a shoddy cloth handbag and extracted cigarette papers and a clear bag filled with what looked to be dried, crumbled weed. "Why, of the thousands of people in and around Boulder, did you have to pick on that crazy old man?"

"I think you do Mr. St. John an injustice. This world seems peopled with lunatics and your grandfather appears more sensible than most . . . at times." Brandy concentrated on averting her eyes from the pictures Lottie had rehung. She called them "posters" but whatever they were, grown men had posed naked to be photographed. "How any of you keep your wits about you is beyond me."

"You sure talk funny." Lottie sat on the foot of the bed and drew in on a cigarette, holding the smoke inside her, releasing it gradually through her nostrils. A sweet smell drifted over the covers toward Brandy, heavy, unlike any tobacco she'd ever been around before. "Almost like you aren't one of us. Did they send you off to school in a foreign country or something?"

"I'm no foreigner." In Brandy's world foreigners were all foolish if not suspect.

Lottie drew her nightgown up to bare her legs, pulled a foot high until it lay—dirty sole upward on top of the opposite thigh, and crossed the remaining foot over to do the same on the other thigh. She pressed her bents knees against the covers, making a folded crisscross of her legs that should have pulled her hip joints from their sockets.

Brandy looked away from the embarrassing spectacle only to have her eyes meet the reclining figure of a man with dark hairs on his chest and arms . . . and other places as well. The hairs reminded her of Marek Weir. She lowered her eyes to Shay's folded hands resting on the hump of stomach.

"That one turns you on, doesn't he? That why you took the posters down? He's not bad but I've seen better pricks."

"Pricks?"

"Yeah. Look, why don't you just go home and not tell anybody where you've been? Like I told you, you're too far along for an abortion."

"Would you have me locked away in some asylum, Lottie?"

"Anybody who could've had an abortion and didn't, belongs in one." Lottie affixed a hairpin to her cigarette and holding it by the pin smoked it down till Brandy feared she'd burn her lips. The cloying smell made Shay's head ache.

"If you're not found out before, you will be when you go to the hospital to have the kid. And if you think Gramps can afford that trip, think again."

"Hospital? It's a baby, not an illness."

Lottie unwound her legs and stood. She swayed and had to steady herself against the bedposts. "Man, that must have been good stuff." Her eyes appeared larger.

"Now there's a prick for you." She pointed to one of the pictures.

"Makes you wonder if they didn't do some trick with the negative or something."

"Lottie, must we have those disgusting things here?"

"Disgusting?" Lottie backed away as if to observe them all at once. "They're supersensational. Probably fags, but certainly put together right."

"They're unclothed." Brandy rolled over to face the window.

"They're more than that, they're bare-assed." Lottie came around the bed to block Brandy's view of limp curtains. "And what's the matter with that?"

"No decent woman looks at pictures of naked gentlemen in her bedroom or . . . anywhere." Brandy fought tears, but Shay's cheeks and the pillow were damp with them. She couldn't cope with this world.

"Decent? You're the one who's pregnant. You didn't get that way staring at a big star in the East either. And don't tell me he raped you with all his clothes on or something. Hey, don't cry . . . I mean . . ." Lottie sat beside her, put a comforting arm on her shoulder. "Shay, I didn't say there's anything wrong in being pregnant. But it's kind of rough on a kid to let it be born if you can't take care of it. Seems wrong, you know?"

"No, I don't know." Brandy rolled over the other way and closed Shay's eyes on naked men. "I've never even lain with a man."

"So, you did it standing up. It's a free world." Lottie gave a snort of disgust. "Jesus! Do you have some old-fashioned hang-ups."

Of the treasures from the Gingerbread House, the wedding mirror and a wooden rocker were all that found their way to the floor of the auction barn the next morning.

Antique dealers from different parts of the country had cleaned out the other items long before dawn. Thora K.'s buffet now sat, carefully padded, in the dark interior of a truck bearing California license plates.

Although the auction had not yet begun, the barn was a busy place. Prospective buyers threaded their way through old and sometimes odd merchandise deciding on biddable items.

Cindy Wilson checked the numbers on tags tied to a row of castiron cherry pitters, of which her shop had an overload this year, and bent to force closed a drawer in an antiquated spool cabinet.

"Excuse me. Can I get through here?" A man in coveralls stood behind her, a roll of extension cord wrapped around his arm.

As Cindy stepped back to let him pass, something cold and sharp poked through her blouse in several places along the ridge of her spine. She turned to find bronze hands coiled about each other, the overlong nails on the little fingers jutting out slightly.

The hands framed a full-length mirror of ancient glass with a crack across the top. Cindy patted her tightly sprayed hair and then shook her head.

She and Ned had been in the business for five years now but this monstrosity had to be the weirdest thing she'd seen to date. Ned's wavy reflection appeared in the mirror as he came up behind her.

"Honey, have you seen this?"

He gave the mirror a cursory inspection and made a face. "It's godawful."

"I know. So godawful it's almost interesting. Put it in a display window and you'd sure get the curious in off the street."

"Or scare them away," Ned said dryly and wandered off.

"Coming through again." The man in coveralls approached, unwinding his extension cord as he passed.

Cindy stepped over it and picked up her clipboard to continue checking her numbers against the tags on the remaining odds and ends from her shop.

The cord pulled tighter as the electrician reached the auctioneer's platform and slipped up over the claw base of the wedding mirror. There were several frayed places along the cord's length, exposing wires no inspector would have deemed safe. One of these places lay up against a curved index finger that supported the mirror's weight.

"One . . . two . . . three . . ." droned a voice from the platform, reaching to speakers throughout the cavernous building, echoing over the conversations of excited antique nuts. "Testing . . . one . . ."

Cindy stuck her pencil behind her ear and turned at the humming sound behind her. The tangled bronze hands seemed to glow. She blinked and looked around into the glass.

Cindy Wilson blinked again and dropped her clipboard.

Brandy McCabe closed the oven door on the loaves of bread she was baking and staggered back to the sofa as the familiar feeling came over her.

Her granddaughter must finally have discovered the secret of the mirror. *Oh, Shay, hurry!*

Brandy leaned back, trying to relax, to give herself up to the fog rising in front of her eyes instead of fighting it as she had before. She strained to lean into the tugging motion inside Shay's body rather than pull back.

But the fog was so thin. She could still see the kitchen through it, and Lottie stepping out of the bathroom.

"Shay? Oh, God, you're not going to have a miscarriage on us or anything?" Lottie's voice sounded far away.

Brandy began to fall and swirl. A forest path and pine trees, an overturned bucket tilted in front of her. But still she could see Lottie behind them. Lottie's mouth moved now without sound.

. . . the smell of earth . . . the sound of wind rushing through layered pine needles above her . . . the sickness . . . the sweating . . .

Brandy fought to sink deeper but the tugging weakened. The forest path and the bucket slowly receded.

Lottie loomed above her, fully seen and heard.

Ned Wilson watched his wife anxiously as the ugly mirror was carried onto the platform. He'd never seen her so pale. "Well, okay, if you really want the damn thing. But you bid more than a hundred and I'll take it out of your hide."

When the mirror sat upright and in full view, the crowd hushed. The auctioneer did a double-take and checked the papers in front of him.

A woman in the audience giggled.

"I tell you, it's magic," Cindy whispered. "If you knew the things I saw—"

"The occult is for adolescents. Darling, what's gotten into you?"

"But I saw scenes or . . . things and people. And clouds of smoke. Not myself. And I was standing right in front of it."

"Bidding begins at fifty dollars," the auctioneer said with a grin, and the crowd laughed.

But Cindy Wilson raised her hand.

14

Lottie threw the dishes into the sink and broke a plate. "Gramps, it was like a fit. Her eyes rolled back. Maybe she's epileptic."

"Don't believe so." Ansel held the newspaper at arm's length, his head tilted back as if he were underscoring each line of print with the end of his nose.

"Will you get your brain together long enough to listen to me? She could be up there right now dying of a miscarriage or—"

"Just looked in on her. Sleeping, peaceful and healthy. She'll be all right by tomorrow. Tough as nails when she needs to be."

Lottie pressed the newspaper down on the table. "She's pregnant and hasn't even been to a doctor. If she did die what would you do?"

Ansel wrung a mashed pea from his beard. "When people die you bury 'em."

"Where? Out in your graveyard? Put up a cross with 'Stina Mark'? Gramps, they're liable to call it murder and kidnapping. If she's dead she can't tell anybody she wanted to be here."

"She can go anytime she wants." Ansel lifted her arm from the paper, turned a page. "Will you look at this? Marek Weir."

"Who's he?"

"Says here he's a scientist at the National Center for Atmospheric Research." He pointed to three small photographs lined up at the head of several columns. "Local scientists search for the key to the destructive nature of stormclouds," he read aloud.

"So what? We have a problem and it has nothing to do with scientists or stormclouds."

"Does so. This is the baby's father, Lottie."

Ned Wilson loaded the mirror onto an already crowded van.

His wife was the business head in their family. She knew what to buy, whom to hire, what to pay for salaries and merchandise and how to haggle.

But Cindy did make mistakes. This mirror was one of them. The bidding had gone to a hundred. Ned felt sure the other bidder was a plant to force up the price.

He was the sensitive part of their family-business partnership. The one who could entice a wavering customer. And the only person he knew who could understand and cajole his sharp-witted wife.

He draped the mirror with a cover and tied the strings to hold it in place, then dusted off tingling hands. High blood pressure? He'd better get in for a checkup.

"It's not really you that's got me worried," he said to the shrouded shape in front of him. "It's her. It's why she went bonkers over you and thought she saw things she couldn't have."

Ned had checked the mirror. There was no projection equipment concealed in it that could explain Cindy's visions. She didn't see visions. She didn't see past money and success unless she was hit over the head.

"Ready to go?" Cindy stood at the van's door, looking normal enough.

"Yeah. You drive this and I'll drive the truck."

"I just talked to Myrtle on the phone. Colorado got some snow last night. Do you think we can drive right on through to Denver?"

"Let's stop over one night. I think you . . . we need to slow down a little." He jumped to the earth and slid the van's door shut.

"Why? Ned, we have a shop to run." She pushed at strawberry-blond curls disheveled by the winds of a Texas plain.

"Because we haven't horsed around in a motel for far too long." He raised an eyebrow and tried to plead with his eyes. "And motels turn you on." He gave her his winsome sigh.

"Will you never grow up?" But she smiled. Another woman would have giggled. "Well, all right. One night in a motel." She slid into the driver's seat. "But I expect champagne . . . at least."

The truck and the van with Colorado license plates pulled out of the rutted field in convoy.

Jerry Garrett drove the Oldsmobile into the alley behind the Gingerbread House. He needed more shirts.

He got out of the car and paused to look at the house through entwined and leafless branches. He needed more than shirts. He needed to pull himself out of his resentment of the place. No one held him here any longer. He could find no one else to blame.

Jerry needed to come to grips with his losses, the loneliness that seemed a part of his body.

A few hours before, he'd had Thanksgiving dinner with his in-laws in Remy and Elinore's apartment. Dan and Ruth had crossed the hall from theirs and the women combined their efforts to make the first home-cooked meal he'd eaten in months and to make the twins behave. Jerry basked in their sympathy, envied the tangible smugness of people whose marriages worked, ate to the point of discomfort.

And then Remy voiced everyone's thoughts. "Hope Rachael isn't eating alone today. We sent an invitation through Marek but she wouldn't come."

"It's Shay I'm worried about. Poor kid," Dan said.

"She's dead." Jerry felt better saying it aloud.

The women rattled dishes to distract the conversation, made a pretense of clearing the table.

"I won't believe that till she's found." Dan was always the one to start an argument. "And don't you either, Jerry. Damn world. Everybody gives up hope at the first excuse. Remember starting out in California during the depression, Rem? We made it because we didn't give up."

Jerry excused himself after pie and coffee.

Rachael's car wasn't parked along the side street now. He wondered if she ever came back to the Gingerbread House for anything or if she was too far away.

Flakes of snow feathered on the air, landing finally to melt on warm earth.

Jerry lifted the latch and pushed at the gate. The wrought-iron fence tilted toward the house. "What the hell?"

The gate was wired shut. Jerry squatted to investigate it, leaning his shoulder against a spear-tipped post.

The entire section of fence between the gate and the corner fell over into the backyard.

* * *

Brandy leaned back against the sofa, feeling better since her nap but still weak from the sickness that was receding as had the thin view of another world, the tugging that'd almost claimed her.

Her granddaughter must make the mirror work properly, and soon. Brandy couldn't stand another disappointment.

Lottie stood in front of her, hands on her hips, her feet spread, her expression worthy of Mr. Shakespeare's shrew. "Why can't this Marek guy help you if it's his baby? He gave you a diamond, didn't he?"

"Of all people, I can't go to him, Lottie."

"Why not? You're even still wearing the ring."

"My hands have swollen so that I can't remove it."

"Didn't used to be. Had it on when you came but you didn't take it off then." Mr. St. John hovered at Lottie's elbow.

The ring isn't mine to take off. Neither is the finger it's on. "You can't turn me out now, Lottie. I beg of you."

"You're too far along for an abortion. You're . . ." She made a pretense of slapping the side of her head. "What am I going to do with you two? Do you know I'm supposed to be in Nederland? How can I leave with all this going on?"

"Your three men friends get tired of you?" Ansel asked.

"I have a new boyfriend and a place to live up there. But, Gramps, I can't leave you in a mess like this."

"Seems to me the mess started when you came. We was doing fine. Go on up to Nederland. I'll take you in the truck if you want."

"How am I going to have any fun up there worrying about you down here all the time? You're worse than a kid. Can't leave you alone for a second but what you don't get into trouble."

Lottie kicked one of Stina Mark's kittens off a chair with her bare foot. She flopped down and laid her arms on the table in a pleading gesture. "You're getting to be too much of a responsibility for someone my age."

Ansel St. John assumed a wounded air and scooped up the adopted kitten which was fast on its way to becoming a cat. "That DOES IT!" He handed the kitten to Brandy and grabbed his coat from the back of the chair. "I'm going into town and buy some coffee. Lots of coffee. For Shay and me, and you can't have a drop."

His lips formed a pout over his ill-fitting teeth. "So there, Carlotta Ralston. Think you can run things around here," he muttered and slid the glass door shut behind him.

Lottie screwed up her face for crying. "What am I going to do with the old bastard? I mean . . . I just got his diet straightened out."

"Lottie, you can't treat your grandfather like a child." Brandy stroked the offended cat. "He surely knows more about life than you after all his years of living." She couldn't understand the relationship between these two. There was obviously love here but it made the grandfather childish, the granddaughter churlish and overbearing. "He must worry about you living with men to whom you're not even married, smoking, the scandalous language you use. And you seem to have no respect for your grandfather."

"Respect? He's old. He's crazy. One of these days he's going to pull his last screwing fuck-up and I'm not going to be able to get him out of it. And I've got the feeling you're it. People live too long anymore. That's the problem."

"They can hardly help how long they live. That's in God's hands."

"God? Oh, great, we got a Jesus freak among us. Shay Garrett, I don't know what he's going to do next. You don't know. Gramps is getting scarier by the year and if I were you I'd get out of this. He's unpredictable."

That was one argument Brandy couldn't counter. "Lottie, who is Stina Mark? Not the cat and the goat but—"

"My grandmother. His wife. Mark was her maiden name."

"Is she buried out by the fence in one of those graves?"

"I don't know." Lottie hugged herself and whispered. "And I don't want to know."

Shay's baby kicked her bladder and Brandy winced. *Granddaughter, please get back to handle things, and soon.*

51

When Rachael called Marek that evening he told her of the burglary of the Gingerbread House. She packed and hurried her little car back to Boulder, seeing the thirty-mile stretch of turnpike through guilty tears.

She'd been selfish, abandoned the home that had sheltered and protected her and generations of her family. And someone had hurt it.

First her mother, then her daughter, then her husband. Gone.

And now the violation of the Gingerbread House . . . how much more could she take? What other shocks could there possibly be left for fate to throw at her?

Lights blazed in every window when she drew up beside the house, reminding Rachael of the night she'd returned to find the house lit, her father on the living-room floor, her mother bending over him, trying to breathe life into his stilled chest and pushing on it . . .

This was the first time it had occurred to Rachael that Brandy Maddon had been attempting a not-too-accurate form of mouth-to-mouth resuscitation and heart massage, a technique Rachael'd been unaware of until recent years.

Stepping over the low concrete wall and a portion of a wrought-iron fence that'd traveled the prairies on a wagon train, she looked up at the house with a mental apology.

When she stepped into the kitchen she saw her daughter's pink ruffled bedspread draped over the kitchen stool. The room looked dirty but she could see nothing missing.

She pushed open the door to the hall. Her husband and a man she didn't know stood talking where Thora K.'s buffet should have been. Jerry held a green book in one hand, gesturing with it.

Rachael had the sensation of rising out of her body, hovering above them and herself. She looked down, surprised to see she was clutching Shay's bedspread. The beginning prickles of a hot flash swarmed over her and she glided back to the floor as Jerry turned.

Relief, sympathy, but only guarded involvement on his face. "Here she is now. Rachael, this is Detective Grant from the police depart—you don't look so good. Want to sit down?"

"No. I'm fine." Her voice sounded as far away as his and her arms wouldn't let go of the bedspread. A jumbled pile of tablecloths and odds and ends from the buffet lay on the floor.

"We've dusted for prints, investigated the house and grounds, Mrs. Garrett," the detective said. "I've talked to your husband and brothers."

Rachael moved away from Jerry's supporting arm and trailed the bedspread into the living room. The lights seemed to flicker and dim in the periphery of her vision but stopped when she looked at them squarely.

"I stayed on to have you confirm the list of stolen items." He waved a piece of paper. "A very professional job. They loaded a truck at the back door. Probably at night. No witnesses."

"Yes," Rachael's voice said. The loveseat, chairs, tables, the Tiffany lamp shade, the chandelier. Gone.

"It seems to have been only the valuable antiques. Not the usual easy-to-turn-over items—TV, stereo, silver, jewelry, that type of thing."

"Yes." The cabinet Great-Grandmother McCabe had brought from France. Gone. Rachael's blue-glass collection lay on the rug.

"Someone who knew antiques and what was in the house. Do you know of anyone who might—"

"No." Rachael wandered into the dining room. Her feet seemed to float above the floor. Nothing left here but the contents of the drawers of the buffets, the lesser articles from the china cabinets.

The set of Haviland china that Aunt Harriet Euler had given Sophie McCabe as a wedding gift. Gone.

In the bedroom, clothes and bedclothes, jewelry and personal items littered the floor. The bed, wardrobe, dressers and chairs. Gone.

The men followed her in. Jerry handed her the green book. "Remember Bran's diary? Found it in the hall. It must have been in the buffet."

"Where were you when this happened?"

"In Nederland. I . . . hadn't been living here while you were gone."

"The place to move this stuff is antique sales and auctions," Detective Grant said. "We'll get tracers out tomorrow if you'll complete the descriptions and check the list."

"Nederland. Yes." Rachael clutched her mother's diary to her breast with the hand that wasn't holding her daughter's bedspread.

Lottie left for Nederland, promising to return before the baby was born and threatening to call Marek Weir, the Gingerbread House, and the police if Shay was still in residence by then.

Ansel St. John refused to be concerned by the threat. "Won't be back for a long time. Means well, does Lottie, but she'll get interested in affairs up there and put off coming down. Makes her own fun. Lottie may get VD but she won't get ulcers worrying over me."

He grinned and rubbed his hands together. "What say we have us a cup of coffee?"

"But, Mr. St. John, what will we do if—"

"Now, don't worry." He spooned coffee into the pot. "Besides, I told her the baby was coming in March. By the looks of you, we'll be lucky to get through Christmas."

Brandy thought it more likely to be February but Shay's body was expanding alarmingly.

". . . burglary at Boulder's historic Gingerbread House," the radio box said. "KBOL learned today that sometime in the last few days priceless antique objects and furniture were stolen from the home of Mr. and Mrs. Jerrold Garrett."

The coffeepot bubbled on the stove. Ansel stared pop-eyed at Brandy. "That mirror, do you think? Stolen?"

Brandy shrugged. She couldn't imagine the mirror a priceless antique, but if it were stolen at this end of time it could make little difference to her. Shay had it with her at her end. She must make it work from there.

"Sure do hate the thought of that thing running around loose," Ansel said.

* * *

Brandy prayed nightly for God, the wedding mirror and her granddaughter to get busy and send her home. Brandy didn't want to have Shay's baby, had no idea how Ansel would deliver it himself or what she could do to help.

The thought of Christmas without her family was beyond bearing.

A week before Christmas, Ansel found her weeping in the barn, heedless of Hooligan's noisy and violent displeasure.

"Now, no need for tears. Having a baby's as natural as oatmeal and breathing."

"It's just . . . that I want to be home for Christmas and—"

"Kind of miss that young buck, Marek?"

"No. I mean home . . . to my own people and time."

"Hooligan, you quiet down. Shay Garrett, dry your tears and come back to the house. We'll have a nice hot cup of coffee."

"My name is Brandy McCabe."

"Just get all that out of our head." He helped her over a strip of ice on the path. "You're going to be a mother soon and you have to learn to get on in this world for the sake of the little one."

Wind creaked the branches of the dead cottonwoods, sent dried weed pieces dancing across thin patches of hardened snow.

"I can't stay here forever, Mr. St. John," she said desperately.

"It's lonely for you I know, with just old Ansel and his animals. Things'll be different when the baby comes." He led her through chill lifeless rooms to the warmth of the oil heating stove in the kitchen.

"Tell you what, Shay Garrett," he said over the supper table. "I'm planning a special surprise present for you for Christmas. Ought to give you something to look forward to."

How I would like a hearty beefsteak for a gift. Answering juices flowed in Shay's mouth. Brandy stabbed a tasteless potato with her fork.

Later, on her way to Lottie's cold room, Brandy stopped at the parlor window to stare out at a moonlit night.

The lights of a flying machine blinked in the sky. On the ground a shadow rabbit leaped from the protection of rusting debris and raced across the grave of a Stina Mark to wiggle through the fence and disappear into the open field beyond.

Rachael Garrett wandered through echoing rooms. The thieves had stolen the heart from the Gingerbread House.

She was alone again. Jerry'd stayed a few nights, sleeping on the couch in the den, until assured she'd be all right.

Nothing had been taken from the basement and she'd worked long hours to finish her book. She felt lost without it.

When rested, Rachael felt it possible to start over, bury herself in the writing and, if none of her treasures were returned, busy herself hunting for things to fill the sadly empty places in these rooms.

But at night when Rachael was void of words and energy, tired of her own company, the sadly empty places in herself plagued her and she doubted her strength to go on.

She wandered into Shay's room and backed out. Nothing but pain here, raw and crushing.

Boxes sat about everywhere, holding that which no longer had drawers. In the guestroom across the hall from Shay's, Rachael knelt to riffle through ancient photographs. Elton McCabe leaned stiffly against the wrought-iron fence, Rachael's mother sat on the grass in front of Sophie and John McCabe. The picture had darkened so the features were unclear, the expressions hidden.

A very old picture of Great-Grandmother Euler sitting on the porch with Great-Grandfather McCabe, both bowed with age, he with a beard and leaning forward, his hands resting on the head of a cane.

Once Rachael'd drawn comfort from these friendly ghosts who'd always inhabited the Gingerbread House, had felt reassured and safe with their vague memory presence.

But now, at night, they lamented and tormented in hushed, angry whispers.

Rachael turned off the lights and descended the staircase.

"Where's me buffet from uld Cornwall, you?" Thora K. demanded.

Rachael shivered and went into the dining room to switch off that light.

"You think you can actually *replace* the Haviland?" Sophie McCabe scoffed. "We trusted you, Rachael."

Rachael hurried into the living room, knowing that once she began to answer them she was lost.

She lay down on the mattress brought from Shay's room, reaching for her mother's green leather-bound diary. She needed to feel her mother's closeness.

By the light of a bare-bulbed lamp, devoid of its Tiffany lamp shade, Rachael opened the diary and began to read.

The ink had faded and the clumsy, messy handwriting was hard to decipher . . . but so familiar . . . so like Shay's. She'd never noticed before the similarity in the way her mother and daughter formed their letters.

The first page made no sense at all and she went back to read it again.

By the second page, Rachael began to read aloud as if the sound of her voice, hollow in the empty room, could make the words believable.

By the third page she was sitting up, uncomfortably bent over the book. Her voice trembled and tears blurred the words. But they held her captive until two o'clock the next morning, when she finished and set the diary aside, every bone, muscle and joint aching

"It's impossible and I don't believe it," she said flatly to her image in the bathroom mirror as she swallowed a sleeping pill.

After breakfast the next morning Rachael brought the diary into the bright cozy kitchen, poured another cup of coffee and began to read again from the beginning.

Rachael giggled helplessly when she came to the place where the writer warned, "I don't think you should tell Rachael any more than you have to. Her life has been upset enough by all this."

Wind slammed into the Gingerbread House, rattled hanging cups in the cupboard, whirled snow at the windows. She couldn't see out. She was enclosed in the dimmed room with the diary and the past.

Brandy (strange calling you by the name I've answered to for so many years), I found a small replica of the mirror in Hong Kong. It sits on a table in the home of a British couple. They said they knew

> nothing of its origin. The wife picked it up in a curio shop that had since gone out of business. At the top of this one the fingers held a large glass stone and the bronze was lacquered red and black. Otherwise it was the same. (Except smaller, as I said, and the mirror glass was newer and better.) I don't know if all this means anything. I was afraid to destroy our mirror in case it might hurt us in some way. But I think you should discuss it with Jerry and see what he thinks should be done. Perhaps buried deep where it will never be found and can't . . .

The end of the sentence was scrawled in the margin because it was the last side of the last tightly written page, but it was impossible to decipher.

Extra pages of stationery had been folded and taped onto the inside of the back cover. Odds and ends of things the writer wanted to add or had forgotten. The very last of these was ominous.

> During that first year or two I would see you sometimes, have awake dreams or visions of you in my body. Be very careful. The last time I saw you screaming and a hand with blood all over it coming toward you. I've hesitated to mention it because I know it will worry you but I thought you should be warned.

Rachael was laughing when the door chimes sounded. Wind still howled around the Gingerbread House and it was growing dark.

Remy stood at the door trying to keep from blowing away. The air felt warmer than it should.

"Well, you're sure looking happier than I've seen you for months." He struggled in with a large basket and helped her close the door. "What's so funny?"

"Oh, Rem, you just won't believe it. The most fantastic, incredible . . ." She hugged him and led him to the kitchen.

"Since you wouldn't come out for dinner, Ruth and Elinore sent it here and me to share it with you." He pulled out a bottle of wine. "Merry Christmas, Puss."

"I'd forgotten it was Christmas Eve. This couldn't be better."

"There's steaks to broil and I've got orders to put the salad in the refrigerator and the hot dishes on warm in the oven." Remy looked around uncomfortably. "Is . . . ah . . . Jerry around? There's enough here for the Chinese Army."

"No. But if I can catch him, he's got to see my surprise too. You put the food away and I'll call."

There was no answer in Nederland. "I wonder if he's still at the office." Rachael and her brother watched her finger tremble as she punched the numbers.

"Jerry? Could you spare me a few minutes this evening? I've got a Christmas present for you."

Remy was staring at her.

A pause on the other end of the line. "Rachael . . . have you been drinking? You don't sound like yourself."

"No. Listen, Remy's here. Meet us out front of your building. We'll drive by and pick you up."

"To go where?"

"That's the present. Jerry, you'll never guess what's happened." Rachael laughed, and when she could stop she said, "I've found Shay."

16

Brandy McCabe sat in Ansel St. John's kitchen, Shay's head buried in her arms on the table. Stina Mark rubbed against her ankles. Wind gusts rocked the house. The radio box sang Christmas carols.

At home Nora would be making preparations for tomorrow's dinner. The house would be filled with the smell of sausage and cornbread readying for the stuffing. The goose and the ducks picked and clean. Perhaps carolers outside the window, friends laughing in the parlor. "Temperance" punch in the cut-glass bowl. Men adding whiskey to theirs when their wives weren't looking.

Last year Brandy and Elton went caroling with their young people's group from church. Silly Terrence Doogle had tried to hold Myra Trevors' hand and Myra'd boxed him smartly with her muff.

After their dinner of boiled eggs, bread and home-canned peas, Ansel had driven off in his truck.

Last year, over seventy years ago, her father'd been alive and Aunt Harriet stayed with them over Christmas week. After church on Christmas Day and a gay dinner where twenty-five people crowded into the dining room of the Gingerbread House, John McCabe had hired sleighs and hay wagons with runners brought to the door.

Her father was in his cups and demanded to drive the lead sleigh himself. Then he led the caravan about the streets bellowing for people to come out and join the party.

When the caravan was overloaded and other carriage-sleighs had joined them spontaneously, off they set across open rangeland to the north and east.

Brandy sniffed and pulled Stina Mark onto Shay's knees. "We could have driven over the very spot where this old house stands now, kitty, and it was only last year."

They stopped once to let the children run and Aunt Harriet became entangled in her skirts while stepping from a sleigh. She fell and turned an ankle.

"Aunt Harriet's quite stout," Brandy told the cat. "And there was much ado to raise her up. Pa, instead of helping, gathered a snowball and hurled it at her backside at just the right . . . well, the wrong moment." Brandy stifled a giggle and then hiccuped.

"It really wasn't that funny, but I couldn't help laughing behind my hand. Ma wouldn't speak to him the rest of the day and it almost spoiled the fun. When we came home there was hot spiced cider and popcorn."

Happy barked outside the glass door, startling Stina Mark, who jumped to the floor and hid under the bed.

"Hush now, Happy." Ansel's voice raised above the wind. He slid back the door and stepped inside. "Get your coat, Shay Garrett. It's Christmas Eve."

"Coat? Where—"

"Don't talk. Just hurry. Promised you a Christmas present, didn't I?"

"Deck the halls with boughs . . ." the radio box said.

Jerry Garrett slid into the back seat of Remy's car, relieved to see Rachael wasn't driving. "What's all this about—"

"Take it easy, Jerry," Rachael's brother said, a warning note in his voice. "Where to now, Puss?"

"Columbia Cemetery."

"Cemetery," Remy repeated, as if struggling to understand and humor his sister at the same time.

Cemetery, Jerry said to himself and the hope that had flared since his wife's phone call was snuffed out. "Rachael, tell me what—"

"Trust me," Rachael cut him off and turned her face to the windshield as an enormous slab of what looked to be plywood flew across the car's hood and crashed into somebody's porch.

"We get out in this wind and we could get hit by something," Jerry warned when they'd parked at the cemetery entrance.

"It'll only take a minute." Rachael got out and wind slammed the door.

"Remy, Shay couldn't be buried here without our knowing it, could she?"

"I don't know. Let's just go along with Rachael and keep her calm until we get to the bottom of this. Frankly, Jerry, I'm worried."

"About Shay?"

"About my sister."

They stepped over the chain across the vehicle entrance, wind flopping Rachael's hair into her face, grinding stinging grit into Jerry's eyes.

"You're not going to believe this," Rachael yelled, and ran on ahead.

Tree limbs flayed at the sky. Threatening cracking sounds snapped all over town.

"She keeps saying that. Believe what?"

"Hasn't told me any more than she's told you." Remy pulled up his coat collar, turned sideways and shouldered into the wind.

Rachael stopped at the grave of her mother, a distant streetlight cutting through the dark enough for Jerry to see her half-shadowed face. It looked as if she was smiling.

"There she is." She pointed at Brandy Maddon's grave. "There's . . . Shay."

A nasty gust hurled a dirt cloud toward them and Jerry pulled out one side of his overcoat to shelter her, drawing her against his chest as he drew it around her.

Rachael's body shuddered with spasms. She was either laughing silently or sobbing.

Brandy still had the hiccups. They'd begun to hurt.

Wind roared at the truck, trying to force its way in, pinging sand and snow against the windows.

"Are you taking me back to the Gingerbread House?"

"Nope." He leaned over the steering device, squinting to see the road.

She should have known better than to trust such an erratic person as Ansel St. John.

"All these years and I never will get used to the winds. Seems they're getting worse. They have 'em in your day?"

Just last winter Mr. Arnett's hen house blew away, scattering his chickens . . .

"There's more town and debris for them to stir up now," Brandy said stiffly, sure that he lied and was taking her back.

Where streets met and crossed each other, electric lanterns with red, yellow or green lights bounced on wires overhead. They looked to be heavy and Brandy wondered if they ever broke from their wires and fell on vehicles below.

Ansel parked in the shadow of an unlighted building. "Now, you wait here. I got to check on something. Be back in a minute." His beard flying in the wind, he hurried across a street and disappeared, to return minutes later and insist she follow him.

The wind caught her hair and tugged most of it loose as he took her wrist and pulled her along.

Pulling aside a board in a high fence, he shoved her through the gap and said something that blew away, as did the board.

Ansel led her to a gate in a roofless enclosure, across a rough sandstone area and through a sliding glass door.

Brandy waited until he'd switched on a light and pulled heavy curtains across the door.

A deep red rug, stone fireplace, enormous sofa . . . "What is this place?"

"You'll see." He whirled and raised his arms, obviously delighted with himself. "Your Christmas SURPRISE."

"Am I to live here?"

"Up to you, Shay Garrett. Nice place like this, this day and age, and that patio door's never locked. Makes you wonder, don't it?" He studied a hand-drawn map of some kind on the wall above the sofa. "Looks like somebody's sure been busy."

"Mr. St. John, I fail to see what—"

"Come along and I'll show ya."

In the next room, a giant bed without bedposts, the coverlet tucked inside the wooden framing. Ansel pushed down on it, creating a billow under the bedclothes that moved like a wave to the other side. "Now, what do you think of that?"

"I'm not sure I think well of any of this business and I demand to know exactly what—"

"Bet your granddaughter liked it just fine." He caused another ripple and then stared at her in his lidless fashion. "Got to do something about you, though."

Taking a brush from the bureau he brushed out Shay's hair. "You shouldn't braid it at night. Makes it all rumply." He pulled off her coat and inspected her. "Sure could use some color. Don't you have any lipstick?"

"I do not paint my face like a . . . Mr. St. John, what am I doing here?"

"One thing you got to remember, Shay Garrett. I'll be in the closet there. Don't keep looking at it and don't slip and mention my name or we're done for."

Marek Weir swerved the Porsche to miss a wire down in the street. Sparks snapped from its broken end, showering onto the pavement like a Roman candle.

He'd had to detour two blocks because a giant tree limb blocked the way, and just when he thought he'd be clear of the confusion a man in front of a Public Service cherry picker flagged him down.

"You want to wait just a few minutes and we'll have this cleaned up? Probably safer than trying another street right now," the man roared in his ear when Marek lowered his window. "Police and state patrol are asking everybody to stay home tonight till the wind calms down," he added in a rather bored tone, maybe because he knew it would do little good.

Boulderites tended to go about their business in these windstorms, much to the consternation of authorities.

Marek turned off the engine to wait for the Public Service Company to clear his way.

"Look for the good," Louise Weir had taught her sons. "The bad happens anyway."

Marek decided the only good thing about a windstorm was that it gathered up all the wastepaper wrappers and cups around McDonald's and blew them to Nebraska.

On the ranch in Wyoming, when hail ruined the hay crop or heavy snow killed the spring calves, Louise shrugged it off as "just life."

One day before another Christmas, Bill Weir's heart stopped forever on the back porch while the rest of the family was in town.

When they arrived home hours too late, their arms filled with Christmas packages, to discover their father already stiffening, Marek's older brother cried. And he was almost fully grown. "He died alone."

"That's the way we all die, Arnold," Louise had said cruelly. "Alone. Trick's not to live that way."

When Louise Weir died, all three of her sons stood at her bedside. But she died alone, not even coming out of her coma long enough to know they were there. Had Shay died alone?

"World owes you nothing but pain," his mother'd told him. "If you want more, you have to go out and get it. And that's easier than you think. Look at the clouds, son. Ever seen anything so beautiful?"

Marek hadn't appreciated the clouds that day. He couldn't now. But he had in between, and he would again.

A car honked behind him and then passed. Marek was startled to see the cherry picker and crew gone. He headed the Porsche home.

His search for Shay was hopeless, busywork to keep from facing the fact he'd have to adjust to one of life's little alterations.

Marek pulled into his reserved parking area. Wind carried the sound of sirens to him as he shielded his face and ran for the door.

He had an open invitation to several parties tonight. Singles tended to band together on holidays to pretend together they didn't mind being alone. Maybe he should go to one. He fumbled for his key under the light in the hall and decided he'd go to all of them.

Marek noted instantly the drapes pulled on the patio doors, the lights on. A thudding noise from the direction of the bedroom.

He slipped out of his jacket, chiding himself for leaving the patio doors unlocked just in case she . . .

He deserved to be burgled. He moved quietly on thick carpet toward the bedroom doorway, tense, thinking he was ready for anything.

But he wasn't.

Streaming platinum hair with odd ripples . . . longer than he remembered.

Marek choked in an effort to breathe. She turned at the sound, reaching for a corner of the dresser as if in astonishment.

He was unwilling to believe that as often as he'd rehearsed this moment his first reaction should be anger. "All this time, God damn, and you're alive. And you let me worry?"

Leaning against the doorframe, he felt it tremble with the windstorm blasting Boulder and the apartment building. Marek clasped one hand with the other because they wanted to shake her until her teeth fell out.

Her hands moved to reddening cheeks. The ring finger on the left one still wore his diamond and she wore a shapeless thing with long sleeves that hung from the shoulders like a nightgown and extended to the floor. Beneath it she was huge.

The baby. He'd forgotten the baby.

Shay drew herself up and pointed her nose at the ceiling with an expression like an insulted librarian. "Mr. Weir, I did not expect this—"

"What the hell did you expect?" Marek crossed the room in spite of himself. In spite of the baby.

His approach and probably the look on his face took the starch from her. She crumpled. "Oh, how could he? This is awful." She backed away.

"How could who? What? Where have you been?" He reached for her.

Shay dodged. "How could . . . you get your fiancée with child and leave me with the results? She must have been—"

"She? She's you. And she got that way—you got that way right there!" He gestured toward the bed behind her. She jerked away and fell onto it.

The water bed rolled and heaved beneath her and she grabbed for the board frame. "John McCabe would have killed you for this."

"Who?"

"I want you to leave me be. Do you understand?"

"Then why did you come here?"

"I don't know. I mean I do know." She struggled off the bed. "I came because . . . well . . ." Shay bit her lip, looking every bit as furious as he felt. "Because I want you to stop searching for me."

"I'd already decided to do just that."

"You did? That's . . . good to hear." But she looked disappointed.

"Shay, does someone want money for you? Is this a setup? Are you being held somewhere against your will?" Was someone hiding behind the bathroom door with a gun to be sure she said the right thing?

"No. I'm perfectly safe and . . . I know I must seem a silly goose to you but—"

"Silly goose?" He hadn't heard that expression since his grandmother died.

"I'm happy and well cared for and wish to be left in peace."

"Cared for by another man?" Why would anyone take on the trouble of a pregnant woman half the country was searching for?

"Certainly not!" Shay drew in her breath and blinked. "Another man . . . yes. Yes, that's it. So you see you must forget all about me." She posed again with her nose in the air and started to walk past him.

He had her by the shoulders, fighting the urge to violence. "And the baby. I'm supposed to forget about him too?"

"It will probably be a girl and no great loss to you. I assure you I'll do everything in my power to care for her."

"And your parents? Their lives have been ruined by your stupidity." An odd smell had crept into the room. "What do I tell them?"

She gave a little scream as he tightened his grip and she looked over his shoulder.

Just as he realized the import of the direction of her glance and before he could turn to defend himself, something thick and dark came down over him, tightened quickly around his arms before he could move. That smell overwhelmed him now even as he recognized it and did exactly the wrong thing. . . .

Marek drew in a choking breath, instinctively planning to let it out in a roar of fury at this final insult in an evening filled with them.

The roar never came. He stared down and someone gently lowered him to the rug.

"You mustn't hurt him." Shay's worried voice, far away.

". . . just sleep awhile. Looked like he was going to get rough." A harsh whisper. "Thought you needed help."

When Marek came back to the light in the room nothing covered his face or bound his arms.

He had a staggering hangover.

Rolling, he pushed on carpet until he was on his knees. His head and stomach shuddered together, his vision slid in and out of focus.

"Shay?"

Marek pulled himself to his feet, holding onto the dresser, and made for the door across a tilting floor.

"Shay?"

Wind swirled red drapes into the room, howled derision.

A patch of white on the drapes. He stumbled over to find a piece of paper pinned to them.

Dear Mr. Weir,

I am truly sorry for the inconvenience I have caused you. I would have returned your engagement ring but my fingers have swollen and it cannot be removed. Please forgive me and please do not try to follow or search for me any longer. Nothing useful can come of it.

It was unsigned and neither in Shay's words nor her handwriting. But in the same flowery script as the message on his blackboard.

He found the blanket he kept on his closet shelf on the patio. It smelled of ether.

The gate was open.

Shay was gone. Again.

Marek crumpled the note and leaned his face against the brick wall, wind screeching a cover for the groans his voice made as he forced himself not to cry.

17

The wind stopped suddenly, as it had begun. A warm chinook wind, it'd taken the snow with it, brought the nighttime temperature to an unseasonable sixty degrees.

It left nerves frazzled, piles of fine dirt on the insides of windowsills, tree branches hanging broken over roofs and sidewalks, Christmas decorations stripped from streetlights on the downtown mall, shingles lifted and torn, a few houses under construction flattened, and a fire raging in a mobile-home park where a trailer had been torn from its gas connection.

Now that it was gone, the city seemed inert and bizarrely silent. A line had gone down somewhere and the Gingerbread House was without power. The stove was a gas range, the hot dishes had kept warm and Rachael broiled the steaks.

Jerry sat between his wife and brother-in-law, a Christmas candle lighting their dinner. And yet this was not a festive meal. The silence outside seeped into the kitchen. The grating of a knife cutting through meat against the surface of a plate seemed to scrape on the nerves.

Rachael insisted they eat before she reveal her surprise, the reason for their visit to Columbia Cemetery.

Remy watched her with open concern.

She kept her eyes on her plate. Candlelight added to her pallor. She seemed too intent in her concentration on cutting her food, directing it to her mouth.

"Bran would have had a snit once about the cholesterol in this meal," Jerry said, trying to find a common and safe topic to lighten the mood.

Rachael lowered her fork to her plate, the broccoli still on it, her eyes wide with an expression suggesting hysteria. "Remember the fuss Mom made about all the bacon and eggs you used to eat for breakfast, Jerry?"

"Yeah. And that was years before I even heard the word 'cholesterol.' "

"And, Remy, remember on the ranch when she'd make us scrape up and down between our teeth with pieces of thread?"

"It kept breaking or fraying and getting stuck. Sure was glad when dental floss became available."

"Did you ever know anyone else whose mother insisted on that . . . then?"

"No, not that I'd remember anyway." Remy refilled their wineglasses. "But Mom was always ahead of her time. It was uncanny the way she—"

"I'll make some coffee." Rachael's silverware rattled as she took her half-eaten dinner to the sink.

When the table was cleared and the coffee poured, she handed Remy their mother's diary and lit more candles.

"I want you to read this aloud, Rem. I don't believe a word of it, you understand, but . . ."

"Do you think we should? This is a private thing."

"She meant for it to be read by . . . someone."

"Rachael, I know you're troubled. Can't we just talk it out?" Jerry asked. "I can't stay all night to hear your mother's diary."

"You'll change your mind when you've heard some of it," Rachael said too calmly.

" 'Dear Brandy.' " Remy began reading an odd account of Brandy telling herself what had happened to her as if she hadn't been there, using words no lady would have used in 1900—the date of the first entry. It dealt with her first marriage and the death of her father. " 'He died in my arms, Brandy, thinking I was you.' " Remy looked up. "It doesn't make sense."

"Go on to the next entry." Rachael turned to Jerry. "It's dated 1946 and it's after our dad died."

Remy lifted his reading glasses to rub his eyes and then continued.

> As you can see by the date, the mirror didn't reverse us and I think I should tell you of your life that I led. It looks like you will live out my life and I can't fill in all the gaps in your knowledge to deal with that but I can explain something of the family and times you missed. I can't imagine how you'll deal with being Shay Garrett but—

"Shay Garrett didn't exist in 1946," Jerry interrupted.

The diary related eventually how, when she was seven, Rachael brought home a little boy named Jerry Garrett and Brandy dropped a bowl of potatoes because she recognized the name if not the face of the man who would be her father for twenty years.

"Rachael, this is one of your stories written up like a diary or something. That mirror couldn't have switched Shay and Bran . . ." Jerry had a quick memory vision of Shay in the mirror, dressed as a gypsy, and the young Brandy watching the mirror being unloaded from a wagon. "No. I still don't believe it."

"Of course not. It's obviously impossible." Rachael laughed. "The funniest thing about it is how well it would explain the sudden change in Shay."

"And how my mother knew things she couldn't have known." Remy stared at the cupboards. "Like what professions we'd get into."

"And that I'd marry Jerry. And that I'd be a writer. She even told me the title of my first book before I wrote it."

"Rachael, this is some kind of hoax." Jerry's dinner wasn't sitting well.

"You read for a while." Remy handed him the diary. He was as pale as his sister.

Jerry tried to ignore the fact that the handwriting bore a close resemblance to Shay's. He'd been reading about ten minutes when the phone rang.

Rachael pulled the receiver into the hall by its overlong cord to talk and Jerry wondered if there was a man on the other end.

When she came back, she lit a cigarette off a candle and smiled without humor. "That was Marek. He's coming over."

Jerry groaned. "Why do we have to have that—"

"Shay was at his apartment tonight. Or Brandy. Whoever. She's alive."

By morning the four of them had exchanged stories, compared countless details on how the diary explained both Shay and Brandy and how the note left in Marek's apartment came to be in an unfamiliar handwriting. They all agreed at one time or another that the whole thing was preposterous.

"We're too tired to make sense of this nonsense," Jerry said.

"I don't think we should say anything to Dan. At least not yet," Remy said. "He's hotheaded and—"

"He won't believe it anyway," Rachael said. "That the mother who bore and raised him was born his niece."

"There's no scientific basis or . . . or any basis to account for a mirror that could . . ." Marek gave up and shook his head.

"I think we should keep Gale and the police out of this."

"Yeah, or we'll all end up in padded cells."

The conversation dwindled to stares, nervous gestures fed on coffee nerves, fatigue and shock.

"Have you ever had the feeling of lifting up out of yourself and looking down on you and . . . everyone?" Rachael pulled her eyes from the green leather book. Her expression blank. "Does it ever happen to anyone else?"

"You're just exhausted, Puss. And you've been through so much."

"Rachael, you don't really believe this?" Jerry picked up the diary.

"Of course not. It's impossible. But . . . what do you do . . . how do you cope if the impossible happens anyway?" Her face looked serene. Her entire body trembled.

The men sat watching her until Jerry whispered, "I'll stay with her. You two go on home."

Thirty miles away, the wedding mirror reflected a black coffee grinder and part of the oak pedestal table on which it sat.

Wilson Antiques, Ltd., closed for the holiday, stood barred and darkened.

Tiny dust particles floated in the air, many coming to rest on antique chairs and cabinets. But when they drifted onto the wedding mirror, they slid off, fell to the carpet below, collected in faint ridges that ringed the mirror's base.

In January, a cold snap hit Colorado and temperatures fell below zero at night. The weather warmed enough to snow and then turned frigid again.

The combination made the search for Shay unpleasant and difficult. Remy Maddon divided the map of Boulder County with Marek and they started all over again in a race to find her before the baby was born.

Jerry didn't offer to help. He felt ambivalent about finding his daughter now. Not, of course, that he believed the diary. And then he was too busy with Rachael.

He moved back into the Gingerbread House, buying twin beds for the ransacked master bedroom and hiring a retired nurse to stay when he had to be at the office. He couldn't possibly leave his wife now, not in the state she was in.

Rachael sat all day and stared at the wall, lay awake at night after her sleeping pill wore off and stared at the ceiling. She answered when spoken to and took an interest in nothing. She was beginning to put on weight, a thing she'd never allowed herself to do before.

One day the nurse found Rachael in the bathroom holding a razor blade to her wrist.

Jerry gave up and took her in to Gale Sampson, worried she might spill the fantastic story of the diary but not knowing what else to do. If she told him about the wedding mirror, Gale didn't mention it. He put Rachael on antidepressants.

Now Rachael didn't feel bad anymore. Rachael didn't feel anything. The nurse, at least, was relieved.

In Denver, the wedding mirror stood, unsold, in Wilson Antiques, Ltd. The store was located one block and around a corner from the Brown Palace Hotel.

In early February, it warmed up. The snow melted. And one night the wind returned. . . .

Brandy heard the first gust rolling in off the mountain range to the west, felt it slam into the house as she reached over Shay's stomach to wring out the dishrag. The rim of the sink vibrated against the baby. The baby moved sluggishly.

Ansel looked up from his newspaper, listening.

Silence.

As if the wind sucked in its breath.

Then a far-off murmur that grew to a growl as it approached. It swept by with a roar. Roof joists creaked in agony. Brandy could taste the dust on the air.

Again stillness, muffling all.

Ansel cleared his throat. "Drought wind. Better see to the animals."

Brandy rubbed Shay's back when he'd gone. Standing was uncomfortable, sitting anguish, and lying down not much of a solution.

The quiet lasted. Perhaps this wasn't to be a storm after all, just a few stray gusts.

Happy let out a long wailing howl and Shay's teeth ground together.

Brandy slid open the glass door to see if he'd become entangled in his chain.

He bared his teeth and lunged at her, snapping.

"Happy, what–" She lost her awkward balance and fell into the room on Shay's backside.

A twinge of pain from Shay's private parts. An even stronger one from her posterior.

Happy barked, snarled, tugged on his chain until he stood halfway over the doorsill.

"Stop it, dog! I know we're not the best of friends but we've managed nicely. I've even put food out for you."

Stina Mark pushed through the cat entrance and spat at him, arching her back and dancing on her toes in angry fear.

A gust Brandy hadn't heard coming hit the house and Happy snapped at her worn canvas shoe, teeth clicking shut inches from the toe.

"You've gone mad, hound. Out with you." She pushed a chair at him, rolling to her knees to slide the door closed, almost catching the end of his nose as he retreated.

The room was filling with cats, not only Stina's brood but several from the barn. They prowled the kitchen, mewing, sniffing.

Brandy pushed and pulled herself to her feet, using a chair and the table. A small puddle glistened on the floor where she'd fallen, her skirt and legs were damp.

Surely she'd have known if she'd wet herself.

A sickening ache in Shay's lower back.

A barn cat sniffed at the puddle.

Wind shrieked outside. Happy howled.

Pain cramped around her middle, forcing her to bend over the table. The bread toaster fell off the corner and onto the floor. "Ma!"

Brandy held her breath till the pain eased, then drew in so much air it made her dizzy. Shay's legs felt weak.

She half-sat and half-leaned on the sofa with the bed pillows she'd brought from Lottie's room against the small of her back.

Brandy knew nothing about childbirth, but instinct told her she was about to have a child she hadn't conceived.

"Dear Lord, please bring my granddaughter back before this happens."

She'd come to accept the apparent inevitable as this time approached, and, terrified and trapped, she'd refused to think about it.

For the first time since the night she'd raced through the dark alleyways of Boulder, Brandy sensed she could lose control of this body. It seemed alert. Turned inward. Waiting for commands other than hers.

Even the baby was still for once.

Walls and rafters creaked. Windows clattered in their frames.

A cracking snap and the floor shuddered as if some windblown thing had hit and broken against the old farmhouse.

"Having a baby's as natural as oatmeal and breathing," Ansel St. John had said.

In her world no one discussed the fact that a lady was to have a baby, particularly with the other children. Dresses grew voluminous and the lady added weight all around, not just out front as Shay had. The baby appeared suddenly to the great rejoicing of friends and relatives and the mother recovered quietly in bed.

By the time Sophie McCabe miscarried her last baby Brandy was old enough and should have noticed, but she hadn't known one was expected. She had, however, noted a great deal of water being put to boil before she was shunted off to bed. From this she'd deduced it was a messy business.

Brandy filled Ansel's two largest pots with water and lit the gas fire under them.

In a lull in the wind she heard goats bleating and wondered if the old man was having trouble shutting them up.

She walked carefully through the cold portion of the house to the back, thinking to call him in. When she finally forced the door open against the wind she was met with a frenzied hen who entered squawking before she could shut it out.

Dark. But not so dark she couldn't see that the largest of the old sheds, the one Ansel called a barn, had disappeared.

"Mr. St. John?" The wind blew her words back into the house and tried to slam the door in her face.

He'd been gone too long, might have been injured, or worse, if he was in the barn when it gave way.

What would she do if she had to have the child without his help? As curious as she'd always been, why hadn't she asked more questions on this subject? As long as most women had babies, why weren't they trained on the details as they grew up?

Sophie and Nora had a way of shutting themselves away from her when it came to delicate subjects. Just their expressions could put Brandy off.

She slipped outside to look for Ansel. It seemed a foolish thing to do and yet it would be inhuman not to. He could be in as much need of her as she of him. Odd to have only one other person to depend upon in a crisis.

Brandy tried to listen for the old man above the wind.

The body listened to itself. The legs felt weighted. The grinding ache in the back made Brandy feel sick and dampened Shay's skin.

"Mr. St. John!" Her hair came loose and blew about her face. She grabbed a rusty metal hulk to steady herself. Frightened chickens huddled on its protected side.

Arvid and Luvisa frolicked near a section of collapsed roofing.

Praying that Ansel was not lying dead beneath the broken roof, Brandy made her way toward it, battling dirt-filled wind and Shay's increasingly reluctant body.

She was so intent on the broken roof she didn't see him until she'd tripped over him, barely catching herself up on a fencepost.

Ansel lay on his face, one arm stretched out. He felt warm when she turned him over. No sign of bleeding, his eyes closed. He looked alternately pale and dark in night shadows flickered by tossing skeleton weeds and debris.

Brandy felt the cramp returning. She curled over his body, fighting pain and panic. It lasted longer than the first time and it hurt more.

When it passed, Ansel hadn't moved. But she could feel the vibration of his heart in his chest. She couldn't stay out in this storm, and neither could he.

"Only rabbits give up for fear," John McCabe always said.

Brandy crawled until she knelt above the old man's head, then slipped a hand under each of his armpits and struggled to get her feet beneath her. Using his weight as ballast, she leaned backward and pushed with her legs until she was upright.

She dragged him toward the house, his limp body pulling on her arms, easing the ache in Shay's back. It was a slow business with her clumsiness and her inertia, with hair in her face and no free hand to sweep it away.

She prayed another cramp wouldn't force her to drop him, feared she couldn't get either of them up again.

A clicking of hoofs sounded in the quiet between gusts. A goat came to a halt at the corner of the house. A poised and alert satyr shadow . . .

Hooligan. She'd forgotten that with the barn gone, he'd be on the loose.

Fear of him gave her extra energy and she pulled harder at her burden, hoping to reach the door before he charged.

Brandy was but five feet from her destination when Happy's eerie howl sounded from the front of the house and wind screamed out of the west as if bent on making up for the lull.

Hooligan reared on his hind legs and came down on the run, head lowered, little horns prodding the air.

Brandy dropped Ansel and stumbled toward the house. She reached the door but hadn't time to open it, tried to flatten Shay's vast body into its recess, felt Hooligan brush against her skirts as he passed.

In the instant he turned for another charge, she pulled out the door and flung herself inside. The goat's second lunge rammed the door shut.

Brandy lay on the floor listening to Hooligan and the wind outside, the hen clucking nervously in the corner, the sizzle of water boiling over in the kitchen and then the involuntary sounds coming up Shay's throat.

The clutching pain that made her double over before stretched her out now.

18

Brandy McCabe lost track of how long the cramp lasted. When it released her, she lay breathing deeply, aware of tears on her granddaughter's cheeks and the blessed absence of pain.

She'd have liked to lie there forever but over the low moan of a quieted wind she heard another moan. Ansel.

She drew herself up by the knob to a sitting position and eased the door open.

Ansel was also sitting up, holding his head. No sign of the goat.

"Mr. St. John, the baby—"

"Help me, Shay Garrett." His voice but a whine, a whisper. Behind it the wind gathered for another blow.

"You must help *me*. The baby . . . can you crawl on your hands and knees? At least tell me what to do." But the wind shrieked in to close the door.

"Oh, dear God, please . . ." Brandy clawed the doorframe until she stood, leaning against it. Sickly stickiness coated Shay's skin. A spreading sensation between her legs.

As Brandy reached to open the door it tore from her grasp and the old man stepped in to lean against the other side of its frame.

The sound of their combined breathing almost drowned out the wind.

"Mr. St. John, what . . . what is the boiling water for?"

He stared blankly, rubbing his head and wincing. "Boiling water?"

"When a baby's due, someone always boils water."

He laid the side of his face against the wall and closed his eyes. He looked ghastly. "To wash your hands with."

All that water for hands? Another pain came upon her. She took this one standing up, letting the air out of her lungs in grunts that ended in a tiny scream.

"I think I'm having a baby."

"Don't worry." He held her arm and they moved toward the kitchen, he staggering and she waddling. "Nothing to it."

Steam filled the kitchen, coated the glass door to opaque. The water in the pots had boiled off by half.

Brandy added cold from the faucet and washed Shay's hands, finding neither sense nor reassurance in the act. "Now what do I do?"

"See if there's any bleeding here." He showed her a swelling on the back of his head and she cleansed a trace of blood from the scratch on it.

Ansel washed his hands and then sat on the sofa looking as if he could never rise again. "Clean sheets on the shelf in the bathroom. Get 'em on that bed over there and take off some of those clothes."

Brandy shooed a half-dozen cats off the bed before she could begin to make it up, and pain attacked again before she finished.

It felt good to be rid of the sticky confining clothing and finally she lay naked between cool sheets not caring about propriety as the body writhed out of control.

"I feel . . . light-headed—"

"Stop breathing so deep then. You're hyperventilatin'."

The pains came faster now, leaving her little time to relax between.

"Is it . . . is it supposed . . . to hurt . . . this much?"

"Mostly in your head." He was washing his hands again. "Just relax."

"Shay's body won't obey . . . obey me. Help!" Shay's hands clutched at the poles of the brass bedstead.

"Women make such a fuss over a little hurtin'. Thought you was different. Animals got more sense." He lifted the sheet from the bottom. "Looks like you ain't going to take forever anyway."

Once he disappeared and she called out for him.

"I'm here. Just sittin' on the floor. I don't feel so good either, you know."

Stina Mark's yellow eyes glared at her from black fur. The cat stood next to her head, coldly appraising her agony, hissing when she cried out. Ansel stood again at the foot of the bed. "Now bring your knees up and push down, Shay Garrett."

Shay Garrett pushed down without Brandy's help. Brandy was losing consciousness. She was in a strange room watching her own body slide off a chair to the floor. It wore a black dress.

An untidy woman, with a loose look about her, knelt over the still form of the Brandy McCabe on the floor and began to slap her face.

Wind shrieked in the background and a woman's voice rose to join it, but they were from a different world, a different time.

Cindy Wilson heard about the winds in Boulder over the radio on her desk. She looked up as the newscaster mentioned the town because in her hand was a list of stolen articles from a house in Boulder. A printed list circulated by the police. And on it, a standing bronze mirror frame with entwined hands. "It couldn't be the same one. I bought it in Texas."

Cindy took the description and stepped out of her little office. Ned was on a buying trip and she'd decided to work late to catch up on paperwork. The store was empty, locked.

The mirror hadn't sold. No one had reported seeing anything other than themselves in it. Cindy'd begun to think she'd imagined that episode in the auction barn.

She stood before it, checking it with the description. It had to be the same mirror.

If she returned it, would she and Ned be suspected of stealing the other antiques from that house in Boulder as well? Who could be more suspect than an antique dealer?

Cindy Wilson was not a thief. But she was a businesswoman.

She tore the description into tiny pieces, put them in her sweater pocket and decided she would *not* tell Ned of this. Inching the heavy mirror along by lifting its weight onto one of the hand-claws of its base and shifting the other, over and over, she had it about a yard from the storeroom when she paused to rest. She'd defy anyone to find something in the mess in there.

The mirror seemed to grow warm in her hands. She let go, stepping back as that odd but familiar humming began. Gray clouds formed on the glass.

Cindy Wilson sat on the rug to watch.

* * *

"You sure don't do things by half measures, do you?" Ansel St. John said. "Here, hold this."

The sheet had slipped off Shay's body and he laid something slimy across her chest.

"What . . . is it?" Brandy managed to ask between moans.

"A baby. And here comes another one right behind it. What do you think of that?"

When the second baby had been delivered, he added, "See? Told you so. Nothing to it."

"Nothing to it . . ." Brandy stared at him through a blur of sweat and tears. Then she passed out.

Lottie sat behind her new boyfriend, Roger, on his motorcycle and pointed to her grandfather's house.

As Roger turned into the drive, she stretched up to his ear. "Go around back." Happy would probably take his leg off if given the chance.

It was a warm day in March and the clothesline was full of gently fluttering clothes.

Lottie stared. Roger turned off the motor and waited for her to dismount.

"That fries it!" Lottie said. "Let's get out of here."

"I thought you wanted to see your grandpa."

"Look at that clothesline. Diapers. Rows of them. The old shithead—should of known I couldn't trust him. Come on. We got another stop to make."

Jerry Garrett was leaving the Gingerbread House to go back to his office after lunching with Rachael and the nurse. A motorcycle stopped on the street in front and a girl got off the back before the guy driving could get the kick stand down. She ran to meet him at the gate.

"Mr. Garrett? I'm Lottie Ralston. And I want to talk to you about your daughter."

By her appearance Jerry sized her up as one of the idle young, the voluntary poor who infested the area.

"She's had her baby and she's living with my grandfather. I don't want to get him in trouble and I don't want the reward, but—"

"What do you want, Lottie Ralston?" Jerry asked suspiciously.

"I want you to get her and that kid out of there. He can't afford them and you can. She's sponged off him long enough."

* * *

Jerry turned the Oldsmobile into the drive and stared at the dilapidated house, the litter of junk automobiles and ancient farm machinery. How could she have been this close to town and gone undiscovered?

A fat dog barked on the end of a chain.

Jerry swallowed back the acid taste coming up from his stomach. He didn't want to face what was in that house. If the diary were true . . . if she wasn't Shay . . . he didn't want her back.

"Selfish bastard," he muttered at himself and got out of the car.

The dog made it obvious he wouldn't allow Jerry near the front door. So he followed the drive around the house, where more junk sat rusting and rows of diapers flapped on a clothesline.

A black cat with yellow eyes sat in the sun on a crumpled car hood.

And his daughter bolted from the back door, dressed like a destitute hippie and carrying a plastic clothes basket.

"Shay?" It came out choked but loud enough for her to hear over the protesting cries from the clothes basket.

She threw him a terrified look over her shoulder and kept running.

He started after her and then stopped. "Brandy?"

She paused at a gate in a board fence to stare at him.

"Brandy McCabe?" He tried to keep the anger out of his voice. She slipped through the gate as he approached. "We know about the wedding mirror, Brandy McCabe."

The intruder in his daughter's body watched him warily. Unfamiliar expressions played across a familiar face.

"We know. There's no need to run anymore. We . . ." Jerry Garrett felt suddenly tired. "I want to help you."

Bruised shadows around her eyes. Reddened hands clutching the basket so tightly the soft plastic folded inward. He tried to feel sympathy for this stranger . . . but his own loss was too great.

"I will kill you," she whispered, still poised as if to run if he should startle her, "before I let you harm these children."

"Children?" He tried to peer over the gate and the yellow rim of the basket but she backed away. "There's more than one?"

"You are the grandfather of identical twins, Mr. Garrett." She showed him two tiny heads, fine black hair fluffing around white faces, eyes screwed shut against bright sunlight, four little fists purposelessly flailing air. "Your daughter has two fine sons." Her voice softened as she looked at them. "And I intend to keep them safe until she returns."

"She's not returning, Brandy."

"Of course she will. She must."

"No. It looks like you'll have to take care of them. I guess they're yours now . . . and Marek's."

Lottie and friend arrived to add to the confusion. And a few minutes later, Ansel St. John in a rattletrap truck.

Jerry worked hard to convince him he meant the mother and twins no harm, that there had been a misunderstanding, that he wanted only to help them.

"She's of a legal age to do what she wants," Ansel decreed. But then he admitted the three of them were getting to be a handful for an old man.

Finally, Ansel shooed Lottie and Roger from the kitchen and made Jerry write on paper that he would not send his daughter to an institution.

Jerry signed it knowing it had no legal value but hoping to placate Ansel. "You see, when she overheard us speak of institutions and such, we didn't know she—"

"Was Brandy McCabe?" Ansel St. John seemed to know the whole story and he'd swallowed it without blinking.

The man had to be crazy and it made Jerry more determined to get his grandsons out of there . . . grandsons . . . he peeked into the clothes basket. The twins slept.

He told Ansel he'd move them into his cabin in Nederland. "They'll have everything they need there. I'll see to it."

"Good. Boulder's a little raw for an old-fashioned girl to start out with." Ansel turned to the woman in Shay's body. "And I'll be up to check on you. He tries to pull anything and this paper goes right to THE POLICE!"

Brandy still seemed nervous about the move. But, after writing the old man a generous check for his trouble and expenses, Jerry loaded her, the twins and a ton of swiftly folded diapers into the Oldsmobile and drove off.

"The reason I can't take you to the Gingerbread House is your mother . . . I mean . . . your daughter . . . Rachael has been hit hard by all this. We're worried about her. I think she'll have to take you on gradually."

He made a quick stop at the Gingerbread House, leaving them in the car, to pick up the diary and ask the nurse to stay late.

"What are you going to do about Marek?" he asked as they started up the canyon.

"That I will leave for Shay to decide when she returns." Brandy fiddled with the diamond ring. "It's not for me to—"

"She's not returning!" Jerry took a curve too hard and fought the Olds back off the shoulder. "Don't make this any harder for me than it already is. Looking at you, knowing inside you're not her—"

"I must get home, Mr. Garrett. Then you can have your Shay back inside as well as out. Perhaps if I could have the mirror with me in—"

"It's gone. Stolen. Along with almost everything else. You'll understand more when you've read the diary."

Brandy marveled at how the canyon had been cleared, at how quickly they reached Nederland along the sweeping road, at the dam built below the town. Ice covered the water behind it, spread over what she'd known as a vast mountain meadow.

Nederland was in its proper place, but held nothing familiar to her. Pines covered the surrounding slopes now and smoke puffed into a leaden sky from chimneys hidden among them. Snow lay in grimy drifts along the edges of the streets.

Shay's father drove through the town and across a bridge, passing a railroad sitting by itself in a field.

"Did they finally bring the railroad to Nederland then?" Brandy looked back wistfully. Here at last was something familiar.

"It came through someplace up closer to Caribou. That's just a fancy antique shop. I don't know how they got that old caboose in here."

"Antique, yes." It was awful to be an antique oneself. "Caribou, I remember well. Is it—"

"Hardly even a ghost town. Nothing left but the cemetery. And not much of that."

"Ghosts are all that's left, it seems." *And I should be one of them.* Brandy wouldn't believe she must stay trapped here.

Jerry stopped before an odd building in the trees. It was shaped like a capital A, its front of glass, its frame and full-length porch stained reddish-brown. Stacks of chopped wood lined one end of the porch.

He leaned over to stare across her. "This is the spot where the Strock cabin used to stand. I lived in it once when I was a kid."

"Where I shall live when I return. But not in so grand a building, I'm sure." Corbin Strock seemed a remote phantom.

Jerry drove up a steep incline beside the cabin and parked behind it. A rusted lift pump stood on a platform of broken concrete, reminding her of the one at the trough for the carriage horse at home.

"Well, this'll be your home. For a while at least." He carried the diapers in and she the twins.

The air was sharp on the mountainside and chilly in the cabin. "I'll light a fire in the fireplace and turn up the thermostat. There's not much here. I'd better run down to the store."

Brandy sat before the fire and hurried to nurse Shay's infant sons before his return, feeling the prickly relief as Shay's breasts emptied.

This structure would hardly have passed as a cabin in her time. Cushioned furniture sat deep in rugs thicker than those in the Gingerbread House. One vast room, with kitchen and parlor combined, a railed balcony at one end on which she'd seen a bed. Jerry Garrett did seem intent on making them comfortable rather than causing trouble. The place had a soft pillowlike atmosphere, protective, enclosed.

When Jerry came back he made several trips to the car for paper sacks filled with food. And meat. All cut to size on paper plates and wrapped in that clear filmy substance she saw so often in this world.

"You're going to fry T-bones?" he said when she began to prepare supper. "Whoopee-twang . . . as Shay would have said."

He seemed to sober at his own words, stood for a long moment staring into the air, jingling coins in his pocket. Finally he shook his head and poured himself a glass of scotch whiskey. When the supper was ready he did full justice to the meat and the potatoes fried in its grease.

"Mr. St. John didn't approve of eating flesh. He was very fond of animals. It's been so long since I've tasted meat."

"I'll look the other way if you want to nibble off the bone." He managed a smile. "You can call the local store for anything you need and put it on my account. Mrs. Tyler said she'd find some schoolkid to deliver it. I'll bring Shay's clothes up tomorrow."

He showed her another bedroom in the cellar and a clothes-washing machine and dryer.

As he slipped into his coat, he bent over the basket from which much cooing and gurgling emanated. "Have you named them?"

"I'm sure their real mother will wish to do that, but for now I'm calling them Joshua and Elton after my brothers."

"Read the diary," was his only answer.

Brandy watched him drive away through the front wall of window. Snowflakes fell across the lights of the automobile's lanterns.

She washed the dishes, bathed Shay's babies at the kitchen sink and treated herself to a steamy shower in the bathroom off the kitchen.

After building up the fire, Brandy reached for the green leather book she'd seen the night of her abortive visit home.

Wind sighed a timeless winter lament without, making all seem snug within.

Elton twitched comfortably. Joshua snored an infant sound.

Brandy laid the diary aside unopened and curled up on the deep sofa to sleep until the next feeding.

19

"They got the Maddon eyes, that's for sure." Remy knelt stiffly beside the clothes basket and let Joshua clasp his forefinger.

"Yes, and Marek's hair." Elinore Maddon bent to touch Elton's cheek.

"Your Uncle Dan knew you weren't dead, Shay." Dan set a large flat box against the wall. "Nation full of quitters, that's what we are." He glanced at Jerry Garrett in a grouchy fashion and stood beside his brother to admire Shay's babies.

"You and Marek fix it up fast. Kids need a name," Dan Maddon continued. He had the decency to blush. "I don't hold with these one-parent families." His wife, Ruth, tried to hush him up with an elbow in his ribs. Her stiff-curled hair had a bluish tinge to it.

Dan ignored her. "These boys raise half as much hell as two sets of Maddon twins did, you're going to need a man to knock heads together."

Jerry brought in another flat box and the men began to assemble baby beds by the fireplace. The aunts helped Brandy hang Shay's clothes in a closet on the balcony and then sat at the table drinking coffee while their husbands bickered over the meaning of the printed instructions that came with the cribs.

"You're breast-feeding twins?" Elinore Maddon said when Brandy explained why she didn't need more baby bottles. Her eyes widened until the creases in her plump face came together. "I suppose you delivered without anesthetic and the doctor laid them on your tummy and everything. Ruth, are you listening to this?"

"I think this back-to-nature kick can be carried too far." Ruth Maddon made a clucking noise like Nora used to. "All those years of developing painless, safe ways of doing things and then shucking them to the winds. Shay, tell us the doctor put you out."

"There was no doctor," Brandy said. Jerry'd warned her that only Remy knew the trick the wedding mirror had played on them all. "But Mr. St. John did lay them on my . . . bosom until he could attend to them."

The sisters-in-law glanced at each other and turned shocked faces to Brandy as if they were puppets attached to the same string.

"No doctor," Ruth repeated.

"Mr. St. John . . . the old man you stayed with?" Elinore sat back in her chair as if she needed it to brace her. "He delivered the twins?"

"Yes, and as you can see they're—"

"Jerry"—Elinore set down her cup with exaggerated care—"did you know those kids were born in that . . . that farmhouse?"

But Jerry and the uncles had stopped quarreling and were already gaping at Brandy.

There followed a heated discussion on birth certificates, eyedrops, inoculations, and "pediatricians."

"Shay, I'm surprised at you," Ruth said. "After all you've done to Marek and your poor mother. And now this."

Brandy was relieved when the Maddons departed.

"I haven't called Marek yet," Jerry said uncomfortably. "He knows . . . knows you aren't Shay. I suppose he does have some rights here though." He stared into the cribs as if his grandsons were incriminating evidence.

He insisted on making an appointment with a doctor to examine the twins and his daughter's body.

When he'd gone Brandy saw to the infants, watched the television box and tried not to think.

The green diary sat on the low parlor table in front of the sofa.

The twins looked tiny, each in his own bed. Sometimes she resented them for the pain they'd caused her and for all they demanded of her days and nights. Brandy shocked herself with these unnatural feelings.

She prayed to God for forgiveness. She was beginning to resent him too. And that made her feel even worse. Brandy had pork chops for dinner, built up the fire and opened the diary.

She stopped reading only to nurse the twins and to cry.

When she finished, the fire had burned down.

Brandy huddled on the sofa, stared at the embers and saw memories.

The picnic beneath the Flatirons. Pa chasing a squealing Joshua across the mesa top where Marek's devil castle now stood. Joshua captured. His plump little body brought back over Pa's shoulder, dumped on a blanket and tickled till it could laugh and squirm no more . . .

Grandfather McCabe and Grandmother Euler sitting on the shaded porch of the Gingerbread House, discussing days long gone in the quivering voices of the old. Aunt Harriet sitting between them, translating because Grandmother Euler spoke no English . . .

Sitting on the back step with Ma, their aprons filled with string beans to snap, peas to shell or apples to peel . . . chatting pleasantly of nothing much while they worked . . .

Canoeing on Weisenhorn Lake with Elton. Sunday train excursions to Mount Alto to pick wildflowers. Giggling over naughty phrases in the Latin grammar with Violet and Bessie in the cloakroom at preparatory school. Even Nora's scolding seemed dear to her now.

Brandy looked into the cribs. Joshua, Elton and a few gravestones seemed the only continuity left in her life.

She removed the gleaming diamond from her granddaughter's finger and placed it on the diary.

The next morning, while forcing down a breakfast she couldn't taste, Brandy heard a familiar sound.

She opened the back door to see Ansel St. John's truck come to a stop by the lift pump. He carried a box filled with bottles of goat's milk.

"Better for a nursing mother than cow's milk," he said by way of greeting and tracked snow across the rug to the baby cribs. "Sure look comfortable here. Appears Mr. Garrett's keeping his promises. With that money he gave me for caring for you I can pay my taxes and put up a new barn."

Brandy spent the morning telling him the contents of the diary.

"She's lived your life, now you got to live hers. It's done, happened. Nothing you can do. Least you won't be cursed with knowin' things ahead of time like she was."

"But don't you see, Mr. St. John? It's all my fault. All these lives confused because I let the mirror—"

"All you can do now's to get rid of the mirror so it don't do this to somebody else. If your granddaughter's suspicions are right, it's even chalked up a score of killings."

"It was stolen when thieves broke into the Gingerbread House."

"Well, you'll just have to take good care of this little family here then. And I wouldn't worry over that bloody-hand business she writes about. Probably me delivering twins."

He refused to stay for lunch, saying he wanted to stop by and see Lottie while he was in town. "Surprised that Marek fellow hasn't stormed in here yet." The faint smell of goat lingered after he left.

Brandy drew thick curtains across the window wall to shut out a foreign world. But it invaded the cabin that afternoon in the form of Shay's parents.

Brandy was startled by the grim change in Rachael Garrett. She'd grown plump but the added flesh wasn't firm. Her skin was sallow. Thick hair had gone lifeless with patches of gray at the roots.

Dull eyes searched her daughter's face to find only Brandy, then turned to her grandchildren. "I'm glad they're not girls," she said listlessly. "Daughters are so . . . so much heartbreak."

Rachael held first one twin and then the other in shaky arms, Jerry hovering over her as if he feared she'd drop them.

"Maybe you could start a book about twins," he said hopefully.

She looked up from the babe in her arms, her cheeks wet but a sudden spark in her eyes. "Jerry, we've got to find the wedding mirror."

"What good would it do now? Shay's gone, and where would we look?"

"We owe it to Shay and to Joshua and Elton."

"We might drive around to the antique stores in the area on weekends and at least ask about it." His sudden interest had more to do with the spark in his wife's eyes, Brandy suspected, than any hope of finding the mirror.

"We could look for furniture for the Gingerbread House while we're at it, Rachael. Would you like that?"

Brandy donned Shay's puffy, slippery mackintosh and fur-lined boots. She left them with their plans and their grandsons, knowing the sight of her must be torture to them.

Standing on the concrete platform of the lift pump she stared at the A-shaped cabin, trying to visualize another cabin almost eighty years ago and the life her granddaughter must have lived there.

But the odd-angled roof and the narrow strip of cloud that crossed the sky from horizon to horizon now made any association with them difficult. Ansel'd explained such cloud trails were left by flying machines soaring too high above the earth to be seen.

How would it feel to be that far up looking down?

She turned to the trees across the clearing. The smell of pine would be the same forever.

A break between tall trees shaped the path where Shay'd walked to the spring on Brandy's legs. Scattered young pine, chest height or shorter, tried to fill in the disused walkway.

She followed it to a heap of weather-gray boards that poked through a low drift. Kicking aside snow, Brandy found a rotting plank with a smooth-edged hole. It broke along an old crack at the touch of her boot. The seat to an outdoor privy.

Wind fingered her skirt as she lifted it to traverse a drift. Snow trickled cold into the tops of her granddaughter's boots.

What use was there in seeking connection to a past she'd never reach? But Brandy continued to the cave in the mountainside where the couple in the cabin had discovered the wedding mirror and a grisly result of its deeds.

Snow and juniper bush covered the lower half of the entrance. The door Shay'd spoken of in the diary was gone but a piece of its frame hung across a hole that looked like black pitch against the snow.

There'd apparently been no more glimpses between the two lives after the birth of the twins. Did it mean the Garretts would succeed in finding and destroying the mirror? Or merely that it would be removed too far to have power over those lives it had tampered with?

When she returned to the clearing the Garretts' automobile was gone, in its place a familiar silver-green vehicle.

Marek Weir bent over Joshua's crib with his hands clasped behind him as if afraid to touch his tiny son.

He must have heard her enter but didn't turn as she removed the coat and boots.

"They have my mother's chin," he said defensively when she stood beside him, the intimacy gone from his voice and expression.

"I'm deeply sorry for what happened to your fiancée."

"I can't believe you're Shay's grandmother. It's impossible."

"Yes. I know. Nevertheless—"

"But if you are, it must have been strange having twins by a man you'd never slept with. Must have been damned strange."

Brandy closed her eyes on the hard stare and shivered even though burning with embarrassment. "Would you care for some coffee, Mr. Weir?"

"Yes, please, *Miss* McCabe." He was right behind her. "Oh, shit. I don't believe this. It's not . . . I just can't . . . in my world things like this don't . . ." He made a choking sound and flopped into a chair.

By the time she had the coffee measured and brewing, milk was soaking through her granddaughter's bra and dribbling down her rib cage.

Brandy excused herself to carry Joshua and Elton up to the balcony, wishing she could escape the angry frustration of the man who paced and cursed below.

"If you're not Shay . . . even if you are, what are we going to do about them?" He watched her zip the twins into soft blankets ingeniously made into pajamas complete with feet. He still hadn't held or touched them, as if by doing so he would commit himself.

The twins chose not to sleep.

"I mean if you are Brandy McCabe, how will you raise them? You'll have all you can do to learn the ways of this world yourself."

Elton drooled happily. Joshua cried. Brandy took Joshua in her arms to comfort him. Elton began to cry.

"Why don't you answer me?"

"Here." Brandy pushed Joshua at him and picked up Elton.

Marek and his son looked at each other for a surprised second. The son puckered up his face and screamed.

By the time both babies slept, Marek had lost his bluster and the coffee'd sat warming in the pot so long it was too bitter to drink.

"Are they always like that?" Marek whispered as Brandy stirred batter for cornbread.

"Several times a day at least. One seems to give the other the idea."

"People should be married awhile before they have children."

"That thought came to you rather late, I think."

They made a meal of sausage, cornbread and stewed tomatoes.

When she'd served him fresh coffee he lit a pipe without bothering to ask her permission. The smell of it brought back memories of her grandfather, James McCabe, and the time he spilled hot ash from his pipe, starting a fire in his beard. She began to tell Marek the story but fell silent at his look of suspicion.

"I don't believe that diary." He tilted his head and stared at her but seemed to be looking inward. "It's just that it explains so much." His knee touched hers under the table.

Brandy hurried to gather the dishes and take them to the sink. But he was at her side, shelving each in the dishwasher as she rinsed it.

"And I wouldn't know what to do with a good old-fashioned . . . prim . . . simpering . . . Victorian girl."

"I have no idea what you mean by Victorian, Mr. Weir, but I do not simper."

"Victoria. Queen Victoria. She set moral standards for years. She—"

"Is a foreigner, and worse, an Englishwoman. The Queen of England has nothing to do with . . ." Brandy saw the kiss coming and was fascinated at Marek's power to immobilize her with a look. Or was it her curiosity again? *Si fueris Romae,* she thought.

She couldn't blame her granddaughter's body for the rash feelings touching him set in motion. She knew she should pull away. But she didn't.

Marek did.

Brandy held to the edge of the sink to keep upright with the suddenness of his release.

He moved around the door of the dishwashing machine and the shelves of rinsed dishes. "You can't be Shay. She never . . ." His eyelids narrowed over eyes as drained of color as his skin. "Do you know how long it's been since I've screwed a—"

Brandy gulped air. "Screwed?"

Marek Weir walked to the door.

"Please . . . don't go. It's so lonely being Shay."

"I'm going to go think . . . drink . . . run . . . jog. I'll be back, but . . ."

Automobile lanterns swept light over the window above the sink, as he backed the Porsche to drive away. She'd been foolish to think he could love her when he found she wasn't Shay.

One of the twins fussed behind her. Brandy McCabe turned to see Shays diamond was gone from atop the diary.

Cindy Wilson held onto her husband's arm in the storeroom of Wilson Antiques, Ltd. "But, Ned, just let me try rubbing the frame again. Maybe it'll—"

"I don't want to hear any more about that damn mirror, and we're not taking it out to the house. It's no more magic than I am."

"Then why does it never need dusting? Never tarnish? And when it's going to show pictures it makes a sound."

"What kind of sound?"

"Sort of an electrical buzzing . . . or hum like . . . . like power lines make sometimes. And it seems to work on electricity . . . or static electricity if you move it or rub it or—I wish there was some way we could plug it into a wall socket."

"Has Myrtle seen these pictures?"

"No, she's flaky enough the way it is. I didn't tell her about it for fear she'd quit. But, Ned, at first I kept seeing this blond girl. I even saw her having a baby. Then it was just clouds or gas or something."

"Look, honey, I love you. But I've reached the limit of being able to even discuss this thing. We're going to make another appointment with Myrtle's analyst and you're going to keep it this time."

"Ned, I'm not mental. I've really seen these things."

But he led her firmly from the storeroom and closed the door on the wedding mirror.

20

Marek returned, but only to deliver a stack of books, stand over the twins' cribs, eye Brandy suspiciously and leave.

The books dealt with the history of the twentieth century and were written for school-age children. Brandy found the recital of events overwhelming, much of it—such as that German, Hitler, and the fact the United States would involve itself in foreign wars—every bit as fantastic as the wedding mirror.

But in general this history she'd not lived seemed as remote as Caesar's conquest of Gaul. Reality was two babes wanting to eat every three hours twenty-four hours a day. She started them on cereals and mashed potatoes.

Rachael and Jerry visited often. He seemed to prefer this broken, colorless woman to the slim, capable beauty Rachael'd been when Brandy first came to this world. With all the advances touted by the history books and the "liberated woman" proclaimed by the television box, men did not seem to Brandy to have changed overmuch.

The local doctor determined Joshua, Elton, and Shay's body to be in good health and started the twins on a series of inoculations he claimed would keep them safe from almost every disease Brandy'd heard of and a few she hadn't.

Swaths had been cut through the forests on the western peaks and black dots moved down the slopes all day long. Marek told her they were people skiing. Brandy'd seen Norwegian miners race down a mountainside on wooden skis once.

Marek brought round flat pies for their dinner. He called them pizzas. Brandy thought them too highly seasoned. They were not comfortable with each other. He left early.

And then it was April.

Brandy found Shay's life dull.

Remy Maddon strung a clothesline from a corner of the cabin to a tree so she could hang out diapers. Remy wasn't comfortable with her either. His visits grew fewer. So did Ansel St. John's.

Brandy felt cut off from other people.

And then it was May. Brandy wondered what had happened to Easter.

Warm winds melted snow to water. Cold winds turned it to ice at night.

Marek visited again. He seemed warmer, more interested in the twins and Brandy until the Garretts arrived unexpectedly.

Marek announced he intended to take over the support of Brandy and the babies.

Jerry bristled. "Some support. A Porsche, luxury apartment. With your life-style you've got to be in hock up to your ears. NCAR doesn't pay that well."

"I have money from my share of the sale of the ranch and other investments. My only debt is the one I owe these kids and . . . Brandy."

Brandy slipped into Shay's coat and walked out on the raised voices.

She didn't wish to be anyone's "debt."

The sky was dreary, the air unexpectedly warm. It smelled sweet with impending rain.

Mud, dirty snow, stretches of yellow grass. The world looked a dowdy place to Brandy as she walked along the road. But a robin hopped ahead of her, calmly pecking gravel bits.

It felt good to be released from the cabin.

When she came to the train antique store, Caboose Antiques, she found there were really two railroad cars. The one in back headed into the one in front to form a T.

Inside, a girl sat behind a desk idly turning the pages of a colorful magazine. Brandy wandered down the aisles fingering familiar objects, remembering. She came to a stove, identical to the one she, her mother and Nora cooked over.

Finally she picked up a potato ricer and took it to the desk.

"Oh, those are cute." The girl smiled. "My mother has one she hooked on the wall and a little flowerpot nesting in it with ivy hanging down."

"I intend to rice potatoes with it." Brandy pulled out the roll of narrow bills Jerry Garrett had given her and paid more for a potato ricer than John McCabe had paid for their cookstove.

"Potatoes?" the girl said as Brandy left.

At the bridge spanning Middle Boulder Creek, she stopped to look upstream at the abandoned mill, its gray metal roof jutting into a sky of the same depressing hue, its lower edge sagging toward rocks, still rust-colored, in the creek below.

Behind a store building across the bridge a horse grazed on dead grass. Brandy stood at the fence and tried to smell him.

The concrete sidewalk stopped and, for perhaps thirty feet, stretched an old board sidewalk—weather- and shoe-leather-smoothed. Brandy walked back and forth, listening to its sound.

On the other side of the street men laughed over twangy discordant music in a rough-timbered building. The door opened and a beery, stale smell reached her, reminding her of passing Werely's Saloon. A man emerged, shirtless under an open black vest with silver buttons all over it. He didn't even look cold. He looked mean.

He stared across at Brandy and stretched heavy arms above his head, their skin disfigured by odd varicolored markings. When he lowered them, they encircled Ansel's granddaughter as she stepped out from behind him. She managed to wiggle from the apelike grasp and give him a shove.

"Aw, come on, Lottie."

"Fuck off, you big . . ." Lottie was halfway across the street. She stopped when she saw Brandy. "Well, if it isn't *Miss* Mother Goose."

"Hello, Lottie." Brandy started back the way she'd come.

"Hey, wait." Lottie fell in beside her. "It was nice of your dad to pay Gramps all that money. I won't have to beg up the taxes this year."

Brandy turned and was relieved to see the black-vested gentleman walking in the other direction.

"Look, I'm sorry I had to blow the whistle on you, but if anything'd happened—I mean, I didn't want anybody nosing around the place."

"You mean in his graveyard?"

"Yeah. I think my grandma's buried there. I think you're supposed to bury people in cemeteries. He was good to you. You won't tell, will you?"

"Lottie, if you're trying to convince me your grandfather killed his wife and—"

"Not with a gun or anything. Grandma was sick. Gramps treated her awful. Wouldn't take her to a doctor. Worked her tail off."

"That still isn't murder and it doesn't sound like Mr. St. John."

"Yeah, well, he changed. When she got so sick even he could see she was dying, he just . . . changed. Knocked out part of a wall in the kitchen and put in that sliding glass door and then moved her bed in front of it so she could see out. First decent thing he ever did for her.

"I went East to visit my mother who was into another divorce. When I got back the bed in the kitchen was empty. No Grandma, no death notices, no funeral, no nothing."

"Didn't you ask him?"

"Sure. He just said she was dead and buried. That's the last word he's ever said about her. Started naming goats and cats Stina Mark." Lottie turned back as they reached the bridge.

Brandy looked after her and shrugged. She'd known Ansel wasn't "right," but he'd been kind to her. She'd say nothing against him.

The paved road made a sweeping westward curve up ahead. An angular depression in the earth like a wide trench, unnoticeable unless one looked for it, took off up out of the valley from the top of the curve.

Several automobiles came around the curve as she made her way to the odd dip in the ground, the old mountain road that led to Central City and Denver, that used to lead to the Brandy Wine.

The sky lowered to hide mountaintops. What did flying machines do in weather such as this?

Brandy followed the ghost road over rocky outcrops, receding snow fields, claylike mud. John McCabe had called her "precious baggage," lifted her to his shoulder and named a mine after her. Brandy didn't know how much she remembered from being there and how much she'd been told by adults present at the time. But she thought she'd been delighted with all the attention, could remember looking down on cheering faces.

She crossed a ridge and the paved road which had switched back on itself, climbed a fence and came to a heap of mine tailings, old and rusty like the rocks in Middle Boulder Creek below the mill. Clouds swept fog fingers down the ghost road as she climbed the tailings.

On top, heavy boards were nailed across the entrance. The cloud mist turned to drizzle, soaking into her hair and clothes, running down her cheeks as she read the signs posted on the boards. PRIVATE PROPERTY. KEEP OUT. NO TRESPASSING. VIOLATORS WILL BE PROSECUTED.

Marek was gone when Brandy returned to the cabin, and the Garretts anxious to leave.

"We have to go look for the mirror some more," Rachael said vaguely.

They didn't bother to tell her who'd won the argument about her support. Brandy didn't ask.

It rained the next day too, but cleared by early afternoon. She took a basket of diapers out to the clothesline.

The rain had taken most of the snow around the cabin. Tiny wildflowers had blossomed overnight.

Brandy could smell spring.

Turning to pick up the empty basket, she saw a figure walking toward her down the old path where the privy had been. It was Corbin Strock.

Sunlight glistened on raindrops clinging to pine needles above his head.

He was looking directly at her, but didn't seem to be seeing her, his expression that of a man preoccupied, in a hurry, with shocking news to tell.

Corbin walked through a young pine tree and disappeared . . .

"She's not here anymore, Corbin," she called to the empty clearing, and felt both foolish and frightened. "The girl you knew as Brandy is in her grave."

She dropped the basket and slid through the door. "In her grave," she repeated to the window over the sink, rubbing fear-sticky hands along her blue jeans. Her breath rattled in Shay's throat.

The clearing was still empty. Brandy watched it for a long time, trying to convince herself she hadn't seen him, but seeing still the way his hair fell across his forehead under his hat, the very wrinkles in his shirt.

The diapers were still on the line that evening when a boxy-looking automobile drove into the clearing.

As Marek stepped out, Brandy grabbed the basket and hurriedly pulled clothespins off diapers, feeling braver with someone solid for company. "You have a new automobile."

"It's a station wagon." He grinned as if making a joke on himself. "And here's a set of keys for you."

"But I can't drive a—"

"You can learn."

Brandy stared at the machine. "Yes . . . I suppose I could."

"You have to come out in the world sometime. You can't hide here forever."

"No." What would it be like to drive an automobile?

"My project at NCAR has been extended another two years." He followed her into the kitchen. "That's three years I can count on working in this area."

Brandy sat at the kitchen table and folded diapers. She'd liked Marek better when he thought she was Shay. He wasn't so stiff then.

"We've all been trying to give you time to adjust, but—"

"Do you think I could drive a flying machine too?"

"An airplane? You might try riding in one first. But what I wanted to say is, I've bought a house in Boulder."

"Yes . . . there are ghosts here." Brandy glanced at the window. It was growing dark outside. "But then for me there'll be ghosts everywhere."

"Look, I don't know how men got around to this in the old days but—"

"This is now." Brandy removed the pins from Shay's hair. Combed her fingers through it. How had Shay kept it out of her cooking? "This world can't be as impossible as it seems. After all, it produced my granddaughter. And she must have been a very brave person."

He squinted, stuffed his hands in his pants pockets, then took them out. "Just what the hell are we talking about?"

She turned back to the pile of diapers. "Nothing . . . I guess."

"Brandy?" His breath tickled the top of her scalp, a hand warmed each of her shoulders. "I'm not doing this right, am I?"

Did he have patches of hair all over him like the men in Lottie's posters? She folded a diaper wrong and flung it to the floor.

"Hey, I'm trying. It's just . . . you're so different. I don't know how to–"

"Because every time you look at me you see Shay." Why did tears always come to women at the wrong time?

"It's because I don't want to scare you." He forced her to face him, studied her face and grinned–again as if at a private joke. "And because sometimes you scare me."

Marek drew her to the cribs by the fireplace and whispered, "How long before these tigers go off again?"

"They ate shortly before you came."

He led her to the stairs to the balcony bedroom. "Do you want a drink?"

"Why?"

"Might loosen you up." His expression reminded her of the satyr goat Hooligan. "But then maybe you don't need it."

Embarrassment heated her skin, left a chilled place behind her ribs that deepened with every stair she ascended. "You're laughing at me."

"No."

"I don't know what to do with this." She fingered a small box on the bedside table nervously. "It doesn't play music or turn on the lamp."

"It controls the electric blanket. Heats the bed." Marek pulled her shirt up over her head, slid the blue jeans down over her hips and kissed her. "I don't think you'll need that either."

When he lay naked beside her, Brandy couldn't look at him. "Is . . . is everything electric in this world?"

"Some things still come natural." His hands were warm and everywhere.

The mushy soreness of her granddaughter's body contracted to tight tingles. "This isn't easy for me. . . ."

Marek chuckled. "Easier than I thought it'd be, Brandy McCabe."

FORWARD

Wilson Antiques, Ltd., closed for two weeks after the death of Cindy Wilson.

When it reopened, Ned was still out of town attempting to recover from his shock over his wife's suicide (she'd hung herself from a rafter in the storeroom one night), and an employee, Myrtle Teagop, was doing her best to run the business without him when a lady in a red pantsuit entered the shop for the purpose of browsing.

While she did so she explained to Myrtle that she'd flown to Denver to help her daughter and family pack up for a move back East and that there was nothing in the store she couldn't get cheaper at home and that the mountains were pretty but the air too dry here.

And then she ignored the EMPLOYEES ONLY sign and disappeared into the storeroom. Myrtle followed, protesting, but the lady chatted on, poked about in the dust and confusion and stopped to stare when she'd pulled the cover off the old mirror with hands for its frame. The one poor Mrs. Wilson had refused to sell and Mr. Wilson had been threatening to get rid of for months.

The lady declared she had another daughter at home who was soon to be married and who went in for "weird stuff" and this would be a perfect wedding gift to decorate the couple's new apartment. Myrtle Teagop, as anxious to be rid of the pushy intruder as her boss was the ugly mirror, sold it for twenty dollars to the lady in the red pantsuit.

Two days later the wedding mirror sat in a trailer behind a station wagon, a tarpaulin that covered the rest of the contents pulled tightly around it about three-quarters of the way up its frame, an old beach towel tied over the top fourth.

The station wagon pulled out into the traffic, leaving Denver on I-76.

"Well, New York City, here we come," the man behind the wheel said to his family, and wondered how far the moving van that had left the day before had traveled by now.

The people in the car were unaware of the way the tarpaulin rubbed against the mirror's hands, of the image playing across the hidden glass. An image of a slender platinum blond with a dark-haired baby on each hip, her head bowed as if in prayer.

The wedding mirror rode cold and inert in the trailer with U HAUL IT emblazoned on its sides through the middle portion of the country, but as it reached the more densely populated and damper section of the continent the beach towel began to tatter and fray in the winds whipping behind the station wagon and the bronze talonlike fingernails of its frame poked through to freedom.

And one day the towel ripped to expose the grainy glass itself. In its surface were reflected a wealth of electric power lines and a sky charged with summer thunderclouds.

And thus the mirror continues its journey. . . .